Christopher Jelinger, John Adams

Usury Stated Overthrown

Usuries champions with their auxiliaries, shamefully disarmed and beaten

Christopher Jelinger, John Adams

Usury Stated Overthrown
Usuries champions with their auxiliaries, shamefully disarmed and beaten

ISBN/EAN: 9783337382209

Printed in Europe, USA, Canada, Australia, Japan

Cover: Foto ©Andreas Hilbeck / pixelio.de

More available books at **www.hansebooks.com**

USURY STATED OVERTHROW OR, USURIES CHAMPIONS

With their Auxiliaries,

Shamefully Disarmed and Beaten:

By an Answer to its chief Champion, which lately appeared in Print to defend it.

AND

GODLINESS EPITOMIZED

By *Christopher Jelinger*, M. A.

Beza upon *Matth.* May a Man with a safe Conscience lend upon Usury? No surely.

And Holy *Usher*, Arch-Bishop of *Armagh*, in his Body of Divinity, *pag.* 300.

Q. What is that which we call Usury? It is Lending in expectation of certain Gain. So he well stateth it against Usury ill stated by *T. P.*

Q. What do you think of it? If we speak of that properly, which the Scripture condemneth, it is a most wicked and unlawful Contract; which if we live and die in, without Repentance, we are excluded out of the Kingdom of Heaven. *Psal.* 15. 1, 5. *Ezek.* 18. 12, 13. and *Chap.* 22.

But there is much questioning, which is that Usury which the Scripture condemneth. Therefore it will be our wisdom wholly to forbear it, and not to put our Souls, which are of more value than the whole World, upon nice Discourses, and subtil Distinctions. *Thus this Holy Man.*

Plato in Gor. *fol.* 313. *Non de rebus parvis instituta est Disputatio, sed de his, quas & scire pulcherrimum est, & nescire* ἄισχιστον, *turpissimum.*

LONDON, Printed for *J. Wright*, at the Crown on *Ludgate-Hill*, and *J. Sampson* at the *Wonder-Tavern* in *Ludgate-Street.*

Most High and Mighty Monarch,

CHARLES II.

By the Grace of God,

King of *Great Britain*, *France* and *Ireland*,

DEFENDER of the FAITH,

Grace and Mercy be multiplied.

Your Majesty's Acceptance of a Treatise of Your most humble Servant tending to Immortality; and of a large Latin Poem, bidding Your Majesty welcome into those Western Parts, in Your Royal Fort of Plymouth, *emboldned me to offer and to dedicate these my Theological Labours also, which are comprised in this Book; hoping that they will be Graciously accepted, as the former were: and that so much the rather, because this said Book brings to You, as to a Great King, that Great King whose Name is* Jesus, King of Kings, *Rev.* 19. 16. *to keep Your Majesty Company in your Solitudes; and for Your Majesty to spend your time with His great Majesty both Day and Night, according to this Book, wherein Godliness is Epitomized; and wherein alſo are contained ſome Eſſays made againſt that odious, and far-ſpreading Sin of Uſury: which will need the Protection and Support of an excelſe and mighty* Atlas *to ſupport ſuch a weighty Frame, and ſubject Matter, becauſe it will meet with bitter and potent Adverſaries which will be ready to oppugne it, to keep their great Goddeſs* Diana, *Uſury I mean, and her Silver Shrines. Which hath neceſſitated me, in all Humility, to betake my ſelf to ſuch a mighty Shield as Your Majeſty's great Power and Protection is, under which a wary Combatant may lie invulnerable. Nor am I the firſt that made ſo bold as to dedicate a Book of this Nature to a King. When famous Biſhop* Downam *wrote againſt Uſury, upon* Pſal. 15. *as I do now, he dedicated his Book to the King of Scholars, King* James; *and it was accepted: Anſwerably hereunto, I promiſe my ſelf a Gracious Acceptance likewiſe. But I deſire to end with praying to the King of Kings, that Your Majeſty may be kept by His mighty Power and Protection from all Treacherous Conſpiracies; may long ſway the Sceptre of your three Kingdoms in* Halcyon *Days; and after that Your Majeſty hath ſuperated the ſpaces of your Humane Life, you may, being elevated to the Horizon of future Felicity, and entranced into Heaven, there reign alſo, as one of the Kings of that other World, with the*

King

King of Kings, 2 Tim. 3. 12. Rev. 2. 20. *far ſcattering the bright ſhining Rays of your Inenarrable Glory.* Amen.

Your Great Majeſty's

Obedient, Loyal, and

Moſt Humble Subject, and

Orator to the Throne of Grace,

Chriſtopher Jelinger.

To His Grace, Chriſtopher, *Duke of* Albemarle, *Lieutenant General of* Devon, *and one of His Majeſty's moſt Honourable Privy Council,*

Grace and Peace from Jeſus Chriſt, the Prince of Princes.

WHen Your Grace's and this Kingdom's Father was flouriſhing and living upon Earth, It pleaſed him to caſt a favourable Aſpect on me, the unworthieſt of all God's Miniſters; ſo as that I could not but mind you, his Honourable Son and Heir, alſo, in the publiſhing of this Book, by a moſt humble Tender, and Dedication of it to your Honourable Self, and to your great Name; and that ſo much the rather for this too, becauſe you are the General of our Weſtern *Militia*, and this Treatiſe conſiſts of Fighting, and ſets forth a Battel (a Paper Battel I mean) fought in the Weſt of *England*, whereof you are a General, between two Weſtern Warriers, *Pro* and *Con*, about the thing called Uſury; of whom, one, who is a profeſſed Enemy to it, deſireth to put himſelf, firſt under the great God's, and next under your Grace's Protection, by this moſt humble Dedication: wiſhing withal, by a Digreſſion, that, becauſe ſuch a Paper Battel is too low for ſo great a Person to take any great notice of it; I say, wishing that your Grace may mind much more that Spiritual *Militia*, which is called Wrastling with the God of Heaven for Heaven, which is held forth in and by *Godliness Epitomized*, which is a piece and part of this Book; so as to practise it during your Natural Life here on Earth, for the gaining of Eternal Life hereafter in Heaven.

But not being contented with wishing only, your Graces most humble Servant desires to fall a praying for your Grace thus.

The Great Majesty of Heaven enable, strengthen and animate your Grace with his Grace so successfully to wrestle for Heaven in Prayer, as that when you shall have superated the spaces of your Humane Life, you may, being born in the Arms of Angels, be carried up to the Head of Angels, the Lord Jesus, who is the Generalissimus *of all Generals and Christian Soldiers, and for ever sheweth forth the Rays of his pleasant Face to the Vessels of Mercy which are destinated to ever-during Glory.* So ends with Prayer,

Your Graces

Most Humble Servant, and

Orator to the Throne of Grace,

A Palatine Exul for Religion's sake. *Christopher Jelinger.*

TO

To the Right Honourable Lord, *John Roberts*, Earl of *Radnor*, Lord President of His Majesty's most Honourable Privy Council, Mercy and Peace from Jesus Christ the Prince of Peace.

Right Honourable,

SO *ancient is the Mode of Dedicating Books to Great Persons, that we shall find it practised even in the Apostles time, and shortly after; for* Luke *himself, though he was inspired by the Spirit, yet dedicated his Book, called* The Acts of the Apostles, *to* Theophilus, Act. 1. *And S.* Austin *dedicated that most excellent Piece of his, which he wrote against the Epistles of the* Pelagians, *to the Noble* Bonifacius. *Answerably whereunto, I also here dedicate this Book, most Noble Sir, my great Favourer, to your Lordship, to manifest my grateful mind for all your great and undeserved Favours extended to me, and cumulated upon me, the unworthiest of all the Ministers of Jesus Christ: hoping, that as your Lordship hath accepted of the Dedications of others, so you will be pleased to accept of mine; and that my God will bedew these my Theological Sudors and Labours with his Celestial* *Bene-*

Benediction; ſo, as that when your Lordſhip has peruſed and read the ſame, you will uſe them alſo for your Eternal Good, labouring as for Life, to have that ſweet Society with Jeſus Chriſt which Saints have both Day and Night, by an Holy Walking with his Great and Glorious Majeſty in his Celeſtial Galleries and Walking Places, Cant. 7. 5. *and fighting the good and great Fight of Faith, as one of his valiant Warriers, wreſtling with God moſt mightily, to overcome God. O Great Sir! may it pleaſe your Honour, to give your mind to theſe great things more than ever, and to do them; for then how rich you would be in God on a ſudden! and how ſure of Heaven! for Heaven would then not only be above you, but alſo in you:* Rom. 14. 17. *and you would be able to ſay truly, Now I have enough: for, loe what a Life I now live, living by the Faith of the Son of God who loved me, and gave himſelf for me!* Gal. 2. 20. *and ſpending my whole time with my Love Chriſt, by Night as well as by Day, to ſatiate my longing deſire with his moſt ſweet Society! and Oh the unexpreſſible Peace that I now have within; being aſſured in my Heart, that with everlaſting Bliſs I ſhall be bleſſed! and Oh the longing Joy which does now ſurround me! and what a Globe of Glory becircles me! Oh, Noble Sir, 'tis true Nobility for a Man to be a Worſhipper of God, a good Reader*

of

of God's Book, a good Keeper of Holy Communion and Society with the highest Majesty; for that will bring us to the greatest Riches and Felicity. As for this World's Riches, you have enough of them, blessed be God: but one dram of Spiritul Grace, one Glimpse of Jehovah's *Face, one Glance from one of Christ's Love-like Eyes, one Drop of his precious Blood, one Draught of his sweetest Wines of Love, one Sip of his Divine Consolations, will do you more good than all this World's Goods. And therefore, let that be thought upon, and laboured after, above all things: for then, I say again, you will be able to echoe forth these Words from your very Heart, and from an undeceiving Experience: Oh, what an Ocean of ineffable Delights do now overflow me, and what a Mass of Heaven's Bliss surrounds me! But I intend to close up this Epistle with praying thus. May Heaven's Blessing be dropped down upon my poor Labours, and upon the Head of this Noble Lord to whom I exarate and write these Lines; that he, reading and practising the same on Earth, may reap the benefit thereof above in Heaven; receiving an Eternal and Immarcessible Crown of Glory.*

Your Lordship's

Most Humble Servant,

Christopher Jelinger.

TO

To the Most Noble Charles Pawlet, *Lord Marquess of* Winchester, *Grace and Mercy be multiplied.*

Highly Honourable,

May it please your Lordship to permit your most humble Servant to make this Address to your Honour. And first to give an Account of my boldness therein shown; Your Honour knows how long I have been a Tenant to your Noble Father, and to your Honourable Self also; and I remember how ready you have been to offer me a Spiritual Living for my Preferment; so that I could not but reflect upon that, and all other Favours with Thankfulness, and to erect, as it were, a Monument of my Gratitude by dedicating this Treatise to your Honour: hoping that if you will be pleased to improve it, Godliness Epitomized, contained therein, will bring you to be so familiar with Christ, that great King of Kings, as that his Majesty and your self will seldom or never be asunder: and that thereupon you will say like *David*; *When I awake I am still with thee*, Psal. 139. 18. and, *I am Prayer*, Psal. 109. 4. (so it is in the *Hebrew*) being all for Prayer, and spending a great part of your time

time in Prayer. I have read of a Godly Minister, that of twenty four Hours, he spent eight in Prayer; which is not expected of every body, nor required of your Honour; but that you, and all Christ's Saints spend much time in Prayer: Pray often, and even by Night as well as by Day, *Luk.*18.1,7,8. Well, Great Sir, I trust in God that he will lead you into all the Truths and things which here you are pointed to: and that thereupon you will lead such a Ceraphical, Celestial and Transcendental Life for Holiness, as that being ecstasied in your Spirit, you will be able to say, O! what a Heaven! what a Paradise! what a Beatity doth circumscribe me! Heaven being in my very Heart, and my Heart in Heaven. Heaven is high, I confess; but not too high for Strivers, Wrestlers, for holy Livers: and therefore let us strive, Great Sir, as for Life, to enter into Life by a sweet and holy Living with our dear Jesus, whose Life was a most strict, most pious, most Heavenly Life indeed; that we may live with his most blessed Majesty in Bliss and Beatity, Greatness and Gladness, Peace and Prosperity to all Eternity. Which that it may prove so, I humbly beg that the great and mighty Lord of Heaven and Earth would write these Lines that are written in this

Book

Book with his own Holy Finger, as with the Pen of a Diamond, in your Honour's Heart, and in mine too, and in all the Hearts of thoſe which ſhall peruſe and pervolve the ſame. *Amen, Amen.*

Your Honour's

Moſt Humble Servant,

Chriſtopher Jelinger.

A FEW

A
FEW WORDS
To the Courteous
READER.

AND, 1. About some chief things which were omitted; or, at least, but slightly touched in this Writing against Usury: *viz.* That the Expositors which have written upon the Ten Commandments, and others, have brought Usury under the Eighth; which saith, *Thou shalt not steal*: Making it a Moral Evil, and breach of the Moral Law, which is eternal. At present I shall instance in (*a*) *Ambrose, Usher*; And two *Germans*; (*b*) *Piscator*, who, expounding the eighth Commandment, saith expresly, that God in the eighth Commandment commands us to lend to him that needs to borrow without Usury. The other is a great *German* Divine too; famous (*c*) *Ursin*: who, in his *Sum of Christian Religion, pag.* 913. reckoning up the Vices forbidden by the eighth Commandment, names Usury; saying, *That it has not the lowest place, and is that which is taken above the Principal, in regard of the Loan only.* Besides whom a very great number of Expositors, besides those in the Margin, will be brought hereafter, which in like manner bring in Usu-

(a) *Who makes the Usurer a Thief*, l. de bono Mortis. Usher, *in his Body of Divinity, upon the eighth Commandment.* Dod, *upon the eighth Commandment.* (b) Piscator, *in sua Catechesi, upon the eighth Commandment.* (*c*) Ursin, p. 910. Peter Lombard *may be added, saying, In the eighth Commandment is prohibited Usury.* Polanus *also, in his Synt. And Bishop* Hall *making it Theft. With Mr.* Powel, *in his Posit.* Bart. Westhimerus, *in* Psal. 15. *And Mr.* Smith; *who saith, Christ expounding the Commandment which forbids stealing, saith,* Luk. 6. 35. *Lend freely.*

ry as a prohibited Theft by that Law. If now the Usurer will adventure upon the breach of that Moral Precept, pretending that it is a prohibition of a political Law, he may to his own peril.

2. About the great and * most learned *Spanhemius*, my Cousin, because he is as much stood upon as any Author, and extolled more than any by Usuries Patrons, as if he were one of their best friends. I intended to set down his Opinion in my Title Page: but upon second thoughts, resolved to reserve it for this place; setting down his own words, which he wrote after he had said what he could say for Usury, to shew, it may be, his Parts, and the Acumen and greatness of his wit, for which he was sent abroad of purpose by the Prince Elector *Palatine*, into Foreign Countries, to greaten the same more and more. I say, that his own words I resolved here to set down: *viz. But this I shall freely say; that it must be confessed, that it is far better for thee to bestow thy Money either in Husbandry, or in Merchandizing, or any other honest way to increase thine Estate, than to lend it upon Usury.* So that *Spanhemius* has left the poor Usurer in the plain Field: which I greatly rejoyce at because of his transcendent Parts and Excellencies, which made him so famous, as that the greatest Protestant Divines in *Christendome* (named in the Margin) desired his Friendship, and were of his Acquaintance; besides many great Noble Men: To whom may be added the renowned (*a*) Queen of *Sueden* her self, which saluted him by her Ambassador, and wrote to him how much she was delighted with his Works, and (*b*) esteemed him.

3. About my future proceedings: That I intending to content my self with my promised three practical Usury Books, to whom three or four more will be added, I shall no more so immerse my self, as I have done, into the controversial Sea of Usury, because I am so much stricken in age, and may, like aged Sea-men, well be excused from going to such a Sea again; as one which desires to labour for Heaven above all Terrene Concerns, and to end the remainder of his little time in a Calm; striving most of all to enter into that everlasting Rest

* *So called by Dr.* Bernard, *in* Usher's *Life, and* Tho. Hall. (a) Clark, *p.* 511. (b) *Not to speak of* Usher, *Dr.* Twisse, Prideaux, Moulin, Rivet, Garrisotius, Mestrosa, Drelincourt, Cameron, Tossanus; *all highly prizing him.*

which

which is to come, by believing, and a practical maintaining of good works, according to *Tit.* 3. 8.

But if any shall oppose what I have already written against Usury in this Book, and in my former, I may happily answer by a few Animadversions upon that which was never before objected, and answered. And so I will close up this third *About*, with that notable Saying of that most wise King; *And further, by these, my Son, be admonished, of making many Books there is no end; and much study is wearisomness of the Flesh,* [especially about controversial matters.] *Eccles.* 12. 12.

4. About this present Writing, let the Reader take this Advertisement. 1. That altogether unexpectedly, I have been assaulted and abused by cruel mockings, according to *Heb.* 11. 36. and grievous charges of things which I never did or practised; and Usury it self by name: which made me stir for my defence, as the least Worm that is will do when it is trod upon. 2. That his and other Men's Letters about Usury sent to me, I shall not *(a)* answer here. 3. That I was sent unto by a certain Messenger which is yet living; who told me expresly, that I must answer first such a one, who had written against me, before I did print my other three Books which are to come. So that I was even challenged and provoked to write, for the saving of my Credit. 4. That being informed how the same Pamphlet which was sent to me, was sent up to be printed, I still waited to see it published very near two Years, that I might answer so as that we might not differ in Copies. But when I saw that no such Pamphlet did come forth, I resolved to tarry no longer, being ready, and much spurred on by others who did long to see my Answer to the said Pamphlet, scattered up and down to my disgrace, I resolved to tarry no longer, but to proceed to the publishing of my Answer to the said Manuscript: but in civility, I would not divulge the Author's name, nor any others, which since the publishing my Treatise against Usury, have written to me: imitating blessed *Bolton*, who did the like; contenting himself with putting down of these two Letters, M. S. only. I add, that I was willing to follow in this, B. *Downam* also; who, in his most excellent Book against Usury, upon *Psal.* 15. confutes a great

(a) *For just causes; imitating in it Dr.* Stillingfleet: *who also would not answer his Adversaries Letter, but his Book called* Sure Footing.

part of a Manuscript, without naming the Author thereof: and well known it is, that a number of other Writers besides, have done the like. Now, my most hearty prayer to God is, that he will bedew this my Confutation with his Celestial Benediction; so as that his holy Name may be glorified, and many a poor Usurer's Soul rescued from everlasting Burnings, and graciously entranced into God's holy Hill, called Heaven; there to dwell in fulness of Jucundity, unutterable tranquillity, blessed Immortality, immortal Felicity, to all Eternity.

But upon new Incomes, I must,

5. Declare yet farther, that in this my proceeding, I am resolved to build and to depend principally upon the sure foundation of the holy Scriptures; which my Adversaries are destitute of: and not upon Man's Reason; though secondarily I use Reason too. If there were a difference between me and my Antagonists about Men's (a) Apparel, which the Scripture does not plainly inform us of, what form it must be of, (As there was such a difference once between the Emperor *Severus*, who would have a distinction of Cloaths to be ordered for all sorts of Men; and his Lawyers, *Ulpian* and *Paulus*, whose Reasons were stronger than his against it; and made him yield to theirs) I should be apt to yield to the Carnal Reasons of Usuries Defendants, as the said Emperor did to those of his skilful Lawyers: but in such a weighty matter as Usury is, I dare not. For how far Reason will go, and yet without deciding, that most learned Man, Doctor *Cudworth*, in his *True Intellectual System on the Universe*, sheweth. For, notwithstanding his indefatigable Labours and pains exantlated and taken therein, he must be a Sceptick in several things and places. I will instance but in two.

1. 'Notwithstanding all which, *saith he*, that has been here 'suggested by us, we shall not our selves venture to determine any thing in so great a Point; but sceptically leave it 'undecided.

2. He saith; 'Now, how these *Præludiums* of an immortal 'Body can consist with the Soul's continuance, after death, in 'a perfect separation from all manner of Body, till the day of 'Judgment, is not easily conceivable. Which thing considered,

---

(a) *About which, no certain form is prescribed unto Christians. Revius*, de Usu Capillitii, p. 254.

minds

minds me of a saying of great *Erasmus Roterdamus*; who saith, 'I could say something for Usury too (meaning that 'he could according to carnal reason) but I dare not, because of those (*a*) immortal Souls, *&c.* In short, he durst not, because the holy Prophets, and Fathers, and Martyrs are against it, and make me also to be against it, notwithstanding all the carnal reasons which the Wit of Man doth or can bring for it; I am for the holy Scriptures before all them.

6. But besides, I cannot omit here a most memorable Narrative which was brought to me after the writing of this Book, concerning a certain Usurer; who living not far from the place of mine aboad, and having got a very great Estate by Usury, though (as I am told, he took Use but after the ordinary rate of this Land, and no more) fell sick; and sent for a most Godly and learned Minister, who was named to me; and confessing how heavy that Sin of Usury lay upon his troubled Conscience, desired him, that as he would answer it at that great day of Judgment, he would declare unto him his judgment concerning that Sin. Whereunto the said Godly Minister returned this Answer; that, *Except he repented, and made restitution, he could not be saved.* Whereupon he departed. As for his Estate, that as the Relater told me, did melt away. Which I desire may awaken Usurers, and deter them from their cursed practises.

7. I advise the Reader, if he be an Usurer, that he will no longer delude himself with this, That multitudes follow that trade, and put out their Money upon Usury: considering that multitudes also, both in *England*, and beyond the Seas, in *France*, in *Germany*, and in *Holland* especially, break and prophane the Christian Sabbath, by working, shooting, buying and selling, as I have seen; saying, that the Law which requireth such a strict keeping of the Sabbath as the fourth Commandment mentioneth, was given to the Jews, and does not bind us: and that those which are so precise in the observation of our Lord's Day, do Judaize: Even as Usuries Defendants and Committents say now, that the Law made against Usury concerned the Jews, and doth not bind us. Both which I refer to answer for what they say, to that great day of the Lord,

(a) *Sitting upon those Thrones*, Rev. 20. 4. *Videatur* Tossanus, *in Annot. ejus in Bibl. de illis thronis, quid sint.*

which is to come; adding no more to this Paragraph now, but this; that we must not follow a multitude to do evil.

8. I shall super-add this; for that because some may blame me because I stand so overmuch in this Controversie upon the ancient Fathers, which, with *Erasmus*, I call those Immortal Souls, joyning the holy Prophets with them; I shall therefore thus Apologize for my self. If I were to dispute of the Opinion of the old Millenaries, whom the new ones follow, or of the time of Antichrist's coming: which two things I name, because of our late Fifth-Monarchy-Men, and those which hold that the Pope is not that Antichrist which the Apostle speaks of; (*a*) (but the same is yet to come) in the end of the World; I say again, if that were it, I should not much insist upon Fathers; because in both, they write so one against another, and contradict one another. As, 1. In the Millenary Opinion, (*b*) St. *Austin* writes against the Millenaries Opinion as fabulous: And contrarily, (*c*) *Papias*, who is held to be the first, (*d*) *Tertullian*, (*e*) *Justinus Martyr*, (*f*) *Nepos*, (*g*) *Lactantius*, (*i*) *Victorinus*, (*k*) *Pictaviensis*. Where, by the way, let me tell you how they contradict one another in this. Some say, that *Papias*, the first Author of the Millenary Opinion, was a Hearer of St. *John*, as if he had been so instructed by him, whenas he himself confesses that he never saw nor heard the holy Apostle. 2. As for the time of Antichrist's coming and reigning, loe, how they contradict one another also! (*l*) *Irenæus* holds (and it is said, he had it of *Papias* too) that in the end of the World Antichrist should come, and hold it not full four Years. But *Justinus*, who is elder than he; yea, as some say, the eldest of the Fathers, denies it: and saith he is ἤδη ἐπὶ θύραις, *Even before the door*. After whom, in cometh *Tertullian*, his σύγχρονος, affirming the same, that Antichrist is even at hand. Next to him steps in St. *Cyprian*, asserting, that the times of Antichrist are appropinquant, and very near come. Thus they disagree

---

(a) *Which is confuted by* Rev. 20.4. (b) Aug. *de Civ. Dei*, *l.*20. *c.*7. (c) Papias *in* Euseb. *l.*3. *c.*33. *Idem ibid.* (d) Tertul. *l.* 3. *contra* Marc. (e) Justin Martyr, *in Dial. contra* Tryph. (f) Nepos *Ep.* Ægypt. *confut. à* Dionys. Alex. *in* Euseb. *l.* 7. *c.* 10. (g) Lact. *l.* 7. *Inst. c* 3. Irenæus *l.* 7. *c.* 5. Feuardentius *in princ. op.* (i) Victorinus. (k) Pictaviensis *in* Apocal. (l) Irenæus *apud P. in Apoc.* Justin Martyr in *Dial. cum* Tryp.

in

in these two things; but as for all Usury, that all the holy Fathers, with one mouth, one consent, one spirit, condemn as unlawful, and interdicted by the holy Scriptures; and therefore I am so for those immortal Souls, the holy Fathers I mean, which also must sweetly harmonize with those immortal Souls which we call the Lords holy Prophets, *Sitting upon Thrones*, Rev. 20. 4.

9. But I must needs add this Codicil unto that which I have said already about the holy Scriptures; that such is the power thereof, as that when holy *Nehemiah* had spoken these words (which are part thereof) *I pray you, let us leave off this Usury*, all the Usurers in the Commonwealth of *Israel*, the Nobles not excepted, were convinced and converted; and so Usury then was put down: *For they said, we will restore them, and will require nothing of them: so will we do as thou hast said.* So effectual was the word of God spoken against Usury there called המשא a burden, as it is; and not נשך biting, purposely; because Usurers stand so much upon *Neshek*, biting, which they say is only forbidden.

So how powerful have been those other places set down in holy Writ? as, *Psal.* 15. 5. *Ezech.* 18. 12, 13. and in the new Testament, that famous saying of our Saviour, in *Luk.* 6. 35. *Lend, hoping for nothing from thence*; in that all the holy Fathers and Councils, and all Antiquity have been convinced thereby of the unlawfulness of Usury, and quoted those places still, and so put it down, as that an Usurer then was, *Rara avis in terris, A rare Man in the World*, scarce one in a City, because these places were still brought against them: and so, since the Reformation, and when *Luther* lived, much above a hundred years ago, Godly Ministers preached and wrote against it, *(a)* still bringing those very same Scriptures to bear upon them, so as that it was put down at *Augusta*, by *Charles* the Fifth, and the whole Assembly of all the States of the Empire. O wonderful! for on a sudden fell that great *Babel* called Usury in all places of that great Empire, even as in one night all the Images in the *Netherlands* fell, and by the people were thrown down, and even in *Antwerp* it self, to the astonishment of the Popish Party; as appears by that which *Fabianus Strada* has written of it, and that after and upon the

(a) *As B.* Down. *upon* Psal. 15. *asserts it.*

preaching of Gospel-Ministers, which by the Scriptures cried them down. And may not the like be said of *England*, wherein, in King *Edward*'s time, all Usury was put down by an Act of Parliament, which was impowred by the holy Scriptures so to do. For so that Parliament grounds the forbidding of all Usury upon the holy Scripture in these words, saying expresly, *That Usury is by the Word of God utterly prohibited, as a Vice most odious and detestable.* Whereupon down tottered Usury in *England* also, like the Popish Images aforesaid in the *Belgick* Provinces: which shews the Power of God's Word seen in the putting down of Usury, above all carnal and humane reason: Which makes me chiefly to stand upon it, because I find it so experimentally, by my preaching and printing, how thereby it is thrown down.

10. And whereas some may mislike my repeating of some chief and most notable sayings of some renowned Authors by me quoted, I shall briefly apologize for my self thus: That 1. My Adversary has compelled me so to do, by his frequent repeatings, and bringings in against me of Mr. *Hughes*, Dr. *Rivet*, Dr. *Spanhemius*, and their *ad nauseam usque* reiterated distinctions and expressions. 2. And did not Christ himself repeat his own sayings, *Luk.* 13. 3, 5. and elsewhere? So *Paul Gal.* 1. 8, 9. and *John* 20. 30. and 21. 25. See also *Eccles.* 1. 2. and 2. 15. how that King of Preachers repeats the self same words: all which puts me in hope that the courteous Reader will pardon my necessary reiterations.

A

A POSTSCRIPT, ABOUT

Two things left out in the Writing of this Book, *viz.*

PART I. NUM. 28.

I. *About the* Heydelberg-*Catechism, which my chief Adversary pretends to make for Usury against me; whereunto I have three things to say, having read the said Catechism, and the Exposition of it; yea, having learned the said Catechism by heart, when I was young.*

1. *The first is, that I find no such thing in the Catechism it self as favours Usury; nor could there be, because* Ursin, *who made it himself, was against Usury as well as my self, as in this Book I shew it.*

2. *That the Author of the Exposition of it could do no other but write of Usury as he doth, and as others do, if he would be suffered there.*

3. *That I do highly commend him for all this, because he writ more precisely for the strict keeping the Lord's Day than any of that Country, that I have seen.*

II. *About the unjust charge, whereby I am charged with Popery; because the School-men, and I, with my Brethren, are joyntly against Usury. The words of the charge are these,* The Man is become as one of them. *Whereunto I desire to answer a little more fully than yet I have done, and that three ways.*

1. *He might as well have said that I am become a* Mahometan, *because* Mahomet *is against Usury too.*

2. *That I am become a Heathen, because the Heathen and I agree in the point of Usury: they writing against it, as I do; even most bitterly too.*

3. *I answer, Am I as one of the Papists? who,* 1. *Because I would not become a Papist, chose rather, like* Moses, *to suffer Affliction with the people of God, and to lose, and to leave all that I*

was

was owner of, and to live as an exiled man in a strange Country. 2. *And whereas some British Divines do question it, whether the Pope be Antichrist, or whether the great Antichrist be yet to come; have lately declared, and do declare, that it is as clear to me as the Sun, that he is the Antichrist, and that* Rome *is* Babylon: *it being so evident to others also, even Papists themselves, that it is,* viz. *(a)* Alcassar, *(b)* Clemanges, *(c)* Ribera; *yea, (d)* Bellarmine *himself; little considering that in his name is the number of the Beast, 666. in* Rev. 13. 16. *if it be written in* Hebrew *thus.*

ב ע ל ל ר מ · י נ ו ס · י ע ס ו א י ט א

1 9 10 1 6 60 70 10 60 6 50 10 40 200 30 30 70 2

And so the Hebrew *Name,* ת י י מ ו ר } *makes*
400 10 10 40 6 200 } 666.

III. *About* Erratas, *I must beseech the gentle Reader to overlook them, and to pardon me for letting any of them pass: for being a Stranger, and not able to write so legibly as Natives can, I was necessitated to employ both Ministers and others to transcribe my Copy: in which Transcription I found innumerable faults, because the Transcribers could not well read many words and letters: so that I was forced to take extraordinary pains, and much time, to correct so many faults; which notwithstanding, many were left uncorrected, and could not be mended by me, unless I would spoil all by correcting. Which puts me in hope that those* Erratas *which are left will be imputed to transcribing, and not to me; whose case is like that famous Authors,* Jonas le Buy Sr. de la Perie, *in whose French Paraphrase upon the* Apocalypse, *I find* 130 Erratas.

IV. *About Prince* Rupert, *because I am jeered by one of my Adversaries for my Prophecy concerning him, by me alledged in my Dedicatory Epistle to his Illustrious Highness, out of a certain Author in Print; and did, since the writing of this Treatise, meet with a far greater* Encomium *then given to the said re-*

(a) Alcassar, (b) Clemanges, (c) Rivera, (d) Bellarminus. (e) Romana nimirum חיה *Bestia* חיה רומיית *Romana Bestia, Jonas le Buy,* in *Appeal.* p. 443.

nowned

nowned Prince my Gracious Lord, by Doctor Titus Oates, *I thought it good to transcribe it, and here to insert it. His words are these;*

(a) '*I have presumed to dedicate this* Pl. Dis. *to your Illustrious Highness, to whom, under God, our Gracious Soveraign is chiefly owing a very considerable temporal deliverance to this Nation. For, without your Highness's great Zeal (and some miraculous Providence intervening) it had hardly failed, but that Might and Craft had stifled the Truth in weak Hands, and brought a dismal Deluge of Blood and Slavery upon the Nation. And a little after he saith,* '*It is not for my weak Pen to recount the Merits of your Highness,* &c.

V. *About a certain brag, which one, since the writing of this Book, made to me;* viz. *That five hundred to one of my friends would be against me in this matter. For answer whereunto, though I could bring an infinite number of Authors, and of other impartial men, to stop such a one's mouth, yet will I at present quote but one, who is a Country-man of mine, even a chief one among the* Germans *(whom yet some falsely give out to be for Usury) His name is* (b) Keckerman, *a most learned and famous Writer; who confesseth,* '*That even all the* Greek *and* Latin *Fathers, almost all our Reformed Divines, and all of the Romish Church, do hold Usury to be a Sin. Where note that he makes no distinction between biting and toothless Usury; oppressive, and harmless or moderate; as my chief Antagonist would have me to make.*

(*a*) Doctor *Titus Oates*, our Preserver, under God, in the Dedication of his late Sermon to Prince *Rupert*. (*b*) *Keckerman*, in his *Oeconom.* ch. 7.

A Letter

A Letter ſent by a Godly Miniſter to the Author about this Treatiſe.

Reverend Sir,

I Have received your Lines, wherein you deſire me to diſcover my Sentiments concerning your Anſwers to the Uſurer's Champion: and therefore I ſhall ſay thus much; *viz.* That I am very well ſatisfied with them; and do heartily deſire that your ſucceſs of them in the World might be anſwerable to your deſign. It is to me a matter of great lamentation, that a crime (in my opinion ſo notorious) ſhould find any Advocate to plead for it: for I am ſenſible how much greater influence thoſe Arguments have on the credit of Mankind that comply with their carnal intereſt, than thoſe which deſign their greater benefit, and to bring them into the obedience of the ever bleſſed God, and his Son Jeſus Chriſt. However, let your Examiner paſs never ſo ſevere a cenſure on you, whilſt you plead the Lord's Cauſe, you have this comfort, that your reward is with him. And though truth may be ſuppreſſed by its Adverſaries for a while, yet the force of it is ſuch, that it will prevail at laſt. It were indeed to be wiſhed that men would open their eyes to behold it betimes: but if the World hath ſo far bewitched them, that they either cannot, or will not; ſure I am, that the day of Tryal will make it clear. I pray God that men would ſuffer themſelves to be convinced, before the Judgment-day. Sir, I have no more to ſay, but that I am and ſhall be an Orator at the Throne of Grace for you, that the ſame holy Spirit that hath hitherto moved you in the defence of ſo good a Cauſe, would aſſiſt you ſtill, both to the perfecting of this work, and what elſe you may have deſigned for the Glory of God, and the profit of Man-kind; and that you may never want Champions for God's Cauſe in theſe famous Iſlands; that Satan's Kingdom may not only be ſhaken, but altogether ſhattered, and Glory may dwell in our Lands, that we may be the Field which the Lord God delighteth to bleſs. Which muſt be the concluſion of the hearty Lines of him who is ſincerely,

Reverend Sir,

Your aſſured Friend and Brother

March 7. 1679. *in the Work of Chriſt,*

J. W.

THE

THE CHIEF

CONTENTS

Of things added to this

ANSWER.

Viz.

1. *A Citation for Usurers to answer at Christ's Tribunal for their Usury.*
2. *Bishop* Babington's *Prophecy of Usury's Downfall.*
3. *Two notorious Usurers buried by Satan in his own Chappel called Hell.*
4. *An Usurer's last Will and Testament before his Death and Burial.*
5. *A Figure of two Ways: A Dangerous, which is the way of Usury, leading to Hell; and a Safe, which is without it, leading to Heaven: for the Reader's Choice.*

USURIES

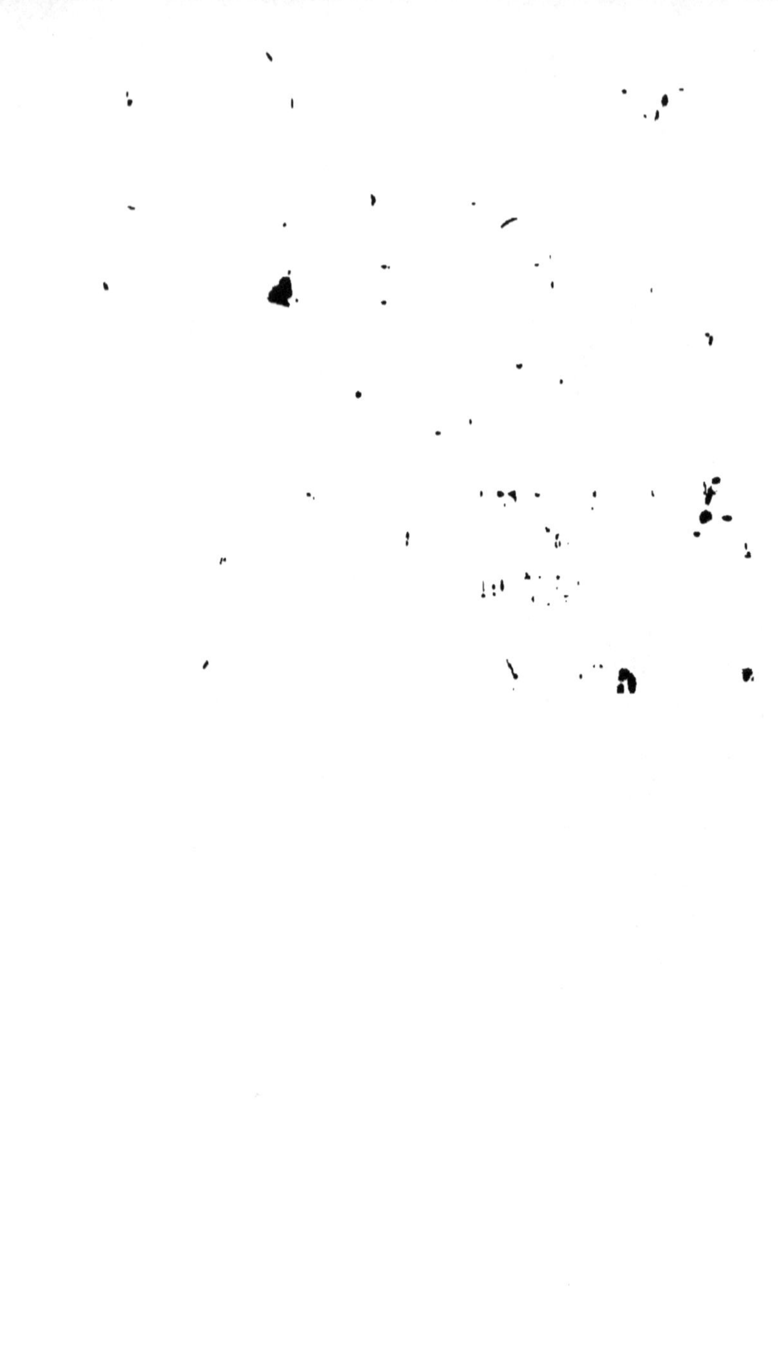

USURIES CHAMPIONS AND AUXILIARIES SHAMEFULLY DISARMED, AND LAMENTABLY BEATEN.

PRELIMINARIES.

NUMBER I.

HAving received since the coming forth of my *Usurer Cast*, several Papers and Letters sent to me by sundry persons, Ministers and others: some being for me, to encourage me; and others against me, to daunt me:

I thought it necessary to vindicate the truth, and the (*a*) honour of my Profession, and to resolve tender Consciences too, by answering what is asked of me, and also is objected against me; and especially, a certain Pamphlet, wherein I am called, *The Censurer examined*. And that for these causes.

1. (*b*) Because it is carried upon the wings of fame, that thereby I am confuted, because my Opponent would not be silent.

(a) *The honour of our Profession must be defended*; Phil. Cæsar. *against Usury*. (b) Facile est aliquem videri respondisse si tacere noluerit. *August*.

2. Be-

2. Becauſe it was given out that I could not anſwer it. But withal, I reſolved to name no man or Author of that or any other writing, for great and weighty cauſes; and alſo to omit what might put any of my adverſaries in any danger: contenting my ſelf with this, that it is granted me by my chief Antagoniſt, that the Biſhops alſo *decry all Uſury*. Which maketh mightily for me, that ſuch learned, renowned and great men, of whom ſome have been glorious Martyrs, which have given their bodies to be burned for Chriſt, have decried all Uſury, as well as my worthleſs ſelf, and are on my ſide, and therein agree with me, as I with them. But to the matter.

As for the Title given to my Book, *Uſury's Champions ſhamefully diſarmed and beaten,* I ſhall now give this account for it.

NUM. II.

1. I ſtile it ſo, and take my Examiner to be the chief, and *The Champion*, as he calls me *The Cenſurer*; becauſe he is, or at leaſt will be accounted ſo, as preſuming to encounter with the moſt famous, holy and learned men which have flouriſhed in old time, and of late; *viz.* thoſe of the Council of *Nice*, and that of *Agatha*, and Biſhop *Hall*; whom he goes to confute in his Pamphlet: and famous *Bolton* too, and learned *Trap*, and *Drexelius* and *Bertoldus* alſo; as if he were ſuch a man as could examine and confute any learned man, though never ſo much eſteemed and admired by others, which are his betters. So that the Uſurers of our time, I ſpeak Ironically, could not have ſuch another Champion if they had gon over all *Devon*, yea, all *England*: for none elſe doth appear ſo againſt ſuch Worthies as he doth: which compelleth me to ſtyle him *The Champion*. But I ſubjoyn withal,

Firſt, *Shamefully (a) diſarmed*; like bleſſed *Bolton*'s Adverſary, *M. S.* of whom famous (*b*) *Bagſhaw* writeth thus. *That being a man of no great Note, and of leſs Learning, he thruſt himſelf upon the greateſt infelicity of War: as firſt to be* Diſarmed, *and afterwards to be killed in the Field with his own Weapons.* [And with their Auxiliary Forces lamentably beaten.]

(a) *Arma autem ſunt exceptiones, replicationes, triplicationes. Doctor* Freig. *in ſuis Rudim.* (b) Bagſhaw *in* Bolton'*s Life.*

Whereby

Whereby I underſtand Replies, Exceptions, Allegations and Abetters: which being compared with thoſe mighty and numerous Forces and ſtrength of Uſuries Adverſaries, are but as Pigmees and Graſs-hoppers to them, and therefore could not ſtand before them; but were forced to put themſelves to flight, (*a*) and ſo totally routed. For how can Error ſtand before Truth, and Stubble before the fire of God's Word? which utterly forbids and condemns Uſury to the pit of Hell?

Thus much concerning this Title.

NUM. III.

Now, before I enter that Controverſial Sea of Matter, I will do as I did firſt, when I prayed, ſaying, 'O my God, 'do thou ſtand by me, a poor weak feeble Creature, as thou 'ſtoodſt by *David*; for I mean to go againſt this *Goliah in thy* '*Name*, &c. So I will pray again, becauſe the Lord did then hear me graciouſly; and this ſhall be my Petition: 'O thou 'Lord of Hoſts, forſake me not in this new and ſecond en-'counter, for I put my ſole and whole truſt in thee; and thou 'haſt formerly heard me graciouſly, when I cried unto thee, 'ſaying, Lord help me: anſwerably whereunto, I will cry 'unto thee again three times, Lord help me, Lord help me, 'Lord help me, againſt my Adverſaries, as the people of (*b*) '*Merindal* once did cry againſt the Duke of *Savoy*'s Armies; 'hoping to prevail, as that people did then.

Thus I frame my Supplication here.

'And thou, Lord, knoweſt; how, as I went on from time 'to time with the writing of this Book; ſaying alluſively, like '*David*, as he went; O *my Son* Abſalom, *would God I had* '*died for thee*; O Abſalom, *my Son*, *my Son*, 2 Sam. 18. 33. 'So, O *Abſalom*, *Abſalom*! poor Uſurer, who art a Rebel 'too, as *Abſalom* was, againſt thy Father by Creation; would 'God, I could perſwade thee to die to that great, that grie-'vous, that loathſome, that damnable ſin of Uſury, that 'thou mayeſt not die for it everlaſtingly.

And ſometimes thus: 'Lord, let that good and mighty 'Wind, whoſe name is the Holy Ghoſt, now blow upon me, a 'poor weak Veſſel of thine; that being ſet upon by mine Ene-'mies, in this controverſial Sea of Uſury-matter, I may pre-

(a) *And ſome to recant.* (b) *As* Fox *reports it.*

'vail; and thereupon many a poor ſoul that fought under Uſuries Banner may be overcome, won, converted and ſaved: So that I cannot but expect a joyful iſſue; only be thou my Helper, O my God and Deliverer. *Amen.*

And one thing more I cannot conceal from the poor Uſurer caſt; That when I had ended this Treatiſe, I could not but, *David*-like, who faſted for his enemies, *Pſal.* 35. 13. obſerve a day of Humiliation for him alſo, that he may be converted; which God grant.

NUM. IV.

In the next place, I ſhall, according to my uſual proceeding, premiſe a Preface, and place it next to my Prayer.

The Heavens, which are ſo clothed with ſhining light, ſo beautiful with a Canopy of gayeſt colours, ſo beſpangled with ſparkling Diamonds, [*the Stars I mean*] declare the glory of God, *Pſal.* 19. 1. But ſo do not our *Uſurers*. For they do rather, as much as in them lieth, unglorifie God; in that,

1. They [*I mean ſome of them*] do lend their Mony wittingly upon Uſury to ſuch as will ſpend it upon their luſts, (ſome of them) and upon their drunkenneſs (others,) and in playing it away in Carding and Dicing (others,) as long as they can borrow any Mony after Six in the Hundred, which they call moderate Uſury, to the undoing of their Wives and Children.

2. They are ſo far from declaring the Glory of God, and honouring that great and glorious Majeſty, as that they give great occaſion to the enemies of the Lord to blaſpheme, as did *David* by his Adultery and Murther, Both which, grave and great *(a)* Writers paralel with Uſury.

2. In that they make men to blaſpheme the God of Heaven, like thoſe, *Rev.* 16. 11. becauſe of their Plagues, *ver.* 9. Becauſe men do look upon uſuries and Uſurers as the Plagues of the World, like theſe which God ſent againſt, and into the World, according to the aforeſaid place; which maketh men ſo to blaſpheme, and to *(b)* charge theſe Uſurers, with their preſſures, to be the cauſe thereof.

(a) Ambroſe *de* Tob. *c.* 15. Cato *in* Cic. Calvin *in* Pſal. 15. Phil. Cæſar *againſt Uſury*, p. 3. (b) *Obſervabis iſta Uſurariis potiſſimum objici.* Guat. *in* Amos 8.

2. They

2. They dishonour God; causing men to (*a*) curse, not only God, but themselves also, for their cursed Ttade of Usury; whereby they ruin themselves and their families, and many others besides, according to *Jer.* 15. 10. *Every man does curse me.*

I know my chief Adversary will be very much displeased with me for this, [*though others also say and write the same*] as his Papers sent to me do prognosticate. Concerning which,

1. I will only say thus much in this Preface, that I do not regard his displeasure at all manifested and [illegible] in it.

2. That when first I saw it, I wondred, that after so many mortal Wounds given by so many sharp Pens of a number of holy and learned Writers, to that *Absalom*, that Rebel, that damnable sin, called Usury, which so rebelleth against God; yet it should perk up again and lift up its head again, and be defended, even by some Ministers of the Gospel, against the Gospel, for filthy lucres sake, and contrary to so many sacred Councils which have prohibited it.

And I wondred also, that when all other Ministers were silent; yea, diverse both Prelatical and Anti-prelatical Divines encouraged me by Letters and otherwise, by and in discourses, he only should rise up in Arms against me, in detestable Usuries Defence.

NUM. V.

But when I considered (*b*) how easie it was for a man which is enamoured with that profitable and soul-destroying Evil, and for this young man, my Adversary, to collect together some Arguments out of those new Writers, which defend a certain kind of Usury, with Cautions, and then vent them, to get a Name, and to give out

---

(a) *Unde* Musculus *in* Psal. 109. 11. *vocat fœneratores, maledictionis Ministros. And Bishop* Jewel, *in* 1 Thess. *saith, Usury is always the Curse of God and the People.*
(b) *Which, what an unbeseeming thing it is for a Minister, that of* Eusebius, *out of* Apollonius, *about* Montanus, *Doth a Prophet exercise Usury? does sufficiently declare.*

that he has confuted me. And I was told besides, that this same young man himself also, putteth his Mony to Usury. I left wondring, because I saw then the cause of his writing against me, and entring into the Field of *Mars* with me, by his contending with me, even as M. S. blessed *Bolton*'s Adversary, did contend with him about Usury, to defend it, by reason of a Sermon which that holy man preached against Usury, whereof he was guilty; as that learned and noted Parliament-man, Mr. *Bagshaw*, reports it. (a) And so to go on with this my Preface, I resolved upon three things.

1. That I would not hearken to him, but God; as blessed *Austin* adviseth me, saying, *I have not written it*; *viz.* what is written, *Psal.* 15. 5. *He that putteth not his Money to Usury. Hear God, and not a Minister*; He may be an Usurer himself.

2. I resolved to value his sayings and barkings against me the less, because I remembred what a most able and learned Author (*b*) writeth in his Dedicatory Epistle, prefixed before his Book against Usury, to the Arch-bishop of *Canterbury*, in these words: *Your Grace is reported to be one who neither lendeth nor taketh upon Usury*; *which is not in this Age every such man's commendation*: *and therefore, being free from that sin, you may the more freely give sentence upon the ungodliness thereof.* According to which saying, I thought this young writer to be very unfit to meddle with this controversie, and to judge me, and to pass sentence upon me after examination: (to reflect upon his Title) and so resolved to slight his appearing for Usury against me; who, together with a Cloud of able, holy and learned Divines, old and new, appear against it, and all the Defendants of it.

3. I resolved also, that, seeing Providence has so ordered it most remarkably, that this Champion should rise up against me in Arms, as it were, and to rowze me up by all manner of provocations, given me from the beginning, and first line of his Paraphrase, to the very end thereof, wherein he would fain make a Usurer of me also, by a false report: I say me, who never lent any Mo-

---

(a) Aug. *in* Psal. 15. (b) *Mr.* Mosse.

ney upon Usury in all my life time, that by God's mighty help, I will now go to the very bottom of that most deep dead and dangerous Sea of Usury, which has overflown a great part of this and other Countries also, in our *European* Orb, to the spoil and ruin of many thousands, thousands, thousands, who make a most sad out-cry about it, like those in *Nehemiah*. 5. 1. so that their cry goeth up, even to Heaven.

The Lord my God strengthen, assist and enable me to go thorow with this great, noble and mighty work *(a)* with a prosperous success; so as that many a poor Usurer's soul may repent, and not continue any longer in that great and grievous sin; be saved, and not damned; live, and not die to all Eternity, according to that most dreadful sentence, *H'as given forth upon Usury*, בנשך, *and h'as taken encrease*, ותרבית, mark, *any encrease*, or overplus; not נשך, *or vehement biting only*: shall he then *live? he shall not live, he shall surely die, his blood shall be upon him*, Ezek. 18. 13.

NUM. VI.

But to the main matter it self, after this Preface; which I will methodize after this manner: dividing it into four Sections, and distinguish each Section into Numbers, as our new Casuists do; because my Adversary will needs make me a new Casuist too.

The First Part will comprize his Examinations of the two first Chapters of my *Usurer Cast*.

The Second, My Answers given to the Examinations of my third, fourth and fifth Chapters; together with some certain Numbers joyned with the rest, as concerning the same Subject.

The Third, My Defence made against his and other Opposites, Impugnations and Insults made against my Sixth and Seventh Chapters.

(a) *As* Daneus *calls it.* (b) Martin *ab* Alpiseuet, *and others.*

... Fourth, my Resistance made against his and other ... aries encountring with, and assaulting of my Eighth ... th Chapters.

... several Additions; *viz.* of a Narrative, and the ... ast Will and Testament, mentioned in the Table of the chief Contents of this. Together with sundry Exhortations, and some Transcripts; And a final Supplication.

THE

THE FIRST PART.

NUMBER I.

HIS Title is, *The Censurer examined: or, a Consideration of Mr.* Jelinger'*s Usurer Cast.*

The later part whereof I have nothing to say to; but the former I cannot but discuss and deal with according to its desert.

And First, Not to speak much of the Name he bestoweth upon me, calling me *The Censurer*; as if there were none like me: but only this more, besides that which I have said already upon my Title which I give him; that those Judicious Readers, which have read my Book, and Bishop *Downam's*, and Mr. *Bolton*'s, have given this verdict upon the three; that both the one, and the other have dealt more roughly with the Usurer than I.

Secondly, In the second place, I shall observe in the word *Examined*, this Man's

1. *Arrogancy.*
2. *Boldness* and Impudence.

1. *Arrogancy:* That, being but one of the lower Form of Scholars, he will take it upon him *to* (a) *examine* such as are passed and gone from Form to Form, and from University to University; yea, (which I must needs add) will examine the *Theses* in the University of *Wittemberg* disputed against Usury, so as to condemn them for bringing Usury by their reasonings

(a) *I say, examine others, when he should have put an Answer first to Mr.* Smith'*s Examination of Usury in his Second Sermon against Usury.*

(as if his reasoning were better) into greater credit and request than some are aware of, in his 97th Page. Which, whether it be not height of Arrogancy, let the Reader judge.

NUM. II.

2. *Of his Boldness.* That, being but a young Man, he would presume to examine such a deep Subject; and to be Defender, yea, Judge of such a Controversie, when all his other elder Brethren in this Country, and elsewhere are silent. But I do, upon this Observation, remember, 1. What my old deceased friend, Mr. *Hughes* did write of such another young Man, who would needs dispute with him, and challenged him for it; that he was *Omnium Juvenum audacissimus, Of all young Men the most audacious.* *(a)* Which may well and most fitly be applyed to this also. 2. I remember also, what I have read in a certain Author; who writing against Usury, as I do, dedicated his Book to an old great Lord; saying, *The Question of Usury being controverted in these days among many Divines, requireth an Arbiter of much reading and experience. And if no Man chuseth a young Man for a Judge, or a Guide, because there is no sufficient evidence of their Wisdom; then should I have shewn my self a very young Man, if I had chosen any that is young to be a determiner of this Controversie.*

Let the Reader apply now this old grave Author's Saying to the present case. I, for my part, will close up this Observation with that noted saying of *Oecolampadius:(b) De Usuris judicare non est omnium: Every Man is not a fit Judge in this case of Usury.* And *Aristotles* Verdict concerning young Men; *Quod non constat eos esse prudentes : That it is not evident that they are so prudent.* That is, prudent sufficiently.

(a) *A Defender of that most odious sin of Usury, properly so called, and now practised by our Usurers. Where I desire to cite, for the Impudency of this Defence, that Illustrious saying of* Lavater, (*Comment on* Ezek. 2. Homil.) Our Age wants not Men of whom *Usuries*, and other Crimes, (*Mark. he calls Usury a Crime*) are most *impudently* defended. (b) Oecolampadius, *Epist.* 16. *l.* 1.

Having done with this Man's Title, I proceed to his Premisses, And,

First, I have this to say therein of this young Philosopher; who so begins with his Philosophy, when he should inchoate σὺν θεῷ, *with God*, and with his holy Word, to make his matter good; that his wrong which he doth me, charging me with Confusion and height of uncharitableness, is so great, as that I must needs vindicate my self in a more than ordinary manner, because he assaults me so hotly in such an unusual manner, beyond the bounds of all Civility, and the example of all others that have written of, for, or against that dreadful sin of Usury. So that he must expect to have the like measure measured out unto him, with which he measures unto me, in this my Defence. And,

1. Whereas he chargeth me with a *Chaos*, because I couple, as he saith, the grossest Oppression and most griping Exaction with the least Expectation; be it a Mite, or Cup of cold Water, upon the account of Mony lent: and because I do not distinguish as he would have me, *viz.* between griping Usury and moderate. I must thereupon needs retort, and tell him, that his Pamphlet is a Confusion and a *Chaos* indeed. For, 1. Where are his Parts, his Sections, his Divisions, throughout his whole Pamphlet? Is not the whole Body of it out of Joynt? Which caused one who read it to say, that it had neither Head nor Tail.

2. Doth he distinguish between the several kinds of Usury as he ought (save only between the most griping Usury and his moderate, which is for his tooth?) No, no.

3. As for me: Because he finds such fault in me for not distinguishing, I will therefore now distinguish more than yet I did, though I know he will not like it.

And First, between that which is (a) manifest, and the cloaked, which, in all likelihood, is omitted by him, because palliated Usury comes too close home to his Lending. For Divines tell us that it is committed thus.

(a) *Quæ aperta facie est quod dicitur.* Erasmus, *in* Psal. 15.

1. When a man who is a Usurer taketh any thing above the Principal without an express Compact, but by a Tacite, custom it self tacitely making the Compact: as between infatuated Harlots, and those that commit Fornication with them, Custom maketh the Agreement, themselves being silent. Thus my Author compareth Usurers to Harlots in this thing.

2. When a Man palliateth Usury with Partnership, in that he will be the borrowers Partner: But how? In his Gain, but not in his Loss. Which this Champion's own (*a*) *Authors* in their Cautions disallow; because the Usurer is so unjust, as that he will have the Borrower to take the pains, and himself will take the gains.

3. When the Usurer maketh a Translation: that is, when he will not take Money beyond the Principal, but bushels of Corn, of the Borrower, or his labour for it, or some other thing, contrary to *Deut*. 23. 19.

4. When the Usurer makes a Translation *de persona ad personam, from person to person.* As thus: When the Usurer will not be seen in the taking of Usury, because it is an odious thing, and will bring a scandal upon him (especially if he be a Minister or Professor) but employeth another: as some do their Wives; others some noted common Usurers, which can best put out a Man's Money upon Usury, because they are still resorted unto: Yea, others there are who will employ the very Jews, whom famous (*b*) Doctor *Pareus* calls therefore *Christianorum famulos, The Christians Servants.*

Here now I distinguish indeed, but little, I suppose, to the Champion's liking, though he finds fault with me that I do not distinguish in my *Usurer cast.*

5. Palliated Usury is committed also, saith the famous (*c*) Bishop *Downam*, by counterfeit exchanging; which I, for my part, shall call Exchange bordering upon Usury. The manner of its committing is this; When Money is delivered upon Bills of Exchange, with mention of the places, not that the Bills should be transported for the satisfying of the Creditor

(a) *As Mr.* Baxter, *and others.* (b) Pareus *in R.* (c) B. Downam, *in* Psal. 15.

beyond

beyond the Seas; but that the Lender, keeping the Bills at home with him, may have the like Allowance which Merchants have for the same time, dealing by Exchange and Rechange betwixt the places named.

The reason of this practice is, because their Gain is greater than any other; which is tolerated by some Magistrates: Insomuch that they which put forth their Money in this counterfeit Exchange are supposed to get after 16 or 20 in the 100. So that therefore this Exchange may be called *Cambium siccum*, *Dry Exchange*, because it is void of Charity.

6. There is also a kind of adventuring, which is but a cloak of Usury; When a Man covenants for Gain in lending under a pretence of hazard, when all the while he intends to ensure; and so the Principal is not hazarded. And so many a Man lendeth fifty pounds, if himself and two or three others which he shall name, or any of them, shall be alive at the twelve Months end, that the Debtor shall pay him fifty five pounds; otherwise he shall pay but forty five pounds: For if he should name but one, it were twenty to one that he should be living at the Years end; but naming three, it is more than twenty to one, but that some one of the three shall survive.

This famous *Downam* also judgeth to be a cloaked Usury.

7. There is likewise a kind of pretended free Lending, which is but a Cloak of Usury. As, when a Man lendeth fifty pounds; much of it being light Money, and such as will not pass; as being clipped, or Brass coloured over, with this condition, to pay him again so much in good and passable Coyn. Such was the Usury which some practised in *Ezekiel*'s time, a little before the Captivity. For, as some write, they having ordained a new Shekel, exceeding the old thirty two Grains; so that whereas the Civil, or *Mosaical* Law, which was but half of the holy Shekel, weighed an hundred and sixty Grains, the new weighed an hundred ninety and two: they would lend after the old Shekel, but they would be paid according to the new.

More, much more could be said of this Palliate Usury: for it is just like one *Perielimenus*; who, to beguile others for the enriching of himself, sometimes would be like a Fowl, sometimes like a Bee, sometimes like an Ant, sometimes like a Serpent; yea, saith my Author,

—εἶχε δὲ δῶρα
παντοῖ᾽ οὐκ ὀνομαστά.

So

ſo many ſhapes he had, as no Man can expreſs. Anſwerably whereunto, Uſurers alſo appear ſometimes in one ſhape, and ſometimes in another: yea, they have ſo many a quillity, and ſo many a ſubtilty couched in their diſtinctions, as no Writer is able to diſcover. But I muſt be briefer than I have been, having much other matter to utter: and therefore I will haſten to

NUM. V.

A Second Diſtinction, between Natural Uſury and Unnatural, The Natural is, Whereby a Man deals with (*a*) Mother Earth, which the holy Fathers in old time uſed by God's own Inſtitution; and which (*b*) *Aretius* ſaith, is only lawful; excluding all other interdicted Uſury. Which alſo maketh againſt my Adverſaries.

2. *Unnatural*: *viz.* That which, againſt Nature, Uſurers would have to come of ſuch a barren thing as Money is; and which that renowned and pious Biſhop *Hall* brings as an Argument againſt Uſury, (ſee my *Uſurer Caſt, p.* 44.) but hereof more hereafter. In the mean time let me add, that for this unnaturalneſs, Uſury is called by ſome, *Sodomia Naturæ*, *The Sodomy of Nature.* O abominable! And if any do not like Biſhop *Hall*'s Reaſon, as this Champion doth not, I prove the unnaturalneſs of it thus; becauſe the poor Heathens, by the Light of Nature, have written and ſpoken againſt it: yea, becauſe the Light of Nature, called the Law written in Men's Hearts, accuſeth Uſurers for the unrighteouſneſs of their practiſing Uſury.

NUM. VI.

Thirdly, I diſtinguiſh between (*c*) *Metaphorical Uſury, and Proper*; or, properly ſo called. The *Metaphorical* is that of Gifts, and Graces, and Parts; whereby we may gain ſome benefit, encreaſe and excreſcency (as *Aquinas* calls it) of good Works; as Alms-giving, *&c.* to be underſtood by that Uſury

---

(a) Turner, *pag.* 12, 13. (b) Aretius *de Uſura.* (c) *Whereof the one gains Heaven, the other Hell; ſaith* Chriſoſtome, *Hom.* 5. *in* Matth.

which

which Chriſt ſpeaks of, *Matth.* 25. gotten by the Talents; that is, Gifts and good Works there mentioned. And ſome think that Chriſt there meant Miniſters and Paſtors of the Church eſpecially; that they ſhould ſo lend forth their Gifts and Parts, as that he may receive his own with Uſury; that is with a Spiritual Increaſe: as *Marlorate*, with others, is of that mind. Whence is that of (*a*) *Origen*; *Behold all ye to whom I ſpeak theſe things, do take theſe my words as Money lent to Uſury; This is the Lord's Money, which you muſt uſe to Encreaſe.* Thus he underſtood Chriſt's Parable. But of this alſo more hereafter. In the mean time, this ſheweth that this Parable doth nothing at all favour Uſury, properly ſo called; which I muſt ſpeak of next: ſhewing, that it is not only biting, but alſo Encreaſe, called in *Hebrew*, תרבית. any Pleonaſme, or Overplus, Uſurariouſly taken; *Ezech.* 18. 13. *H'as taken Encreaſe.* So that theſe two words, *Neſheck* and *Tarbith*, are both one; that is, Uſury. Which is ſo acknowledged by *Rabbi Kimki*, upon *Ezech.* 18. that *Neſheck* and *Tarbith* are all one. So by *Calvin* himſelf; that is, both Uſury, forbidden Uſury.

NUM. VII.

Fourthly, I ſhall diſtinguiſh between *Mental Uſury* and *Actual.*

To begin with *Actual*: that is, A kind of Uſury, whereby actually and outwardly, encreaſe is made by the (*b*) uſe of a thing. So it is by learned Men deſcribed: And it is that which hath ſpread it ſelf, and is grown moſt common in the World; and of it (and not of moſt griping Uſury only, as the Champion would have it) moſt Writers of all Countries do treat, ſaith a moſt famous Author.

2. *Mental*: Which is a kind of Fœnory, conſiſting in the mind, and hope of Gain, without any Covenant (ſaith a famous Writer:) Whence is the name *Mentalis Uſurarius*, *A Mental Uſurer*; that is, one who committeth Uſury with his Mind. So that if a Man's purpoſe, deſire and expectation, note *expectation*, be, that the borrower ſhould not bring his Goods weeping home, but that he ſhould tender him Conſi-

(a) Origen, *Homil.* 3. *in* Pſal. 36. (b) *Whence it is called Uſury, from Uſing, jus Canon. p.* 466.

deration

deration for the uſe of his Goods. Such a Man, in his mind, has committed Uſury before God, ſaith a renowned Writer.

And the ſame was ſaid long before of him by bleſſed *Auſtin*, whoſe words I formerly quoted in my firſt Book; *viz. If thou lendeſt thy Money to any, of whom thou expecteſt to receive more than thou didſt lend, thou art an Uſurer.* And ſince, by another famous Writer; whoſe words in *Engliſh* are theſe: *Mental is committed without Covenant, when a Man lendeth with hope of receiving ſomewhat that is Moneys worth, above, or beſides the Principal.* Which thing I intend more fully to confirm by the unanimous conſent of the School-men, and other Divines, and their Scriptural Proof for it.

I know the Champion will miſlike this as much as any thing I ſaid yet: but I muſt diſcover God's Truth; Will he, Nill he.

N U M. VII.

4. I will diſtinguiſh next between the ſeveral values of Uſury, which are and have been from time to time; and are all called Uſury; and are, and have been interdicted by God and Men: *viz.* 1. The *Centeſima*: that is, A certain Uſury which was gathered Monthly, and amounted to twelve pounds by the Year. The Second is called *Semiſſalis*, Six in the Hundred. The Third, *Trientaria*, Four in the Hundred. The Fourth, *Exbeſſe*, Eight in the Hundred. All which are Uſury, and called ſo by all ſorts of Writers; and as they all are ſo, ſo they are all interdicted; as I ſaid, 1. By God, who forbids all Uſurious Encreaſe, *Ezec.* 18. 12, 13. *Thou haſt taken Uſury and Encreaſe.* As if God ſhould ſay, which thou oughteſt not to have done, becauſe I have interdicted it. Mark, *Encreaſe*; any Encreaſe, as well as *Neſheck*, *Biting*: Whereof more in a fitter place. 2. By Men: All theſe kinds have been interdicted, and taken away quite by degrees. Thus the ancient *Romans* firſt brought Uſury to one in the hundred; and by the Laws of the twelve Tables (which Biſhop *Hall* alſo cites) ordained, that if any Uſurer ſhould take above One in the Hundred, he ſhould be puniſhed fourfold; whereas a Thief, by the ſame Law, was to be puniſhed but twofold. (Whereby you may gather, ſaith *Cato*, how much they eſteemed an Uſurer to be a worſe Common-wealths-man than a Thief.)

Thief.) Within one Year after that, it was (*a*) reduced *ad Semuncias*, saith *Tacitus*, to half a pound in an hundred: and the next Year after, that also was abolished, *Genuncia rogatione*, saith *Bodin*, *whereby it was enacted, that it should be unlawful at all to lend upon Usury*; as *Alexander ab Alexandro* informs us. And Bishop *Downam* brings and names many ancient and famous Philosophers and Law-makers, who have absolutely been against all such Usury.

But more of this hereafter also.

And has not the Champion brought his Ware to a good Market (by his *Chaos*) which yields him such Returns. I hope we shall hear no more of his congealed Water for the future: he may do better to keep it for his own *Chaos*.

3. But I do not desire to evade this way only, nor altogether; and therefore, to shew that I minded distinguishing, before he sent me to the Philosopher to mind me of it, I will send him to the third Chapter of my *Usurer cast*; where I distinguish between Usury compacted for, and expected: and to my fourth Chapter, wherein I distinguish Usury, properly so called, from Inter-Usury, and Interest, and Ship-loan, and Liberal Increase, held lawful.

4. And if this be not sufficient, let him pervolve the Writings of the holy Fathers, and other learned Authors, as I and others have done; and see whether they so distinguish still between the most griping Usurer and the more moderate. I am sure they do usually speak in general, without such distinguishing. And therefore why must I be so branded as I am by this censorious Champion, and my Treatise compared to cold Water that congealeth and hardens in the same lump things of a far differing Nature: if my Treatise be so, then hundreds more of far greater Authors are so too.

5. Yea, are they not most famous and learned Men, who in very deed couple together (to use his own words) even expresly and distinctly those which for their taking of five Guilders for the Loan of a hundred Guilders: and maintaining pertinaciously, that this quantity was to be lawfully taken for the said hundred Guilders, they say are to be censured for Robbers and Hereticks; mark, ROBBERS AND (*b*) HERETICKS: and them (whosoever they be) that take any thing for Money lent, though it be but a Mite, or a Cup of cold

(a) *Duilia Rogatione.* (b) *So* Archidiaconus, Q. 1.

Water.—— (*a*) So the University of *Wittenberg* couples them, not I; I do but quote them, as also doth learned (*b*) *Aretius*: and therefore why doth he so run out upon me?

6. But I'll go higher yet. Doth not God himself couple those which take *Nesheck*, (*c*) נשך, *Biting*, and them which take *Tarbith*, *Encrease*, which is more than the Principal, as learned (*d*) Expositors do aver it. Which has caused a famous (*e*) Author to say those words which the Holy Ghost confounds, *Let not us distinguish*.

NUM. IX.

1. *I pass on to Uncharitableness*, wherewith this Champion most fiercely and hotly chargeth me to defend my self against this his heavy, dreadful and spitish Charge, and Imputation, set down by him in these words: *That my not distinguishing*, whereby he meaneth, as his words shew it, my not distinguishing between the grossest oppression, and the least Encrease and moderate Gain, in his first and fourth pages; wherein he wrongs me, as it is to be seen in my fifth page: where I do distinguish *Nesheck*, Biting, or gross Oppression, from *Tarbith*, Encrease; which may not be grosly oppressive, and yet is Usury too, forbidden as well as *Nesheck*, *Ezech.* 18. 13. and threatned with death(*f*) and damnation in the same place. I say, he saith, that *My not distinguishing is the Inlet to all that monstrous Uncharitableness that runs through my whole Treatise.* And how is that; *In that I sentence all that are concerned therein* (Usurers he must needs mean) *to Hell-Flames.* Yea, he addeth, that *Within this Scheme, I take in by far, the greatest part of the Nation.* And not content with these Tautologies, he addeth a third, saying, by a direful Gradation; *Thus Doctrinally he damneth for this one practice the whole Nation, excepting few, himself, no doubt, and two or three more, without Repentance: And to leave little hope from the after Remedy, he tells us farther*, Usurers seldom repent.

(a) *In the* Wittemberg *Positions disputed, where* Mordesius *proceeded Doctor.* (b) Aresius *de Usura.* (c) *In which word is a* Dagesh *for it in the letter* נ, *which denotes much Biting, as I said.* (d) *As* Ambrose *l. de* Tobia, *c.* 15. & *in* Levit. 25. (e) *Bishop* Downam. (f) G. Powel, *p.* 28.

Which

Which falſe and fearful Charge to anſwer, I ſhall firſt break out into this Exclamation, becauſe (*a*) Eternal Salvation and Damnation are no ſmall things.

Oh, that a Miniſter of the Goſpel ſhould ſo forget himſelf, as to draw ſuch a formidable and groundleſs Conſtruction from my harmleſs and ſure-footed Expreſſions. God forgive him; for, as much as in him lieth, he laboureth to render me as odious as poſſibly he can to this whole Nation: Which, if this Charge were true, and he could make it good, might juſtly ſtone me to death, for ſending ſuch an infinite number of Men, Women and Children to Hell. But my comfort is, that that famous and holy (*b*) Arſhbiſhop *Uſher* ſaith as I ſay; that Uſury is a wicked and unlawful Contract, which, if we live and die in, we are excluded out of the Kingdom of Heaven; *Pſal.* 15. 5. *Ezek.* 18. 12, 13.

3. I ſhall haſten to my particular Reſponſes and Anſwers which I have fitted for this heavy Charge, to defend my ſelf againſt it.

NUM. X.

And Firſt, Do I damn, and ſend the whole Nation, for this one practice, to Hell, ſave my ſelf and two or three more excepted? and that leaving but little hope for the after-remedy, which he calls Repentance, becauſe I ſay, that Uſurers ſeldom repent? How can he make this good? Becauſe I ſay, that in my Anatomy, which is to come, few will eſcape, as if he had ſeen the ſaid Anatomy: But I would have him to know, that when I ſay in my Anatomy few will eſcape, my meaning there is not that (*c*) few will eſcape Hell: but my Diſcovery, meaning Borderers upon Uſury properly ſo called, *viz.* ſuch as are guilty of Uſurious Dealings in Buying, Selling, Setting, Letting, &c. and who may, and very many times do repent; as is to be ſeen, 1 *Cor.* 6. 10, 11. whereas Uſurers properly ſo called, whom I chiefly aim at, and preach and write againſt (like bleſſed *Bolton*, whom I deſire to

(a) *Non parva res eſt æterna ſalus & æterna damnatio*, Leſſius *de Relig. c.* 1. *p.* 2. (b) *Arch-biſhop* Uſher *in his Body of Divinity*, *p.* 300. (c) *Though in ſome other reſpect few will eſcape Hell, becauſe few are choſen*, Matth. 20. 16. *which yet are many thouſands*, Rev. 7. 4.

imitate therein) very *(a)* seldom repent. So as upon most of them we spend our breath in vain.

Secondly, Do I damn the whole Nation, excepting a few, two or three, besides my self? how can he speak it? and how will he make any one that is in his Senses believe it, that he speaketh true? for, are all, or most Men Usurers in every Parish throughout *England*? Do we not know, that in many Parishes there are none, in others but two or three, in some but one; as *(b) Peraldus* tells us, that there was but one Usurer, who kept it very private too, in a whole City. And if so, how can he say that I damn the whole Nation, excepting so few?

Thirdly, But if I had Hyperbolically said such a thing as he charges me with, which I did not, he might have more charitably construed my words, as that great Apostles words must be construed; *There is none righteous; no, not one: and there is none that doth good; no, not one: that all the World may become guilty before God*, Rom. 3. 10.

NUM. XI.

Fourthly, But I must come closer to the matter, saying, that I am so far from damning the whole Nation, as that, contrary to his fearful Charge, which is, that *I censure and condemn many of his Brethren to Hell*, pag. 2. I do *(c)* exempt and except all those Godly Ministers, my dear Brethren, which, though they are for some Increase (as I also my self am, *viz.* for a Gratuity) yet are no common Usurers, properly so called: observing the Godly Cautions which blessed *Calvin*, pious and learned Mr. *Baxter*, and *(d)* others prescribe; and which being observed, do make that which by some is called Usury no Usury, but Partnership. As when Men are con-

---

(a) *So seldom as that we Saint a Man who does but give over this Golden Trade of Usury*, Capel *in his Tempt. p.* 264. (b) Peraldus *de Usura.* (c) *Only let me use St.* Austin's *holy Admonition to my Brethren, that they be not moved with the reasonings of vain Men, nor imitate them in this perverseness in Opinion*, c. 31. (d) *Of whom I will name but one more, Mr.* Durham, *who in his Exposition upon the Commandments, has these notable Cautions.* 1. *We should consider what the Borrower makes of our Money.* 2. *And we should not be swayed by our own Gain only, as most Usurers are.*

tented and minded to ſhare, not only in the Borrowers Gain, but Loſs alſo, which the abovesaid famous (*a*) Mr. *Baxter* and others require. And yet farther I ſay, that I hope in God, that I ſhall meet with thoſe holy and reverend Miniſters in Heaven, and that there we ſhall enjoy one anothers Society to all Eternity.

5. *I anſwer*, That I except alſo from that foreſaid Condemnation, thoſe Godly Chriſtian Hearers which obſerve the ſame Godly Cautions, which likewiſe make that which by ſome is improperly called Uſury, no Uſury, but Factory; and would not take any Gain for their Money if they were convinced that it is unlawful for them to take what is proffered: for I ſhall ſtill ſtick to that which I have ſo often ſaid with and after a number of other Divines, who ſay the ſame; that it is lawful to take what is unexpectedly offered. I add, that I have a very charitable Opinion of ſome Chriſtians beyond the Seas alſo, which in their ſimplicity and ignorantly follow *Abſolom*, like thoſe two hundred Men which followed *Abſolom* out of *Jeruſalem* in their ſimplicity, knowing nothing of it, that Rebellion was in it againſt *David* the King, 2 *Sam.* 15. 11. I ſay it again, that I do not condemn ſuch ignorant Souls, becauſe they are not convinced of the Evil of all Uſury properly ſo called, even as they are not convinced that they offend God by not keeping our Chriſtian Sabbath ſo ſtrictly as we keep it in *England*, accounting it *Judaiſm*: So that in the *Netherlands* they will carry burthens, and do ſervile work without control, as I have ſeen it: and at *Geneva*, after the Afternoon-Sermon, will go a Shooting in their *Plimpalee*, ſo called, which mine eyes have beheld alſo; and which, if Chriſtians, profeſſing Godlineſs, ſhould do here, they would be cenſured to ſin damnably. Which maketh me to judge charitably of ſuch a People as ſinneth ignorantly, not being convinced: *For the time of ignorance God winketh at; but withal, commands all men every where to repent*, Act. 17. 30. Which has ſtirred me up to perſuade all Men every where to repent of Uſury by name, and to leave it, with the very expectation of gaining by it, leſt that tremendous ſaying of Chriſt, *Joh.* 15. 22. *If I had not come and ſpoken unto them, they had not had ſin, but now they have no cloak for their ſin*, become applicable to them. Now, in this charitable Opinion I am not alone;

(*a*) *In his Directory.*

but there is (a) one besides me, who writeth as bitterly against all Usury as ever I did, and maketh it damnable, as I do, in one place of his Book; and yet in another speaketh thus dreadfully of it: *The sin is hainous, and the danger desperate; and the more dangerous when it is covered and shrowded: as a consuming Fever, that cannot be espied before it grows incurable.* And yet addeth withal, these words; *I know there be many, otherwise good Christians, that entertain this UGLY MONSTER, who would not do it to gain the World, if they knew their Trade were damnable Usury.* So saith he.

NUM. XII.

Obj. You will say, Why did not you tell us of this first?

I answer, Because I feared that all common Usurers would abuse this precious Cordial, intended for tender and troubled Consciences, and thereby be hardned in their Trade of Usury; pretending that they also are not convinced about this point, and therefore hope to be saved notwithstanding their most cruelly biting Usury: when God knoweth it, that they are fully convinced in their own Consciences, that their Usury is naught and damnable, because it stares in their faces now and then; and they will not call it, nor have it called Usury, but Interest, the Rent of their Money, and honest Profit, and Consideration, and Satisfaction. Whereof more hereafter.

NUM. XIII.

Sixthly, And this brings me to those which I chiefly aim at in this my Subject, *viz.* professed common, impenitent, resolute, obstinate, convinced Usurers; who, though their Consciences check them, and accuse them for their sinful practice, yet go on in that damnable Sin, and will not forsake it; of whom (being compared and conferred with some good people who observing the Godly Cautions prescribed by Godly Divines, whom I shall ever highly honour, lend their Money and take some Profit as a Gratuity of the Borrower, or ignorantly expect Gain for Money lent, as not being convinced yet, that even the expectation of some Usury and Increase i

(a) *Gabr. Powel.*

Usury,

Usury) I shall say as *Joab* once, to the wise Woman of *Abel* said, of *Sheba* the Son of *Bichrie*, 2 *Sam*. 20. 20, 21. *Far be it from me, that I should swallow up and destroy*, meaning that peaceable People of *Abel*. *The matter is not so : but* Sheba *the Son of* Bichrie *has lifted up his hand against the King, even against* David. So, far be it, far be it from me, that I should swallow up, by my preaching against impenitent Usurers, Death and Damnation ; or destroy, or go to hit the peaceable People of God, who truly fear God, and intend no War at all against God by any wilful Usury. The matter is not so ; but Sheba *the Son of* Bichrie, the wilful and obstinate Usurer I mean ; otherwise, the common Usurer who makes a Trade of that Usury which God interdicts and condemneth, called *Nesheck* and *Tarbith* ; that is, Usurious Encrease, *Ezek*. 18. 13. who lifts up himself against the King of Kings, and rebelleth against him, and his Commands concerning Usury ; against him I preach Damnation, as one who may well be called *Sheba*, because he hath *Seven Abominations* in his heart, as the Scripture speaketh of the Wicked, as he is, if any be among us, the Son of *Bichrie*, as some read it, because he is in *Aries*, which is not only a Celestial Sign, but also a Warlike Instrument used against a place or King besieged, and rebelled against, as the Usurer is, who is an Instrument acted by Satan, and used against the Great King, against whom he fighteth : against him, even this Usurer, I say, that I am ; telling him, that *except he repent, he shall surely die* ; that is, he shall be damned, and burn in the flames of Hell everlastingly, *Ezek*. 18. 13. and never dwell in God's Holy Hill above, as those who do not put forth their Money to Usury, *Psal*. 15. Nor am I alone in this ; for, besides these holy Scriptures, I shall bring against impenitent and common Usurers several Great, Learned, Pious and Renowned Writers, and their Writings ; who say the same, and condemn the Usurer to the flames of Hell, as well as my self ; *viz*.

1. (*a*) St. *Chrisostom*, Who saith, *Usuries prepare Hell*, without distinguishing, or once naming Griping Usury.

2. (*b*) St *Ambrose*, *If any Man takes Usury, he commits Rapine, he shall not live*. Which is also cited by others for such a purpose as well as by me.

(a) Chrisost. *in cap*. 1. *Math*. *Hom*. 5. (b) Ambrose, *lib. de Bono Mortis, & habetur*, 14 *q*. *Can*. 4.

3. (a) *Leo*, *We are to flee that Iniquity of Usury, because the Usury of Money is the Funeral of the Soul.* Thus he.

4. But why do I name but these *Three Fathers.*

Famous Bishop (b) *Downam* tells us, *The Fathers of the Church have with one consent condemned Usury, even* TO THE PIT OF HELL.

5. (c) *Adams* also hath these dreadful words against the Usurer, condemning him *to the Flames of Hell: Infinite Excuses, Evasions, Distinctions, Paintings, are invented to countenance on Earth Heaven-exploded Usury. God saith,* Thou shalt not TAKE USURY: *Go now, dispute the matter with God,* HELL FIRE *shall decide the Question.*

6. Next to this famous Man, let blessed (d) *Bolton* pass his Sentence. *Out of the wideness of the Conscience of some wicked Men proceedeth mincing and excusing in many Interpretations, favourable Cnstructions and distinctions of Sin. As for example, That Usury is of two sorts; Biting, and a Toothless,* (as also saith the Champion and his Brethren) *holding for it; when* ALL KIND OF USURY IS MOST CERTAINLY DAMNED BY THE BOOK OF GOD.

7 (e) *Francis Whiddon* the Elder preached the same, that *The Usurer's Portion will be* ETERNAL DAMNATION.

8. Add (f) *James Spotwood*, who from *Psal.* 15. 5. tells us, that *Usurers are excluded from Eternal Life.*

And I will add to those two Modern, most Learned, most Renowned, most Valued and Pious Bishops.

1. (g) Bishop *Jewel* tells the Usurer, *How darest thou look up to Heaven? Thou hast no Dwelling there.* And, *Usurers shall die the Death*, Ezek. 18. 13. meaning the Death of the Soul.

And 2. (h) Bishop *Sands*, besides Bishop *Downam*, already quoted.

(a) Leo *de Jejunio Decim. mensis, Serm.* 6. (b) *Bishop* Downam, *in* Psal. 15. 5. (c) Adams, *in his Works, pag.* 15. (d) Bolton, *in his Discourse of True Happiness.* (e) *As his judicious Hearers informed me when I was putting forth this Treatise.* (f) James Spotswood, *in his short Discourse concerning Usury.* (g) *Bishop* Jewel, *in* 1 Thes. *p.* 145. (h) *Bishop* Sands *Serm. upon* Rom. 13.

And 9. I will now close up this naming of Authors with that terrible Doom denounced against the Usurer by Doctor (a) *Williams*; who tells the Usurer, that *The punishment of Usurers in Hell shall be greater than most Sinners.* O dreadful! Tremble at it, O Usurer.

NUM. XIV.

But when the Common Usurer, who takes and expects Use above his Principal, hears this, that he is chiefly meant, he will be apt to make these two Objections.

Object. 1. That these Writers may and must be understood, as speaking against Oppressive and cruelly Biting Use and Usurers.

Whereunto I answer, That this cannot be their meaning, because they also shew what that Usury is, and those Usurers are, which they write against.

I'll instauce in two only, reserving many more for another Answer, which is to come upon another account.

The first is, (b) St. *Ambrose*, whom but now I mentioned; and who saith expresly, *Et esca Usura est, & vestis Usura est, & quodcunque sorti accedit Usura est*; that is, *And Meat is Usury, and a Vestment is Usury, and whatsoever exceedeth, or is taken above the Principal, is Usury.*

The Second is (c) *Brentius*; saying, *Men do define Usury to be a Gain that is added to that which is lent; or, when over and besides the Principal, any thing is paid for Lending.* Which doth not cross free Lending, and a free Gratuity, because it is a Gain arising from the very Act of Lending; whereas a free Gratuity ariseth from Thankfulness.

Object. 2. The condemned Usurer will object and reply; I hope that I cannot be, nor shall be condemned to the flames of Hell, living under the New Testament, though Usurers, living under the Old, were sent to those everlasting Flames, because the New Testament neither interdicts Usury, nor condemneth the Usurer.

(a) *Doctor* Williams, *in his tr[illegible]hurch*, p. 438. (b) Ambrose, *l. de Tol. c.* 14. (c) Bre[illegible]us *Comment in* Levit. 25.

Where-

Whereunto I return these Responses.

1. That Usury is interdicted in both Testaments. In the Old first, by a general consent; and in the New also, as well as old, by the Verdict of whole Councils and Universities.

I'll instance in one of each. And,

1. In the *Lateran Council*, twice it is asserted by two hundred and sixty Bishops, or more, *That Usury is forbidden in both the Volumes of the Bible.* And again, *The Crime of Usury is detested by both Testaments.*

2. In the University of *Wittenbergh*: Whose words are in its first Thesis or Position, *Forasmuch as Usuries, not only by a positive Law, but also by both the Old and New Testaments, are, as in themselves evil, prohibited by God,* &c. See the rest in my *Usurer Cast*, p. 47.

Whereupon it followeth, that Damnation must needs follow, if what both affirm be proved. So that,

2. It may be made good by Arguments and Proofs, that in the New Testament, Usury is interdicted, as well as in the Old; and so consequently condemned as a breach of God's Prohibition.

NUM. XV.

Now, to prove it, I shall

1. Lay down this Position, That that is Scripture which, by a necessary Consequence, is inferred from the Scripture; according to a Maxim which we have in Divinity, and which *Gregory Nazianzen* used against the *Arrians*; saying, *That some things are said to be, and are in the Scripture; and some are, and are not mentioned in Scripture*; that is to say, consequently. As for Example,

The prophaning of the Christian Sabbath is not mentioned, nor interdicted expresly, but consequently, because it is called The Lord's Day, *Rev.* 1. 10. Whereupon it followeth, that we must do the Lord's Work; and not prophane it, by doing the Devil's work.

And the like may be said of Usury; that, at least, consequentially it is forbidden; *Luk.* 6. 35. *Lend, hoping for nothing again.* For, as *Beza* worthily reasoneth, if, *as some say, we must not, by vertue of this place, look for the very Principal again, then much less may we look for Usury.* But yet let it be remembred, that by a great number that place is understood

thus,

thus, hoping for nothing again, that is, *no Usury*. So that famous Mr. (*a*) *Poole* in the opening of that place, placeth this Expofition firft, *Hoping for nothing again*; that is, NO USURY; whereof more abundantly hereafter. For I fhall, before I have done with this matter, in this very Book, bring a Cloud of Witneffes, afferting that the meaning of that place in *Luk.* 6. 35. even now mentioned, is this, *Lend, hoping for nothing again*; that is, *No Ufury*.

NUM. XVI.

2. (*b*) I anfwer to that other part of this Objection; which is, *I hope I fhall not be damned to the Flames of Hell, living under the New Teftament, for Ufury thus.* As that moft Learned most Pious, and moft Famous Doctor PAREUS, my ancient Friend of bleffed Memory, who alfo was an Enemy to Ufury, as many others are, when he was writing his Learned Commentary upon the *Revelations* (the beft of all which I have feen) had a Prophefie fent him concerning the Deftruction of the Pope and Turk, with the Effigies or Defcription of that great Monarch who fhould deftroy both, (*c*) which he inferted, and fet down in his Book So, as I was writing this Book, a Letter was written by an Able, Noted and Godly Minifter, living at a great diftance from me, after he had read my late Book, and therein, *The Ufurer Caft*, I fay, a Letter was written for my encouragement in my proceedings, and fent me concerning a late great Ufurer's Damnation. Which Letter I will alfo, like PAREUS, here infert and communicate, that Men may fee, and Ufurers efpecially, what becomes of Ufurers *under the New Teftament*, as well as under the Old.

The Letter it felf now follows, containing this Narrative.

'Mr. *Grefham*, a Merchant, failing from *Falerno*, where dwelt 'the aforefaid great Ufurer, called *Antonio the Rich*; who 'at one time had two Kingdoms mortgaged to him by the 'King of *Spain* (who is a great Borrower) and being croffed 'by contrary Winds, was conftrained to Anchor near

(*a*) *Mr.* Pool, *upon* Luk. 16. 35. *naming his Author.* (*b*) *Second Objection anfwered.* (*c*) Pareus *upon* Rev. 17.

Mount

'Mount *Ætna*. Now, about Mid-day, when for certain 'hours it accustomarily forbeareth to flame, he ascended the 'Mount with eight of the Sailers; and approaching as near 'the Vent as they durst, amongst other noises, they heard 'a Voice cry aloud, *Dispatch, dispatch; the rich* Antonio '*is a coming*. Terrified therewith, they descended; and 'anon the Mountain evaporated Fire: but from so dismal 'a place they made all the haste they could when the Winds 'were still. And desiring much to know more of this mat-'ter, they returned to *Falerno*: and forthwith enquiring of 'ANTONIO, it was told them, that he was dead; and 'computing the time, did find it to agree with the very In-'stant that the Voice was heard by them. *Gresham* repor-'ted this, at his Return, to the King; and the Mariners 'being called before him, confirmed by Oath the Narra-'tion. In *Gresham* himself (as it was reported) it wrought 'so deep an Impression, that he gave over all Traffick; di-'stributing his Goods, a part to his Kinds-folk, the rest to 'good Uses, retaining only a Competency for himself; and 'so spent his time in a voluntary Devotion.

Oh dreadful! Oh, that the poor condemned Usurer would seriously mind all this, and give over his damnable Usury, that he may not come and be cast into these everlasting Burnings! for that will be the Portion of every impenitent Usurer; after he hath breathed out his last, most ugly Devils will immediately carry his Soul into that Lake that flameth like Mount *Ætna*, and burneth with Fire and Brimstone, which is the Second Death, threatned against the Usurer, which takes Biting and ENCREASE, *Ezek*. 18. 13. Confess I do, that the more cruel a Biter any Usurer is, the hotter (if any can be) and the deeper Damnation he will have for his Part and Portion: but he that shall have the least Torment in that woful place, and merciless fire, shall have so much as will make him cry out with horrid and hellish Anguish; *Who can dwell in these everlasting Burnings*, Isa. 33. 12. And therefore, as that Merchant called *Gresham*, hearing what was said of *Antonio*'s, that great Usurer's, coming and bringing to Hell, was quite changed and converted, so let the threatningly condemned Usurer repent and live; for why will he die, poor Usurer? that to him I may apply that in *Ezek*. 18. 21.

NUM.

NUM. XVII.

But I desire to answer yet farther to his charging me with monstrous Uncharitableness; as thus, that I cannot but wonder how an Usurer can censure one which is no Usurer for Uncharitableness, when in very deed THE USURER standeth deeply charged for his Cruelty and Uncharitableness by a number of great and famous (*a*) Authors, which tell him that his Usury is directly against Charity, and that there is no such Toothless Usury as is talked of by some, because either the Borrower or Commonwealth is bitten; for which cause he is called a Biter, מַשִּׁיךְ, and the Borrower, נָשַׁךְ, that is, Bitten.

Lastly, who will believe this Man, that I am so uncharitable towards the poor Usurer as he makes me, and that he is charitable, when he doth his utmost to harden him in his Sin? For, how do they rejoyce that one is come to defend Usurers, by so many others condemned? taking themselves to be but moderate Takers of Usury after Six in the Hundred; and how I am told, where I come abroad, that my Book is answered and confuted? And how they name *Grotius*, a Foreign Divine, who hath written somewhat favourably of some Usury; as some few others, with Cautions and Limitations; which none of our common Usurers do observe, whereas they never heard of such a Man, before my Adversaries Pamphlet was brought among them, which maketh mention of him. So that my former Labours would prove altogether fruitless and abortive, if I should not answer him; telling the condemned Usurer, that my Charity towards him is such, as that I labour to my utmost to convince, to convert, and Ministerially to save his Soul from Hell, and his Estate from Ruin, according to my Cordial: So that he will find in the end, that I am one of his best Friends which he has in the World, because of both, and especially because of that which I have written of Restitution, which will undo the richest Usurer in *Devon*, unless he be forgiven; because, being an Heir to a departed Usurer, he must restore that also which

---

(*a*) *As Doctor* Rainold, *Who in his Book of Divorce*, p. 8. *holds, that distinction between Biting and not Biting Usury, used by some late Divines, to be but a meer flam.*

by

by Usury was gotten, as Mr. (a) *Powel* giveth his Reasons for it.

Of other *Biters*, which my Adversary speaks of, I intend to write hereafter.

All this while I have answered but one side and a little more of the Champion's first Leaf, and spinning out the thread of my Discourse to such a more than ordinary length, by reason of his extraordinary charging me with a confused *Chaos*, and with monstrous Uncharitableness; telling the World, that I send the whole Nation, except two or three, to the Flames of Hell. So that of necessity I must crave the gentle Reader's Pardon, promising to study Brevity for the time to come.

NUM. XVIII.

My next work will be to come to the strange Vision which this strange Man writeth of; saying, *It ill becomes Mr.* Jelinger, *upon that late Vision, wherein he was seen mounting Triumphant to Heaven (he knoweth what I mean) to be so far lifted up with Self-conceit, as to censure and condemn so many of his Brethren to Hell, for the things here under debate: to me its no doubt, but that of our Saviour meets with such as these, viz.* Judge not, that ye be not judged. Whereupon he brings in, as he supposeth, against me Mr. *Vines*, writing thus; *To render a Sin manifest and notorious, , I suppose, first it is requisite that it be manifestly a Sin; and this is* Quæstio Juris: *For a thing may be commonly cried down under the name of an Enormous Crime, and yet indeed be very doubtful: I instance in Usury,* &c. *Thus Mr.* Vines; *who, no doubt, had as much skill and ability to weigh what was written on both sides concerning this Subject, as Mr.* Jelinger.

To all which I answer thus. And,

1. To the Vision.

2. To Mr. *Vines* Saying.

3. To what he saith concerneth my Skill and Ability compared with Mr. *Vines*.

(a) *The Canon Law, l.* 4. *tit.* 7. *p.* 469. *And* Gregor. *de* Val. *To.* 3. *Disp.* 5. *q.* 21. *punct.* 3. Gabriel Powel, *in his Positions, p.* 70. *And* Capel, *in his Treatise of Usury, p.* 268.

1. *As for the Vision*; that I will relate first, and so clear up: Which done, I shall add some Observations.

For the first, Let me tell the courteous Reader, that there was a certain Man of great Parts and Gifts, for whom, being fallen sick, and like to die, I was sent for to visit him, and to pray with and for him. Whereupon (to be short, he being recovered the same Night, sent for me the next Morning to give me thanks; telling me, that he had seen me in Heaven, *&c.* and wrote a Book of it, and left it with me, but what became of his Book I know not. Which sheweth what confidence I placed in it.

Now, let the Reader judge what fault I have committed in this. Suppose twenty more should tell me the same, that they saw me Triumphant in Heaven, can I help that?

NUM. XIX.

2. But I shall raise some Observations next upon this Vision. And,

1. *I observe my Adversary's great Spight.*

2. *Great Indignation.*

1. *Spight*, Which is such, as that by this Vision he thinks to render me and my Book contemptible. Which I hope he will never be able to do, because I see the quite contrary already; some of Quality being lately, as well as others formerly, convinced by my first Book, and changed graciously.

2. *I observe his Indignation against me*, In that he laboureth by this Vision to be revenged upon me for my writing against his DIANA, Being,

1. Like, therein, to his Grandfather, *M. S.* Who also was so angry (as he is) as to pick a Quarrel, and enter the Lists for Usury with that most Learned, most Godly, and most Famous Man, Mr. *Bolton*, of blessed Memory, for a Sermon of his preached against Usury, as Mr. *Bagshaw* reports it.

2. And like *Demetrius* and his Crafts-men, who so cried out against *Paul*, as he against me, because he and they saw that by his preaching their Craft and Gain was like to go down: for so said *Demetrius*, *Sirs, you know that by this Craft we have our Wealth*; meaning his and their making of Silver Shrines for *Diana*: which brought no small Gain unto the Crafts-men, *Act.* 19. 24, 25. Even as *Usury* doth now to *Usurers*, who make a Trade of that great and grievons Sin. *Moreover, you see*, crieth he, *that not only this our Craft is in*

danger to be set at naught; but also, that the Temple of the great Goddess Diana *should be despised.——— And when they heard these Sayings, they were full of Wrath, and cried out, saying, Great is* Diana *of the* Ephesians, vers. 26, 27, 28. Even as now also our Usurers, being full of Wrath when they and their Usury is spoken against by God's *Pauls*, as it has been of old by all the holy Fathers, within the space of fifteen hundred Years, cried out against. I say, *Great is our* Diana, *Great is our Gain which we make of our Usury-money.* Let the *Vision-teller* apply all this as it may be applied, (I, for my part, must be brief, because I promised it) and let none blame me for using this Comparison; for so famous Mr. *Bagshaw*, a Parliament-man, makes use of the same in blessed *Bolton's* Case; saying *The Gain that* M. S. *made by that* SILVER SHRINE *whetted his Invention to maintain by Humane Argument what he was loth to part with by Divine Commandment.* Where note withal, that he quoteth in the Margin this same, *Act.* 19. 24.

NUM. XX.

2. As for his Citation of Mr. *Vines*; To that I answer thus.

1. That I say, as he, that to render a Sin manifest and notorious, it is requisite that it be manifestly a Sin; adding withal, that so Usury has been manifestly proved to be a Sin; I mean, both *Nesheck* and *Tarbith*; that is, (*a*) Encrease, by God himself forbidding, and threatning both with Death and Damnation, *Ezek.* 18. 13. and by a World of holy Writers, New and Old, which I shall bring against the condemned Usurer. At present I will name but

1. (*b*) Gregory Nyssene, *Apud Divinam Scripturam & fœnus & Usura sunt prohibita*, (that is, both Encrease, which the (*c*) *Latins* call *Fœnus Fœnorios*, and the *Hebricians, Tarbith:* And also, Usury, which the *Latins* call *Usuram*; the *Grecians*, τόκος· the *Hebricians*, *Nesheck) are forbidden in the Scriptures.*

(*a*) *As Doctor* Kinchus *upon* Ezek. 18. 12, 13. *doth make it clear, saying, that By that place Usury is expressed what it is; namely, Encrease: that is to say, what is more than the Principal.* (*b*) Greg. Nyssenus. (*c*) *As saith a famous Author.*

2. St.

2. St. *Ambrose*, upon *Lev.* 25. *Generaliter omne sortis excludit augmentum*: that is, *This Sentence of God doth generally exclude all Encrease above the Principal.*

Whereunto, Thirdly, may be Repetitionally added Bishop (a) *Downam*, (who, I hope, had as much Skill and Ability to judge of Usury as Mr. *Vines*, and a little more) saying, *My Assertion concerning Usury is this, That all Usury (which I have defined to be Mutation, or Lending for Gain) whether it be Mental, or Actual, whether Manifest or Covert, whether Simple or Compounded, is simply, and in its own Nature, utterly unlawful: however, some Usury is worse than other.* And farther he saith, *Which Assertion I will not only prove by Testimonies of Scripture., but also defend and maintain against the Objections of those who hold the contrary Opinion.* Which is more than ever Mr. *Vines* did, or could do.

NUM. XXI.

2. And whereas Mr. *Vines* stands upon this, that its a Question whether the Sin in Question be Usury, and what Usury is; I shall cite against his Saying so cited,

1. The same Great and Learned Prelate even now mentioned, Bishop (b) *Downam* I mean, whose words are these; *In* Luther'*s time, and in all Ages before him, although many practised Usury, as they did other kinds of Theft and Robbery, yet there was never any Controversie among the Learned concerning the Lawfulness of Usury more than other kinds of Thefts, but all with one consent have condemned Usury, and Usurers to the Pit of Hell.*

With him blessed (c) *Bolton* doth Symphonize thus, *The Covetousness of these times has made a Controversie, which in former Ages was never doubted of.* And what Rational Divine will not hearken to these two great Writers, rather than to Mr. *Vines*, in this thing?

2. To Mr. *Vines* great Names of Learning and Godliness, who deny all Usury to be sinful, I shall oppose far greater Names and Numbers, even *(d)* hundreds, and hundreds, and hundreds, of as Learned and Pious Men, assembled in at least thirteen *Councils* as ever Doctor *Vines* was; besides an infinite

(a) *Bishop* Downam *upon* Psal. 15. 5. (b) *Idem ibid.* (c) Bolton. (d) *I had almost said thousands.*

number

number of particular Fathers, Doctors, (*a*) publick Persons, and (*b*) Who have all generally condemned all Usury, properly so called, and by them defined to be that which is Usuriously taken above the Principal, as I have already shewn it, and shall make good yet farther by these following Quotations of some of them; who have been even super-eminent for depth of Learning, and height of Holiness. As namely,

1. Renowned (*c*) Doctor *Fenton*; *There was never any Church or Church-man, carrying the name of a Christian, who defended in writing* ANY BRANCH *of Usury, for the space of fifteen hundred Years after Christ: Neither was this for want of occasion given; for it has been both practised and written against in all Ages. Neither can we with modesty impute it to the ignorance of the Church: Her Writers in Cases of Conscience, for matters of Morality, were most exact.*

2. With this Pious and deep Learned Doctor, I joyn also that aforesaid great and highly esteemed Prelate, Bishop (*d*) *Downam*: Who, speaking of our latter times, since the fifteen hundred Years spoken of by Doctor *Fenton*, elapsed, has let fall these words, *The Godly Learned Divines of this Age; and namely, of this our Church, do for the most part inveigh against it.*

3. (*e*) *Oecolampadius* also declareth his mind against all Usury, as simply evil: And addeth, *And this has been the general Judgment of the Church for above fifteen hundred Years, without opposition.*

4. But lest Usurers should despise these Sayings, as coming from some particular persons *against all Usury, I will subjoyn the Judgment of a whole* English *(f) Parliament, consisting of a most Wise and Learned King,* viz. *King* James, *and of most*

(*a*) Viz. *Emperors, Kings, Law-givers.* (*b*) *Christian and Pagan.* (*c*) *Doctor* Fenton, *p.* 142. *with whom I may joyn the Holy and Learned* Richard Capel, *saying in his Tent. p.* 5. *Edit. p.* 293. *There is an* English *Manuscript carried about from hand to hand, said to be written by a Great Man, and Learned Clerk. He takes it for granted, that all Usury is unlawful; which confutes, those that say the contrary, and justifies me. And so great* Tostatus *too; who saith, that All Modes of Usury are unlawful, in* Levit. *p.* 516. (*d*) *Bishop* Downam *upon* Psal. 15. 5. (*e*) Oecolampadius, *a* German *Divine, upon the Lesser Prophets.* (*f*) Jacobi, 13.

Judicious,

Judicious, Able and Erudite Bishops, and other great, and deeply Literate Lords, besides hundreds of Commons, Gentlemen of great Piety and Experience.; who with one Consent made a most noble Act against Usury, to restrain it: with this Introduction, Forasmuch as ALL USURY, *being forbidden by the Law of God, is Sin, and detestable.*——

What can you say to all this now, Champion? Will you speak against all these Holy and Learned Men, which are against all Usury; and against this Wise, Great and Glorious Parliament too, as you are against me? Are the *Names* which Mr. *Vines* so stands upon as great as these which I have named, and can name? Can they compare with mine for Godliness and Learning? Here let the Learned judge.

NUM. XXII.

Object. *If my Adversary object, That these are Humane Authorities.*

I Answer, *And are not his too?* as blessed *Bolton* answered *M. S.* and only Humane Authorities? But my chief Basis is the Holy Scripture.

5. *I Answer thus*, because the Champion adds to Mr *Vines*'s Saying, these words are added. First, *With what a more tender Hand, and prudent candid Spirit did Mr.* Vines *write.* And afterward it is said, *Mr.* Vines, *who, no doubt, had as much skill and ability to weigh what was written on both sides, concerning this Subject, as Mr.* Jelinger.

That 1. I will not gainsay what he saith of Mr. *Vines*'s Hand, that it was tender, and his Spirit prndent and candid: But whose Hand was more tender, and Spirit more prudent and candid, must be left to God to judge, as himself saith in his words foregoi g.

2. That he had as much skill and ability to weigh what was written on both sides, concerning this Subject, as Mr. *Jelinger*; yea, more, I must in modesty acknowledge. But even therefore, that Mr. *Vines* may be equally matched, and that the Truth which I am maintaining against the Damnable Sin of Usury may not suffer through my Insufficiency and Inability, I will oppose against his citing of Mr. *Vines*'s words against me, the words of as great a Name and Divine as ever Mr. *Vines* was, to match him indeed; *viz. Gabriel Powel*, a famous Man, and great Scholar indeed: who, living at *Oxford*, in

that Peerless and Famous University, wrote his Position against Usury, which Men may see in Print, and was never answered, as far as ever I could Learn, though there were then, and are now so many Great and Learned Doctors and Scholars, which, as one should think, would have taken the pains to confute him if they had thought it feisable. To be short, his words are; *I have read all that ever I could come by, Fathers, Canonists and Modern Writers, and made choice of what I judged best out of them all; which I have couched together concisely and methodically, so as the Reader may compendiously, as it were, with one Prospect, take a view of what has been written concerning Usury.* After which words, he sets down among his Positions, this Apodictical Syllogism in *Barbara, A definitione rei, From the Definition of the thing. All Gain, that contrary to the Word of God, is expected, or exacted, above the Principal, for the very Duty of Lending, is unlawful and damnable.*

Usury is such a Gain.

Ergo, *Usury is unlawful and damnable.*

The Assumption he proves by six places of Scripture; *Exod.* 22. 25. *Levit.* 25. 37. *Deut.* 23. 19. *Psal.* 15. 5. *Ezek.* 18. 13. *Luk.* 6. 34, 35. Where let the Judicious Reader chuse whom he will believe; that great *Oxford* Scholar, who was never yet (b) confuted, as far as ever I could hear, being armed with his six holy Scriptures; or Mr. *Vines*, who brings no Scripture along with him at all.

NUM. XXIII,

6. And against Mr *Vines*'s great Names, of *Godliness in special*; who, as he saith, deny what I now, and others heretofore, have asserted, of the sinfulness of Usury, properly so called, I can produce the Sayings and Names of Men as great for *Godliness* as any he could name; who have proved this my Assertion in Books at large. For, was not blessed *Ambrose* who wrote that excellent Book of *Tobie against Usury*; defining Usury thus, *Whatsoever is more than the Principal, is Usury*

(a) *Which* Calvin *counts the best way of Arguing.* (b) *Also Doctor* Pye, *writing a Book in Latin at* Cambridge *against Usury, was never confuted: which is very remarkable, that in both the Universities none should appear to take Usury's part.*

A.

An extraordinary holy Man? Oh, yes; if we will believe his Master, the Emperor *Theodosius*; who told his Courtiers, who would have him go to receive the Sacrament of him, after he had been kept from it a great while; *I know him to be such an Holy Man, that he will not admit me.* He is such an Holy Man.

And what may we think of (*a*) *Hierom*, who writes of Usury thus? *Some think that Usury consists in Money only; which the Divine Scripture foreseeing, takes off all that is over and above that which is lent, from every thing lent, that a Man should take no more than he gave.* Was not he a holy Man? Oh, yes; if we will believe what he writes of himself; That when, to live a more Godly Life than he could live at *Rome*, he lived in *Eremo*, a Wilderness, and saw Visions.

So Great (*b*) *Basil*; who, besides many other things written against Usury, which, reading him, I have extracted, has penned and published a whole Sermon, made upon *Psal.* 15. against it: and more especially in his Homily against those that will be rich, has let fall these words; *What? Gold begets it self, in that by Usury it comes to an Encrease* (which the Hebrew calls *Tarbith.*) Thus he. And was not he a Godly Man? Oh, yes, an extraordinary one; for he sold his great Estate, and by it relieved the Poor in a time of great need.

And what shall I say of blessed *Bolton*, who has preached so much against all Usury, as that he was forced to defend his Preaching against it, in and by that famous Book of his, called *A Discourse concerning Usury*; which I wish all good people, and Usurers especially, to read. Was not he a Godly Man? Oh, yes, if we may believe him who wrote his Life; and herein tells us, that he was wont to pray six times a day; twice with his Wife, twice with his Family, and twice by himself solemnly. And when he was dying, told his Parishioners, which were come to see him, *I am as full of Christ as my heart can hold.* All which, I wish Men would consider, and such as defend Heaven-exploded Usury especially; and that for this Consideration also the rather, because a great Name, both for Learning and Godliness, Bishop (*c*) *Downam* I mean, has left these words for the Patrons of Usury to pause upon: *And I will, out of* (*d*) *their Writings, manifestly de-*

(*a*) Hierom *on* Ezek. 18. (*b*) Basil *Magnus.* (*c*) *Bishop* Downam *upon* Psal. 15. 5. (*d*) *Holy Authors against Usury he meaneth.*

monstrate before their eyes, that the Usury which is practised in the World is not allowed of any GODLY DIVINE. Thus he.

6. I add, that because I am so much cried down and blamed by this Champion, my Adversary, for being so much against all Usury, properly so called; and Mr. *Vines* so extolled; I will therefore produce,

NUM. XXIV.

Yet more, two great and famous Writers indeed, who will speak as much for me, as possibly he can say against me; and that by way of Commendation: *viz. (a) Beza*, and *(b) Poole.* Both which joyn in one and the same Saying: The one speaking, or rather, writing first; the other after. The Words are, and deserve to be, printed in Letters of Gold.

Sed hac de re acturus (dicit Beza*) illud primum præfabor probare me eorum PIETATEM, qui totum hoc lucrandi genus sublatum vellent e rebus humanis quando multa inde nasci mala manifestissimum est.*

*That is, (*saith *Beza) Being to treat of this thing, viz. USURY, I will first make this Preface. That I do commend their PIETY, who would have that WHOLE, mark,* Whole *Kind of Gaining to be taken away from among Men, because it is most manifest, that much Evil comes by it.* Which way doth the Champion now look, when he readeth these words? I, for my part, would not give them for much Silver; and I value these two famous Men above an hundred Usuries Patrons. And yet I cannot but confess that I have a reverend Esteem of Mr. *Vines* too; for I knew the Man, and heard him preach excellently well, and hope that he and I shall meet in Heaven hereafter; but yet I must prefer his Betters before him for what is one such Man to so many hundred Holy Men, me

---

(a) Beza, *and (b)* Pool *upon* Luk. 6. 35. *Against whom some usually object, that he is but a Collector. But then, why may not I quote him for my self about Usury, as well as M. B. for himself about the Sense of the Spirit in* Lev. 1. 77. *in his Syn. p.* 104. *Part* 1? *(c) Which is also Syllogistically said, and set forth by* Philip Cæsar *plainly, and Rhetorically by* Ockerfor *in his Orations, and made good by Doctor* Wilson, *that it is commendable.*

in at least thirteen Councils, which, in my answering of his Sayings, I hinted at? And what is he to so many Godly Fathers, and Learned Writers more, both new and old, which are on my side, being all against all Usury, properly so called? And Lastly, What is one such Divine brought against me, to those two great Names which I named last, *Poole* and *Beza*: *Poole* being a Man, whose Learned and Laborious Commentaries upon the whole Bible will be famous over the whole *European* Orb; which Mr. *Vines* never can, nor will be; because the one writ so much, and all in *Latin*; and the other so little, and in *(a) English*, which few have yet seen, nor read in *England*? And as for *Beza*, who can commend him enough? I, for my part, and so all my Brethren, which hold with me in this Point of Usury, have cause enough to commend him as much as we are able, because he commends them, and their PIETY, for being against all that kind of Gain which comes by Usury, and because he is worthy of all Commendation: For, Oh, What a Man is he for Learning, for Fame, for Piety! For Learning first; For how his Learned Works are made use of in Printing, and Preaching, by our Tribe, even almost the whole Tribe of *Levi*? And when a Dispute was to be maintained against, and with the Papists at *Paris*, before the King and Queen, *Vivente* Calvino, *Calvin* being yet alive; who must be sent to carry on that Dispute, but Learned *Beza*: And, for his fame, how? Oh, how it shines every where among the Protestants! And when the King of *France*'s Army marched into *Italy* through and by *Geneva*, how the great Commanders went to see famous *Beza*? And Lastly, Such was his Piety, as that, when the *Sabandian* Army had by a Scalade assaulted *Geneva* by Night, and was entred half way into the City, *Beza*, with Old Men, Women and Children, did betake himself into St. *Peters*, and there prayed; and praying, so prevailed, as that the *Sabandians* were beaten out again, and never returned *(b)* since. And thus much may suffice to be spoken about *Beza*'s Commendation of those Men's Piety, who are against all that WHOLE Kind of gaining by Usury.

(*a*) *Which beyond the Seas they do not understand.* (*b*) *As more of this I shew in another Treatise.*

NUM. XXV.

In the next place, I will view and anſwer the Champion's Charge, whereby he charges me for being a Name caller. His words are, ' His Charity diſcovers it ſelf yet farther, in ' the Titles that he giveth the Men of his Indignation: Thoſe ' Expreſſions that any of the Fathers, or other Writers, in- ' tended againſt Oppreſſive Uſury, and Exacting Vſurers, ' he has been at the pains to collect (or receive from others ' hands) and Crown the Heads of all ſuch he calls Vſurers ' with: So that with him every Vſurer (*i. e.* every one that ' expects Advantage upon Money lent) is like the Devil, is a ' Dog, an Extortioner, an unjuſt Perſon, a Biter, a Thief, ' made equal with Adulterers, Covetous, a Deſtroyer, to ' be of the Generation of Vipers, a Mercileſs Perſon, is not in ' Caſe to give (*a*) Alms, is a Murderer, a Baptized Jew.

Whereto I anſwer,

1. That I am not (*b*) the firſt that has been ſo taxed for calling Names.

2. That for ſuch Names, I cannot only bring Fathers, and other Writers, but their Definitions and Deſcriptions alſo of Vſuries, and Vſurers, which they call by theſe Names. As for Example,

1. (*c*) *Peraldus*, having defined manifeſt Vſury, what it is, *viz. When a Man delivereth numbred Money, weighed or meaſured, with this Compact, that ſomething be given him beſides the Principal.* I ſay, having ſo defined Vſury, he ſaith not only, that the Vſurer is like the Devil, but *very like him*; his words are, *Eſt valde ſimilis Diabolo:* Which is more than ever Mr. *Jelinger* ſaid yet. And therefore, Why is this Man ſo angry with me?

2. So (*d*) St. *Ambroſe* having ſaid, that *Generally that place in* Lev. 25. *excludeth all Encreaſe, and Augmentation of the*

(*a*) *Which I have learned to ſay of the famous* Phllip Cæſar; *who, in his Diſcourſe againſt Uſury, ſaith, that Alms received of Uſurers is Abominable. So St.* Auſtin, Dona iniquorum non approbat Altiſſimus. (*b*) *The Author of* The Arraignment of Vſury *has been ſo taxed alſo, p.* 7. (*c*) Peraldus, *that Learned B. in* Spec. Avar. (*d*) *St.* Ambroſe *de* Tob. *c.* 15.

Principal, maketh the Vsurer a Murderer; saying with *Cato*, *That to commit Usury is to kill a Man.*

3. And St. *Basil*, having made Vsury to be an Encrease, calleth Vsurers *Vipers*; and their Vsuries, *Generations of Vipers*, upon *Psal.* 15. 5. which is my Text.

N V M. XXVI.

4 And doth not God himself, who maketh, not only *Nesheck*; that is, *Biting*; but also, *Tarbith*; that is *Encrease, Usury*, call the Vsurer an *Extortioner* in the Original, *Psal.* 109. 11. and couple him with Bribe-takers and Defrauders, *Ezek.* 22. 17. and with *Idolaters*, *Ezek.* 18 12, 13. For so *Tremellius* reads that place by an Apposition, *Has lift up his eyes to Idols, committing Abomination*, (and then it followeth immediately) *giveth to Usury and Encrease*. Not Vsury only, called *Nesheck*; but also Encrease, called *Tarbith*. which Coupling, (*b*) St. *Ambrose* also takes special notice of, saying, *Lo, how the Prophet in this place has coupled an Usurer with an Idolater, as if Usury did run equal and parallel with Idolatry.* Thus this holy Father.

I thought to end with God's Coupling and Calling; but because some other Names afterward were brought to my mind, I hold it good to add them also, and so to go on.

And 5. I will name St. *Chrisostom*, who calls him *Cursed*; saying, *The Usurer is, above all Merchants, cursed.*

And 6. After him I will cite (*c*) Mr. *Wheatly*, who calls him *Unjust*, (which the Champion saith, that I call him) His Words at full are these, *The Usurer maketh sure for himself to have part only, and infallibly, in the Profit; and therefore serveth himself alone, and not also his Brother. And for this cause, the Usurer is set among those who cannot dwell in the Mountain of God; which he should not be, were he not unjust.*

7. After this good and famous Man, in comes the University of *Wittenberg* again; which calleth Vsurers *Robbers and Hereticks.*

And lest some should say, that it meaneth Oppressive and Exacting Vsurers, as the Champion is pleased to make the

---

(*a*) Basil *Homil. in Ditesc. p.* 152. *Making Usurers also worse than Dogs.* (*b*) *St.* Ambrose *de* Tob. *c.* 15. (*c*) *Mr.* Wheatly, *in his* Caveat for the Covetous. *p.* 71.

World believe, that when Writers call Vſurers ſuch Names, they mean ſuch ; the ſame Vniverſity tells us, that thoſe which take but Five in the Hundred are Vſurers, *&c.* Its whole Deſcription of Vſurers the Reader may peruſe in my *Uſurer Caſt*, pag. 5.

8. (*a*) *Lavater* couples Vſury with Drunkenneſs and Adultery, and to make the Vſurer as bad as a Drunkard and Adulterer alſo.

9. And, as *Auſtin*, *Jerom* and *Bernard* made Vſury Theft in old time, ſo Reverend Mr. *Dod* did in his time : ſaying, In the ſame colourable Theft is that common Sin of VSVRY : And ſo making the Vſurer a Thief. After whom,

10. (*c*) Mr. *Williams* makes the Vſurer the worſt of all THIEVES.

11. Famous Biſhop BABINGTON calls Vſurers (*d*) *Canker-Worms*.

12 BALDVS the Lawyer calls the Vſurer a Defamed Perſon.

13. I will add to theſe a few Heathen Authors too. And,

1. (*e*) *Plutarch* who calls Vſurers Devils ; ſaying, *Theſe curſed Uſurers being turned into DEVILS.*

2. (*f*) *Ariſtotle* makes them Bawds : ſaying, *Uſurers and Bawds may well go together.*

3. *Julius Cæſar*, the firſt Emperor, I ſhall bring in hereafter.

By all which Names, the Reader may ſee how the Champion.

1. Wrongs me ; ſaying, that I do ſo call the Vſurer, as if none elſe but I did give him ſuch Names, when ſuch worthy Men do ſo call him, and worſe too.

(*a*) Lavater *in* Ezekiel, *Hom.* 5. *Who alſo, in his 70th. Hom. defines Uſury to be Gain beyond the Principal.* (*b*) *Mr.* Dod *upon the Commandments, like* Auſtin *and* Jerom, Bernard *and* (*c*) *Mr.* Williams *in his* True Church. (*d*) *Biſhop* Babington, *upon* Exod. 8. *In Latin called* Melolontha ; *which are Worms very fair and green, but of a devouring nature, as* Calepinus *writes : even as Uſurers, in like manner, are very fair alſo in their Speeches, making a great flouriſh, pretending much Kindneſs and Good, but devouring Creatures.* (*e*) Plutarch, *Hiſt. Natural, l.* 33. *c.* 3. (*f*) Ariſtotle *apud Dr.* Wilſon.

2. How

2. How, through my sides, he striketh at these great and famous Authors (besides God himself.) Among whom I will now leave him, chiding them, why they will call his dear Friend, Master VSVRER, such woful NAMES. Adding,

3. But (*a*) one great Author more, because he is my Country-man, a *German*, and will be willing to second me in this Combat, as one of his own Native Country. His words are, *Usurers are called Wasters, Pollers, Thieves, Murderers, Idolaters, Cousins to Fools, as ill as Mad-men, worse than Pagans, which are without Religion, Wicked, not believing there is a God. To conclude, They are likened to poysoned Serpents, to mad Dogs, to greedy Worms, to Woolves, Bears*: he adds, *yea*, Luther *doth almost think to be very Devils.* O sad! For Men to be turned into Devils. *In a word, They are like to Vessels full of stinking Carrion and Filth.* Thus he, not only seconding me, but outgoing me; for I did not call the Vsurer so many names as these.

I know what the Vsurer will say, I warrant you, this *German* was no Saint; if he had been, he would never have called any Man such names. Whereunto I answer, that I can name a Saint, which also saith, *That Usurers do more stink in the sight of God, than any Filth in the eyes of Men.*

How uncivilly and causlesly he compareth me with the Quakers, calling Mr. *Baxter* Dog? for, did I ever call Mr. *Baxter* so; a Man whom I do most highly value and esteem, for his Fame, Learning and Godliness.

N V M. XXVII.

I add, that he injureth me also very highly in that,

1. He casts this Aspersion upon me, that I have been at the pains to collect, or receive from some other hand, those Expressions which the Fathers use against Vsurers.

For Answer whereunto, I must let him know, that I had no need to receive such Expressions from some other hand, because I have my self read, not only Writers handling this Controversie of Vsury, but the Councils also, and the principal Fathers throughout; and drawn them out of their great Volumes, into my common places; tying my self, for the per-

(*a*) Philip Cæsar *in his General Discourse against the Damnable Sect of Usurers*, p. 3. Saint *Bridget*.

pervolving of them to so much an Hour, so much a Day, so much a Week, so much a Month, so much a Year: which had almost killed me, for it cast me into a desperate Sickness, wherein Physicians left me for dead, but God, who had mercy on me, was pleased to restore me, having more Work to do for me; and it may be this, which now I am doing.

2. As for the holy Fathers, and other Writers, how he injured them; asserting, that they intended the Sayings which in my former Book I cited, against oppressive Usurers, and not others. That I shall evidence to the World in my following Answer to his Premise. Which is,

That there is a damnable Usury which is condemned in Scripture, &c. *and has been deservedly made infamous by Laws, Punishments, Restraints, and by the Censures of Godly Persons of the respective Ages, and then this takes in a cruel Griping of the Poor, a merciless Exacting*, &c. *which is the Usurer's old Song*. So that I shall be forced to give some old Answers among new ones. And,

1. Seeing this his *Premising* consists of two Parts.

1. Of a Confession.

2. *Application*.

N V M. XXVIII.

To answer to his Confession, I shall

1. Acknowledge that I am glad to hear him grant, that there is a *Damnable Usury*, because I know that he must prove it by the same *Moral Law*, and such Scriptures which are quoted against all Usury, prohibited by the same Scriptures.

2. And because he and some of his Brethren do not speak for or against any Usury all the Year long, as their own hearers tell me, whom I appeal to in this thing. I, for my part, can witness this, that when I did preach once against Usury, I was taxed for it, and told, that it was not usual to speak of such a thing as Usury is in the Pulpit: and so I must preach no more in their Pulpits, because they suppose that I will cry out against their DIANA, and her SILVER SHRINES, like Mr. *Bolton*.

2. I answer, That, yet farther, I observe two things in this Confession, which I must utter.

The First is, That this Champion brings out this *Damnable* with a נקף נטן, to speak as the *Hebrews* do; that is to say, being low, and not very high nor hearty, as others that are against

against all damnable Usury in earnest, and cry it down indeed to the Pit of Hell, as Ministers ought to do.

The Second thing is, That he wrongs those Godly Persons which he writeth of, that they made this damnable Usury infamous in their respective Ages, if his meaning be, that they were against excessive Usury (*a*) only, which he calls a cruel Griping, a merciless Exacting of Money, a taking of all Advantages, an exceeding of those Bounds which Law and Equity prescribes, *&c.* Whereunto he adds, as it is taken notice of in the Exposition of the Catechism, used both in the Low-Countries, and in his own Country, the *Palatinate*; wherein it is added, that we must make a difference between occupying of Usury, and taking of Usury, *&c.* I say, if this be his meaning, he is most injurious both to the Holy Scriptures, and those Laws, and Godly Persons; for I can make it good by sufficient Proofs, that the Scriptures and the said Godly Persons have spoken against all Usury and Usurers, properly so called: and that accordingly, Laws, Restraints and Punishments were made and ordained to suppress the same in all their respective Ages. Whereof my Proofs are these,

First, *Scriptural*, From the Holy Word of God.

I. Psal. 15. 1, 5. *Lord, who shall abide in thy Tabernacle?* &c. *He that putteth not his Money to Usury.* Where,

1. Let it be noted, what a (*b*) famous Author writeth concerning this Scripture; because some did say of him, that in his preaching against Usury, he alledged, nor could alledge nothing but the fifteenth *Psalm*; *If I could alledge no more than the fifteenth* Psalm, *yet were that alone sufficient to stop the Mouths of all the Usurers in the World.* Thus he. And well he might say so: for, though some would shift off this Stripture, as if it did only make against cruelly Biting, and Oppressing Usurers, because the word נשך, is made use of therein, which signifies *Biting*; yet doth it not follow, that cruelly biting Usury is only meant, but also Usury, properly so called, and commonly practised. For these Reasons.

(*a*) *As it is like, that it is, to wrest these holy Men's Writings, as it is an easie thing for a Contentious Person to do; as* Calvin *tells us of the Sayings of the Fathers. Inst. l.* 3. *c.* 4.

N V M.

N V M. XXIX.

1. Because *Nesheck* is the usual word, which signifieth Vsury, and also all that Encrease or Excrescency, which is taken above the Principal, for the Loan of Money, which is soon to be demonstrated by the words *Marbith* and *Tarbith*, which are usually joyned with *Nesheck* by the Holy Ghost, ἐξηγητικῶς, that is, *by way of Exposition*, to shew that they are *Synonimas*, as appeareth, and it can be proved by *Lev.* 25. 36. *Prov.* 28. 8. *Ezek.* 18. 13. and 22. 12. where *Marbith* and *Tarbith* are set after *Nesheck*, as words signifying the same. Which is also confirmed by Doctor *Kimchi*, upon *Ezek.* 18. as I said formerly, *That both are mentioned together, and condemned.* Mark, *Condemned together.* So that though a Man do not so cruelly bite as some, yet if he takes but *Tarbith* or *Marbith*, he is condemned for it, saith this Author. Where give me leave to shew what this *Marbith* and *Tarbith* signifies, *viz.* An (*a*) Encrease; that is, Gain above the Principal, as famous. Which the *Grecians* translate πλεονασμὸν· *That is*, saith *Balsamon*, *Nysseni Shiolastes*: *when a Man doth lend any thing, to receive more than he gave.* Thus he.

2. I find that in this *Psal.* 15. 5. *Nesheck* is not set down with a *Dagesh* for it, as it is in some other places. Which affords us this Criticism; that it holds forth two things. 1. *Biting, any Biting.* And 2. *Such Biting also, inclusively, as doth not so cruelly and vehemently bite as some, and yet biteth too.* For we have a Rule in Hebrew, that when there is a *Dagesh forte* in a word, it implieth Vehemency: Whereof more hereafter.

All that which I have said yet concerning this Scripture is but a Touch, whereunto I will add but this more.

That this one and first Scripture is so strong, as that from it, many, both Councils and particular Writers, have, in their respective Ages, proved the unlawfulness and damnableness of all sorts of Vsury, properly so called. At present I will instance only in the most famous Council of *Nice*, *Can.* 18. which the Learned may peruse at their leisure: observing what it saith, not only of the *Centesima*, but also, *de quolibet tali lucro, of any such Lucre.*

(*a*) *By the Hebricians also called* יותרן, *that is,* aliquid amplius, *somewhat more than the Principal.*

2. My

2. My second Scripture Poof is, that in *Deut.* 23. 19. *Thou shalt not lend upon Usury to thy Brother.* Mark, Brother, whether he be rich or poor; for still he is our Brother, as he is either born of the same Parents, or a Christian of the same persuasion, &c. as (a) *Clemens Alexandrine* expounds that Law-saying (as I have read it long ago in him so expounded.) *The Law forbids to lend upon Usury*, saith he to our Brethren, *under the name of a Brother; comprehending, not only him which was born of the same Parents, but him also which was of the same Tribe, and of the same Opinion, and partaker of the same words.* Whereof more hereafter.

Not a word of the *Rich*, to which the Defendants of Usury hold it lawful to lend upon Usury, because this Law admitteth an exception of a Stranger, which I intend to clear up at full in another place, and another time, being contented to say but a word or two about it at this time, *viz.* That if the Lord intended it so, that it should be lawful to lend upon Usury to the Rich, here was a fit time to mention the Rich, as well as the Stranger, because *The Rich we have always with us.* But that Stranger, which there is meant, *viz.* one of the seven Nations which God would have destroyed, were destroyed, and by degrees consumed in *David*'s time, as Divines from Holy Writ collect it: which now makes all that Plea which Usurers plead from the Stranger void, and of none effect, as I shall have an occasion hereafter to evidence it at full. Now, one Word more I will add, that I take special notice of in this Scripture, of a Word which I find of the Stranger, *vers.* 20. לנכרית שיך *Unto the Stranger thou shalt lend upon Usury*, as *Junius* also renders it; not *Thou mayest*, as the English has it. Which sheweth, that God commandeth it that his People should bite him; for so much the Hebrew תשיך, signifies: as in another place he saith, *Thou shalt consume, destroy and cut him off*, Deut. 7. 20.

Where note also, that if it be Lawfull to lend to the Rich, because of this Exception of a Stranger, it will hold also, that he commands it, that the Rich should be so *Bitten*. Which, how absurd it is to think so, let the Reader judge.

3. But because these places mention *Nesheck* only, therefore I will produce a Scripture, which makes this thing called

(a) Clemens Alexandrine, *Strom. l.* 2.

Usury

Vſury more plain, *viz. Ezek.* 18. 13. where *Neſheck* is joyned with *Tarbith*, and joyned thus, *Has given forth upon Uſury, and hath taken Encreaſe*, ותרן, (of which word I have even now ſufficiently ſpoken) *Shall he then live? He ſhall not live.*

Where note firſt, How the Lord placeth his words.

1. *By way of Interrogation*, and ſo the more Emphatically; as if he ſhould ſay, Is there any reaſon for it?

2. *Moſt Comprehenſively*, Poſiting Lending upon Vſury to be underſtood by *Giving forth* firſt, and then *Has taken Encreaſe*, to defeat thoſe Vſurers which think themſelves to be no Vſurers, becauſe they take no Bond, nor Bill, nor Promiſe, and yet expectedly take it when it comes.

Note alſo what bleſſed *Calvin* here ſaith upon this eighteenth Chapter of *Ezekiel*, and concerning this whole matter of *Neſheck* and *Tarbith*, *viz. That whereas Uſurers avoided the name* Neſheck, *which ſignifieth Biting, as they do the name Uſury among us, as being odious; and therefore they took not* Neſheck, *but* Tarbith; *as among us, they will not be thought to take Uſury, but Conſideration, Uſance, or Intereſt. Therefore the Lord forbiddeth as well* Tarbith *as* Neſheck, *whereby he condemneth generally,* Quamlibet ſortis acceſſionem, ſaith he, *Any Addition*, mark, *any Addition, or Encreaſe above the Principal.* And, upon *Ezek.* 18. eſpecially, he ſaith, *Not only* Neſheck, *which ſignifieth Biting; but alſo* Tarbith, which he tranſlateth *Incrementum, Encreaſe: Hoc eſt quicquid ſibi avari homines conciliant ex mutuo:* that is, *Whatſoever Gain Covetous Men do get to themſelves by Loan.* Thus *Calvin.* Whereas ſome may wonder, becauſe Vſurers take him to be their chief Friend; and will be ready to ſay, that I take out of him what ſeemeth to be for me, leaving out that which maketh againſt me. But to this I anſwer, that I can and ſhall give a Reaſon hereafter, (when I ſhall come to ſpeak more fully of *Calvin*) why he writeth after this rate and manner.

NVM. XXX.

And now, paſſing over many Scriptures, beſides the forequoted, I ſhall paſs over out of the Old Teſtament, into the New; and, by name, to that noble and famous place, *Luk.* 6. 35. *Lend, hoping for nothing again.* From thence, and that ſo much the rather, becauſe ſome give out that Vſury is not interdicted or condemned in the New Teſtament at all. For Anſwer whereunto, one which is a moſt famous and learned

ned Writer, *Gabriel Powel* I mean, ſaith thus: *It is a monſtrous* BLASPHEMY *againſt the Goſpel of Chriſt, to affirm, that the New Teſtament giveth more Liberty to ſin than the Old.* With whom I joyn the renowned Mr. *Capel*, ſaying, *We have Uſury forbidden in the New Teſtament, when Judicials were out of date*, Luk. 6. 35. Thus he.

As for me, becauſe I have already touched this place in this Book, I ſhall therefore ſay the leſs now: but I intend to ſay much hereafter of it and in a place fit for it. Only this I will boldly averr now, That it is to me as plain, and as clear as the Sun, that Chriſt by it forbids Vſury and Encreaſe. Becauſe, 1. He ſaith, *Lend, hoping for* NOTHING, in Greek, μηδὲν. 2. Becauſe he ſaith ἀπελπίζοντες· which is a Compound, compounded of ἀπὸ, *A Bind*, from thence; and ἐλπίζω, *I hope:* So that the Senſe of ἀπελπίζοντες muſt needs be, *Hoping for nothing from thence*; that is, from your lending, *non ampliùs*, *no Overplus*; that is, no Vſury. 3. Becauſe the words foregoing evince it: for in *verſ.* 34. Chriſt ſaith thus, *And if you lend to them, of whom you hope to receive, what thank have you? for Sinners alſo lend to Sinners, to receive as much again.* The Greek is τὰ ἴσα, which will bear a double Conſtruction. As, 1. *The like*; that is, the like Sum in the like Coyn, though not the very ſame. 2. Τὰ ἴσα· that is, *The like Courteſie.* As namely, for a hundred Pounds by you lent to them, an hundred Pounds lent to you by them; which I like beſt. Whereunto, if you add the word *Hope*, *If you lend to them of whom you hope to receive*, viz. *the like, what thank have you?* The words following muſt needs be plain; *but lend (ye) hoping:* as in the foregoing Verſe, the word *Hope* is uſed with this difference only, that ἀπὸ is joyned with ἐλπίζειν, *hoping*, to cut off Vſury, even all Gain above the Loan, by μηδὲν, *nothing*; and by name, even the Loan, of ſo much too; another time, for the Loan of ſo much this time, which is worth Money too, and a kind of Vſury too. So that I do not wonder now, why moſt Expoſitors have ſo explained that place, as I do here, not denying that Chriſt's words may be extended in ſome Caſes, to the Principal too; that a Man muſt not hope for the Princcipal neither, if the Borrower be not able to pay it:

(a) Rich. Capel, *of Uſury*, *p.* 267. *of* Luk. 6. 35. *(b) Nothing, not* μηδένα, None, *as ſome have groundleſly read it, perverting the Scripture.*

Where-

Whereupon in cometh that acception of the Compounded Word ἀπελπίζοντες μηδὲν ἀπελπίζοντες, *Nothing despairing*, as some understand the word, that is, nothing despairing of a better Reward than any Man can give you; which I hope will give content to some pious Men, who are much taken with that Exposition, and that without any offence given thereby by me to any, because the Compound ἀπελπείζειν signifieth also *to despair*, though I, for my part, insist mostly upon my premised Exposition, as most likely in my Judgment. But more fully I shall handle this Scripture hereafter, shewing the very Expositions of it, and bringing a Cloud of Witnesses, witnessing for and to the true meaning of it.

NUM. XXXI.

At present I will only resolve one Case, which will be in all likelihood proposed. As namely, whether a Man may not lend, and afterward crave the like Courtesie in his need. Whereunto I answer, Oh, yes, provided he look not for it when he lendeth, because Christ saith, *Lend, hoping for nothing again*; mark, *Nothing at all*.

Secondly, From these Scriptures, I pass to Godly Men and Authors, which, in their respective Ages, have declared against Usury, properly so called, and the Defendants of it: And withal, have made it generally DAMNABLE, as also do the Scriptures.

And 1. *(a)* I will briefly recite what they have voted, being assembled in Councils for their respective Ages against all Usury and Usurers, and their Defendants.

2. What they have written apart against both.

For the first, I will instance in *(b)* the Councils of *Carthage*, the Sixth and Seventh; both which having caused the *(c) Nicene* to be turned into Latin, approved of it; and so, by name of the eighteenth Canton against all sorts of Usury, condemned by it out of *Psal.* 15. So that thereby all these three Councils, joyning together their combined Forces, did put down Usury at that time, and for their respective Ages.

(a) I say briefly, because I have already said something to the same effect, and shall say much more yet hereafter, in its most proper time and place. *(b) Concil.* Carth. 6. & 7. *(c) Concil.* Nicen.

2. I

2. I will subjoyn the (*a*) *Parisian* Council which has set it self as much as any against that damnable Sin of Usury; declaring openly, that *The Kingdom of Christ is endangered by it.*

3. Next to the *Parisian*, I will place that of (*b*) *Vienna*; which has discharged a most dreadful Canon against the Defendants of Usury, *whereby it condemneth all for Hereticks, who hold Usury to be lawful.*

I name but these few, but could bring many more; and there is one, blessed (*c*) *Bolton* I mean, who goeth farther, saying, *I may oppose* (*viz.* against *M. S.* his Adversary, eighteen Men quoted by him, as being for some Usury) *all other Councils that ever mentioned Usury:* But there will be a fitter time for me to make use of so many when my Third Book cometh forth.

NUM. XXXII.

2. At present I advance nearer against the Adversaries Hold, which he calls his *Premise*, by alledging those Godly Persons and Authors, which have severally, and apart, let fly their most keen and sharpest Arrows against all Usury, as it is, and has been generally and usually practised in their respective Ages. And,

1. I shall bring up with me some of the Ancient, most Learned, and Pious Fathers, as chief Leaders in that great Army which has been Militating for fifteen hundred years together, against that Enemy of Mankind, called USURY, ALL USURY.

2. Next to them, I shall fetch some new Leaders also, who, since those fifteen hundred Years past, are risen up to second them.

To begin with the old experienced ones, I shall let you see them, and you shall hear them speak too. And,

1. (*d*) *Lactantius*, the Churches Secretary, who wrote of her Secrets more than any other I know, saith, *Let a Christian take this Course, that in Lending, he take not USURY; for that is against the Law of Lending.*—— Lo, how this old Father is against all taking of Usury.

(*a*) *Concil.* Paris. (*b*) *Concil.* Vien. (*c*) Bolton *in his Book against Usury.* (*d*) Lactantius.

2. (a) Saint *Ambrose*, in his Book of *Tobie*, *chap*. 14. saith to the Usurer thus. *If Usury be lawful, why dost thou shun the Name? why drawest thou a Covering over it? If it be unlawful, why receivest thou ANY ENCREASE?* mark, ANY ENCREASE.

3. You shall hear St. *Hierome* speak too, upon *Ezek*. 18. thus. *He that taketh more than he gave* (writing of Usury) *cannot live, but shall die in his Blood.* Thus he maketh what is taken beyond the Principal, *Damnable.*

Many more such holy Leaders and Fathers you will see at the Usurer's Funeral, in my Third Book, which is to come. For the present I will educe and bring up,

NUM. XXXIII.

2. Some chief Leaders of the new Army, risen against the same Enemy of Mankind, after the aforesaid fifteen hundred Years expired: Usury, I mean. And,

1. (b) *Aretius*: who saith, *Sit igitur Usura quicquid ultra sortem accipitur. Sors est elocata pecunia utpote centum coronati, quicquid igitur ultra sortem id qualecunque tandem sit Damnabile esse censamus.* That is, *Usury is whatsoever is taken above the Principal. As for Example, For an hundred Crowns, whatsoever is exacted from thence, we account it Damnable.*

2. (c) *Spotswood*: Who saith, *Usurers are excluded from Eterna Life by* Ezek. 18. 13. *And shut out of God's Tabernacle by* Psal 15. Thus he. And that is bad enough, and *Damnable* indeed: yet this he saith, without excepting the more moderat Usurer, in General.

3. You shall hear again Learned (d) *Powel* speak like Scholar, as he was. *If Usurers be excluded from* Jehova's *Tabernacle, then Usury is a thing unlawful and damnable. Bu the Antecedent is true, as appeareth by* Psal. 15. 5. Ergo, *Th Consequent is true also.*

Now, that you may see what Usury he meaneth, his form Syllogism, by me alledged upon the like Account, will shew

---

(a) *St.* Ambrose. (b) Aretius, *that famous and learned Pr fessor of* Losanna, De Usuris, *p*. 626. *Mark, Less than Six the Hundred, and yet Usury.* (c) Spotswood *in his Short Di course of Usury, p*. 21. (d) G. Powel *in his Posit. calling th Argument*, Syllogismum connexum primo modo a conjugatis

For that runs thus, as, word for word, I recited it formerly; *All Gain that, contrary to the Word of God, is expected, or exacted above the Principal, for the very Duty of Lending, is unlawful: And* Damnable Usury *is such Gain* (as he proveth it) *Ergo.*

4. In cometh after these, (*a*) Doctor *Smith*, speaking thus, *That Opinion which condemneth all Usury is grounded upon evident Testimonies of Scripture*, Psal. 15. 5. Prov. 28. 8. Ezek. 18. 13. *and* 22. 12. What can be plainer?

5. I shall subjoyn the Author of *The Death of Usurers*, who speaks after this Pathetical manner in the Close of his Book. *I would not wish the Usurer to stand upon such Cavils: but seeing, not only the Word of God, but All Ages*, Note, All Ages, *Nations, Laws*, Note, Laws too, [which answers the Champion, who mentions Laws too] *and sorts of Persons do condemn Usury, as a Sin most odious and opprobrious. I would have him to loose the Bonds of Wickedness, wherewith St.* Jerome *understands the Bonds that Usurers wrap others in. So, getting Goods in the fear of God, they will be to his comfort while he liveth, and without prick of Conscience when he dies.* Thus he giveth the Usurer this Godly Counsel (which I wish Usurers would follow) and withal tells us, how Usury, in all Ages, has been condemned: Speaking of it generally also.

6. And Lastly, I must needs again bring in blessed (*b*) *Bolton*, speaking and symphonizing with these *Worthies*, thus. *If the Usurer be pressed with this and other places, his most ordinary Answer is, They are to be understood of Biting, not of Toothless Usury, &c. But what if those, and the like, prove to be rotten Distinctions, and false Glosses upon their Beds of Death, as indeed they are, what is then their Case? as they have leaned in their Life-time upon such broken Staves of Reed, their confidence in that dreadful Hour will be but as the Spider's Web.* Which Words of this holy Man, how applicable they be to my Antagonist, let the Reader judge. I need not now speak of *Laws*, which the Champion mentioneth, because there will

(*a*) *Doctor* Smith *upon* Levit. *p.* 626. (*b*) R. Bolton, *I say Lastly; though, if I would, and there were need, I could bring in, besides these, the Testimonies of many Scores more, even of all the wise and truly learned Men, who have flourished until this present Age. Wherein I am Seconded by that famous Bishop* Downam, *who has a Saying much like this upon* Psal. 15. 5.

be a fitter time for it hereafter; and something concerning them, my fifth Author, even now, did speak.

NUM. XXXIV.

But here I suppose my Adversary will be ready to reply, that all that which I have spoken of Damnable Usury will signifie nothing, nor convince Vsurers, unless I make it more plain yet than I have made it, What that Damnable Vsury, and those Vsurers are which shall be damned, and against whom the Prophets, and all sorts of Writers have written, to make them odious.

For Answer whereunto, I shall say, That if I must needs make it more plain to my Antagonist, and all Vsurers whatsoever, then I will send him and them,

1. To the Prophet *Ezekiel* again: who, not only sheweth what that Vsurer is which shall die, and be damned; *viz. He that has taken Vsury or Encrease*; that is, (as *Calvin* himself expounds it, and as the old Latin Translation renders the Hebrew *Tarbith*) *more than thou gavest*: and as (a) *Ambrose*, *Ad amplius recipiendum*, *To receive more*: But also, most remarkably, hath in the word *Neshech*, a peculiar Note of Difference, scarce observed by any yet; *viz.* a *Dagesh forte*, which is not to be found in other places; yea, a *Double Dagesh forte* in it, and in the prefixed Letter נ, which denoteth, not only Vehemency, but much Vehemency and Strength; that is, strong and vehemently biting Vsury; yea, and an Hebrew Accent, called *Darga*. All which plainly and remarkably ostends and clears it, what Vsurer it is which shall be damned: Namely, he chiefly, and first, which vehemently biteth, and cruelly oppresseth; and he also which taketh more than he lendeth. Vnderstand expectedly (as it was formerly shewn.)

2. I send him again to that famous Vniversity of *Wittemberg* (because I hear that he has been but a little while in an *English* Vniversity) to see the aforesaid *Wittembergish Theses*, and to learn out of them, what Vsurers, by them censured and condemned are. Their Words of five in the hundred are plain: I need not repeat them, because I have already quoted them.

(a) Ambros. *de* Tob. *c.* 15.

NUM. XXXV.

3. I send him to that famous Council of (a) *Agatha*, which, *Nemine contradicente, None contradicting it*, then, when it sate, nor since, determined and voted what Usury, by it condemned, was; thus. *Usury is, when any thing is demanded more than was given, or lent forth. As for Example, If thou lendest ten Shillings* (Mark, but ten Shillings, which is but a small matter) *and seekest more; or lendest a Bushel of Corn,* (which is a very little thing too) *and demandest more.* So strict were the Holy Fathers in this point of Usury, in their respective Ages.

4. I send him to his own Country-man, (b) Mr. *Adams*, who most notably describeth condemned Usurers: What some of them are in respect of their Bodies, and in respect of their Souls; his Character is this, *The Usurer is known by his very Looks often, by his Speeches commonly, by his Actions ever: He has a lean Cheek, a meager Body, as if he were fed at the Devil's Allowance, his Eyes are almost sunk to the back-side of his Head with Admiration of Money, his Ears are set to tell the Clock, his whole Carkase a meer Anatomy*, (of which more hereafter in my *Anatomy*, or Second Book against Usury, which is to come.) *Some Usurers have fatter Carkasses, and can find it in their hearts to Lard their Flesh: but a* Meagerness *is upon all their Consciences.* And then, with *Leo*, sends him to the Pit of Hell for ever.

NUM. XXXVI.

5. If this Man be not full and plain enough, though he speaks plain English, I shall send him to another, and far greater English Author, who speaketh more fully and plainly; *viz.* Famous Bishop (c) *Jewel*: whose words are these; *Usury is a kind of Lending of Money, or Corn, or Oyl, or Wine, or any other thing,* &c. *and then, as if I lend an hundred Pounds, and for it Covenant* (understand tacitly, or expresly) *to receive an hundred and five Pounds, or any other Sum greater than was*

(a) *The Council of* Agatha *in* France, *kept in the days of King* Alaricus. (b) *Mr.* Adams *in his Works, p.* 454. (c) *Bishop* Jewel *upon the First of the* Thessalonians.

the Sum which I lent: *This is that which we call Usury. Such a kind of Bargaining no Godly Man ever used.* He tells us of Five in the Hundred, and of any Sum above the Principal, and of that which is commonly practised. And in another place maketh this Usury Damnable; saying of the Usurer, who committeth it, *He that giveth his Money upon Usury, shall not dwell in the Tabernacle of the Lord*, which he calls Heaven. Thus he, in that respective Age wherein he flourished, not only made cruelly griping Usury damnable, but even Five in the Hundred, and any other Sum beyond the Money lent.

And therefore, let my Adversary now seriously consider his words, together with those which I formerly quoted, especially of expectation out of them three great and learned Authors, and let all *English* Usurers whatsoever, especially, be convinced, and hold their Peace hereafter; ceasing and forbearing to ask this Question any more, *What is Usury? We are not convinced yet about it, what it is: and that such a thing as you call Usury, is that Damnable Usury which you and others so cry down; and which Fathers, and all sorts of Writers have made so odious.* For, Lo, here is brought to you, to convince you, besides many others, your own Country-men, one of your Great and Learned Bishops; who has discovered, cried down, and condemned that Usury which here he defineth, and which is commonly and generally practised amongst us, and has been, besides the most excessive and cruelly biting Usury committed in the Ages which are past.

I would not here obtrude mine own Words and Judgment, to shew what Damnable Usury is; because, if I had, then some would have said, as some do already, *Who but the old* Jelinger *saith so?* Whereas now, if they will find fault with that which hath been spoken, they must say, *Bishop* Jewel *said so.* So that I cannot see how Usurers will be able to shun, and to keep off this mighty Blow.

NUM. XXXVII.

But it is high time for me to advance.

Secondly, To his (*a*) Application, wherein I take notice of three things.

(*a*) *My Answer to the Adversary's Application.*

1. That

1. That he saith, *In things of this, or the like nature, there is none of his Brethren would scruple to joyn with him* : that is to say, They would joyn with me, if I would, against my Knowledge and Censcience, say as he saith, that Scriptures, Fathers and Writers have, in their respective Ages, deservedly made odious his Damnable Usury, as he describeth it to be a cruel Griping of the Poor ; as if that were the only Damnable Usury which they have written, and spoken against ; yea, Condemned : and so consequently, like a *Transfuga*, or a Run-away, should betake my self into the Camp of the Enemies of Truth : Which I cannot do, nor ever will do, by God's Help, because I know, and even now proved the contrary, nor indeed, have cause so to do. For those holy Writers, I mean the Pen-men of the Holy Ghost, and those other Godly Writers which are against all Usury, as it has been, and is now generally practised, are those that will hold with me hereafter, if I joyn with them here, being a numerous multitude, at that great Day, when that small and inconsiderable number of Usurers Defendants, which have spoken bitter words against their Brethren, for speaking the Truth against Usury and Usurers, will be ashamed of their Craft, and of what they have spoken maliciously ; and when God's Holy and Faithful Servants will, with much boldness, hold up their Heads, when Christ himself will be Judge, to judge of what both have said, when himself being Judge, will also be his Servants Advocate ; when being his Servants Advocate, he will advocate and call them to come near him, saying, *Come good and faithful Servants ; come, wear your Crown ; come, receive your Kingdom prepared from the beginning of the World ; come, dwell with me in my holy Hill ; come, abide with me in my Tabernacle*, Psal. 15. 1. *For you are they that bear about you the Marks of Heaven's Citizens, and that by Name :* And especially, which that sweet Singer of *Israel*, here present, sets down in his most sweet Psalm, and Song of his, set down in his Book of *Psalms* ; *He that putteth not out his Money to Usury, shall dwell in God's Holy Hill.* And therefore lift up your Heads with joy, for ye shall now enter into your Master's Joy.

NUM. XXXVIII.

2. The Second thing which I take notice of is, that he addeth, *But whilst he over-doth it, and under the same Condemnation brings all others that take but moderate and regular Gain* (being ashamed to call it Use or Usury) *of Persons sufficient*; (meaning the Rich, as all Usurers hold that Lawful, which must be examined hereafter) *yea, such as take but any thing above the Principal, be it but a Mite, or Cup of cold Water.* Wherein he frets his Malice and Spight upon the University of *Wittemberg*, and that most famous Foreign Divine *Aretius*: for these words, about a Mite, or a Cup of Cold Water, are their words, not mine; I do but quote them, as many other Writers do; leaving the Readers to weigh them. So that he wrongs me very much by this Expression (as he saith) when they say it, who, if they were now alive, would soon answer him, and stop his Mouth. For what is such a Novice, to such Grave, Ancient and Learned Professors and Doctors as they have been.

He goeth further, and saith, *Yea, when there is but an Intention, or Expectation of Gain, he must not think it strange if all Men are not of his mind.*

Whereunto I answer, That I do not much regard it, if such Men as he is be not of my mind, as long as Elder, Abler, Better Men, and a far greater Number of such Men, than the Number of his Men is, are of my mind. Where let the Courteous Reader peruse what I have taken ont of St. *Austin*, Doctor *Chemnitius*, *Gabriel Powel*, and others, concerning *Expectation*, how it maketh an Usurer, and what more abundantly I shall bring forth *(a)* hereafter, to prove this *Expectation* to be Usury, and *Expecters* to be Usurers.

At present I shall speak a little more fully of and against his *Moderate Usury*, Thus.

(a) When that Renowned Arch-bishop Usher *will be brought in, defining Usury to be Lending in Expectation of certain Gain.*

NUM.

NUM. XXXIX.

1. That the Holy Scripture speaks of no such Moderate Usury, much less alloweth it.

2. That those beyond the Seas, which take but Five in the Hundred, as they do in *Helvetia*, where I have been also; and in my Country, which is *Germany*, where they also are contented with Five in the Hundred, will say of our *English* Usurers, who take more, that they are *Immoderate* and *Excessive*. Yea, the very Jews beyond the Seas, who are pleased with four Pounds in the Hundred, (*a*) as a great Merchant (who is a Usurer himself, and has been a Traveller beyond the Seas himself also, and is, being yet alive, able to attest it) told me, I say, that even those poor Jews will say of thee, that art a Christian Usurer, that thou art an Excessive Usurer: and that thy Usury is Immoderate, it being forty Shillings more than his in the Hundred.

3. And if this be not enough, hear what a great (*b*) *English* Doctor, far surpassing you, Mr. Champion, and me too, saith concerning this thing. I will name him, if you will know his Name, it is Doctor *Fenton*, whose most Learned, most Sound, most Excellent, and Unanswerable Book against Usury, I wish every one that will be fully satisfied in this Point of Usury to peruse. His words are these: *After the Defenders of some Usury have examined the Point, and answered, as they think, the Objections which are usually brought against Usury by the Schools; yet, in Conclusion, put all their Limitations together, they can agree upon no Usury at all, as it is before defined: Single them out one from another, there is not any one of them that dareth defend any such ordinary Usury as is amongst us practised, with Greatest Moderation.*

Ah, poor Champion, where are you now? What becometh of your *Moderate Usury* now?

3. I, for my part, I will triumphantly charge on, and march up to your third Thing, to overthrow that too, *viz.* And let him consider whether, by putting in such Companions with them, he doth not take the ready way to strengthen the hands of Griping Usurers, whilst they find the greatest

---

(*a*) *Besides one of that Country, who lately told me the same.*
(*b*) *Doctor* Fenton, *p.* 144.

part

part of this and other Nations taken in with them; and amongst those many sober, serious, pious, learned Persons too. I say again, such confused writing of things and Persons as here is, is a more likely way to harden the most greedy Cormorants in their unjust Practices, than to abate the number of them. Where this Champion seems to make a great Flourish, which yet will soon vanish. For,

1. He brings with him in this Charge, his old already beaten and scattered Forces; I mean, his many vain and weak Expressions about my confused Writing: So that I need not say much to that, because I have already said much concerning that, if not too much, which the Reader may peruse if he please. This only I will say again now, That if my Writing be a confused Writing of things and persons, then what may we think of the Sacred Scriptures and Writings themselves, who joyn, as I said formerly, *Nesheck* and *Tarbith*, which is but an Encrease (which some of the Defendants of Usury themselves very simply call Toothless Usury, as more simply they call *Nesheck* the Lord's Rack-Rent) and make both damnable? *Ezek.* 18. 13.

2. The like may be said of all other Famous and Learned Writers who make such Conjunctions, as I have formerly shewn at full; so as that I need not say the same again over and over, shewing my self to be a Lover of Tautologies, as he doth.

NUM. XL.

And whereas he addeth, that this is the ready way to strengthen the Hands of Griping Usurers, whilst they find the greatest part of this and other Nations taken in with them; and amongst these, many sober, serious, pious and learned Persons too.

I answer to this his Charge after this manner.

1. That I fear no more such strengthening of such Griping Usurers, than the Ancient *Teutkons*, my Country-men, feared *Alexander*'s Forces (which were far enough from them) when they said to his Ambassadors who were sent to ask them, what they did fear; *Metuimus ne cœlum ruat, We fear lest the Heavens fall.* Which I say, because that which the Champion saith is far enough from me, and from any likelihood that ever it will come to pass. As also, that hardning of them is, which here also he talks of in the Close of his Charge; because

because I have already seen the contrary, since the putting forth of my first Book against Usury, by the Conviction and Conversion of many; among whom, some are Ministers and great Scholars; whereof more hereafter in due place. But let the Champion take heed, lest he strengthen the Hands of the most greedy Cormorants, and common, and most griping Usurers, as I hear he begins to do, in places, unto which his Pamphlet, or the Report of it cometh. Certainly God will call men to an Account for such proceedings.

And Lastly, Whereas he maketh this the Ground of his so charging me, whilst they find, &c. See his words,

To which I shall answer now. And,

1. To the first part of his Ground, which he pretends to have for what he saith, *viz. Whilst they find the greatest part of this and other Nations taken in with them.* Whereunto I have this to say.

1. That it is far from Truth that he saith, they find the greatest part,

1. Of this Nation. And,

2. Of other Nations taken in with them. For,

1. How can he make that good, which he saith of this Nation, when in many Parishes there are no Lenders upon Usury at all, or but very few; as I can say of mine, and so others of other Parishes, there being so many Borrowers every where, which commonly go to some certain Moneyed and noted Usurers, who take Six in the Hundred, and no more usually.

2. And, as for other Nations,

1. It is well known, that in some there is no Usury allowed or practised at all. As among the (*a*) *Indians*; which, as some Geographers write, make up the fifth part of the World. And among the *Turks* too, which claim half the old World, Usury is (*b*) not allowed.

2. And of my Country I will say thus much, that they have a thing there, called a *Commissariat*, with which they deal by way of Partnership, so as that the Lender, or putter out of his Money loseth when the Receiver and Employer of it loseth, as it happened in the late *Germany* Wars; for the Putters out

---

(*a*) *As the Learned and Well Red* Aretius, *in his Tract of Usury reports it.* Culverius *and* Speed. *Because* Mahomet, *in his* Alcoran *interdicts it.*

of

of their Money had nothing at all for their Money these twenty Years, because of the Receivers Losses which the Employers of such Money sustained by Wars. And many such Instances for that Country I could give. So that they need not there be such Usurers as here they be, because they can be such Partners in Loss and Gain.

Which doth not contradict what I have formerly said of some Transmarine Princes, which have espoused Usury, dealing upon Men's Money, as they do at *Frankfort*-Mart twice a Year; because some deal in a way of plain Usury, not all.

NUM. XLI.

To the Second Part of his last Thing, or Saying; which is, *And among those, many sober, pious, learned Men are taken in*: I shall answer next, and last of all, thus.

1. That some Grave and Great Divines affirm the contrary. As,

1. Bishop (*a*) *Jewel*, having spoken against Usury, and shewn what it is, said farther, that *No good Man or Godly Man ever used it*, *viz.* as now it is practised.

2. And before him, Great (*b*) *Lactantius* said, that *A just Man will not defile himself with such Gain.*

3. Bishop (*c*) *Downam. The Usury which is practised in the World, is not allowed of any Godly Divine.*

Here are two great Bishops on my side, and an old Father.

Secondly, Men may be learned, and yet not serious; I mean, so serious as to consider what a great and grievous Sin Usury is. And again, May be not only serious, but also sober, and yet not truly Godly; *Having but a form of Godliness, and denying the power thereof*, especially in these last times, 2 *Tim.* 3. 5. So that no wonder it is if such turn Usurers in such an Age wherein Men are so much carried with Gain: and that so much the rather, because even some Ministers are become Usurers, and shew them the way to it by their ill Example. Which caused a very Able, Learned and Godly Minister to break out into these Expressions after he had seen my

---

(*a*) *Bishop* Jewel *upon* 1 *Thes.* 4. (*b*) Lactantius *de vero Cultu*, *l.* 6. *c.* 19. (*c*) *Bishop* Downam *upon* Psal. 15. 5.

Usurer

Usurer Cast: Ministers now turn Usurers, and therefore so many Hearers turn Usurers too: I am, and ever was against it.

3. But suppose Men be truly Godly, and lend and take Use or Gain, as my Adversary calls it, then the words of the aforesaid great Authors are to be understood thus, that no Godly Man ever used it as it is now practised.

4. Those Godly Men may observe the Cautions which some Learned and Pious Ministers, as *Calvin*, *Farell*, *Baxter*, *Durham*, and others give; thereby making that which is said to be Usury, no Usury, but Partnership, as my Country-men in *Germany*, even now spoken of, is: they being Partners with the Employers of their Money in their Loss as well as Gain: which common Usurers will not do.

NUM. XLII.

But Finally, I must super-add one thing which I had almost forgotten; as namely, That I much wonder at my Adversary's having so much to do here with cruelly Biting and Griping Usury and Usurers, to vent and to excuse his moderate Usury by it. Because,

1. I understand by such as hear him, that in his preaching they shall not hear him speak against any Usury. And,

2. Because it is well known, that there are not so over-many such cruelly biting Usurers, who take all Advantages, Mortgages, &c. to use his own Expressions: I, for my part, hear but of a few, and those few do not go untold of it by me, and my Brethren; but rather a little more than by him and his Brethren. And so they were spoken against by the Holy Fathers (but not only.)

I will instance in Holy (*a*) *Ambrose*; who, when some Usurers were so cruel as that they would arrest the very dead Corpses of their Borrowers, not only spake against them, but also caused the said dead Bodies to be carried to their very Houses: and yet, when he came to shew what interdicted and damnable Usury is, he defined it as I and others define it.

(*a*) Ambrose *de* Tob. *c.* 10.

NUM.

N U M. XLIII.

3. And besides all this, because I observe generally, when I hear Men speak of and against Usurers, they call every Lender upon Usury, and for Gain, an Usurer, whether he be a small one, or a great one, that lendeth Thousands, and is content with Six in the Hundred, which they call moderate Gain, *alias* Usury, and craves and looketh for no more: as also, they call thee, who art such a Lender, and readest these Lines, a Usurer, do what thou canst, and say what thou wilt of and for moderate Usury; and tell as much as thou canst what a damnable Sin excessive Usury is, and how cruelly it gripes the Poor, though very few, if any, will lend to the Poor: Usurers being for the Rich only, that can give them good Security, and pay them punctually. I say, Men will call thee an Usurer, as well as the cruelly biting Lender, as long as thou livest, and livest in the Sin of Usury; And so they will call any of thy Brethren that come after thee, as long as *Nesheck* and *Tarbith*, *Biting* and *Encrease*, stand coupled together, interdicted together, and condemned together in thy Bible, and by name, in *Ezek.* 18. 13. This will be every Usury-taker's Name, from Generation to Generation, to the World's end. I for my part, to tell thee the truth here, thy Name, which is *Usurer*, told almost every Day, though thou art ashamed to call thy self so, and not willing that any of thy Neighbours should call thee so. So that I suppose that by this time my chief Antagonist's Flourish, which even now he made, is come to an end. And that I may now, being out of that Labyrinth which I was in, advance and come to a new Engagement, without any Let or *Remora*. Thus,

N U M. XLIV.

And here he charges me first, saying,

His Text, *Psal.* 15. 5. *He that putteth not his Money to Usury.* I shall pass some Remarks upon the words of the Text which he hath chosen. And what are those Remarks, say I? (to answer him) doubtless, as he thinks, some rare and choice ones: but that we shall see by and by.

[*Has not put.*] The Hebrew word properly signifieth *Giving*; which he must prove, that properly. As for me, I grant, that sometimes it signifies *Giving*: Besides which signification, it it alſo ſignifieth *ponere, to (a) poſite*, and *to put*, and *to put forth*, *Lev.* 16. 13. and *Joel* 2. and to (*b*) deliver a thing over into a Man's Hand, as *Joſh.* 6. 2. where the Latin Tranſlation runs thus; *Ecce, in manus tuas tradidi* Jericho; *Behold, I have delivered* Jericho *into thy hands.*

Again, it ſignifieth *To offer*, ſaith (*c*) one who was a moſt excellent Hebrician: which well befits Uſurers, who will (*d*) *offer* their Money to rich Heirs, to entice them to borrow of them, as holy *Ambroſe* reports it of them. Where, let me put this Remark upon my Adverſary's Remark, that נָתַן *He hath given or put forth, delivered and offered*, ſuffereth a defect, ſometimes in its Front or Beginning, ſometimes in its End, ſometimes in both. For the firſt we have an Example, *Gen.* 24. 35. and *chap.* 14. 19. For the ſecond in *Joſ.* 6. 2. The third in 2 *Sam.* 22. 41. *Thou haſt given me or delivered into my Hands alſo, the Necks of mine Enemies.* All which moſt notably befits Uſurers alſo; who, when they put forth their Uſury-Money, either cauſe the Borrower to ſuffer a defect in the beginning of their Loan, as ſome of them, who take Advance-Money; or in the end, when the Half Year is run out, as others uſually do; or both in the beginning and ending: making the Borrower to ſuffer a defect in his Subſtance, whereof, both firſt and laſt their Uſury bites off ſomewhat with a witneſs, as the worſt of Uſurers, being cruel Biters, and cruelly oppreſſive Uſurers do; who will have Gain upon Gain, even exceſſive Gain.

NUM. XLV.

1. But I ſee that my Antagoniſt, not being contented with this his Saying, in his Remark, has a mind to charge up yet nearer towards me, and againſt me; adding, *And if Giving may be put for Lending.* Mark what he ſaith, *may be*: he dareth not ſay *Is.* Why may not Lending, *Luk.* 6. 35. be interpreted Giving? Which, if granted, overthroweth the whole Fabrick he builds thereon. But of that more hereafter. Which Check

(*a*) *To put*, Pſal. 4. 8. (*b*) *As* Paynine *renders* Lev. 16. 13. Tradere. (*c*) Joh. Reuchlius Papinianiſta, *lib.* 1. *Rudiment. Hebr.* Anno MCCCCLXXIX. *Impr.* (*d*) *As* S. Baſil *ſhews it.*

and

and Charge to repel, and to put off, I shall return unto him this Response.

1. That he doth well that he saith still, *If, If*: which puts me in mind of a Letter which a certain City sent to a certain King, summoning it to surrender it self to him; writing no more in that Letter but *If, If, If,* in Answer to his. Which I leave to the Champion to apply to his *If.*

2. That in *Luk.* 6. 35. Lending cannot be Giving,

1. Because of (*a*) Giving, Christ speaketh expresly, *vers.* 30. and then after that, of Lending, *vers.* 34, and so 35.

2. Because one should think that those grave Translators of our English Bible had a little more Wit and Skill, and so other Translators also, than this Novice, when they used the word *Lend.*

3. Because the Original, δανείζετε, maketh it as clear as the Sun, that it must be *Lend,* because δανείζω is a word, which in no Author I find to signifie *Dono, I give,* but *Mutuo, I lend*: only this some write, that the *Grecians* are ambiguous about it: some affirming that it signifieth to lend without Usury, as I here; others to Usury. Which being so clear, I wonder with what face this Champion, contrary to the Current of so many wise and erudite Interpreters, should put Giving for Lending, Lending being a quite other thing differing from Giving: for Lending is, as (*b*) *Hemingius* tells us, a Contract which transferreth the Propriety of a thing from one to another for no consideration of any Price or Recompence, but only with a Covenant that the same kind of thing be repayed again.

But Giving is, when a man bestoweth a thing with this purpose, that he will have it presently to become his that receiveth it, and never in any wise to be rendred to him again, as (*c*) *Donorif* sheweth it.

Where note by the way,

1. That there are two Acts of Liberality; *Dono dare, & Mutuo dare*: *To give freely, and to lend freely*: The one whereof is mentioned by our Saviour in this place, *Luk.* 6. 35. and not the other: but *vers.* 34. and that most uncivilly, Usury is stept into the Room of its contrary, Free Lending; and thus strangely maintained by this my Adversary's Remark.

(*a*) *As* Aretius *also observeth it.* (*b*) Heming. *Com. in* Jac. 5. (*c*) Donarif, *de Donationibus, & l. don. ff.*

2. That

gh we read sometimes this Phrase in the holy *not give him thy Money to Usury*, Lev. 25. (in some Translations) *He that giveth not his* instead of *put forth*: yet we must not be so hampion is, as to gather from such places, Giving properly; and that the Usurer pra- Giving, because he indenteth, expecteth, the Return of such things as are delivered: never looketh for any such things as he gave For so *Donation* is by (*a*) Civilians defined. *sio aut traditio alicujus rei eâ mente facta, ut exerceatur liberalitas.* That is, *Donation is very of a thing, with a mind that it be his who* onsequently, be not returned) *and that there- xercised.*

ging Addition, which, if granted, overthrows k he builds thereon, I look on it as a meer ell him aforehand, that that which I shall abrick, *Luk.* 6. 35. will make his heart ake it overthrown. But of that, as he, so shall after. So that all this while the Champion vantage at all, much less a Victory, by his her a mark of Disgrace; not being able to fault, in which he has been shamefully repul- back.

N V M. XLVI.

is Remark, my Adversary approaches to *His* e Usurer loveth with all his heart.) Not, *nger.* As if a Man might put out another's dren's Money. Mark his reason, for a Man e of other Men's Sins, 1 *Tim.* 5. 2. which I for if putting out to Use be a Sin, it is the hat puts out the Money, and not the Child's, tive. Understand, for the present, while it is is my Answer partly, but not fully and whol- , that commonly Children, when they are nd continue in the same Sin of Usury, where- d put out their Money brought them. And

---

gius *in Rudim. Instit.* p. 327.

 are

are they not guilty of making themselves pa
Children's Sin of Usury, though they do no
own Money to Usury? So that I am much a
Children, living after, and dying in that d
Usury, unto which such Guardians have en
will, when, as Usurers, they shall be, chained u
of utter Darkness in Hell, they will curse such
them to that unutterable Misery; saying, O cr
if you had not been, we had not been in this wo
place, nor in such Chains and Bonds, for you we
caused Usury-bonds to be made for us to make us
we, poor Souls, knew what Usury is. Thus it
ed, that poor fatherless Children will curse
their misery, who have made them miserable. E
saith of a Man's own Children, that *They wi*
ther; saying, Cursed be you, Father; for you
our Torments; for if you had not shewn us the
your Example, we had never gone that way to H

But let us see farther how the Champion go
work; sad work indeed which he is like to ma
to shew, saith he, *what a Man has should be tr*
civilly his.

And how doth the Champion answer thi
saith, he had no mind on this Text, and m
of Scripture, when he wrote, that *Worldly Good*
to speak according to Scripture, *Psal.* 24. 1.

1. That I spake this upon another Subject
and that according to that *(b)* Scripture by
24. 1. *The Earth is the Lord's, and all that*
what fault have I committed and perpetrated
I do thereof put a gloss upon the Merchant's
he had, meaning, as others also do, his Si
Worldy Goods, as *(c) Lyra* doth; for this
Worldly Goods are not our own: and how so
Scripture, and that fore-alledged Scripture,
Psal. 24. 1. I do not speak it with a respect
of Man, which is the bringer in of *Meum, Tuu*
among Men; and giveth a Man a Civil Prop

(a) Mr. Smith *in his Sermons, p.* 105. *(b)*
44, 45. *handled in my* Spiritual Merchant, *by*
ned in his Margin. (*c*) Lyra *in* Mat. 13.

ıas and possesseth, reserving for God his, mentioned in that
Psal. 24. And whereas he would make me an Offender, be-
ause I say, what a Man has should be truly his, and that this
aying is to shew that: And saith farther, that I had no mind
ı my Text, &c. I answer, Whatsoever he may wrongfully
ıppose, I minded my Text for all, and forgat not the last
Commandment neither, nor other places, as well as he; but
ithal, do and shall still mind that never to be forgotten Say-
ng of a greater, learneder, holier Man than he is; St. (a)
Austin I mean; who saith expresly, *The whole World is a Be-
ever's Wealth, but the Infidel is not worth a Farthing.* Inti-
ıating, that the one has what he hath as a Proprietary, as his
wn; but what the other has, he has as an Vsurper, though,
ccording to the Law of Man, it be called his, in the tenth
Commandment, &c. And so he goes on, *Do we not convince
ll Men, who seem to rejoyce in what they have gotten, and know
ot how to use the same (as Usurers, who abuse what Money they
ave to Usury, putting it forth to Usury) that they possess what
ı not their own (as Usurers also may be said to be such Possessors,
ecause what they get by Usury is not their own, but should be re-
ored to them to whom it belongeth.)* And so progresseth; ad-
ing, and concluding at last, *Omne ergo quod male possidetur,
lienum est*: that is, *All that which is ill possessed is not a Man's
wn.*

2. Note that I say no more than other modern Writers said
efore me, *viz.* famous (b) Bishop *Downam.* And therefore
t the Reader judge what cause this *Zoilus* has to pick such
eedless frivolous Quarrels, which do but recoyl to his own
Dishonour, Opprobry and Shame. See the Margin before I
o farther.

But after all this, he cometh at last to that which he loveth
ıost dearly too, even, to Vsury; which is the Vsurer's great
Diana.

(a) *August. ad Maced. & habetur* 14. *q.* 4. *Can. Quid Dicam.*

b) *It is required (saith this great Man, Bishop* Downam, *up-
ı this same* Psal. 15. 5.) *of every Christian, that he get his
oods justly,* &c. *And therefore why must I be so blamed, who
y the same?*

And what doth he say of that ?

1. *The word signifieth Biting,* quoth he, *and s*
ly granted; and it is thence argued on the other h
Biting Usury is forbidden : That there is a biting
deserves that name, and that is unlawful and fo
doubt ; but that any Emphasis is to be placed in
Sheck, *I cannot be persuaded, because Encrease is j*
ed with it. And whatsoever the import of the wo
vation, yet it seems to me that the Holy Ghost ma
word in a moderate sense. (And here cometh i
again, *Moderate Usury*) without placing any Em
carried Biting in it by way of Aggravation.

Quest. And what say you to this ?

I answer,

1. That I deny what he saith, that only B
forbidden, if he mean cruelly and vehemently
because,

1. As I noted formerly, there is no *Dagesh fo*
ginal : so that it might take in all Vsury, thou
not bite so vehemently as some.

2. And if this Criticism be slighted, then I
plain terms, that all Usury, as it is commonly
bite, as Experience sheweth, actually or po
therefore deservedly is interdicted. Nor is i
only, but many more besides me, affirm the san
Downam, Gabriel Powel, Mr. *Smith*, and others
pear by their own words. And,

1. (*a*) *Gabriel Powel,* who saith, *Usury in He*
Nesheck, Exod. 22. 25. *which signifieth Bitin*
Nashack, to bite, *or* to gnaw as Serpents and
Usury bites and devoureth a Man's Substance very

2. (*b*) So Mr. *Smith, As the name of the De*
what an Enemy he is, so the name of Usury doth a
Enemy she is. That you may know Usury for a Bi
doth signifie Biting. If there were one biting Usur
healing Usury, then Usury should have two Names ;

(*a*) Gabriel Powel *in his Posit. p.* 29. (*b*) *Mr*
first Sermon against Usury, p. 96.

nd another of Healing: but all Usury signifieth Biting, to shew hat all Usury is unlawful.

3. And blessed (a) Bolton addeth, *Biting is individual and sential both to the Name and Nature of Usury; it ever biteth nd stings one or other, less or more; either the Borrower, or the mmonwealth; either, like the Morning-Wolf, it sucks out the ife, the Blood and the Marrow of a poor Man; or, like a Mastiff, snatches a piece and portion out of the Borrowers Substance; or ke a Wasp, or the Dog-Fly, it stings him one way or other in his tate. All sorts of Usury, even from that* Centesima, *the hun-edth part Monthly paid, which* Nehemiah *complaineth of, which Twelve in the Hundred, unto that* Semiuncianum, *which is n Shillings in the Hundred, has Teeth; some more empoysoned ody than other, but all bite. In every* Tarbith *there is a* Ne-eck, *a Tooth in every Usury.*

Thus Mr. *Bolton*, that Holy and Learned Author, now tri-mphing in Heaven, after his Glorious Victory won and got-n over his Adversary, *M. S.*

(b) Again he saith,

Nesheck *is the common and ordinary Name whereby all Usury gnified in the Hebrew Tongue,* &c.

4. I add Learned and Famous (c) Mr. *Trap*, mentioned in *Usurer Cast.*

5. In cometh (d) Mr. *Turner*, *There is no Usury but bites more ess: that which is but moderated, or qualified (as Men think) haps Five in the Hundred; yet, what is this but as it is in Greek Proverb, to shave to the very Skin; and like the Dog- to draw some Blood? So that although all kind of Usury bite alike, yet there is no Usury at all that is toothless.* Thus he. ny more Ancient as well as Modern Writers I could cite, these few may now suffice, because I must strive to be brief-han I have been.

. Only one more cometh now into my mind, which I must omit, *viz.* (e) *Justus Lipsius*; who, writing Annotations n a Heathen Author, called *Tacitus*, which also was an my to Usury, as a multitude of Christians are, has this ression; that *By the* Romans, *after they had moderated y, and brought it to Thirty Shillings in the Hundred, and*

) R. Bolton *in his Discourse concerning Usury*, p. 13. (b) *Idem* . (c) *Mr.* Trap *upon* Prov. (d) *Mr.* Turner *in his Ser- against Usury.* (e) Just. Lipsius *in* Cornel. Tacit.

ſaw the inconvenience of that moderated Vſury, ...
ken away. So that the very Heathens were a...
Vſury.

N U M. XLVIII.

But I muſt and ſhall haſten to that which ... ſwered, and uncloath my mind therein with ... vity, becauſe I have been too prolix hitherto ... cauſe moſt things of greateſt moment are cle... ſwered in my former Diſcourſe : ſo that I ſhal ... ſo long as I have been, hereafter ; and eſpecia... full of Tautologies ; repeating the ſame thing ... which he chargeth me with, again and again ... Modern Authors, which are his chiefeſt Proo... tute of Scriptural ones) in words of a great ... much Latin, only by him quoted ; which, t... frivolous Reviling, Jearing and opprobrious L... up his Pamphlet, as that of neceſſity I muſt b...

Now, 2. I anſwer, that what I ſay of *Ag*... my Saying only, but bleſſed *Bolton*'s alſo ; ſo ... he muſt grapple, becauſe of him I have it. Neſheck *doth metaphorically intimate and impo*... *tion of the Sin, not a Diſtinction of the kinds of* ... *and Originals ſerve more to amplifie and exagge*... *ſtinguiſh.*

3. As for the Stranger, I will ſay no more b... ing to handle that matter more largely in it ... That whereas he taketh the reſtraining of the ... *Canaanite* to be a groundleſs phanſie, I ſh... which I have already written formerly about ... him firſt three famous Men indeed, who give t... *Canaanite, viz.* (a) St. *Ambroſe*, St. *Jerome* ... which I believe every impartial Reader will pre...

(a) *To which three Fathers I add* Paulus Fag... *who, in his Annot. in the* Chald. *Paraphr. und*... naanite. *And Learned Mr.* Pool, *Extraneo iſti*, ... *naanorum quos paulatim conſumi volebat, in Hebr*... Gabr. Powel, *p.*42. *By the name Stranger in t*... *the curſed* Canaanites, *and God doth not licenſe t*... *Vſury of any but of their Enemies, whom they mi*...

Novice as he is, as being better grounded than he is, who calls their Exposition *a groundless Fancy*. And if this be not enough, I will subjoyn famous Mr. *Smith*; who saith in Answer to what he quoteth out of *Deut.* 23. *It is said*, Of a Stranger thou mayest take Usury: *I perceive no Scripture speaketh for Usury*; Of a Stranger, *saith God*, thou mayest take Usury: *but thou takest Usury of thy Brother, therefore this condemneth thee, because thou usest thy Brother like a Stranger. Here Stranger signifieth the Lord's Enemies, whom they were commanded to destroy. Therefore, mark how much this maketh against Usury, which they object for Usury. God doth not license the Jews to take Usury of any but their Enemies, whom they might kill: They might not be Usurers to any, but to them of whom they might be Destroyers: Whom they might slay, of them only they might take Usury. Shewing that Usury is a kind of Punishment; and such a kind of Punishment, as if we were to kill a Man, it were a very fit Punishment for him; and therefore the* Jews *might take Usury of none but those whom they might kill. I hope Usurers will alledge this Scripture no more.* Thus that renowned Author.

And will you, Champion, call this a groundless fancy too?

And Lastly, In my Margin I quote three Authors more, *viz. Paulus Fagius*, Mr. *Pool* and *G Powel*, who second me, and make seven great Authors that hold with me.

N V M. XLIX.

4. That place in *Exod.* 22. 27. doth not patronize him, because it concerns the Stranger converted, who is called גר, *Advena, a Dweller among the* Jews, though he was no *Jew*; and therefore was not to be vexed nor oppressed by Usury, as another Stranger of the seven Nations unconverted, and called נכר, which signifieth *Hostem, an Enemy*, otherwise *an Alien*. See *Obad.* 11. and *Lament.* 5. 27. and one whom they might kill, *Jos.* 3. 24. contrarily whereunto, the Proselited Stranger was not to be oppressed, because he was become a Brother, *Deut.* 23. 19. even as now also, a Convert is become a Brother by Religion. So that I wonder with what face he could make this Addition after these words, *Thou shalt not vex him, and yet they might take Use of him*; when there is not one word nor syllable there for Usury, and when the word *Vex* doth absolutely take off all taking of Use, because Usury is a vexing

thing; because it afflicts and brings low, as the Hebrew word עני, denoteth it; because it signifieth to afflict, and to bring low: so the word ולא תלחצנו, nor oppress him, takes off all Usury, because Vsury is Oppression, yea, Extortion; because the Vsurer will have his Vse, and exact it. So as that an Vsurer is also called an Extortioner, *Psal.* 109. 11. an Extortioner in the English, and an Vsurer by all other Translators. The like may be said of *Ezek.* 27. 7. His jeering me for my *Rabbinical* Learning I pass by, being resolved to make use of the Hebrew Punctations; not to make them my Foundation, but for Illustration, as my great Friend and Instructor *Buxtorfius*, that great Hebrician, has taught me: Let him jeer both him and me, we regard it not. What he saith of my Doctrine, *Chap.* 2. *That no Usurer, living and dying in the Sin of Usury, can be saved: That it is made up of strong Presumption, rash Judging, monstrous Uncharitableness,* &c. whether it be or no, let the Reader judge when he shall have read what I shall say about it, and to it. As namely,

1. That it is such a Doctrine as has convinced and converted Souls. I will instance at present in one or two. A certain great Gentleman of mine Acquaintance, having heard this my very Doctrine, word for word, preached, and pressed since my Book against Vsury came out; was thereby so convinced and converted, as that he left that damnable Sin of Vsury, (though he took but Six in the Hundred) and made Restitution: Whereupon, he died shortly after, and had a Funeral Sermon preached; at which it was publickly related, how he was converted, and restored his Vsury again. Which remarkable thing was told me by a Godly Man which heard both the first and second Sermon, and will assert it to any for truth, and can bring many more that heard the same. And very lately, in this Year, 1679. about *Midsummer*, another was thereby so wrought upon, as that she, being a Gentlewoman, resolved to send her Restitution-money as far as *London*, where it is due.

2. That I shall desire my Reader to peruse, and to read over what I have formerly quoted. 1. Out of *Ambrose*, thus Reasoning in *Psal.* 15. *If he be blessed that has not put his Money to Usury, then, doubtless, he is cursed that has.* 2. Out of Bishop *Jewel*, *How darest thou* (Vsurer) *look to Heaven? Thou hast no Dwelling there.* 3. Out of Bishop *Sands*, *God, as he has threatned, excludes thee out of his Kingdom.*

NUM.

NUM. L.

Vnto which three great Men, I shall add two more. As,

1. *Gabriel Powel*; who writes thus. *It is impossible for them that wittingly and willingly persevere in this Sin of Usury to be saved.*

2. The pious Mr. *Francis Whidden* the Elder; who, having been an Vsurer, as I am informed, repented of it, and left it, and made Restitution, and afterward preached many Sermons against it; and delivered this this very Doctrine against it, *The Usurer's Portion will be Eternal Damnation.*

Now judge, Courteous Reader, whether these great and holy Men do not deliver and maintain the same Doctrine which I have derived from my Text; and whether this Champion, censuring me and my Doctrine so rashly as he doth, do not judge them so too, as well as me.

As for his Quotation out of *Dixton*, an obscure Author, I need not value it much, as long as I have such greater, and more illustrious, and famous ones on my side.

Nor indeed can Mr. *Dixton*'s reasoning from the Judicial Law, disposing of Commodities, and from the Year of *Jubilee*, and from the end of six Years, and from lending to a Stranger, that obsolete, and so often and fully confuted Argument convince me, that Vsury is Lawful, and not Damnable; I say, me, who have proved it, and can and will prove it more strongly hereafter, that the Law against Vsury is *Moral*, and not *Judicial*, than he can prove the contrary; instancing in dispensing of Commodities, *&c.*

As for my dear Cousin, Doctor *Spanhemius*, his words by him quoted, I hold with him in this; that *David*, in my Text, doth speak, *De fœneratore expilante fratres Usurâ rodente*; that is, *of a Usurer corroding his Brother with corroding Usury*. But I add withal, not only because *Nesheck*, as I have already proved it, doth not only signifie Corroding and Biting Vsury; but all manner of Vsury. Nor doth my Cousin's Addition make good what is said by him, that the words must be understood *Limitate*; that is, *Limitately*; as many other Aphorisms in the same Psalm; because he doth not demonstrate and prove it, but only saith it. Where I cannot but mind what a greater Man than my Cousin, *viz.* famous St. *Austin*, saith; *If I prove what I say by the holy Scriptures, believe me; if not, believe me not.*

And

And this I am the more bold to declare, becauſe divers Great and Learned Men have ſo learnedly confuted and contradicted this; *viz.*

1. Biſhop (*a*) *Downam*, *Let not us upon this frivolous Diſtinction build our Practice, or hazard the Eternal Salvation of our Souls.*

2. Bleſſed (*b*) *Bolton*, ſpeaking of and againſt diſtinguiſhing of Sin, ſaith, as for Example, *They ſay there are two ſorts of Uſury, Biting and Toothleſs; when all ſorts of Vſury are certainly damned by God.*

3. (*c*) Mr. *Smith*, *They ſay, becauſe Vſury cometh of Biting, the Biting Vſury* (by (*d*) Doctor *Spanhemius* called Corroding) *is only forbidden, and none but the biting Vſury: Why then all Vſury is forbidden, for all Vſury cometh of Biting.*

4. In cometh next Learned (*e*) Mr. *Turner*, in his Sermon upon Vſury: *Let not theſe poor Evaſions of Biting and Toothleſs Vſury deceive us; they are but as Fig-leaves ſhapen by ſome indulgent Wits, to cover the Nakedneſs of that which the Law of God, of Nature, and Equity have diſcovered to be deformed and naked in it ſelf: as if there were ſome Vſury without the meaning of God's Law; or, as if God had never meant to condemn Vſurers, but only to muzzle them.*

Let me add, 5. (*f*) Dr. *T.* in his *Progreſs of Saints*, p. 96. *Men deceive themſelves in their Diſtinctions.*

NUM. LI.

To his Speech about my perſonating of *David* ſlaying *Goliah*, that it had been better I had let it alone, leſt I hit ſome that truly fear God, *&c.* and ſo be brought to Confeſſion and Recantation, with *Job*'s Friends that ſpake not right of God, and to the Grief of his Servant *Job*. To this my Anſwer is, that I fear no ſuch thing, nor need to fear it, becauſe (*g*) I hear from ſeveral Parts in *England*, and out of *England*, where they underſtand Engliſh, by Letters, and by Confeſſions, Acknowledgments and Relations, of the Approbations of my *Vſurer Caſt*, and of the Convictions and Converſions of ſun-

---

(*a*) Downam *upon* Pſal. 15. 5. (*b*) Bolton *in his Diſcourſe of True Happineſs.* (*c*) *Mr.* Smith *in his firſt Sermon upon Vſury, p.* 105. (*d*) Spanhem. *in Dut. Evang.* (*e*) *Mr.* Turner *in his Sermon upon Vſury.* (*f*) *Dr.* T. (*g*) *To God's Glory be it written.*

dry

dry Persons, both Ministers and private Christians, which have declared it to their (*a*) Friends, and to my self; giving me hearty thanks for it, and blessing God, who has wrought so great a Change in them, as that they have made Restitution of the Vsury-Money which they have taken. But of this more hereafter.

At present I will say a word or two concerning the two Disciples which, *Eliah*-like, would call down Fire from Heaven upon the *Samaritans*, &c. because he applieth that Narration to me. And my Answer to it is this, That those two Disciples did (as *Calvin* glosseth upon it in his *Institutions*, *Book.* 3. *chap.* 20. *p.* 549.) inconsiderately do it, desiring such a thing out of an Emulation of *Eliah*; whereas I, for my part, had no such emulous thoughts; but did considerately, and in the fear of God, I hope, and calling upon his Name (he is my Witness) write what I wrote concerning this matter; as knowing what Spirit I must be of, and how I must not rashly condemn my guiltless and innocent Brother: The Vsurer being the Man, who, because he putteth his Money upon Vsury, shall not dwell in God's holy Hill and Tabernacle.

NUM. LII.

I add, Nor do I fear that I have not spoken right of God, because I have written just according to this very Scripture, which is the Word of God, and proceeded from the very Mouth of God, as an Oracle, or Answer to *David's* Question, *Lord, who shall dwell in thy Tabernacle? who shall dwell in thy holy Hill? He that has not put his Money to Vsury*, Psal. 15. 1, 5.

(*a*) *Which will be ready to attest it.*

THE

THE SECOND PART.

Taking in the Third, Fourth and Fifth CHAPTERS.

NUMBER. I.

ABout the several Names given to Usury he will not concern himself, he saith: Nor will I concern my self about many frivolous things, and Tautologies, not worth the answering thereof. I will subjoyn only this; That whereas he saith, that all the Names given to Usury properly belong to that rigid Exaction and Oppression in the World under the Name of *Usury*: My Answer is, that I have answered that already formerly, denying it; and saying, that though chiefly they do, yet not only; and that I also my self am as much, and chiefly against that Oppression, *&c.* As when Men must pay so much to the Usurer's Agents and Servants, to procure so much Money upon Usury, and so much to the Usurer himself, *viz.* twenty or forty Shillings more. And when they must pay Use upon Usury, which the very Civil Law prohibits in these words, (*a*) *Usury of Usuries*, &c.

But to the Name *Interest* I will say something, because he adds these words to his former; *But Interest he will not have it called. And why not? Surely that is an Overplus above the Principal, which the ancient Doctors of the Church call Usury: But Interest with him is lawful, because properly it is Damage,* &c. Whereunto I answer,

(*a*) *Lib. 6. placuit, 29. ff. de Usuris.*

1. That

1. That not I only will not have Usury called (a) Interest, but others also, far greater and learneder than he and I, will not have it called so; I say, others; even both Civilians and Theologians, because it is another thing, and not the same, as I will make it appear by and by; quoting for it,

1. *Civilians*; and by Name, famous Doctor (b) *Vulteius*; who defineth Interest thus, *That it is an Incommodity which happeneth* ex mora, by a delay. And then shewing what *Mora*, or such a Delay is, a *Culpa*, or fault of him which doth not answer the Convention, or Agreement made between the Creditor and Debtor, for an Opportunity, (c) Place and (d) Time where and when Payment is to be made.

It is also called (e) *Pœna*, or *a Punishment*, in the Civil Law, which the Creditor stipulateth for. Whence is the Appellation of Penal Stipulation.

As for Usury, that is defined by (f) *Hottomannus*, *Gain, which for Loan is required at certain times.*

And, as *Civilians* do thus distinguish between Interest and Fenory, so do *Divines* also apparently put a difference between Interest and Usury, and will not have Usury called Interest; saying, (g) *That whereas Men pretend to the honest Name of Interest to their gainful Usury, it is pernicious Sophistry*, saith (h) *Melanchton*; who also saith farther, that *Interest is a Debt, which he oweth by the Law of Nature, that has been to another an effectual cause of Damage and Loss; or indeed has hindred his just and lawful Gain.* But Usury to him is Gain which exceedeth to the Loan of Money, &c. As it is also with (i) *Selneccerus*, (k) Doctor *Chitræus*, (l) *Aquinas*, (m) *Vignerius*. I add,

(n) The Author of *The Arraignment of Usury*, who is more full; saying notably, *The way for the Discovery of the Usurer's Evils is, that howsoever the World is wont to confound the Names*

(a) *Interest, because we may say,* Interfuit mihi hæc habuisse. (b) *Doctor* Vulteius, *Jurispr. l. c.* 34. *so called.* (c) Cinacius *de Paratittis.* (d) *L. Si soluturus* 39. *de solutione.* (e) *L. Stipulatio ista,* 38. *S. alteri D. De Usura. D.* Vult. *l.* 1. *Jurispr. c.* 34. (f) Hottomannus *his Definition of Usury.* (g) Melanchton, *l. de Difinit.* (h) *Idem ibid.* (i) Selneccerus, *Hist. Chrift. Relig. p.* 2. (k) Christ. (l) Aquinas *in his Sums.* (m) Vignerius, *Instit. Sect.* 3. *Theol. c.* 5. Lavat. *in Exod.* 22. (n) *The Arraignment of Usury.*

of Interest and Usury; and Men are wont to say, that they take Interest, and lend upon Interest, when indeed they take Usury, and lend upon Usury: yet there are two manifest and essential Differences between Usury and Interest, which do so distinguish the one from the other, as that they cannot possibly be confounded. One Difference is this; Usury is an Overplus, or Gain, more than was lent: Interest is never Gain or Overplus above the Principal, but a Recompence demanded, and due for the Damage that is taken, or the Gain that is taken, or the Gain that is hindred through Lending. Another Difference is this; Usury accreweth aud groweth due by Lending, from the day of Borrowing, unto the appointed time of Payment: Interest is never due, but from the appointed Day of Payment, forward; and for so long as I forbear my Goods after the Day in which I did Covenant to receive them.

And I add, that *Usury is against Equity, Conscience and Reason: Interest stands with them all*, saith blessed *(a) Bolton*; whereof more hereafter.

So that if once I have lent freely unto a certain Day, I shall not demand Interest for any Damage sustained, or Gain hindred, during that Term of Time for which I have lent to another. But if at the Covenanted time I receive not mine own again, then what harm soever do betide me after that Day, for the forbearing thereof, Reason will, that it be recompenced by the Borrower. Thus he also.

Ah, poor Champion! What are you to these famous Men, who, in this grand Point, are so fully for me? And why do you blame me for this Damage, as they and I call Interest, as if none but I did call it so?

NUM. II.

But he will have me prove it by Scripture.

Whereunto I answer two ways.

1. *Retortiug*, And so let him prove his regulated and moderate Vsury by Scripture. As for me, I hope to prove Damage by it thus.

1. That as the word ὁμιούσιος, though it was not *verbatim* in the Scripture, yet it was generally received; because, by a necessary Consequence, it was proved by Scripture, and so

(a) Bolton, *p.* 58.

approved

approved as Scriptural by the Catholick Fathers. So, though these very words be not in the Scripture, that Damage is to be paid for keeping back a Man's Money, and delay of Payment; yet in general, Damage for Hurt done is by the holy Scripture allowed and required. Whereupon consequentially, in cometh Damage for Money freely lent, but not paid at the time appointed, to a Man's hindrance: As thus, Damage is allowed and required by God, if a Man be hurted or hindred in or by any thing. As for Example,

1. Damage is required if a Man's Beast or Ox be hurted: Whereupon it followeth, that much more if himself be hurted by not paying what is due to him at a Day, *Exod.* 21. 22.

2. A King must not receive Damage by his Subject, for *Why should damage grow to the hurt of the King*, Ezr. 4. 22. whereupon I infer, and why should Damage accrew to one who is a Citizen of Heaven, and is a King too, *Rev.* 1. 5. and lends his Money freely, as God would have him, *Psal.* 15. 5. by the keeping back of his Money so lent at the day nominated, to his great hurt and hindrance.

3. If a Man hurt another Man in his Eye, Hand, or Tooth, or Foot, Recompence must be made for it, *Exod.* 21. 24. And if so, why should not Recompence and Damage also be allowed, required and given for any other hurt?

4. The Borrower, who borroweth ought of his Neighbour, is to make good the hurt which his lending Neighbour receives, *Exod.* 22. 14. Money is not named, but cometh in by a Consequence.

As for my Cousin *Spanhemius*, whom he quotes, as speaking against the School-men, because they are for Damage because of Gain ceasing, I need not dispute it with him, because he is against the School-men, not me; and the School-men are of Age, and such able Men, as that they can and do speak for themselves, and that at large, as my Cousin confesseth, *prolixe*; whereas he is but short. But if he had spoken against me, I am of Age too, and have read as much as I could concerning Usury, and this matter of Damage: So as that I may say after *Gabriel Powel*, *I have read all that ever I could come by, Fathers, Canonists, Councils and Modern Writers*; and therefore can speak for my-self; yea, and for the School-men too, *viz.* That they are not so simple as they are made by the

(a) *Exod.* 21. 24, 25. *and* 35, 36.

Champion,

Champion; nor for *Effugias* of words, and shifts, as his *Grotius* is pleased to upbraid them in his second Citation: which I therefore the less regard, because he is unsound also in other things, and because so many Holy, Learned, Orthodox Writers are for that Damage which I maintain. As, besides the above-cited, I could quote a World of them: But I desire to return to the School-men, and to let the World see how serious, and far from *Effugias* of words and shifts they be in this Point, I will alledge but one of them, instead of more, about Damage, especially Covenanted for, *viz.* *(a) Gabriel Biel*; which, because I have him, I do often make use of in serious matters, relating to Vsury especially: His words, being weighty, I wish were written with Letters of Gold; but I will write them with Ink, which I hope will be as much accepted as if they were written with Gold. *If a Man lend any thing, and take the Borrower's Bond for the Payment of it, with an intent, that at the Day, the Penalty* (of which I spake even now, when I wrote of Interest) *shall pay for the forbearing of the Money; then certainly he is an Usurer. Now, it is to be presumed,* saith the same Learned *Biel, that the Lender imposeth a Penalty upon the Borrower, to cloak the act, or to avoid the danger of Vsury; whereas either the Lender wishes rather that the Borrower would pass his Day, and so he might take the Forfeiture* (or Damage,) *than that he should pay him at his Day, and so avoid the Penalty* (or Damage:) *Or else, when the Lender knoweth, at the time of Lending, the Borrower is not like to make Restitution* (or Payment) *at his appointed Day. Or Thirdly, If the Lender imposeth (and so taketh) a greater Penalty* (or Damage) *on the Non-payment, than his Damage can possibly be for the forbearing of his Goods.* Which words I do with all willingness here subscribe unto, for they are good and honest.

NVM. III.

Where note by the way,

1. That Damage is called תַּכְלָא, *a Cord*, because it binds a Man like a Cord to make Satisfaction, and that with God's Approbation, to be made and determined by Judges, *Exod.* 21. 22. *He shall pay as the Judges determine.* Which, 1. Takes off all Aspersions cast upon this Doctrine of Damage,

(*a*) *Gabriel Biel.*

to be given, if at the Day nominated, the Money freely lent be not payed; as if then a Man might make his Market, and make the Borrower pay what he pleaseth, which is false; for as the Scripture doth, so do we put it to the Determination of others to be Judges, (as also the Civil Law, according to God's Law, doth, *Tit.* 47. *l.* 7. *c.*)

Whereunto I will add what blessed *Bolton* saith to the same effect, *pag.* 57. *That the Estimation of the Interest must not be referred to the Creditor's own Arbitrement, but to the Judgment of some other honest and discreet Men.*

2. It serves as a Bridle for the Lender, that he may not exceed in his Damage demanded. So that therefore under the Hebrew Word an Accent is put, which the Hebricians call *Meteg, a Bridle*; as the same is to be seen in the Hebrew Text.

Let (*a*) *Panormitanus* be seen also of Damage arising from Gain, both emergent and ceasing.

NUM. IV.

But here my Adversary will say, this makes for me, who am damaged by the Borrower, if, keeping my Money for half a Year, he pay me nothing; because, if I had had it, I might have gotten by it. But,

I answer, Not at all it makes for him; because Lending here must needs be that which we call free, and is commanded, whereas his is Usurious and Interdicted, *Deut.* 23. 19.

2. But I have not yet done with the Holy Scripture, which makes just Damage allowable.

Consequentially in the New Testament also; for, in 2 *Cor.* 8. 13. that great Apostle, speaking of Alms, saith thus; *For I mean not that other Men be eased, and you burthened.* Whencefrom a great Writer deduceth this Inference, in these words, *The Apostle will not, that even in the Giving of Alms, much less in Lending and Borrowing we should so deal, as other Men should be eased by the grieving of our selves.* Now, if I lend to pleasure another, and for want of mine own at the appointed time, I am indamaged in my Credit, or hindred of my lawful Gain.

(*a*) Panormitan. *c. conquest. de Usur.*

Whereunto I add that great (a) *Downam*, who infers the same from the same Scripture.

3. Damage is grounded upon Equity and Equality, which the Holy Scripture requireth of us, to be observed by us, 2 *Cor*. 8. 13. But by an Equality, from whence also Divines maintain by a Consequence the Doctrine of Damage; as you may see in the Margin, who is cited for it.

4. It is due by the Law of Nature; for this is the Law of Nature, and Natural Equity, (b) *Nemo locupleretur cum alterius injuria*, *Let not Man enrich himself by hindring of another*, saith that great Divine, *Melanchton*. And again he tells us, that *Damage*, alias *Interest*, *is a Debt due by the Law of Nature*, &c. And again, having asserted Damage arising from a Contingent Loss, and from Gain ceasing, he saith, that *The Reason is drawn from Natural Justice*.

And as for the Law of Nature, that is made Scriptural and Divine, by that great Apostle, in two places. 1. *Rom*. 2 15. where it is called, *The Law written in the Heart*; that is in the (c) Conscience, (d) inscribed by God himself. An[d] 1 *Cor*. 11. 14. where he maketh Nature a Doctress, teachin[g] us, that *It is a shame for a Man to wear long Hair*. Which i[s] also applicable to Usury, that even Nature teacheth us, tha[t] it is a shame for a Man to lend upon Usury, and to be a[n] Usurer, which even Usurers themselves are (e) ashamed of to be so called; as one, to shame them, writeth of their saying, that *Usurers blush, and are ashamed to answer for the[ir] Trade, that they are of such a Trade*.

5. We are to think upon whatsoever is just, *Phil*. 4. 8. th[at] is, so as to do it; but to pay and to give Damage is just, be cause it is (f) just to give every Man is due, *Rom*. 13. 7. an[d]

(a) Downam *in* Psal. 15. 5. *inferring and reasoning thus*, *is against Equity, as the Apostle saith in a like Case, that to t[he] Creditor should be* ἄλιψις, *and to the other* ἄνεσις. *Recompens[e] Usury*, alias *Damage*, *is due by the Law of Nature*. Bolton, 54. (b) Melanchton *de Definit*. (c) *Wherein the Law of N[a]ture ruleth saith a Famous Writer*. (d) *The Law of Nature is* Dictamen, *or a Dictate of Conscience, and so a Direction by G[od] himself, put into Men's Minds and Hearts, admonishing the[m] what they must do or omit*. Bullinger. *Decat*. 2. *Serm*. 1. Musculus. (e) John Bromyard, *in Summa præd. Tit*. *Usu[ra]* (f) *Justitia est suum cuique tribuere, neminem lædere*; *Justini[an] in suis Institut*.

ſo conſequently, Damage to whom it is juſtly due. Where give me leave to ſubjoyn the words of a renowned Writer, ſaying, that (*a*) *Damage* (called Intereſt alſo) *is juſtly due.* And adding, *Not only when a Man has lent, and for want of receiving again of his own in appointed time, he ſuffereth Damage; but alſo, when, wanting his own to employ for his beſt advantage, his Gain and Encreaſe is hindred. As for Example, I lend freely,* mark FREELY, *looking to receive mine own again at a certain appointed day. The day came, I received it not; for want of it, I forfeited, at that day, a Bond to another Man; and the Forfeiture is asked of me in part, or to the utmoſt: I doubt not but Reaſon and Conſcience will that I may demand ſuch Recompence of him to whom I lent freely, as I am compelled, for want of mine own, to make to another, to whom my Bond and Obligation by that means is forfeited.* Thus he. And is not ſuch Damage juſt? Is it not to give to all their dues, according to the fore-quoted Scripture? *Rom.* 13. 7.

6. Damage here maintained is according to the Law of Nations (as Uſury is againſt the Law of Nations) which (*b*) proceedeth from the Law of Nature, and is like that written in Men's Hearts and Minds alſo; and, by name, maintaineth a Rendring of Pledges and things lent, and is againſt the keeping of ſuch things back, becauſe it thereby becomes Damage. Whereupon it followeth, that it is a Law founded in Scripture, as the Law of Nature, *Rom.* 2. 15. 16. it being the iſſue of it, as even now I ſhewed.

7. Damage is alſo grounded in the (*c*) Civil Law, which ſpeaks according to the Scripture, and differs from the Law of Nations, in that it is written (*d*) as the Scripture is written, and ſaith the ſame that the holy Scripture ſaith about Damage.

For (*e*) *Juſtinian* the Emperor, who has written thoſe famous Law-books, called his *Inſtitutions*, having diſtinguiſhed certain Caſes from uncertain, did determine that the one ſhould not exceed double, and the other ſhould be determined by

(*a*) Panormit. *de Uſuris.* (*b*) *Quam a Natura proceſſiſſe facile intelligere licet*, Calepinus, *p.* 633. (*c*) *Hoc autem jus Scripto conſtat ut ſunt leges & plebiſſcita, Idem ibid.* (*d*) *Which is the ſame with the Law of Nature, being deduced from it; and unleſs it be ſo derived from it, is no Law, but only an Idol, or falſe pretence of Law, ſaith a renowned Author,* (*e*) Juſtinian *the Emperor, Tit.* 47.

Jndges: which is alſo ſo ordered by Scripture, as I quoted it out of *Exod.* 21. 22. All which ſheweth how Scriptural Damage is.

8. It is according to ſound [*a*] Reaſon, as Uſury is againſt Reaſon; which the Scripture alſo approveth and alloweth, *Act.* 17. 2. *Chap.* 18. 14. *Chap.* 24. 25. *Rom.* 12. 1. 1 *Pet.* 3. 15. *Eſa.* 1. 18. *chap.* 41. 21. and according to which I may receive Damage, as it ſhall be allowed me by Impartial, Godly and Juſt Judges, becauſe there is reaſon for it, and Scripture too, ſtrengthening reaſon, that what one would have another do to him, he ſhould do to another, and which the aforeſaid Law of Nature alſo teacheth: and on the contrary, there is no reaſon for it, that I having lent a Man my Money freely, I ſhould be harmed by him for my kindneſs ſhewn him; he forbearing to pay me, for my need and Indemnity, at the time appointed.

NUM. V.

Here let me ſubjoyn the Verdicts of other Divines alſo.

And 1. That of (*b*) G. *Biel* again; who ſaith, *If I received not my Money, freely lent, at a certain day appointed, and forfeited at that day a Bond; Reaſon and Conſcience will, that I may demand Recompence.*

2. The ſame words almoſt I find in the (*c*) Author of *The Conviction of Uſury,* and deſire may be remembred upon a new Account; *If, at the covenanted time, I receive not mine own again, then what harm ſoever do betide me after that day, for the forbearing thereof, Reaſon wills, that it be recompenced of the Borrower*; Meaning Reaſon warranted by Scripture alſo: Which requires our Reaſons, and ſtrong Reaſons too; as I cited for it even now, *Eſa.* 41. 21.

But Reaſon perſuades me now to make an end of this matter of Damage, becauſe I have been ſomewhat long, if not too long about it, and to go forward; becauſe there remains for me another ſharp Encounter, which I muſt enter into about the Definition of Uſury, which my Antagoniſt ſo much impugneth. Only theſe three things I will firſt add.

(*a*) *Uſury is againſt Reaſon, but Intereſt is not*; Bolton.
(*b*) Gabriel Biel, *in* 4. *Diſt.* (*c*) *Upon* Pſal. 15. 5.

1. That my very Adversary's own Author, Mr. *Mayer*, by him cited, and to be read in this *Book*, 2. *p.* *Num.* 80. herein is for me: for he saith thus, that *If the Borrower do not repay, so as that the Lender cannot have it again in due time for his Maintenance, the Borrower Trading with it from Year to Year; it is not against this Precept to require Recompence.* He doth not say Usury, which is forbidden; but Recompence, which we stand for, and hold with him in.

2. That the very first two great and learned Divines which God raised for a Reformation, *Luther* and *Melanchton*, aver the same, touching Damage, which my Friends and I do here aver. Their words are these,

1. '*Luther*'s, To recompence a Damage is not to give or 'take more than the Principal; but it is a hurt which cometh 'to the Lender, contrary to his Will, whereby he is compel-'led to ask a Recompence.

2. (*a*) '*Melanchton*'s, When a Debter has given a Cause 'of Loss, if he make a recompence for the hindrance which 'his Creditor is come to by his means; such Gain is not U-'sury, nor unlawful. But that Gain is Usury, and unlawful, 'which is gotten only for the Loan of Lending, when no dan-'ger or hindrance is come by the lending.

(*b*) And again saith that Phoenix of *Germany*, *Melanchton*, 'May any thing above the Principal be demanded in conside-'ration of the hindrance had by the lending of the same? I 'answer, that is called Interest; which is either because he 'is damaged, or because some Gain indeed is lost by the lend-'ing, *&c.*

I say, that that deep learned Scholastick, the renowned, and most highly esteemed *Aquinas*, I mean, has written so fully, so groundedly, and so satisfactorily of this thing called Damage, as that when his much and copious Reasoning about it shall be ballanced with that little of (*c*) *Spanhemius* and *Grotius*, by the Champion cited, and brought against Damage, it will be but as a Candle set in the Light of the Sun.

(*a*) Melancht. *in Philos. Morali.* (*b*) *Idem ibid.* (*c*) *Whose All of Usury is but sixteen Leaves, which some do extol above Volumes.*

But here I am desired to answer three Questions:

The First is, whether a Man may lawfully look for something again, when he lends his Money upon this supposition of his delay?

Whereunto I answer, That the aforesaid *Gabriel Biel*, in the forecited Decision, has answered it by that which he has said above of this thing, whereto I subscribe.

The Second is, whether a Jew might receive this Damage of his Brother, if he kept his Money, lent him, beyond his time, suppose a quarter or half a Year longer?

I answer, Doubtless he might if he were much hindred and damaged by it, because God did most eminently provide for the Jews Indemnity by a Law formerly cited, and made for them Primarily, and for us Secondarily.

The Third Question is, Whether a Lender, that puts out an hundred Pounds for a Year to his own Damage, may not as justly receive Satisfaction for that Damage, as well as the next Year, suppose the time be expired, and Payment delayed, *&c.*

For Answer hereunto I have this to say.

1. That blessed (*a*) *Bolton* has answered this fully *pag.* 58. 59. 60. See his Book.

2. That a Lender in some Case must be contented to lose his very Principal, and look for no Satisfaction at all, as it has been formerly shewn, to be partly the meaning of that place, *Luk.* 6. 35.

3. That to Godly wise Men, who do not put their Money upon Usury, it is no Riddle at all (as he saith it is to him) to receive Money upon the Account of Gain ceasing, or less arising; and yet to damn a Man that receiveth any thing back for one, two, three or four hundred Pounds lent for several Years: because the one is against the Law of God, *viz.* to receive Usury, *Deut.* 23. 19. which he calls Satisfaction, as Usurers use to nominate it, being ashamed to call it Usury; and because God condemns it, *Ezek.* 18. 12, 15. But as for the other, it would be against the Law of Nature, which also is God's, written in our Hearts, *Rom.* 2. 16. not to recom-

(*a*) Bolton, *pag.* 56.

pence

pence a Man's Loss which he susteins by the Borrower, after he has lent it for a certain time freely: Which because the Usurer will not do, I shall bring one Learned and Godly Man or other to second me in this; and blessed *(a) Bolton* shall be the Man; who saith Interest or Damage may grow due, say Divines, two ways.

1. By Loss arising.
2. By Gain ceasing, &c.

In which two Cases I may lawfully provide for my Indemnity, by exacting an equal Recompence at thine hands, and thou art bound in Conscience to make good this Use or Hindrance, which by thy default I sustein. And this, he saith, is no Usury, for there is a great difference between them. Thus this holy Man seconds me.

He ends with Jeering, being full of his Jeers.

It is some comfort yet, he saith, *that Interest is lawful with this German Divine*. But what Comfort? A poor and cold One I am confident of; because this *German* Divine, and so many *English* ones too, do combine together and symphonize so as they do in this matter of Interest; making it lawful Damage, and damning Usury and Usurers to the Pit of Hell, as it hath been formerly ostended and shewn.

NUM. VII.

But Reason persuadeth me to make a full end of that great matter of Interest and Damage, because I have been so long about it, if not too long: And to hasten forward, because there remaineth for me another sharp Encounter, which I must enter into about the Definition of Usury, which is Foundation-matter. So that I must, before I enter, implore Heaven's Aid, looking up to the great God of Heaven for his Support in this great Combat.

My fierce Adversary in this, begins his Combat thus.

His Definition of Usury runs thus; Usury is a certain and absolute Gain, compacted for, or expected, and taken for the Loan of things, which may be consumed in the use thereof; or whatsoever is, more than the Principal compacted for, or taken for the Loan of things, which may be consumed in the use thereof.

---

[a] Bolton *in his Discourse concerning Usury*, p. 56, 57, 58.

From this last Definition, I shall say, Gain
ture, which he holds Lawful, is Usury, it bei
the Principal. Thus he goeth to work, even ve
mingling the first with the last Definition : So r
forced to answer him accordingly. And to cut s

1. *Insist upon adventuring most*, which he me
and most ; saying, *Whatsoever Gain* so received
is not absolute and certain, but uncertain an
Besides, [*a*] this Limitation of Absolute and
Scriptural, but added (it's like) to salve adv
Usury, for all the other parts of the Definitio
unto ; So doth *Ambrose*.

Whereunto I reply,

1. That I am for the whole first Definitio
other is added for Brevities sake, as the like is d
and so I shall,

1. Maintain absolute and certain Gain : wh

2. Adventuring.

1. Absolute and [*b*] certain Gain : wh
Scriptural, and to answer his Negative, I bri
place, [*c*] *Exod.* 22. 25. *Thou shalt not lay upon*
Hebrew is, and signifieth thus much, *Thou shalt*
Greek, ὐκ ἐπιθήκης. And [*d*] *Vatabl.* obser
verbatim from the *Hebrew*, *Thou shalt not impose*
sitions are absolute and certain. As for examp
imposed by Law are absolute and certain. As
Imposition is granted by the King and Parliam
lute and certain, and must be paid : and so n
posed be paid, and cannot be called uncertain
pion is pleased to say.

But he thinks to make good his Saying by G
because it is not imposed or compacted for.

Whereunto I answer, that though it be not
presly compacted for, yet tacitly, and so as th
certain enough. Where, to make this evident

---

[a] *And. to distinguish ours, I say, from c*
also learned Danæus *therein agreeth with me, s*
Ship Loan is justly distinguished from commo
[b] *As also* Usher, *that great and learned Ar*
magh, *doth ; calling Usury a certain Gain.* [
Tremel. *translate it.* [d] Vatabl. *in* Exod. 2

1. That by the Lawyers a Compact is called a Covenant, and made [a] both one and the same thing.

2. That there is a twofold Compacting.

1. Expressed.

2. Tacit.

1. Expressed, Which is also twofold.

1. *Nudum*, or Naked.

2. *Vestitum*, or Clothed.

1. Naked, or Bare, by a sole promise. As thus, I will lend you forty Pounds, but you shall pay me so much for the Loan of it. I will, saith the Borrower, and thank you too. So they compact by a bare promise.

2. [c] Cloathed, And that is done three ways.

1. By Deeds, as by a Pledge or Pawn.

2. By Words, as in Stipulations and Fidejussions.

3. By Writings, as Bill or Bond.

All which Compactings make Usury certain enough, as the World well knows; that is to say, *humanitus*. And hereof more hereafter.

2. But besides this expressed, there is a Tacit Compacting. As when an Agreement or Consent is by necessary or probable Consequence intended, although it be not expressed unto others. As for Example, [e] one useth this Instance; 'The Parents of two Children do, in their presence and hearing, conclude a Marriage to be contracted and solemnized between their Children: the Children standing by, hear the Conference and Conclusion of their Parents; but neither demand any thing, nor answer any thing, nor object any thing, nor reply any thing, nor affirm any thing, nor deny any thing that is spoken. In this case is intended the Consent of the Children to the Conclusion of the Parents; And why? Reason presupposeth, that if either Party had been discontented with the Match, they would by one means or other have signified their dislike. Which I apply thus; So I come to a Man to borrow an hundred Pounds: You shall

[a] *Lege* 1. *F. de pactis.* [b] *Quod est contractus, quo res ita creditori obligatur, ut is in credito eo nomine securior sit. Doctor* Fregius, *p.* 333. [c] 1 Pet, 3. 21. [d] Unde fidejussor *is added to a Stipulation*; in novatione res, *as Civilians term it. Doctor* Fregius *Instit. p.* 335. [e] *Summa Angelica, Tit. Matrimon.*

have

have it (saith he] as others use to have it, though I do not mention it. Here the Borrower, and others, know that he looketh for so much Usury; that is, Six in the Hundred: and so taketh the Money, and goeth away with it, saying nothing to it. Which, what else is it but a silent Compact? So that we have a common Proverb for such Cases, *Silence is Consent*. And [a] *Plutarch* hath a Saying to the same effect, *Silence is an Answer to a wise Man.* And such a Compact, though not expressed, yet maketh the Usurer's Gain usually certain too. You will say, How? I answer thus; The Usurer knoweth by experience, that Men which stand upon their Credit will not be worse than their silent consent, and that they use to pay their Usurer punctually; because else they know they shall have no more Money of the Usurer, what need soever they have, if they falter: and they know also the Usurer's mind and practice, that he useth so to lend, because he will not be reputed to be an Usurer, who lendeth upon Usury, and putteth down the Sum with the Principal: but only expects it, and takes it when it is brought to him. And so accordingly brings his Six in the Hundred as punctually and unfailingly as others which compact expresly to pay so much Usury as is imposed by the Usurer.

NUM. VIII.

2. As for Adventuring, or *Fœnus nauticum*, *Nautical Fenory*, to make way for his cavelling about that, he saith, *This Limitation of Absolute and certain is added (it's like) to salve Adventuring from Usury.*

Whereunto I reply, 1. I grant that it is added to salve it from Usury properly so called, not from Usury generally so called, and in a large sense accepted; as *Gabriel Biel* speaks, [b] *Usury is taken sometimes very largely, for any thing which is taken in lending, above the Principal.* Wherewith *Bullinger* [c] also sympothizeth, as I shall shew when I come to my Antagonist's Authors, and to that Saying of some, that *All Usury is not unlawful.* Upon which account it is called *Fœnus nauticum*, *Ship Usury*, though it be not Usury properly so called, because all the parts of my larger Definition, which I have set

[a] Plutarch. *l. de Immod. Verecund.* [b] Gabriel Biel in 4. *Sent. dist.* 15. *q.* 11. *a.* 1. Bulling. *Decad.* 3. *Serm.* 1.

down,

down, and am now proving, do not agree thereto; and by name, Absolute and Certain Gain, even now asserted. So that his catching at St. *Ambrose*, and other Men's shorter definitions (which will admit an Explanation and Amplification) will not stand him in any stead, because I stand not chiefly, or only upon them, though I name them as generally most received.

2. I answer, That whereas he replieth to my Saying, *But the Gain thereof (viz.* of Adventuring) *depends upon the Ship's safe coming and going.* &c. *And so doth the Gain of Loan, and the Principal too, depend upon many Men's single Honesty.* Whereunto my Answer is, that Usury-gain depends not upon Uncertainties and Casualties which Navigation is subject unto, by reason of Tempests, Ice and Pirats: whereas most Usurers will be sure to secure themselves by sufficient Sureties to be bound with the Borrower, and by Pledges, Pawns, Mortgages, and Lands bound, and Judgments to make sure both Principal and Use. So that by a great [*a*] *Council* Usury is interpreted and set out thus: *This is the proper Interpretation of Usury, when men labour to get Gain and Encrease from the Use of a thing which groweth or increaseth not; and that with no Labour or Cost, no Danger or Adventuring.* Which hath caused a great [*b*] Divine to define Usury thus; *Usury is, when a Man, not adventuring the Goods which he lendeth, covenants to receive again more than he lends; even upon this Consideration, because he lent them.*

Which Definition is held to be the best.

NUM. IX.

But here the Usurer will insist upon his uncertain Gain thus. 'You tell of Sureties, Bills, Bonds and Pawns: but 'what if the Borrower himself and his Sureties break, or he 'and they for some Crime may have their Goods confiscated: 'again, he or they may flee the Country, or keep the House; 'Evidence may be stollen, or lost by Fire, or Wars, or other'wise caught out of my hands, as some have been; and Lands 'may be mortgaged or engaged to others before me, I not 'knowing it, and so I may lose all, as some lately, both Mi-

---

[a] *Concil.* Later. *Sect.* 10. [b] *The Author of Usuries Arraignment.*

'nisters

'nisters and others; have lost Hundreds by other Men's 'Breaking: and therefore how can you say that the Usurer 'adventureth not, but is certain of his Gain.

Whereunto I answer,

1. That so every body adventureth all that he has; for he may lose all, as *Job*; either by Fire, by Thieves, by Enemies in a time of War, as I did in the *German* Wars: which notwithstanding, it cannot be said that he is such an Adventurer as the Ship-Adventurer is, who taketh for it sufficient Pawns, or who keeps it by himself, under Lock and Key in a Tower, or strong House, Moated, and having a Draw-Bridge to it, as some have.

To make this more plain, I will illustrate it by this Example.

We have in *England* two sorts of Merchants, Merchant-Adventurers, and Merchant Retailers. The Retailers cannot but hazard much, because he must trust often; sometimes for round Sums, sometimes for a great while, sometimes upon the Borrower's bare Word, or Hand to his Book: which Assurance no Usurer will take: and yet no Man calleth him a Merchant-Adventurer, neither is he assumed into their Hall and Company. How much less then can an Usurer be called an Adventurer of his Goods, who will neither trust to a Man's bare Word, nor for any long time; but only from half Year to half Year, and then not without very sufficient and Landed Men, bound with the Borrower, and such like Securements.

2. I answer to the Usurers pretended Adventuring thus.

There is a twofold Adventuring.

1. *Quoad Eventum*, *In respect of the Event.*

2. *Quoad Media*, *In respect of the Means.*

1. *In respect of the Issue*: So the Usurer adventureth, and no thanks to him for it: for he can do no otherwise, because none can see the end of things when he begins them, because the All-seeing God, by his over-ruling Providence, will work as he pleaseth, sometimes beyond Means, sometimes without Means, sometimes contrary to Means; so that none can tell certainly what will be the End and Issue of things, and so the Usurer also cannot be altogether sure.

2. *In respect of Humane Means*: So the Usurer maketh his Usury as sure and certain as it can be made, and is no Adventurer, nor can be, in Humane Reason. I will instance for the Dilucidation of this, in that which is written, *Act.* 12. 1, 3, 5. where

where *Herod* is said to have apprehended *Peter*, and cast into Prison, and delivered to four Quaternions of Soldiers to be kept, and bound with two Iron Chains; and lastly, that he caused a Watch to be kept before the Prison Door, and about *Peter*'s Lodging, that he should not escape: which notwithstanding, by the extraordinary Providence of God, he escaped. In which case, who will say, that *Herod*, having used all such means for *Peter*'s safe keeping, did adventure *Peter*'s escape. Even so, when the Usurer hath bound the Borrower with Bonds and Pawns, as it were with Fetters (as [a] *Plutarch* speaketh;) and when he hath tied him as fast, and made him as sure as his own Head can devise, or Laws will permit; it may be, that one way or other, not fore-thought or fore-seen by him, God, by his Providence, may defeat him, as some have been defeated by the unexpected Breaking of some great Men, thought to be as sufficient as any, and being accounted very honest Men too. But can or will any wise Man say, that the Usurer adventureth as Adventurers do, or means to adventure the Principal? No, no, For, because he will not adventure, he will not lend but to the [b] Rich, and such as can give him sufficient Security; and not to the Poor, who cannot. *Nemo fænerator pauperi, None will lend to Usury to a poor Man*, saith the fore-mentioned [c] *Plutarch*. Nay, therefore the Usurer will not lend two Years together to a rich Man, but with new Sureties, for fear that he or they should be undone in few Years by Usury; and so, not being able to pay, he should lose his advantage.

I close up therefore this matter with great [d] *Luther*'s words. *And yet will not the Usurer take upon him any Adventure or Hazard, either in his Body or Goods:* And with pious *Bolton*'s, *Usurers love not to be Adventurers.*

N U M. X.

The Champion adds to his Reply, That there is a proportionable Gain (in Ship-Loan) that answereth the Hazard, seeing that he that adventureth taketh three times the Gain, or more, it may be, than he that lends upon Use.

(a) Plutarch *de non fænerando.* (b) *Pleading for such lending to the Rich so much as he doth for that very cause.* (c) Plutarch, *ibid.* (d) Luther *de Taxand. Usura, Tom.* 7.

Where-

Whereunto I answer, And yet I have heard discreet Men say in discoursing with me about this thing, that it is observed that Men, and Usurers especially will rather lend for Six in the Hundred, than adventure their Money at Sea, because of hazard. And I do observe it my self, that our great Men, which are great Usurers, do generally and usually lend for Six in the Hundred upon the Land, rather than for Twenty upon Ships for the same cause; not fearing that the Debtor will break (which the Champion adds) because Usurers have so many Strings to their Bow besides, if he should break.

But some will say, *Who, besides you, is for this Ship-Loan?*

I answer, *both Civilians, and many pious, learned and able Divines.*

1. *Civilians*, By whom it is called *Fœnus nauticum*, *Nautical Fenory*, and defined thus: *(a)* A Creditor's Gain which he gets by his Money lent to one which navigateth, and goeth over Sea, taking the hazard upon himself: where note,

1. That *Justinian* has stinted this kind of Usury at Twelve in the Hundred, that none may be oppressed by its Excess.

2. That that great and Godly Lawyer (*b*) *Hottomannus* doth not also approve of it; but also refels and confuteth those which held (*c*) that the Canon Law is against it: shewing, that either the Text in that Law is corrupted, the word *(Not)* being omitted; because *Gregory*, who is the Author quoted, as being against it, doth expresly exempt Ship-loan from Usury, by him condemned, together with two Cases more: or else, that their Law must needs be very unreasonable, seeing where is Hazard, there may be Gain required, as the due price thereof.

NUM. XI.

2. I subjoyn Divines. And,

1. Renowned and most learned (*d*) *Danæus*; whose words are, *It is a Question put forth by some concerning Nautical Fenory, whether it may be lawful? And my Answer is, That this kind of Usury is justly distinguished by the Doctors of the Civil*

(*a*) *De Naut. Fen.* 22. *D.* 2. *c.* 33. *vult. Jurisp. l. c.* 34. (*b*) Hottoman. *l de Usuris.* (*c*) *Decr.* Greg. *l.* 5. *tit. de Usuris.* (*d*) Danæus *de Usuris.* *Law,*

Law, because in it the hazard of the Money and Principal is by the Creditor taken upon himself.

2. Pious and erudite (*a*) *Bullinger*, whom *Danæus* nominates, as an Aprover of it; quoting his first Book written of that Subject.

3. *Aretius*; who saith, *The Nautick Fenory was granted to Merchants and Sea Negotiators; and that either for their Navigation or for their Return too.*

4. That great and famous Bishop (*c*) *Downam* writeth thus, 'Usury is distinguished from three other things, to which the 'name of Usury especially in the Latin Tongue is assigned, 'but are not this gainful Usury whereof we speak. The first 'of these is Adventurers Usury, improperly so called; which 'in Latin is called *Nanticum Fœnus*, and is Gain, or Allow-'ance made for Money, which is transported beyond the Seas 'at the peril and hazard of the Creditor, contrary to the Con-'tract either of gainful Usury or free Loan, and seemeth to 'draw near to Partnership. The manner whereof is thus, I 'deliver to a Merchant, who is to travel beyond Seas, a sum 'of Money for him to use in Negotiation, as he thinks best for 'his advantage; conditioning with him, that if his Ship mis-'carry, I will lose, not only my hope of Gain, but also the 'Principal it self: But if his Ship shall come safe to Land, by 'the Arrival whereof he is sure of good Gain, I look for an 'Allowance proportionable to that Hazard which I susteined. 'And this Hazard Men were wont to undertake, either for 'the whole Voyage, covenanting for a certain Gain if the 'Ship arrived safe at the same Point from whence it first set 'forth. Which kind the *Grecians* call ἀμφοτερόπλουν. Or 'else, for the one part of the Voyage, as from one Port to 'another, as from *London* to *Venice*; which they called ἑτε-'ρόπλουν, &c.

And a little after he saith farther; 'And therefore Adventu-'rers Money may be allowed, not only *in trajectatia pecunia*, '*in Money sent over Sea at the Creditor's Peril*; but also in other 'cases, wherein the Creditor susteineth the like hazard.

'Provided always, that there be an Adventure, or Hazard, 'in truth, and not in pretence only. Thus this great Prelate.

(*a*) Bullinger. (*b*) *Aretius* de Usuris: *with whom* Rudæus *and* Demosthenes, *do symphonize and agree.* (*c*) *Bishop* Downam *upon* Psal. 15. 5.

NUM.

NUM. XII.

But is not the Scripture against this Adventuring? some will say.

I answer, No; because no such Prohibition: but it is against that Usury only, which is not only more than the Principal, but bites too, (a) as all common Usury doth; either the Borrower, or Commonwealth, or Poor, as has been formerly at large shewed; and that wherein is no adventuring of the Principal, as Divines take that to be the sense of that place, *Luk. 6. 35.* at least in part, that a Man in some cases must not expect the Principal it self. So that the best definition of Usury, which is going, taketh in Hazard and Adventuring, which the Usurer will not be at; as in the said definition by me set down above it is to be seen.

I add, that the Scripture is so far from being against it, as that it commends rather the vertuous Woman for being like a Merchant's Ship, bringing her Food from afar, which maketh her an Adventurer, adventuring in Ships at Sea, because a Merchant's Ship is expresly named, and she is said to bring her Food which she adventureth for from afar, *viz.* far from her home. I add, that her adventuring must needs be by others too, because Women married to Husbands (as she was) do not use to go in Ships (though she be compared to a Ship) but adventure by others in their Ships, as it is well known how usual a thing it is. So that we need not scruple this Adventuring upon this Account, and also because it is a kind of Society, (b) as learned *Downam*, in his fore-quoted place, declareth it, provided,

1. That we do not (c) exceed in the Gain we agree for.

2. That we do consider the Employer of our Money, if he be a Loser, and cannot, when the Ship returns, pay so much as we expected. This I mention, because I will not make my self guilty of other Men's Sins, nor justifie any Iniquity in Traffick, and in Adventuring especially, because I know that

---

(a) *Usura generaliter Serpentis instar mordet*, Arias Mont. Malvend. Besa. (b) *His words are*, Which (*Nautical Fenory*) seemeth to draw near to Society, *Bishop* Downam *upon* Psal. 15. 5. (c) *Which to prevent, the Emperor* Justinian, *as I said, stinted it.*

much Oppression is committed by it, if these Cautions be not observed.

NUM. XIII.

But I must answer a second Question more fully.

And why may I not take Six in the Hundred, when the Adventurer takes Twenty, or more?

I answer, No.

1. Because he may lose Principal and all; which is very usual, the Seas being dangerous: whereas Usurers very seldom lose both.

2. Because Usury is expresly forbidden by the Word of God, and condemned, *Deut.* 23. 19. *Ezek.* 18. 12, 13. and Adventuring is not, as but now it was shewn.

NUM. XIV.

A third Question remaineth yet to be resolved.

And why may not I take Six in the Hundred, when the Merchant or Shop-keeper gets I know not how much by my Money, which he borrows for so small a matter as Six in the Hundred is?

I answer,

1. Because he is at a great cost, if he be an Owner of Ships, to build, repair, and set forth his Ships.

2. His pains are great; but thou takest no pains at all; Usury being a gainful idleness, as (*a*) one calls it, whereby men do eat of the sweat of other mens brows. For whether they eat or drink, sleep or wake, work or play, be sick or whole, their gain cometh in by Usury alike; when the borrower must wake and work, and has scarce time to eat his Meat many times when he is an hungred, and to drink with a Friend when he is a-thirst.

3. His hazard is great; because if he be a Sea-faring man, he may lose his Ship, Goods, life and all by Tempests, Ice, Pyrats, and Enemies: And if his Dealings be upon the Land, he may be undone by bad Debts and Pay-masters, whom he must trust: for his Debtors may break and run away; and then how shall he recover his Money to pay thee thy Usury,

---

(*a*) Bolton *in his Discourse of Usury.*

or the Money which he hath borrowed of thee, being arrested, he may be carried to Prison being able to pay thee? Whereas thou hast Sureties and Leases bound to thee for thy Usu therefore art in no such danger, and in no suc is, unless God by an unexpected Providence cr but seldom happeneth. I have read in S. *Amb* poor borrowers Corps have been arrested for De and their Children carried into Captivity: bu read (to my best remembrance) that Usurers hav because they use to make themselves as sure of and Use as the wit of man can possibly do it.

NUM. XV.

Thus much concerning hazard and adventuring in the next place I must come to Compacting: Fo on proceeds, thus he goeth on, *it is Gain co much thou shalt pay me.*

Reply. Let it be remembred that the Law st the sum, and ordinarily to take what the Law no injustice, *&c.*

For answer whereunto I say, That I do u saying, that the Law alloweth to take what and lest it should be said I deny this out of n and presumption, let that be remembred whi self saith, *in the Statute of* Jacobus 21. *intit gainst Usury, Provided, That no words in this shall be construed or expounded to allow the pra &c.* Which Answer is given by (*b*) *Downam* Bishop was one who was at the making of I ment, and therefore understood the Law better this Novice: His words are, *by the Law it self i pears, that it doth not allow Usury as good, but p*

NUM. XVI.

As for his telling again of Interest, and brin of *Spanhemius*, and repeating of his words *a* I wonder why he will do so: But seeing he dot

(*b*) *Downam* in *Psal.* 15. 5.

to that which even now in this Tract I have so largely handled, to answer him in that which he hath formerly objected against it. *He addeth* (saith he farther) *or expects or intended*, and then tells me (I think a good definition should not be disjunctive) *whereunto I answer.* This sheweth what a poor Logician he is, and how little his skill is in his judging of a good Definition, bringing against him such like Definitions, which have been made by wiser heads then his is And

1. *That of* (*a*) *Dr.* Sanders, 'Usury is all manner of gains, 'which is either bargained or hoped for, (just as I say in my 'Definition) by the force of the Contract of giving to Loan, 'whether Money be lent, or Oyl, Corn, Wine or any like 'thing that is spent, with the first Natural or proper use there-'of; even as I say likewise: where note, that no less than three '*Ors* are in this great Doctors Definition; so that if this great 'Doctor were now alive, I would desire this Champion to 'go to *Lovanium* where he lived beyond the Seas, to learn 'of him to make Definitions.

2. *So the* (*b*) *Wittemborgs* in their Definition, have their two '*Vels*, or O R S.

3. And *Gabriel Powel*, that great *O X F O R D* Scholar, has his O R in his Definition also, as thus. *All gain that contrary to the word of God is expected or exacted* (just as I say) *above the Principal for the very duty of lending, is unlawful and Damnable; and then Usury is such:* and for this he was never taxed or consured by any of that Famous University that ever I heard of. So that if that great Scholar were living at *Oxford* now, I should advise my Adversary to go to *Oxford* and to tarry there a little longer then he did, when he was there, to learn of him how to frame Definitions, so as that they may pass for currant and not be censured as he censureth mine.

N U M. XVII.

But he progresseth farther, saying, This part of the Definition is pleaded from our Saviours Injunction, *Luke* 6 35. *And lend, hoping, or looking, for nothing again.* This is the place of Scripture he builds with so much confidence upon, and

(*a*) *Dr.* Sanders *of Usury.* (*b*) Wittemb. *in Thess.* 2.

so often quoteth to prove their state damnable that expect the least gain from Money lent; in the sense whereof, if he mistake, then down totters his Definition, and all the uncharitable Censures he builds thereon, *&c.*

To all which sayings of his my Answer will be several.

1. That not I only, but far greater Writers than my self, or he, do build upon this place to prove their state damnable, that expect the least gain from Money lent; at present I'le only name one of them again, *viz.* that great *Oxford* Scholar G. *Powel,* who having said (as I quoted him even now) *that all that gain (be it much or little, the word* all *takes it in all) which, contrary to the Word of God, is expected or exacted above the Principal, for the very Duty of Lending, is unlawful and damnable,* (Note, Damnable) *and that Usury is such Gain.* (a) *proves it from* Luke 6. 35. besides others, as I do: And therefore why am I only so harshly censured for uncharitableness?

2. It's well for him that he puts in an *(if),* in the sense whereof, if he be mistaken, down totters his definition; which I hope he will never see while his Head is hot, as it is with Anger.

3. I add, That if I were, yet will not my Definition totter down, because it's not only built on that place, but other also: As for example, that in *Prov.* 16. 28. *The Lord pondereth the Spirits*; which a *(b)* deep learned Author brings as reason to prove; that the very expectation of Gain, above the Principal, is unlawful, and Usury. For by *Spirits*, Wills, are meant Purposes and Intentions: And not amiss is that place so explained, because *Solomon*'s meaning there is to shew, saith *(c)* another famous Writer, that the Lord seeth into the very depth of our ways, and bottoms of our hearts; so that he not onely beholds our works and words, but discerns also, *(d)* *Lavater* tells us, the impulses, motions, and purposes by which we are acted. *(e) Eadem est voluntas lucri sperantis, et non pasciscentis (forte timore Ecclesiæ) & pactum facientis*; that is, He that lendeth hoping for Gain, though he enter no Covenant for it (for fear haply of the Churches Censure) has the same will which he has which covenants for Gain when he

---

(*a*) *See his Proofs*, page 28. (*b*) Alex. de Alef. G. Biel 4 Sentent. Distinct. 15. (*c*) *Doctor* Sand. *of Usury*. (*d*) Lavater *Com. in* Prov. 16. (*e*) Al. de Alex.

lendeth

lendeth: add (a) *Nehem.* 5. 12. *We will require nothing*; just as Christ, *Luke* 6. 35. *Looking for nothing again.*

2. Because it is grounded on strength of Reason: For what saith blessed (b) *Austin? There is so much power and vertue in the intention and purpose wherewith a man goeth about to do a thing, that if it be good, the action is good; if it be evil, the action is evil also.* So he tells the *Manichees.*

And this is confessed by all, that if a man have a lust and intent to commit the sin of Uncleanness with a Woman, it's Adultery, because Christ saith it, *Mat.* 5. 28. And so likewise (c) it's confessed, that he which intends theft, is a thief, though he doth not steal, being hindred: Answerably whereunto it followeth, by strength of Reason, that intention maketh a man a Usurer.

So that I may say and answer here, as one on *Psal.* 15. 5. When some said he had nothing but that place against Usury, answered, That if it were so, that were enough; so if I had no other place but this, *Luke* 6.35. that were enough: (d) and again, if there were no such place at all, yet there is Reason enough to make good what I have said of Expectation.

4. *I answer,* As for my (e) two Authors, because he saith he will bring several that put another Interpretation, and more probable (mark, *probable* only, he cannot say *demonstrative*) upon the Text, I cannot have the patience to stay for his *severals,* but I will forthwith name several that shall second these *two great men,* than which I know he cannot bring more able and famous men. And,

First, I shall name great *Gratian,* whose words are these; *Not only every Gain, but also the very hope of Gain, maketh a man a Usurer:* whereunto he addeth, *As for a Patron to hope for Gain of the Clerk which he presenteth, maketh him a Simoniack.*

Secondly, (f) *John Molanus* calleth this Expectation *mental Usury.*

(a) *Note this, what a famous place it is, so clearly concurring with Christs.* (b) Aug. *de mor.* Manich. *l.* 2. *c.* 13. *to.* 1. (c) *Because the same words in* Luke 6. 35. *which though they be diversly read and expounded, yet in every sense they command the duty of Free lending, which excludeth Expectation.* (d) *So* B. Downam *in* Psal. 15. 5. *tells us.* (e) Austin *and* Chemnitius, *which also make the very expectation of Gain Usury.* (e) John Molanus *Comp. Theol. Pract. tract.* 2. *c.* 28. *Consil.* 6. 2 *sect.* 8.

Thirdly, (*a*) *Bartholomæus Fumus*, who saith, Mental Usury is committed without a Compact, when a man lends with a hope to receive somewhat that is more worth above the Principal.

Fourthly, (*b*) *Justin Martyr* tells us, *That the first Christians were so far from this expectation, as that they would lend to them of whom they hoped not to receive any thing.*

Fifthly, I say, That all the Schoolmen and Canonists, as *Raynerus*, *Gamfredus*, *Hostiensis*, *Alexander de Ales*, *Gabriel Biel*, and the rest, do agree in this thing called *Expectation*. Let the Champion bring more, and more eminent ones, if he can, hereafter.

Answ. 5. In the mean time I shall answer to his two Questions next: And,

1. *To this*, Whether this Expectation was Usury before Christ spake those words, *Luke* 6. 35? That doubtless it was, that being an Explanation and Amplification of the old Laws made against Usury, as the Saying of Christ against mental Adultery, *Math.* 5. 28. so this against mental Usury.

2. Expectation of Gain is included in (*c*) *Nehem.* 5. 12. yea expressed, *Require nothing.*

2. To his other Question, Where Expectation was forbidden under the Law? I answer,

1. That I have already given him a Scripture even now, *viz. Prov.* 16. 28. so interpreted as I delivered it by two great Authors; so that he needs not say, *Shew it.*

2. By undeniable Consequences drawn from Scripture, as I have already shewn.

NUM. XVIII.

Answ. 6. And whereas he tel's me, that he will joyn closer; It was lawful then to take Use from Strangers, and that therefore Gain expected did not lay open this expectation to cen-

---

(*a*) Barth. Fumus *Aur. Armil. tit. Usura, sect.* 37. (*b*) *Mutuo damus iis a quibus nos nihil accepturos esse speramus.* Justin Martyr. (*c*) *For Lenders were required there to take nothing, as these words do shew it*, [As thou sayst, so will we do:] *We will require nothing of them. Whereupon it followeth, That they might expect nothing neither; as those which must require no Bribes, must also expect none.*

sure

ſure : *I anſwer,* 1. That I did already give my Reſponſe at large about Strangers : And 2. ſhall now add a little more, *viz.* what (*a*) St. *Jerome* ſaith : It's ſaid in *Deut.* 23. 19. *Thou ſhalt not lend upon Uſury to thy Brother : but unto a ſtranger thou ſhalt. Note here the going forth of their Law in perfecti-on : In the beginning of the Law Uſury was forbidden to be taken of their Brethren : In this Prophet Uſury is forbidden to all.* Note ALL. So *Jerome.* But hereof more another time.

N U M. XIX.

Anſw. 7. As for his Counſels, That if this be only a Definition under the Goſpel, it falls in with thoſe that hold that Chriſt not only interpreted, but added to, and perfected the Law by new Counſels : *To that I anſwer,* That there is no fear of that : For, as (*b*) one ſaid well, when one told him, being a Papiſt, That he thought the prohibition of Vſury to be rather a Counſel given in God's Word, to avoid the extreme taking of Uſury, than any ſuch Precept as bound men to the obedience thereof, under pain of everla-ſting damnation ; he replied, *Nay, that cannot be ſo ; for the Church hath taken it to be a Commandment, which muſt be kept under the pain of damnation :* ſo ſay I. *He adds* (ſaith my Examiner) *And taken as part of the Definition :* Yea, and part of God's Word too, ſay I, according to *Ezech.* 18. 13. *has taken increaſe* ; to ſtop all gaps, that no uſe may be taken, neither *Neſheck*, nor *Tarbith*, as his words there declare.

N V M. XX.

But the Champion goeth a ſtep or two further, *per ſe, aut per alium, directly or indirectly*, to jeer me, as his following Expreſſions ſhew it : For he adds, *As if it were ſome Bribe or Simoniacal Contract :* Which unawares he ſpeaks againſt himſelf. For a very great (*c*) Writer having declared, That the very hopes of Gain maketh a Uſurer, adds, as hope maketh *a Simoniſt :* As for a Patron to hope for Gain of the Clerk which he preſenteth, maketh him a Simoniſt, or Committer of Simony.

(*a*) Hieron. *in* Ezech. 18. *With whom I joyn learned Mr.* Poole, *that late and famous Writer, whoſe words are to the ſame effect.* (*b*) *Mr.*Moſſe. (*c*) Gratian. *Decr. Par.* 2. *Cauſ* 19 Q. 3.

Loe, Champion, how this great Writer joyneth the Vsurer with a Simonist, and coupleth Expectation with Simony; as if he had foreseen what is here said against me, and would answer for me. Of a Gratuity hereafter.

I'll superadd, saith my Adversary, yet further FOR LOAN: for that is the thing that leavens and (*a*) poysons all. I may receive a Gift from a Rich man, be it Money, House, or Land; but if I expect or receive any thing from the same hand upon the account of Loan, that is the sin of Usury. Who can believe this, save one that hath his Judgment tinctured and prepossessed? Lo, what he makes of me; but no matter, as long as his own Friend, *Car. Molinæus*, the chief Patron of Usury, saith the same, and so must needs be tinctured too, and prepossessed too, and must not therefore be believed neither, as this Champion saith of me. The words of *Molinæus* are these.

(*b*) *It is the common Opinion of all, That Usury properly is not committed, but in Loan:* And yet farther he saith, (*c*) *That Loan is the Subject of Usury.*

With him (*d*) others do harmonise, saying, That Usury, according to all the *Doctors*, consists ONLY IN LOAN, or else cloaked under some other Contract, which may be resolved or reduced unto Loan. And are all these tinctured?

I will name next a few more particularly, and so pass on to other Responses.

(*e*) *Chemnitius* shall be a third man, whom I will cite, saying, *Men say that Usury is only committed in the Contract of Lending.*

(*f*) *Brentius* shall be one more: *Usura fit tantum in mutuo: Usury is committed only in lending.*

NUM. XXI.

Quest. *But why may not I expect somewhat back for lending*, saith the Champion? Because, saith he, Loan ought to be

---

(*a*) *And here he speaks against himself the truth unawares; for usurious lending is by Divines called* Venenum. *So* Bernard. Sylv. de cura rei Famil. *calls it*, Venenum patrimonii. (*b*) Car. Molinæus *de Usura, c.* 8. (*c*) *Idem ibid.* (*d*) *Summa Angel. tit. Usura.* (*e*) Chemnit. *loc. Com. l.* 2. *tit. de Paup.* (*f*) Brentius *Comment. in* Lev. 25.

gratuitous,

gratuitous. *Reply*. Of a truth he is a free Borrower, or rather a bold Beggar (Lo, what he calls me, now a Beggar, then a Carrier.) in begging the Question. *How proves he this, that all lending to men of ability must be free?* Or if lending must be free necessarily, then let him call the Contract by another name, and let it no longer go under the name of Lending, and then all is well, that sore is healed. Take learned *Ames* Judgment, &c.

Whereunto I answer,

1. That if I am a Beggar in this, other great Men are so too, and by name great (*a*) *Bullinger*, who giveth the same Reason, saying, That Usury (*b*) ought to be gratuitous (Mark, it ought to be so; that is his REASON, as it is mine) is committed in Lending ONLY, and not in other Contracts: Where let me add a sufficient Reason, shewing that it ought to be so. (*c*) See the Margin.

2. But I stand upon Scriptures chiefly: And,

1. That in *Exod.* 22. 25. *If thou lend money*; for so it is read in all old and new Translations, and the Greek Interpreter hath it thus, ἐὰν ἐκδανίσῃς.

2. That in *Luke* 6. 35. where Christ useth the same word, which all men translate *Mutuum date, Lend, looking for nothing again.* And is not that gratuitous lending? Whether men be of ability or no, (to answer him) there is no Exception added.

3. *I answer*, It's not the calling of Lending by another name, that will heal the sore; because Lending is defined thus by the Learned.

'Lending is such a Contract (saith (*d*) *Hemingius*) as transferreth the Dominion or Property of a thing from one to another, for no consideration of any Price or Recompence, but only with covenant that the same kind of thing be rendred and repayed again. Thus he of Lending. So that if you call the Contract by another name, and call it no longer Lending, the sore is not therefore healed; as if you call Usury by the name of Interest, as men usually do, it is not there-

---

(*a*) Bullinger *Decad.* 3. *Serm.* 1. (*b*) *Lending ought to be free, because it's one of the Contracts which Civilians call* gratuitous, *and are called* mutuation, commodatum, depositum, stipulatio, mandatum, negotiorum gestio. (*c*) *Tutelæ administratio, pro mutuum & exhibitio, præter quos cæteri sunt Mercenarii.* D. Vast. *l.* 1. *c.* 34. (*d*) Heming. *Comm. in Jac.* 3.

fore

fore Intereſt, and muſt be no longer called Vſury, becauſe Vſury is one thing, and Intereſt another. Anſwerably whereunto, if you call Lending by the name of another Contract, yet is Lending one thing, and Lending ſtill; and another Contract another thing, and is defined after another manner. As for example; If you call ſuch a thing as Lending is, by the name of giving, as ſome do, it's not the ſame; becauſe Giving is defined after another manner, by a *(a)* Learned Author: Giving properly is, whereby a man giveth a thing, with a mind and purpoſe that he would have it preſently become his that doth receive it, and never in any wiſe to be returned again to himſelf. The like I could ſay of other things and Contracts. But note, That there is a two-fold Giving, 1. Of Loan. 2. A Free Gift, or Giving.

4. *I anſwer*, to the quoting of *Ames*, thus.

1. That *Ames* living in the *Low-Countries*, *(b)* where ſome Vſury is defended, and not in *England*, where Vſury is ſo much cried down by moſt (as Learned B. *Downam* tells us), writeth as they uſe to write there; whereof more hereafter; becauſe there is no living there for a Diſſenter to have a Publick place of Profit.

2. That my Brethren and my ſelf in part ſay the ſame, That Vſury (ſo called) is not generally and abſolutely unlawful: For we hold Nautical Fenory (ſo called improperly) lawful, and Recompenſatory lawful, and liberal too; though we hold all Vſury, properly ſo called, and commonly practiſed, unlawful.

3. That if *Ames* held for that (which I hope he doth not), I do not ſee him by his few words prove what he ſaith. The Sayings and Negatives of men, though they may be good men, as he was, are no Proofs to me.

N V M. XXII.

Fourthly, As for his *Clauſula*, or Cloſe, which is, That Lending, if it be not free, paſſeth into another Contract, *nominate* or *innominate*, ſimple or mixt; I for my part cannot

---

(a) Donarif de Donar. *(b) That is, Three pounds ten ſhillings in the hundred; which ſhews that* Ames *will little advantage my Adverſary, and his Vſurers, becauſe they will not take ſo little, but muſt have at leaſt Six in the hundred.*

miſlike

mislike it: for it passes for Society, which we hold lawful, as I quoted for it learned Bishop *Downam*; so that *Ames* is rather for me, saying, That Lending, if it be not free, mark, *if it be not free*, as we say it must be, nothing of that followeth, but that it passeth into another Contract; for then the Case is altered.

5. I answer, That *Ames* doth not well in it, when he saith, It cannot be proved, what we say, That all Lending, with what Circumstances soever it be clothed, (Is his Addition not ours?) ought to be gratuitous: because our Men do prove it. As for example; I can name as godly and well-read an Author as ever *Ames* was, who proveth this Point at full, That Lending must be gratuitous, and not for gain; and that if a Man lend for gain, his Lending is Usury; spending six pages about it, for the proving of it: whereas *Ames* writeth but a line or two, thinking it enough to say, That it cannot be proved that all Lending must be gratuitous; when another (a) Doctor, as great as he, saith expresly, That Loan ought always to be free: Mark, *always*, against *Ames*.

I, for my part, if I had no other Author at all on my side for it, yet should make no question of it, because of these two sufficient Scriptures which command it; *Lend, looking for nothing again*, *Luke* 6. 35. and, *From him that would borrow turn not away*, *Mat.* 5. 42. which must needs be understood of free Lending, because Usurers will not turn away from them that will borrow upon Usury, giving good Security for the Loan, as Usurers do expect it: For, have they not their Agents abroad to procure Borrowers? I add to these two Places, that one most excellent Scripture, *Psal.* 112. 5. which commends it, *A good man is merciful, and lendeth*, viz. freely: because he that lendeth otherwise, as the Usurer doth, cannot be either good or merciful, as it hath been formerly evidenced.

Before I go farther, I will mention one of the Usurer's Tricks, which is, that he is for *gratis* too, as I and others; saying to him that cometh to borrow of him, I cannot forbear my Money so long; but to do you a Courtesie, I will lend you so much for half a year *gratis*, as if he would lend it *gratis*, that is freely, indeed: when in truth he means *gratis* the

---

(a) *Dr.* Sanders, *fol.* 21. *Otherwise it is no Loan at all, but a selling, or setting to hire.* Idem ibid.

Noun,

Noun, that is, ſuch as will be thankful, and pay him Uſe; and not *gratis* the *Adverb*, which ſignifies freely: whereupon ſome Uſurers call their Lending Giving, as I have formerly declared it.

NUM. XXIII.

But I count it high time to advance farther, and therefore I'll ſpend no more time about this.

My Adverſary, in the next place, goeth to anſwer my Citation for proof, out of *Deut.* 23. 19. *Thou ſhalt not lend upon Uſury*; and ſaith, *That it is elſewhere limited to thy poor brother.*

Whereunto I anſwer, That not only to a poor Brother lending upon Uſury is forbidden, but, in this place by me cited, to any Brother; becauſe he ſaith, generally, *Thy brother*, (*a*) whether he be rich or poor, there is no limitation. And by *a Brother* we may underſtand any man, ſaith (*b*) *Aquinas* alſo, (who is an abler man (I trow) to judge of the meaning of *thy Brother* than this Novice) becauſe every man we muſt hold to be our Brother. So that learned (*c*) Biſhop *Downam* makes an Anſwer to ſuch a Cavil, like mine, ſaying, This evaſion (of the poor Brother) is very frivolous; for in *Deut.* 23. 19. there is no mention of the Poor, but all Uſury is forbidden towards a Brother, whether he be rich or poor. Thus he anſwers: With whom I joyn famous Dr. *Sanders*, who goeth farther, even to *all men*, ſaying, *But now ſeeing every man is both our Neighbour and Brother, we may not take Uſury of any man at all*; meaning doubtleſs Uſury properly ſo called.

NUM. XXIV.

The Champion's next On-ſet, in the laſt part of his Definition, is, *for loan of things which may be conſumed in the uſe thereof*, from *Deut.* 23. 19. *Reply.* And what if Money be con-

(*a*) *B.* Jewel. (*b*) Tho. Aquinas 2. 2. Q. 79. *a* 1. (*c*) Downam *p.* 201. *and p.* 203. *he ſaith, And in this general ſenſe, including both Rich and Poor, the Learned among the Jews have underſtood this Law, and unto this day it's obſerved among them, ſaith* Rabbi Abraham.

ſumed

ſumed in the uſe thereof, ſeeing Houſes and Fields, Bargains and Wares remain, which were purchaſed by this Money conſumed? View this from another ſide, and you may take this Aſpect of it. If you have 100 *l.* you may not hire this out for gain; but if you will convert this Money into Fields, you may hire them out, and take yearly gain for your Fields, though not for your Money, *&c.* Thus he.

No more to the purpoſe is the ſelling of Wine, and the uſe thereof; foraſmuch as the Vintner doth and may take ſomewhat for his Wine above the Price laid out, and that is upon the account of his Money disburſed.

And here too *Ames* is before-hand with him; after whom he quoteth *Rivet* alſo: and ſo ends with triumphing, as if he had gotten a notable Victory, and left me in darkneſs, to come off as well as I could.

But *σὺν Θεῷ* I hope to come off well enough, by anſwering all that he hath to ſay againſt me orderly. And,

1. Whereas he ſaith, What if Money be conſumed in the uſe thereof, ſeeing Houſes and Fields, Bargains and Wares remain, which were purchaſed with this Money conſumed? I anſwer,

1. That what I ſay herein, I aſſert, next unto that famous Scripture *Deut.* 23. 19. where Money and Victuals are named, both which are conſumed in the uſe thereof, from more learned and renowned Men, than any he can name, or bring againſt me: For, what a Man is (*a*) *Aquinas*, who writes the ſame? And ſo (*b*) Dr. *Sanders*, ſpeaking of things lent in Uſury, names Money, Oyl, Corn, Wine, and then addeth, Or any like thing, that is ſpent with the uſe thereof.

2. That here is a Confuſion indeed: The lending of 100 *l.* upon Uſury, is called hiring it out for Gain, as Houſes and Lands are, which are let out for Rent: For, as one ſaith notably, that is alſo a Phraſe of Speech which they have among themſelves, namely, that they Let their Money, and therefore call Uſury *the Rent of their Money.* Now *Letting*, ſaith famous (*c*) *Melancthon*, is a Contract whereby a thing is transferred for a certain time, for its uſe, but not as touching the Propriety; for a certain Price, and not for its Dominion:

(*a*) Aquin. 2. 2. *q.* 79. *a.* 1. (*b*) *Doctor* Sanders, *fol.* 3.
(*c*) Melancthon, *lib. Defin. Appell. &* *l.* 2. *P. locat. l.* [illegible]. *Siquis ſervum depos.*

nion:

nion: Whereas Usury is no such thing, because the Money lent becomes the Borrower's Propriety, as has been shewn by Allegations; to which I will now add (*a*) one or two more. In Mutuation, or Lending, saith the Civil Law, there is a transferring of the Property and Dominion of the thing lent, for a certain time, from the Lender to the Borrower; whence *Mutuum*, or Lending, is so called, *quod de meo fit tuum*, Mine, thine, So (*b*) Dr. *Sanders*; Money is of those things which are lent; and consequently, he is not Lord of it that lent it, but he only which borroweth it.

3. I answer, That whereas the Champion standeth so upon this, That by Money consumed in the use thereof, may be bought Houses, Fields, Bargains, and Wares, which may be hired out, and for which I may take yearly Gain, though not for my Money. I answer,

1. That I may lawfully take Money for those Houses and Fields which I purchase with Money, which I have, because I am not forbidden to do it by the Word of God; and Saints have paid Hire for things hired, as is to be seen *Acts* 28. 30. which they would not have done, if setting to hire and letting had been unlawful. And lastly, Because if a thing be hired and hurt, the Hirer of it is not to make it good, if the Owner of it, who set it to hire, be with it; *It came for his hire, saith the Lord, Exod.* 22. 18.

But for the Money which I lend, I may not take Gain, compacted for, or expected, because that is interdicted, and Lending must be free, as formerly has been proved; And I add, That though the Money borrowed be converted into Fields, or Houses, therewith purchased, yet it is illicit, because the Usurer doth not mind that: whether a Borrower buy a House, Field, or Wares, or do not, he will have his Usury, that is his sin: whereas the Borrower, who buyeth a House, or a Field, or Wares, for his need, with that Usury-Money, sins not; because borrowing, especially for need, (and not for (*c*) covetousness) is lawful by the Word of God,

---

(*a*) L. 2. *Appellat. si creditum F. si certum petatur*, 3 *Instit. quibus modis.* (*b*) D. S. *fol.* 22. (*c*) *I add, And to waste the Money lent: For then the Lender is not to lend at all, nor the Borrower to borrow, as* Stephen Egerton, *who translated* Virel, *asserts it, saying, If it be like that the Borrower will spend wastfully that which he borrows, Money ought not to be lent*, p. 137.

Exod.

Exod. 22. and strength of Reason, used by several Authors; of whom, at present, I will cite but one, *viz.* (*a*) *G. Powel,* whose words are these, *For necessity it was lawful for* Adam's *Sons to marry with* Adam's *Daughters, because there were no other Women. For necessity it was lawful to eat the Shew-bread, because there was no other Food,* 1 Sam. 21. 6. *For necessity it was lawful to work, to heal, to fight, upon the Sabbath-day, which was not lawful but for necessity. Therefore for necessity why may not a man pay more than he borrowed? Seeing no Scripture forbids to pay more, but to require more.*

Seventhly, I will add (*b*) Mr. *Smith: It is lawful to suffer injury, as Christ paid Tribute, which was injury:* But it is not lawful to offer injury, because there are six Commandments against it. Now to take Usury, that is, as it were, to offer injury; but to give Usury, is to suffer, as it were, injury: and therefore though I may not take more than I lent, yet I may give more than I borrowed.

Nor will his much ado about the converting of things lent, do him any good at all; because seldom or never do men convert their borrowed Corn or Wine into a Purchase, because they are things absolutely consumed in the use thereof; for we eat the one, and drink the other, which is the use thereof. And as for Money also, where one doth turn his Money borrowed into Fields, hundreds do not, but only spend it, and use it to save that they have, or to trade with it, though they gain but little by it; which notwithstanding, the Usurer will have his Use.

NUM. XXV.

4. And whereas he tells us of the remaining of Houses, Fields, Bargains, Wares, which are purchased with Money consumed in the use thereof: I answer, True, they remain; but how? Not as things lent, but bought with Money lent, and do differ from them very much; because Lending is only of such things as consist of Number, Weight, and Measure, as the Civil Law tells us, saying, (*c*) *Solæ autem res in quantitate consistentes mutuo dari possunt, quæ nimirum ponderari, numerari, & mensurari solent & possunt*: that is, But only those

---

(*a*) Gabr. Powel, *p.* 102. (*b*) Hen. Smith *in his second Sermon upon Usury.* (*c*) *Doctor Vult. Jurispr. l.* 1. *c.* 31.

things

things can be mutuated and lent, which consist in quantity; and are wont to be weighed, numbred, and measured. Now it's evident, that in such things as pass from man to man by number, weight, and measure, the use of them cannot be severed from the propriety, nor the propriety from the use; but they must of necessity pass together, without division or separation, saith a famous Author, who is as well versed in the Doctrine of Usury, as my Adversaries Authors; of whom hereafter. For the present I will use an Example, to make plain what was said even now. I cannot lend a man Money, or Corn, or Oyl, or such like things, but I must make them his fully, to do with them what he will; if I do not, he can make no use of them, nor receive any benefit by them; so as he cannot have the use of them, unless he have the propriety of them. And what shall he do with the Propriety for a time, unless he have the use of them also? which I make over to him with the Money lent, as one entire thing, because the use cannot be separated from the Propriety; whereupon he buyeth, it may be, a Living, or House to put his Head in, or Wares, which is lawful, and may be called the use which he maketh of his Money lent him, and is (as I said but now) one entire thing with the Money lent him, though severed and distinguished, as it were, in a manner; because otherwise (as (a) Divines assert and shew it) in Truth and in Nature, it's impossible to divide the use of those things which are given to loan, from the property and ownership of them, as being things which may be consumed in the use thereof, which use is then gone, when the thing lent is consumed.

5. To his cavilling about Wine, by me instanced in, I answer, That as wise men as both he, and his by-him-quoted Authors, have used the same Instance of Wine; and one especially, above the rest, hath written it in the compass of three leaves three times, (b) as a thing considerable, and to the purpose mentioned; whereas the Champion tells me, That the selling of Wine, and the use thereof, is to no purpose by me mentioned, because the Vintner doth and may take somewhat for his Wine above the Price laid out, and that upon the account of the Money disbursed. Whereunto I reply, And who denieth that? the Vintener's Act and Calling (if I may call it so) not being the Act and Calling of the Usurer, but of

(a) Viz. *By purchasing things which remain.* (b) *Dr.* Sand.

a (*a*) Buyer and Seller, who may gain by his Buying and Selling, not only because Wine wasteth, but also because Buying and Selling is not prohibited kind of Dealing or Contract, as Usury is (*b*), but allowed by God and Man; and therefore is said to be *Contractus* (*b*) *Juris Gentium*, A Contract allowed by the Law of the Nations. Where, by the way, I bless God, that he hath put me upon the study of that Law, and that which is called the Civil, for divers years together, with the study of Divinity, that I might the better handle this noble Controversie, as having collected the sum and substance of the whole *Corpus Juris*, or Body of the Law, and of many other Civilian Authors, into a Manuscript written with mine own hands, and very helpful and useful to me now in this Encounter about Usury.

NUM. XXVI.

6. But I long now to see what his Authors say to all this, and to answer them. And,

1. *Ames*, of whom the Champion saith, And here too *Ames* is before hand with him; (of whose Replies, and many other learned men too, he takes no notice:) wherein he wrongs me grievously. For I have read *Ames* too, and it may be a little more too, long ago; and many other learned mens notable Pieces concerning Usury, and extracted the quintescence of their Labours out of them; and intend, God willing, to answer every one of them, before I get out of this large, deep, and intricate Subject: For I am not afraid of them.

And to begin with *Ames*: Whereas he saith *he is before-hand*, I wonder wherein he is before-hand with him, who can well and truly say, that as great a Doctor as he, yea, both his Authors are, *Aquinas*, whom I cited in my behalf, *is before-hand with Dr.* Ames *in two respects*.

1. Because he is the *senior*, as being one who by the bright-shining Lamp of his Writings did inlighten and irradiate the World hundreds of years before him.

2. Because he is of so great a Repute, as that all other School-men, and Casuists too, light their Candles at his;

(*a*) *Whereas Usury is not.* (*b*) Prov. 31. (*c*) *Dr.* Vult. *l.* 1. 35.

which has caused a great Protestant Writer, (a) Doctor *Boys*, to say, That all of them are but *Aquinas* upon *Aquinas*.

NUM. XXVII.

But to the matter: What saith *Ames*? Here I shall set down his Words in Latin, because the Champion doth so, and not in English, for the Learned. *Allegant in rebus illis quæ usu consumuntur non distingui dominium ab usu atque adeo nihil posse accipi ultra valorem ipsius rei vel dominii ejus. Respondetur lucrum accipi non simpliciter pro usu rei mutuatæ, quoad substantiam, sed quoad valorem, aut proventum, qui manet post substantiam consumptam.* Whereunto I shall now put my Answer thus.

1. That he doth but briefly say, and not prove what he saith; distinguishing between the substance of the thing mutuated, and the value or profit which remains after the substance is consumed.

2. That if that were granted, yet cometh he short of his aim; for it doth not make Usury lawful: nor are those by his Distinction confuted, who hold, That in things which are consumed in the use thereof, their propriety or dominion is not distinguished from the use thereof; and that therefore nothing can be taken for the use thereof, beyond the value or dominion thereof: Because,

1. Usury is forbidden (b) expresly, and therefore is not to be taken, if there were no such Reason given against it, upon the even now mentioned account.

2. And also because what he saith of a Revenue, or value of the thing mutuated, will not hold, at least not generally for when Corn, Meat, or Oyl is lent, that is eaten in the use thereof; so if it be Wine, that is consumed in the drinking of it: because that is the use of both Meat and Drink. And then what remains? Where shall one find it? And if it be Money that is lent, where one purchaseth Land, or Lease, or a House, there are thousands that do not; for most Borrowers are such as borrow for need, to keep themselves harmless, or to get a Maintenance by dealing upon it, and oft-times lose and spend all, Principal, and what they make

---

(a) *Dr.* Boys *in his Postill.* (b) Deut. 23. 19. *and* Nehem. 5

of it, as I have said formerly. And then where is the Profit, which they call that which (a) remains? Surely these Distinctions are but Spiders Webs, which will not cover the nakedness and shame of Usury; for what is so said for it here, is not able to do it.

NUM. XXVIII.

As for *Rivet*, I shall be very civil towards him, because he was my very good Friend in the University of *Leyden* in *Holland*; and so we parted friendly, as his own Hand, wherewith he wrote his Motto in my Book of Friends, (which I have to shew for it) as a perpetual testimony of his Favour and our Friendship, witnesseth: So that I will only set down some Authorities of some of the wisest men that ever lived in the world, to shew how they differ from him in that which is asserted by him; though in other things they may be good Friends enough. That which he holds, is much like that of *Ames*; only he tells of Wine in particular, that some say of it, (meaning *Aquinas*, whom I quote for it), That it and the use of it cannot be severally sold. Whereunto he answers generally, by a distinction of an ambiguity in the Word *Usus*, (as *Ames* also doth) which, saith he, denotes either the distinction of Money, (warily leaving out other things, which are absolutely and utterly wasted and consumed, so as that nothing remains), or the commodity or benefit thereby gotten. Now though the benefit of Money and the right of distraction, or the use, cannot be separated; yet is the distraction it self one thing, and the commodity or gain, arising from that distraction, another: the distra-

(a) *I add, thirdly, That because they stand so much upon Houses, Fields, Leases, Lands, which remain, where Money is consumed and gone; God would have added such an Exception to his forbidding and condemning of Usury,* Deut. 23. 19. Psal. 15. 5. *Except the Money consumed be converted into Houses, Fields, Lands, which remain; if he had thought it good so, to clear this Point thereby, to help those men who so stand upon remaining Fields, Lands, and Houses. 2. That those remaining Fields, Lands, and Houses may be gone with the Money distracted, being made away secretly before-hand, or mortgaged, when the Usurer is sufficiently secured by Sureties.*

ction is but once made and computed, not twice; and gain is reckoned but once, the Principal is rendred for the distraction of the Money, but for an undue Office of lending, and for the time of the Money retained, and that the Creditor could not benefit himself by it, a recompensation is not *immerito* postulated; mark, postulated or required. If my Friend had said, That a recompensation may be lawfully taken, provided it be not expected, against Christ's saying, *Luke* 6. 35. it had been worthily spoken. He concludes thus. Therefore the Reason that the Principal is not twice sold, but a real utility by the Creditor relinquished, and the Debtor received; which is but seldom: even as in the setting of an House, the use thereof is separated from the House. Thus he.

Now to answer what my Friend asserts, and that much more fully than *Ames*, for which I commend him, I will set down the Sayings of those Worthies, which I shall quote, in answer to his, that the World may see how they differ, and judge accordingly.

1. And first, I will begin with the aforesaid most wise and famous *(a) Aquinas*, whose words I will set down more fully than yet I have done; they are these, concerning Wine, thus Englished. "If a man would sell Wine severally and by it "self, and withal the use of that Wine severally and by it "self, he should sell the same thing twice, or should sell that "which is not; and so he should manifestly offend Justice: "And by the like reason he committeth Injustice, which "lendeth Wine or Wheat to another, and demands two Re- "compences for the same; one for the thing it self, another "for the consideration of the use.

2. To answer *Rivet* more fully, I shall quote *(b) Chemnitius*, who observeth, how *(c)* Usurers object, *(d)* That they do not *(e)* sell twice over the Goods or Principal it self, but a real Commodity, which is absent from the Creditor, and present with the Debtor, for the time he borroweth.

Which is answered thus: Grant that to be so, (for who will borrow any thing, but in respect of the real commodity which

(a) Tho. Aquin 2. 2. *l*. 78. *a* 1. (b) Chem. *Loc. Commun. to.* 2. *l. de Paup. c* 8. (c) *As also their Defendants do.* (d) *Because he can do with his Money what he pleaseth, and buy what he pleaseth.* (e) *Mark, Sold, not lent.*

is

is supposed it will carry with it ?) yet by that reason a man may take two Prices for many things that are sold: As for example, I sell a man Bullion Gold: Now Gold, besides the Metal it self, which is precious, yea, and besides the benefit which ariseth from it, being coined, in Buying and Selling, it has also this real commodity, that it's profitable many ways to Physick and Health, as a sovereign and cordial thing. Shall I therefore take one price for the Gold it self, and another for the real commodity of Gold ? What's now this, but to sell one thing twice, and to take two Prices for one Commodity, and so to commit a monstrous Injustice, as the Usurer doth ?

3. The most wise Senate of ancient *Rome* neither would nor did make (*a*) Use and Fruit of those things which are consumed in the use thereof: for it could not do it, as it is declared in the Pandects.

4. And what saith (*b*) *Cajus*? It is not effected by the Decree of the Senate, that there be a proper use and fruit of Money; for Natural Reason could not be changed by the Authority of the Senate.

5. I cite *Ulpian* concerning a Recompensation, which *Rivet* saith, a man may take for the distraction or lending, though a meer Heathen; to shame and to convince our Usurers, who call themselves Christians; and to shew how *Rivet* and them differ: If I deliver Ten, for this end, to make thee Debtor of Eleven, saith *Ulpian* (*c*); *Proculus* thinketh, that no more can be certainly demanded or postulated (to use *Rivet*'s own word) but Ten. Mark how these wise Heathens speak against Usury.

I shall desire that great and godly Emperour (*d*) *Justinian* to speak his mind, because some haply will reject those Heathens, though never so wise. His words are,

Use and Fruit is assigned in Lands, Houses, and other things, saving those which are wasted with the very use. For

(*a*) Usum fructum, *as they word it*. (*b*) Cajus *in Pandect. de Usu fructu, l.* 2. (*c*) Ulpian & Proculus *in Pandect. l.* 1. *de rebus creditis*. (*d*) Justinian. *in Juis Institut. de Usu fruct. I am the larger in all this, because I cannot otherwise chuse, taking great delight therein, as having extracted the whole* Corpus Juris, *or Body of the Law, wherein all these Expressions are extant*.

those things receive no Use and Fruit, neither by Natural nor by Civil means; of the which sort Wine, Oyl, Corn, and Garments are; to whose Nature numbred or ready Money approacheth next, because it is in a manner worn out in the very using of it, by continual Exchange.

Thus this great and pious Monarch delivers his mind concerning that great Debate about things consumed by and in the use thereof, That they cannot receive any Use and Fruit. Unto which words of his, I might add more, whereby he confirmeth what he saith by the *Roman* Senates example, saying, That it also did not make Use and Fruit of such things, (as I also did even now:) So that by this his saying it appeareth also, how he and Dr. *Rivet* differ in this thing, and how he also is on my side.

7. There is also *(a)* one who writeth thus: Usury has its name from using, whereby is meant the Price of the Use of a thing: And because we may use certain things, the substance of them remaining safe, as when we hire another Man's Ground, or dwell in another Man's House, in that case it is lawful to take or pay Rent for the said House or Land; and he saith it again, and goeth a little farther, thus: Those things that may be used and remain safe, may also render yearly Rents or Fruits, and the Lord of them may give or bequeath the Property and Ownership of them to one, and the Use and Fruit to another: I add, Because they may be severed, which thing cannot be done in those Goods which are wasted, because the Use doth diminish the Substance it self; which may serve to answer Dr. *Rivet*'s last words. As in the Location or Setting of an House, the Use is separated from the House it self; which is true in part, that in the Location of an House the Use of an House may be separated from the House: Whereupon it doth not follow, that even so in the lending of Money or Victuals, the use thereof and the things themselves may be separated, because the use of such things as Money and Victuals is the extinction thereof, as the Lawyers use to say.

(a) Doctor Sanders.

NUM.

NUM. XXIX.

8. But I must not omit the most reverend and learned (a) Bishop *Downam*, who saith, The use of Money is the spending thereof, as the use of Victuals is the eating of it; and in all things spent, thou canst not, without great inequality, require one allowance for the thing, and another for the use, which cannot be reckoned apart from the thing, or severed from the property. If thou lend me Ten Loaves, thou shouldst do very unequally with me, if thou shouldst require Eleven; or if having taken the price of the Loaves themselves, thou shouldst also ask a price for the use, which is the eating of them: And in like sort, if having lent me Ten pounds, thou shouldst require Eleven, that is, Ten for the Principal, and One for the Use, which was nothing but the spending of the Money. Which also, together with the former Citation, answers, as one should think, Dr. *Rivet* fully.

NUM. XXX.

9. But the Champion will reply, That his Distinction of the Ambiguity in the word Use, which denotes either the distraction of the Money lent, or the commodity and profit thereby acquired, is not fully answered; and therefore I will alledge a few Authors more, as he doth his two, to answer his Reply, and apply them.

And first, again, I will alledge the words of that pious Emperour (b) *Justinian*, saying, The Senate of *Rome* made not Use and Fruit of those things which are consumed in the use thereof, but by a caution did, as it were, constitute Use and Fruit.

2. So (c) *Cajus*: By a Remedy introduced, there began, as it were, a certain Use and Fruit of Money to be taken: Where note, That whereas it is impossible in Nature to divide the use of those things which are lent, from the property of them, the Civil Law has devised a way whereby it may be done, as the wit of Man could invent it; as thus: That the

(a) B. Downam, *p.* 245. (b) Justinian. *Instit. de Lucr.* (c) *In Pandect.* 2.

Lord and Owner receiving a Caution for the Value, ſhould ſuffer him to whom the Profit was aſſigned to enjoy the ſame thing frankly and freely in the mean ſeaſon, which Caution did ſtand to him in ſtead of his Propriety; and this is that the Emperor *Juſtinian* ſpeaks of, That the Senate made not Uſe and Fruit of ſuch things as are conſumed by the uſe of it; but aſſigned it, as it were, after a ſort.

Which I apply thus: Anſwerably whereunto, it ſhould ſeem, they have found out this diſtinction (*a*) and ſhift, to make that which (*b*) cannot poſſibly be, by ſaying, That it may be done by getting Gain out of things lent, and Money eſpecially, turned into Lands, Houſes, &c. which, ſay they, may be ſeverally computed, and ſo conſequently ſeparated from the things lent. But what is to be thought of it, I'le now declare. And,

1. When the *Romans* deviſed ſuch a thing as even now I mentioned, they did it harmleſly, conceiving that no man would have injury by it, as Divines judge of it, and not to eſtabliſh Uſury by it; for they are bitterly bent againſt it, inſomuch as that their Lawyers and Wiſe men confeſſed it, as (*c*) one aſſerts it, That Uſury is againſt Nature; and do not allow it, but only permitted it, as they permitted Fornication and Inceſt, ſaith a worthy (*d*) Writer: but what harm may come of ſuch Diſtinctions, God knoweth.

2. Beſides, that it will not do the thing aimed at, nor demonſtrate it, that the things lent to Uſury and the Uſe thereof can be ſevered, as by Reaſons and many Authors it hath been proved.

(*a*) *As ſome call the* Romans *device, and this Diſtinction may be called ſo too.* (*b*) *That is to ſay, the ſevering of the Propriety of a thing and the Uſe thereof, in things which are conſumed in the uſe thereof.* (*c*) *D. S.* (*d*) *And that Uſury, if it ſhall become due, muſt be fetch'd about another way, which way is not able to diſcharge any Mans Conſcience, who ſhall take it upon him to follow it, ſaith a Learned Doctor.*

NUM.

Lastly, I will, after all this, put in but one Answer more to the Champions Examination and Opposition made against my Definition of Usury, *viz.* That seeing he so misliketh it, I will profer him sundry other Definitions, for him to make his choice of either of them.

And 1. That of *Cato*, who being asked by the *Roman* Senate, what it was to commit Usury, answered, as (*a*) *Tully* has it, and (*b*) *Calvin* too, *It was to kill a man.* Or,

2. (*c*) *Seneca*'s, What is Fenory, and a Calendar, and Usury, but Humane Concupiscences, Names sought out *extra naturam*, without Nature? He could find a place for it in the Calendar, but not in Nature. Or,

3. If he mislike these, because they were Pagans, I tender unto him Mr. *Turner*'s, who saith, (*d*) That it is *terrestris Piratica, a kind of Land-Piracy.*

4. If that be too harsh, let him chuse that of (*e*) Bishop *Jewel*, which was in his time the Honour and Ornament of our Church, as (*f*) one stileth him.

Usury, saith he, *is a kind of lending of Money, or Corn, or Oyl, or Wine, or of any thing, wherein, upon Covenant or Bargain, we receive again the whole Principal which we delivered, and somewhat more for the use and occupying of the same.*

5. Or else that of great *Tostatus*; We commonly call that Usury, when any thing is taken above the Principal.

6. Or that of the (*g*) *Lateran* Council, counted the best of all: *This is the proper interpretation of Usury, when men labour to get Gain and Encrease from the Use of a thing which groweth or encreaseth not, and that without labour, cost, or danger, or adventuring.* Thus that great Council defineth Usury.

7. Or that of famous Archbishop *Usher*, in his *Body of Divinity, pag.* 300. What is that which we call Usury? It is Lending in *Expectation* of *Certain* Gain.

(*a*) Cicero *in Offic.* (*b*) Calv. *in* Ps. 15. (*c*) Sen. *l.* 7. *de Benef.* (*d*) Rog. Turner *in his Usury Sermon.* (*e*) B. Jewel *upon* 1 Thess. 4. [*f*] Humphred. *Epist. Nuncup. in vita* Juelli, *p.* 4. [*g*] *The* Lateran *Councils Definition of Usury.*

8. Or

8. Or God's own; ANY ENCREASE (above the Principal, expectedly taken) *Ezech.* 18. 8. *Luke* 6. 35.

Now, I say again, let the Champion chuse either of these Definitions, if he will not adhere to mine, nor to that of the Council of *Agatha*, nor that of that great man St. *Ambrose*, he shall have my good liking and approbation in his Choice.

[a] Many more Definitions I could have added, but these may suffice.

NUM. XXXII.

But I see I must come to a new Engagement; for thus he sets upon me, with all fierceness and incivility, which he shews in all his Pamphlet, occasioning thereby a very learned and godly man to say, That he did not act like a Man, nor like a Christian, much less a Minister.

I say, he assaults me thus.

Having made a short and jeering Preamble first, he addeth, We are beholden to him in the next place, that he would let us see what manner of thing Usury is, by its Description. Then on he cometh, charging me, That either I am misled, or would mislead others, by my wonted confusion; and that I rake together whatsoever was spoken by any against grossest Cheats, Oppressions, and Exactions, that have passed under the name of Usury, and distribute the same with a name and punishment attending equally to the most oppressive Usury, and to the most moderate taker of Use for Money lent, with what conscience let him look to it.

Whereunto I answer,

1. That I wish he were not misled himself, nor did mislead others, by his wonted confounding of Rents, Setting and Letting, Buying and Selling, Interest and Damage, with Lending upon Usury; which things are of a disparate nature.

2. I do no more rake, as he saith I do, than the Holy Prophets, ancient Fathers, and Authors and godly Writers newly risen up against that great Idol, which they call Usury in

---

[a] *As* Ludolphi *de Vita Christi*, *part* 2. *c.* 49. Pet. de Anchorano *Consil.* 49. Glanvilli *l.* 7. *c.* 16. Viguerii *Instit. Theol.* *c.* 5. *sect.* 3. Zegedini *Loc. Com.* *p.* 457. Turnbulli *Serm.* 4. *in* *Psal.* 15.

general,

general, not naming the grossest Oppressions, Frauds, Exactions, that passed under the name of Usury, and that any Usurers have ever practised the same: I say, in [a] like manner and as they distribute Blame and Punishments, so do I, as I ought, giving to every one his due, according to 2 *Tim.*2.15. telling Usurers, That the more oppressive they have been, the greater will be their Damnation; and the more moderate, the less: So that I shall not need to trouble my self about the close of this his Charge, With what conscience let him see to it. But let us see how he goes on.

Mr. Jelinger. 1. *Usury is a most abominable thing.* *Reply.* No doubt it is, and has been, as some have handled it: but where is the abomination, or incongruity to Reason or Nature, if my Money being improved by anothers Pains or Skill, prove gainful to us both? What he brings here, and elsewhere, from the Fathers, and Heathen, against Usury, respects the Practice of it in their days, which doubtless was bad enough, *&c.*

Whereunto my Answer is, That I have cause and grounds enough to say, that Usury, as it is spoken of and against, without his Addition and Interpretation (*as some have handled it*) is an abomination, or thing to be abhorred, as the [b] *Hebrew* is rendred by Dr. *Luther, a Grewel* in *Dutch*: (where note, that the old Version also calls it an abomination, an offendicle, in *Ezech.* 20. even a thing to be abhorred by all men) which that the Reader may not too much take notice of, he conceals in his Reply the Lord's calling *Usury an Abomination*; as also he [c] leaves out the most remarkable Expressions of the Authors and Fathers cited by me, *viz.* those of St. *Austin*, *How odious and how execrable the sin of Usury is, I believe Usurers themselves do know*, (not telling us of Extortioners, and griping Usurers.) And Bishop *Jewel* he leaves out also, who calls Usury *the foul and loathsom sin of Usury*: And [d] *Petrus Cantor* he omits, who tells us, That the Usurer's House (mark, the Usurer's House in general) was in old time called *the Devil's House*, and his Field *the*

---

[a] *As my Book sheweth.* [b] *A thing to be abhorred.* [c] *Which will make me to deal so by his new Writers also, and not to set down their Sayings at large, to be the shorter in my Answers.* [d] Petrus Cantor.

Devil's

Devil's Field. Whereunto I will now annex a Codicil of more ſuch Writers, to render Uſury yet more abominable: And by name I will mention theſe three modern Authors.

And 1. (*a*) Dr. *Beard*: *Seeing then it is ABOMINABLE both by the Law of God and Nature, let us ſhun it as a Toad, and fly from it as a Cockatrice.*

2. (*b*) One alſo writes of Uſurers, not naming any griping ones, but Uſurers in general, (as I do) thus: *Thoſe that travel in the* Low-Countries *ſay, That the Uſurer is ſo baſely accounted of,* (and conſequently is ſo abominable and ſo odious there) *as that no body will be in his company; and you ſhall ſooner get one to a Brothel-houſe, than to a Uſurer's.*

3. (*c*) *Peraldus.* to make the Uſurer and his ſin odious, according to its deſerving, tells us, 1. *That he is like a Toad which liveth by the Earth, and will get out of a Vineyard when it flouriſheth and buds, not being able to endure the ſweet odour of it: anſwerably whereunto,* ſaith he, *the Uſurer is for Earth, and leaveth the Church, becauſe he cannot abide the hearing of the Word.* Which we know to be true by Obſervation; for they will not hear a Miniſter that preacheth the Word of God againſt Uſury. They ſerved me ſo, when I preached my Fifteen Sermons againſt Uſury, at my *Kings-Bridge* Lecture.

Now that it may not be thought that he ſpeaks of and againſt griping Uſurers and Uſury only, and not againſt the moderate, ſee his Definition quoted in the (*d*) Margin; and (*e*) *Cicero*, who reckons Uſury among odious Callings.

But I deſire to bring more ancient Doctors, beſides theſe later.

And 1. (*f*) St. *Jerome*, who, to make Uſury odious, tells us. That there is no difference between ſeeking after Uſury and Rapine, or Robbing. And leſt men ſhould think that he ſpeaks ſo liberally againſt griping, exacting, oppreſſive Uſurers and Uſury only, he ſaith further, *Lend to thy Brother, and receive of him again as much as thou haſt given, and ſeek nothing over and above,* (which he calls *Superfluum*) *becauſe what is more, is computed to be USURY.*

(*a*) *Dr.* Beard *in the Theatre of God's Judgments, page* 476. (*b*) *The Author of Uſuries Arraignment.* (*c*) Peroldus *de Avaritia, to.* 2. *p.* 68. (*d*) *Idem ibid. p.* 6, 7. (*e*) Cicero. (*f*) *I* Mat. 28.

With which saying of his, 2. *Peter Lombard,* the Father of the Schoolmen, sweetly symphonizeth, by a Sentence of his, which I have read in time long ago: *viz. In the Eighth* Commandment, Exod. 20. *Thou shalt not steal, RAPINE also and Sacrilege are prohibited, and USURY, WHICH IS CONTAINED UNDER RAPINE.* So odious was Usury in the Schools in old time; and so I leave it as it is, even as a great ABOMINATION, which God hateth, abominateth, and abhorreth.

Nor can his new Writers answer them, nor (in the second place) be able to stop the mouthes of such great and most Learned men (God's own especially) while the World stands; because they neither do nor can prove what they assert of that which intrinsecally is in Usury, and that which is *plerunque, that is, commonly,* (which meerly maketh against those Authors) *is present with it*; and because they would make us believe, that the Fathers had respect, in their Sentences against Usury, unto that Usury which too much prevailed, and was taken in all Ages, against Equity, Honesty, Charity, and Faith: when it's well known to my Brethren, and my self also, who have diligently read, observed, and extracted the Volumns of the Holy Fathers, from the beginning to the end thereof, and have accordingly in this Tract shewn it, what Usury they have been against, *viz.* not only griping and most cruel biting Usury, but all Overplus sought and taken.

As to that of St. *Chrysostom* in *Matth. There is nothing more cruel than the Usury of this Age, nothing baser*; it will not at all evince what he would prove by it, *viz.* That the Fathers uttered such heavy things only against the most cruelly biting Usury of their Ages; because, as other Fathers, so he speaks against all, as well as that most cruel Usury which he mentioneth; yea, and declareth against Usury in general (*a*) more than any of them all, as far as I could see, when I read him over; insomuch as that,

1. He compareth some Usury to a (*b*) Serpent, called *Aspis*, which insensibly stings and poysons, and so brings a man sweetly asleep; answerably whereunto, he saith, that when a man has once taken up Money upon Usury, he liveth

(*a*) *In* Matth. 17. (*b*) *Id. ibid.*

pleasantly

pleasantly upon it (Mark, PLEASANTLY) which a man cannot do when he is cruelly bit in the Hundred, which they count modera may and do.

2. But this is not all: for he saith wi USURY was ever judged a token of extreme

3. He speaketh further; (a) *A great Sickn much study*, (which maketh me study as hard sure) *namely, Usury*. Mark, Usury in general *a great Sickness*. And,

4. (b) He saith, *What more IRRATIONA out, than for those* (he speaks to the Usurer) *t without a Field, without Rain, and without a P causes, those that sow so, shall reap Tares, which red up to the æviternal Fire*. And,

5. He ends thus: *Are there no other ways of to be found out?* He might have said, if he ha derate Usury, as this Champion and some c are, Cannot you leave that griping Usury, a which is more moderate? But he does not; h

NUM. XXXIII.

2. But is it not high time to come to the ption of Usury, That it is a most dangerous t and therefore I will now see what the Champic *Reply*. Not so, surely, where no Rule of Charit stice, Faithfulness, or Honesty is broken, whe Law kept in due bounds and limits, saith the

I answer, And when is that, say I and my are many to his one? Will ye hear them about

1. First hear (c) *Lactantius*, who saith, *That* by him in general, *is against Justice*. His words *more than is lent, is* injustum, *an unjust thing*. ny others.

(a) *Ibid*. (b) *The Learned may read all t against Usury there*, p. 437, 438, 439. (c) Lact *Cultu*, l. 6. c. 18.

2. (a) *Melancthon,* that great Ornament of Learning, as (b) *Fagius* calls him, saith, *It is against Equity, and no man ought to make Gain of another mans Goods. But he that takes Usury maketh Gain of that which is another mans; because the Lending has transferred the Dominion of the Goods from the Lender to the Borrower: therefore it's no equal Gain.*

3. So (c) *Barthol. Capet* makes this want of Equity the principal cause of Usuries unlawfulness.

4. (d) *Turner.* Here is no Equity: The Usurer receives great Gain, clear Gain, without Labour, without Cost; certain Gain, without peril, out of the Industry, the Charges, the meer Uncertainties of the Borrower. A cunning Alchymist, that can extract much Silver, and waste nothing in the Smoak. These are the Kine of *Bashan,* that feed upon the Commons, *Amos* 4. 1.

5. And what saith (e) *Beza* of Charity? *Christian Charity forbids to lend upon Usury.* With whom (f) *Ursin* agreeth, thus writing, *The Question about Usury may be determined by this general Rule; Do not to another that which thou wouldest not have done to thy self: Then may it easily be concluded what is to be thought and judged concerning this Case of USURY, namely, That it will not nor cannot stand with the general Rule of CHARITY.* So (g) *Hemingius; Establish Usury, and the Rule of Love is everted, which God would have to be sempiternal.*

6. To quote one concerning Law, mentioned by the Champion and his onely Author, I will bring (h) *Beza* once more, to give his Judgment in that thing: *Many Magistrates do see, that in respect of Traffick and Dealing among men, they cannot simply forbid Usury: Therefore (which is the only thing which remaineth for them to do,) they stint Usury: But MAY A MAN THEREFORE WITH A GOOD CONSCIENCE LEND UPON USURY? NO, VERILY: FOR THE RULE OF OUR*

(a) Melancthon *lib. Defin. Appell.* (b) Fagius *Ep. ante Chald. Par.* (c) Barthol. Capet *Tract.* Comel. 125. (d) Turner, p. 9. *With whom I joyn Dr.* Beard, *who saith, in his Theatre,* p. 473. *That Usury is so contrary to Equity and Reason, that all Nations, by the instinct of Nature, have always abhorred and condemned it.* (e) Beza *in his Annotat. upon* Matt. 19. 8. (f) Ursin. (g) Hemingius *Comment. in* Jacob. 5. (h) Beza *in his Annot. upon* Mat. 19. 8.

CON-

CONSCIENCE IS TO BE FETCHED NOT FROM THE CIVIL LAWS OF MEN, BUT FROM THE WORD OF GOD; NAY, THE CIVIL LAWS THEMSELVES DO NOT ALLOW, BUT RATHER CONDEMN THAT WHICH THEY ONLY TOLERATE, FORCED THEREUNTO BY THE WICKEDNESS OF MEN. THUS ALSO THE LORD BY MOSES MAKING CIVIL LAWS, DOTH NOT COMMAND DIVORCES, (for so he should have been contrary to himself;) but to such as could not be got to retain their Wives, he commanded them to give their Wives a Bill of Divorcement, that provision might be made for them against their Husbands cruelty: And yet for all that, they which put away their Wives ceased not to be Adulterers before God. What more clear to stop my Adversaries Mouth, than what *Beza* saith here? But I must not be so brief in such a dangerous thing, as he is; leaving out (as his manner is) what maketh most against him: and therefore I will now shew how and wherein it is such a dangerous thing; as namely, in that it dreadfully endangers not only a Mans Soul, and whole Estate, and the very Kingdom of Christ it self, (as for that I quote the *(a)* Council of *Paris*, at which my Adversary doth not touch with the least Finger here) but also the Earthly Kingdom wherein Usury is commonly committed, and the Usurers Life, which he liveth here upon Earth. Of both in order.

NUM. XXXIV.

1. It endangers the Kingdom wherein the Usurer lives. For how many Kingdoms and Countries have been destroyed and overthrown by Usury? To instance in some: Was not *Egypt*, if we may believe *(b) Alexander ab Alexandrinus*? Was not the *(c) Roman* Empire then brought to a decaying Estate, when Usury did over-spread it? Was not *(d) Germany*, my Country, (which durst oppose it self against the usurping *Romans*) then brought low too, wheu Usury came to be high and common in it, and did begin to live in sensual Delights, and wasted themselves by Usury, had lost their Warlike Valour? And was it not almost quite lost in the terrible Wars which

(a) Concil. Paris. *(b)* Alex. ab Alex. *l.* 1. *c.* 7. *(c) Doctor* Wilson *in Epist.* *(d)* Aret. *in suis Probl.* & *Dr.* Luther.

were

were therein in my time, because of Usury? What think ye? And is it not now again almost ruined and burnt by the *French*; for the same great sin of Usury, which reigns there mightily in divers places? I, for my part, must needs think so, because I know the Country, and am not inscious of that horrid grand Evil called Usury, which is there so boldly committed by some, because there be no such *Luthers*, such *Melancthons*, such *Chemnitiusses*, such *Aretiusses*, such *Parcusses*, such *Didericusses*, living there now, as there were in old time.

And may not *Spain* also, though it has more Land in the World than any Monarch upon Earth possesseth, (as a great (a) Archbishop of *England*, in his Cosmography, asserts it) be brought as a sad Example and Participatrix of the same lamentable Misery and Decay, which with other Kingdoms it is fallen into, by reason of Usury, which is paid to the *Venetians*, and *Genoways*, and others? So as that all that Gold and Silver which is imported from the rich Gold and Silver Mines of the *West-Indies* can hardly support it. So that for this cause (b) *Lewis* King of *France* returning from (c) *Dameata*, caused all Usurers to depart out of his Kingdom.

2. As for the dreadful danger of the Usurer's Life, that I will make out by *Similitudes* and *Examples*.

NUM. XXXV.

I. *Similitudes*. For,

1. Usury is like Poyson, as (d) Authors resemble it: And how dangerous that is, all men know it.

2. Like a pestiferous (e) *Tabes*: And is not that dangerous too?

3. Like a (f) Whirl-pool, which doth devour and swallow men up.

4. Like a (g) Cancer it is, saith *Peraldus*: And is not that dangerous also?

(a) Abbot. (b) *Centur.* 13. *cap.* (c) *Alias* Memphis. Joh. Bocinus. Aubanus *de Rit. Gent. l. c.* 5. *num.* 34. (d) *Cited formerly.* (e) Cœlius Secundus *Lect. Antiqu. l.* 12. *cap.* 2. (f) Sext. *Decretal.* (g) *Doct.* Willson, *fol.* 62. (h) Perald. pag. 67.

And the Usurer himself is like one who hath a drawn Sword slenderly hanging over his Head, and ready to cut him asunder: For so the Justice of God holds a naked Sword over the Usurer's head, dreadfully to cut him asunder; and there is nothing but the slender Thred of his Life, which for a little time he has to live, next to the infinite Mercy of God, which hinders it, and keeps it back for a short time. O dreadful danger!

6. The Usurer is like a man who has an Asinary Mill tied to his neck, drawing him down into the depth of the Sea: for so his Usury-money, like a Mill-stone, is tied with the Cord of his Love, which he beareth to it, to his neck, as i were, drawing him down to the Pit, his Grave, I mean, an so to that other bottomless Pit called HELL. And is no Usury a most dangerous thing then? *Ezech.* 11. 12, 13.

NUM. XXXVI.

2. I will add *Examples.* And,

1. I have read of a Usurer who in the Bishoprick of *Coll.* died after this DREADFUL manner: (*a*) Lying upon h Death-bed, after he had been a Usurer of some standing, a taken good store of Usury-money, he moved up and dov his Chaps and Lips, as if he had been eating something in l Mouth; and being demanded what he did eat, he answere his Money, and that the Devil thrust it into his Mouth p force, so that he could not chuse but devour it: In which n serable case he died, without any shew of Repentance, and his Usury killed him dreadfully.

2. And I remember an Usurer, saith (*b*) Doctor *Bea* dwelling in a Town called *Argentall*, nigh unto *Anovay*, u der the Jurisdiction of *Tholosse* in *High Vivaria*, who being Hay-time in a Meadow, was stung in the Foot by a Serpe or some other venomous Creature, unto death: and that cording to *Job* 20. 15, 16. *He swallowed down Riches, &c.* Usurers use to do, *the Vipers tongue shall slay him*: In

(*a*) Discip. de Temp. *who speaks this of an Usurer, with any distinction; and* Swinock *relates such another dreadful story.* (*b*) *Doctor* Beard *in his Theatre of God's Judgme p.* 471.

Heb

(c) Hebrew it is, *the Serpents or Basilisks tongue shall slay him*; for so much the Original also signifieth.

Methinks this should make our Usurers fear, lest when they go out into their Fields and Meadows, they be stung and bitten so too, by a Viper or Serpent, even unto death, for their BITING.

But here some will be ready to object (as their usual manner 's so to do) when Ministers go to make Usury dangerous, That ill this concerns not moderate Usury, but cruelly griping and oppressive Usurers.

Whereunto I answer, That as God himself makes *Tarbith*, hat is, any Usurious Encrease, dangerous, as well as *Neshech*, which is rendred *Morsura*, or *Biting*; so our godly Divines do ikewise: as for example; The (b) *Wittenberg* Doctors make he taking of Five in the Hundred, which is counted MODERATE, *Heresie*; and censure the Takers of it for HERETICKS: Which, I am sure, is so dangerous a thing, as hat the Apostle tells us, that *they which are such shall not inerit the kingdom of God*, Gal. 5. 20, 21.

NUM. XXXVII.

But the Champion proceeds, saying,

Mr. Jelinger *here by the way, speaking of those in* Nehemiah *ntended with upon this account, has these words*; For they id promised him that they would leave Usury, and restore, I would wish you to promise so too. *Reply.* I have heard other Advice he gave lately to one concerned on the same ore, *viz.* Go to the Parties, and ask Forgiveness; though e Party were sufficient to make Restitution. Whereunto my nswer is,

1. That I do not advise Usurers to ask Forgiveness, as in other ases; nor ask one another Forgiveness, when they have ofnded, in WORDS: but to have the Usury-money, which ey have taken, and are to restore, forgiven them, in case they not able to restore. Which Advice I give as I am *verbatim* vised by greater men than he, the Champion, is, even fa-

---

(a) אפעה. (b) *As also* Martin ab Alpiscuet *doth*, *Enrid. c.* 17. *num.* 207.

mous men indeed, whose Consent I have in this, and shall nominate in its proper time and place.

2. That the truth is, that there is one, a Minister's Widow, which is concerned in this thing, and has been convinced by my late Book against Usury, (as others also, both Ministers and private Christians, have been both convinced and changed by it) blessed be God, and has rendred me hearty thanks for it, and hath made Restitution, as all the Country about me knoweth, and talks of it, though she was hardly able to do it, as her Neigbours tell me.

3. I answer, That this Convert took but *Six in the Hundred*, which is, as they say, Moderated Usury; and yet repented of that, and made Restitution of about Thirty pounds, not being dissuaded by me from so doing.

4. That being a Widow, and so consequently not so wel able to employ her Money as Men; and being told, that i was lawful for Widows to lend their Money upon Usury, ye she would leave it, and made Restitution, as aforesaid.

5. That this Friend of mine was much blamed for it, an falsly reported to be distracted, by some who should rathe have encouraged her; and yet would not be discouraged b them, nor taken off from her Godly course, which she too for the easing of her troubled Conscience, for her former ta king of Usury.

6. That I take special notice of it, that such a one shoul be so converted and changed, that very time when my Treati of Usury came forth, for the confirmation of it, and encou ragement and drawing of others to do as she did.

7. That I look upon it likewise as a remarkable ordering God's all-ruling Providence, that such a thing should ha pen in the very same Parish and Village wherein my chief A versary dwells, but a few doors from him, to convince hi that God's Hand is in it, and that he approveth of my Pr ceedings, making it evident to all that see and know t Change and Success, and how she reproves my chief Antag nist for defending Usury.

8. That I have given my Advice to others too, and to so of my nearest Relations, to make Restitution, as she mad which also they did, as I can prove it, to stop my Adversar Mouth.

Descript. 3. But I must speed it, to advance to the Third Description of Vsury, which is, *That it is a most infamous thing*; to defend it against my fierce Antagonist, who replieth, Mr. *Jelinger* quoteth, That whereas others in Writings under-write themselves either Husbandmen, or Spinsters, from their Callings; the Vsurer is ashamed to call himself an Vsurer. This part concerneth only those that make a Trade of Vsury, aud have no other Calling to take up their time and thoughts with: and such were they whom *Austin* calls *shabbed*. After which Words, he cites *Rivet* again to the same effect. Whereunto, together with all that he saith besides, I shall answer, I hope, fully. And,

1. That partly it concerneth such; for, my (*a*) Brethren and I say the same that *Rivet* saith, in part, That such as will lend out of a lazie humour, because they will not be taken up with a Calling, are much to be blamed above others, and not at all excusable. But whereas he goeth farther, and adds, But such as out of an impotency of Merchandizing, or Necessity, as Widows, Orphans, aged Students, and the like, who are otherwise taken up with other Functions; if they enter such Compacts as offend (*b*) not, *&c.* I cannot assent to that, because I do not see it proved, what is said, as it should be proved, *quia sub Judice lis est*, *because it is a thing controverted*, what is said for Orphans and Widows, and must be disputed when Objections come to be answered, and by name that which concerns (*c*) Orphans and Widows. At present I will cite blessed (*d*) *Bolton*, against my Adversaries Citation out of *Rivet*: But what say ye to the Case of Orphans? What shall become of Fatherless Children, Widows, and distracted men of their Wits? Suppose all these for their Maintenance have a Stock of Money left them, and they be not able to employ it. (as *Rivet* writeth) how shall they be maintained, but by the Vse of it? For if they spend

(*a*) *Qui ex professo Fœnerat non ferri debet in Ecclesia.* Poole in Ezech. 18. 8. (*b*) *The rest the Learned may read in* Rivet *himself.* (*c*) *Because some Learned men plead for Orphans much, as* Calvisius, Simler, *and others.* (*d*) Bolton, *p.* 48.

of their Stock, what will become of them when their Stock is gone?

To this that holy man *Bolton* (*a*) answers,

1. I might well be excused from answering this Objection at this time, because our common Vsurers, against whom I now purposely deal and dispute, are not Babes and Mad-men, except it be spiritually, but many times of great understanding and wisdom.

2. If Vsury be sinful in it self, it is evil in all, though in some more, and some less: If it be forbidden in God's Book, as it is in many places directly and clearly, what Circumstances, Good meanings, Motives, Ends, or any thing, can make it lawful, except the Royal Prerogative of the mighty Lord of Heaven and Earth, who is the Law-giver, and whose holy Wil is the Rule of Justice, interpose, and declare the contrary.

Though therefore the Relief of the Fatherless and Widow be good, yet must it not be done by *USURY*; for that is to do evil that good may ensue which is condemned by the Holy Ghost, *Rom.* 3. 8. Thus far blessed and learned *Bolton*; who also proveth (*b*) what he saith by the Word of God, which neither the Champion nor his Author doth. Now let the Reader chuse whom he thinks and judges to be in the right to follow.

2. I answer what he saith of St. *Austin*'s skabbed Vsurers *That they were such as lived without a Calling*, desiring him to prove it, that he speaketh of such, and no other; which I know he cannot do: for some Ministers in his time were Vsurers too, as he saith upon *Psal.* 15. 5. even as now also some are, who take up a double Calling, the Ministerial and the Vsurer's Calling: So that St. *Austin* calling the Vsurer skabbed, doubtless calls him not so because he is idle, as some are living without an honest Calling, but for some other cause also, because he takes no pains for the Gains which he gets by his Money, but leaves that to the Borrower; and because he infects, by his lending upon Vsury, others, as a skabbed Sheep infects many; for though he be a Pastor in some respect, yet he is a Sheep too in another. And how doth he infect, you will say, others, like a skabbed Sheep? I answer,

---

(*a*) *As I also do in this Tract.* (*b*) *Which is also so proved by Bishop* Downam.

1. B

1. By his Doctrine, being a Defendant for and of Vsury; so he spoileth many, who will believe him rather, speaking for their Worldly Gain, than holy *Bolton*, who crieth out against their unjust and unlawful Gain, which they get by the Silver Shrines of their Goddess *Diana*, Vsury, I mean.

2. By bad Example: for men, for the most part, are like *Jacob's* Sheep, *Gen.* 30. led by the eye, and conceive as they see, and say, If Vsury were such a grievous and dangerous thing as some make it, such wise, able, and learned Ministers would not practice it. [Here they name thee, that art a Minister and a Vsurer too, and so art, I will not say a double-beneficed man, because haply thou hast not one, but a man that has a double Calling, the Calling I mean of a Preacher, and the *quasi* Calling of an Vsurer: so I speak to any Minister that is an Vsurer; and therefore let no particular man take exception at my word, for I name none, but others do name some.

NUM. XXXIX.

3. I answer; Though the Champion saith nothing directly to my Speech concerning the Vsurer, That he is ashamed to call himself an Vsurer, whereas others in their Writings underwrite themselves either Husbandmen, or Clothiers, or Spinsters; yet will I say a little more to and of that, *viz.* That others also, as well as my self, have used the like Language, to shew what an infamous thing Vsury is: For so Dr. *Fenton*; *He that is an Usurer, if you ask what he is, or of what Profession he is of, he will not gladly own that Name: Mens Consciences are more troubled at the Name, than at the Practise of a Sin.* But most commonly he is called (and so will be called, say I) one that liveth by his Money; and that is without all exception: For, as the Gentleman liveth upon his Rents, the poor Labourer upon the Sweat of his Brow, the Merchant and Tradesman upon their Adventures, Skill, and Industry; the Husbandman and Grasier upon the Increase of the Earth, and Breed of Cattel: so the Vsurer liveth upon his Money, that yeans, and foals, and calves to him, once in Six Months at farthest. What a Fool then was *Aristotle*, to call Money barren, which yields a double Harvest at the least every Year, and the form r Crop maketh the Seed-corn for the next?

4. I say, That because the Champion takes no notice to divers other things also, which I mention, because he is loth

to hear of them, I will ſay a little the more yet, beſides all that; as namely, That whereas they ſay, that I onely, and ſome few moroſe and ſimple Miniſters, that do not know what belongs to City-Trade, and Merchandizing, and the Worlds Affairs, go to make Uſury ſo infamous, ſo that the Champion doth not think it to be worth the anſwering what I have ſaid; I will therefore cite ſome of the wiſeſt Heads that have been in the World, who make Uſury as infamous as it can be made, *viz.*

1. (*a*) *Plutarch* ſaith, That the Publican was a moſt infamous Perſon, and that Uſurers play the Publicans.

2. (*b*) *Petrarch* alſo writeth, as I have read it in him, That there is not a more filthy Study than that of Uſury; and that in former times Uſurers were ſeparated as Lepers from the Society of Man. And I am aſhamed to tell what woful Names (*c*) *Copernicus* calls Uſurers, and therefore will not relate his words.

3. (*d*) *Geminianus* tells us, That even the Notaries which make Uſury-Bonds and Writings, by it are made infamous, and loſe their Office.

4. (*e*) *Cæſar* himſelf, who, as a General, was verſed in all Military Affairs, and did march thorow many Kingdoms and Countries, and ſubdued them, and came to know thereby all their Dealings and Affairs, and, as an Emperour and Supreme Magiſtrate, ruling and governing the whole World, could not but be inſighted in all Civil Affairs too, did make a Decree, That a Uſurer ſhould not be counted an honeſt man; So that I hope, that as *Geneva* was conquered and ſubjected by this *Cæſar*, in the days of (*f*) *Orgentorixe*; ſo Uſury, which was of late years ſo ſet up and defended by ſome at *Geneva*, will be made more infamous than it has been yet, and ſo conſequently much left, conquered, and put down, by his Authority, Sayings, Sentences, and Decrees, in the World hereafter, when his Fame ſhall be ſo ſpread

(*a*) Plutarch *de non Fænerando.* (*b*) Petrach. *de Remed utriuſque Fort. l.* 1. *dial.* 56. (*c*) Copernicus. (*d*) Geminianus Sur. *l.* 8. (*e*) Lutherus *de Taxanda Uſura*, *To.* 7. (*f*) *The Chief Leader of the* Swizers *riſing againſt the* Romans *in* Cæſar'*s time, as* Carion *reports it in his Chron.*

abroad

abroad, together with his Successors Decree against dishonest and infamous Usury.

NUM. XL.

Answ. 5. But this is not all that I have to say, to make Usury infamous: for this is also yet behind to be spoken, That if the Champion shall think that though Usury hath been so infamous in the days of *Cæsar*, and of old Writers, yet it is not so now in our time, wherein Usury is so common; I, and thousands more, can tell him, that it is as infamous now also among us; for one shall hear both Ministers, that lend their Money upon Usury, and other rich men, though they look never so big, called Usurers by way of disgrace.

1. Ministers: For what do the People say, when a man discourses with them about Usury? Such a Minister, saith one, is an able man, and preacheth well; but he is an USURER, for I know where he hath out so much in such a mans hands, who payeth him use for it; and such a Minister has lent so much, it may be Forty, or Fifty, or a Hundred Pounds, to such a Tradesman, and such a back-handed man, who payeth him Usury for it, who can hardly pay it, saith another. And such a Minister, saith a third, is an Usurer; for I had Hundreds of him, and paid him Use for it; (This I have heard with mine Ears confessed.) I must confess that he abated me somewhat, he addeth: But yet, for the Courtesie shewn him therein, he calleth him Usurer: And so they do all call such Lenders of Money Usurers, that is the nick-name they give them, though some take no more but ordinary Usury, or somewhat less.

2. The like is said of other rich men in common talk, if they be Lenders of Money upon Usury, Such a one is an Usurer too, though he takes Use but after the ordinary rate and stint, yea, even those that take much less: for I am told of one, by a Friend who borrowed Money of him, that he took but Three in the Hundred for Hundreds, and yet is called an Usurer for all that, because he lendeth upon Usury; that is a nick-name, the disgraceful stile and reproachful nuncupation, which is put upon every Lender upon disgraceful Usury; even as in old time also those were called Usurers who took but Five in the Hundred for the Loan of their Money, or much less; for some had but Four in the Hundred, which was cal-

led

led *Usura trientaria*, that which an Emperour of *Rome* practised; as Six in the Hundred was called *Semissalis Usura*, and Eight in the Hundred, *Usura ex Besse*: All which kinds by godly Divines are held to be improbous and unlawful, and condemned by (*a*) Divine and Humane Right, and so are justly called Usurers, by God's own Word condemned Usurers, as here by my Citations it appeareth: And how Usurers will help it, that they may not be called so, by such an infamous and reproachful Name, I see not, unless they will repent, restore if they be able, and leave off this Usury, as *Nehemiah* prayeth them to do; (*b*) *I pray you let us leave off this Usury.*

My sixth Answer is, That whereas he makes me a Carrier and Bookseller, to be avenged on me, saying, (after other Passages) Unless upon the like grounds we shall call Mr. *Jelinger* a CARRIER or BOOKSELLER, because he carrieth his Books from County to County, from Town to Town, and from one Gentleman to another, to get vent for them; I cannot but, 1. break out into this Exclamation; O spite! O bitterness! O spleen! which is and lodges in this Man's Breast, for no hurt or harm that ever I have done to him, unless he count this to be a great injury done to him, that I have published my late Book called *The Usurer cast*, because he lends upon Usury; for which thing I not once named him, as here he names me by a reproachful Name, to disgrace me, if he could: The Lord forgive him; so I prayed when I wrote this.

2. I answer, That he wrongs me grievously; for the truth of the matter is this: I went indeed into a neighbouring County, and there bestowed Four Books upon my choicest Friends, which were Persons of Honour, and great Quality, but sold none. To *London* also I went, where I printed some of my Labours, and took a course for printing more, and presented my Books, which I had dedicated to that Illustrious Prince, and to another Eminent Person more, to which *The Usurer cast* is dedicated, but (*c*) sold none. And in this County of *Devon* I gave Six or Seven to some certain Gen-

(*a*) *Has species omnes judicamus improbas jure divino & humano damnatas.* Aret. *de Usuris*, p. 625. (*b*) Nehem. 5. 10. (*c*) *Though I was much sollicited to send some of my Books, by a Stationer, upon that account.*

tlemen

tlemen and Ladies, to whom I was much obliged, and had formerly dedicated the fruits of my Ministry, but sold none in any Fair or Market, (as it is slanderously reported by him, and some other Usurers, who would gladly cast an Odium and Aspersion upon me, for writing against their *DIANA*:) for there was no need, because I was sent unto from Towns, and by sundry Persons, to send Books for them, and to them, which I can prove sufficiently: Only this I add, That to some in that City, unto whom I had dedicated my Labours, I gave (not sold) some of the said Books, as others of my Brethren that print Books do likewise: and must I only be called a Carrier, above all others?

NUM. XLI.

Answ. 7. And whereas the Champion brings in some noted Authors in the close of his Reply, saying, It's not so infamous a thing, that a Man may be ashamed to own it, seeing so Reverend Divines as Mr. *Baxter*, *Hughes*, *Perkins*, and *Calvin*, have not been ashamed to plead the Lawfulness thereof; I shall now, in the last place, answer his naming of these great Names. And,

1. In general, That neither of these godly Men, nor any other, did ever plead for that Usury which my Friends and I plead against, *viz.* Usury properly so called, and by the Word of God condemned.

2. That I will here set down the Words of famous Dr. *Slater*: (*a*) *May not this Sin wind it self into their Affections, and from thence into their Intellect, till it have eaten out all soundness of judging and discerning between Good and Evil? Usury being a Trade so easie, so gainful, so pleasing; this advantage the Devil hath got by it, that it being so easie, it is easily believed what these Divines say for it.* Thus that Learned Doctor: with whom I will joyn (*b*) Bishop *Downam*, who having alledged Dr. *Luther* upon *Psal.* 15. 5. saying, *That that Verse against Usury had no need of expounding, but fulfilling and practising*, makes this application of his Words; *If* Luther *were living in these our Times, and understood, besides the common practice of Usury openly, and the cunning Shifts whereby it's*

(*a*) *Dr.* Slater *upon* Rom. 13. (*b*) *B.* Downam *on* Ps. 15.5.

cloaked,

cloaked, the open **DEFENCE** *also thereof undertaken, not only by Usurers themselves, but also by divers DIVINES, &c. who have either spoken or written more wittily than truly in favour of Usury, assuredly he would confess, that there is scarcely any one Moral Point which needs more fully to be expounded, and more exquisitely to be discussed; which makes me so to enlarge my self upon it.*

3. That I, for my part, if I might win the World by it, would not defend it, much less practice it, considering, 1. How dangerous a thing it is for a man to make himself a partaker of other mens sins, contrary to 1 *Tim.* 5. 22. And, 2. How a whole (*a*) Council has condemned all for Hereticks who hold it lawful, even as the Protestant University of *Wittenberg* doth likewise.

NUM. XLII.

Secondly, and more particularly, I will now deliver my mind about his Authors. And,

1. Concerning Reverend and Renowned Mr. *Baxter*, That I shall freely and willingly subscribe to his Definition, as I have declared it formerly, and hold with him in this too, That all Usury is not unlawful; because there are Fenories improperly so called, which my Brethren and I approve of also, as I have already said before now: though they and I do speak against all Usury properly so called, and by God himself, and all good men, condemned. And lastly, I do with heart and good will assent to divers of his godly Cautions by him

(*a*) *Concil*, Viennense. (*b*) Richard Baxter.

given.

given, and especially this, That a Lender must as well bear a part in the Borrower's Loss as Gain, which maketh such a kind of Dealing Partnership indeed.

2. As for (*a*) Mr. *Hughes* (who was my Colleague and Fellow-labourer, and whom I have read, as well as Mr. *Baxter*) I have this to say of him, That he is a little too short to decide such a great Question, and to make Usury lawful, (as also Mr. (*b*) *Ames* his third Author is, whom I have read too, and formerly answered) and that I have heard enough by the report of others, who will swear it, how he has declared his mind against Usury, to a godly Minister, Mr. *B. Cl.* since departed, and has kept some from the Sacrament of the Lord's Supper for their Usury; which I hint at now again, because my Adversary alledges him so often.

His fourth Author, next to *Ames*, is (*c*) *Perkins*; which will do him but little pleasure: for in his Exposition on Christ's Sermon upon the Mount, he doth (as blessed (*d*) *Bolton* observes it) ONLY approve Liberal and Recompencing Usury (which my Brethren and my self also approve of, as even now I intimated, speaking of Mr. *Baxter*) and not of Usury truly and properly so called, and commonly practised in this Kingdom, which I here speak against and oppose, I say, with Blessed *Bolton*.

(*a*) *Mr.* Hughes. (*b*) *Together with* R. T. *a late Champion for Usury*. (*c*) Perkins. (*d*) Bolton, p. 72.

NUM-

NUM. XLIII.

His fifth and last Author is [*a*] *Calvin*, who will do him less good: For,

1. [*b*] *Himself having delivered his Opinion concerning Usury, would have no man to stand upon his Judgment for the full and absolute determination of this Controversie.*

2. He saith, [*c*] *That it is more than a rare thing, that the same man should be an Usurer and an honest man.*

3. [*d*] *We must always hold it to be a thing scarce possible, that he which takes Usury should not wrong his Brother.*

4. [*e*] *It were to be wished, that the very Name of Usury were buried, and utterly blotted out of the memory of men.*

5. *And he wisheth, that none would write to him any more about it.*

6. [*f*] And it is believed, that if it had not been for the *French* Exuls, that flock'd and fled to *Geneva*, being persecuted out of *France*, we should not have heard of such defending of Usury. For then it was when *Calvin* was asked, *What those poor Exuls should do with their Money, that they might live, because their Lands they cou'd not carry with them, but only their Money, which they could not adventure at Sea for a Livelihood, because* Geneva *is no Sea-town, but far from the Sea, standing upon a Lake only*, (For I lived there as a Student and Exul too, and there-

(*a*) Calvin *Epist. Resp. de Usuris.* (*b*) *Idem in* Ezech. 18. (*c*) *Idem.* (*d*) *Idem.* (*e*) *Idem.* (*f*) *Dr.* Fenton.

fore

fore can ſpeak it.) *and which would be ſoon ſpent, if it ſhould not be imployed, for a maintenance, one way or other? I ſay, then it was that poor* Calvin *was put to it to reſolve them; ſo as that he was driven to adviſe them to a* quaſi Uſura, *that is, to a kind of Uſury, which was ſo caution'd by him, as that it was rather Partnerſhip than Uſury.* So that Uſurers have little cauſe to ſtand upon *Calvin*, becauſe of his godly Sayings, I add, and Cautions, which they do not obſerve, and which I intend to mention hereafter, together with more of his Sayings.

But I deſire to return again to this bleſſed *Calvin*, to vindicate him, becauſe I love him dearly, and read his *Inſtitutions*, as near as I can, daily, being adviſed ſo to do by a godly Divine, when I lived in the famous Univerſity of *BASEL* in *Helvetia*; I ſay, a godly Divine, who told me that he did ſo himſelf: ſo as that I wiſh that others would do ſo too, it being ſuch an excellent Book, as that one made theſe (*a*) Verſes upon it, which I ſet down in the Margin; and that one may ſay of it, that which (*b*) *Fabricius* ſaith of *Tully*, *Let him know, that he has profited much, which is much delighted in* Calvin.

I ſay again, That I deſire by this to vindicate *Calvin*, becauſe the (*c*) Papiſts do brand him with this, That he and his *Calvinians* hold for that Uſury which is every where ſo much ſpoken againſt, and by God's Word condemned; which is falſe:

(*a*) *Præter Apoſtolicas poſt Chriſti tempora Chartas,*
Huic peperere Libro ſæcula nulla parem. Surius Baſtingius, *to the Reader, upon his Comment upon the Catech. in the County Palat.* (*b*) *Doctor* Fabricius. (*c*) *Videatur* Lorinus *in* Pſal. 15.

and

and because a late Protestant Doctor, a Cousin and Country-man of mine, hath written a Book, wherein he calleth *Calvin That Saboudian Innovator*, to please some, by way of reproach; which I dare not, nor will do, though he be alledged against me in the Point of Usury, which he is as much against as I; Usury, I mean, properly so called, and commonly practised in the World.

N V M. XLIV.

Lastly, I superadd, That if the Champion should bring Forty more to these Four, and Forty to them over and above, I should be no more troubled at it, than at the having of One only; because these holy and learned men, who have somewhat favourably written of some Usury, have, like Mr. *Baxter*, and *Calvin*, spiced it so with such Cautions, as make it no Usury, properly so called, but another Contract, and commonly that of Society: I will instance in famous *Virel* (in his *Catech.*) who holds *this Usury lawful, if*, 1. *The Borrower besprinkle the Lender with part of his Encrease, rather out of his voluntary thankfulness, than by way of exaction.* 2. *If the Lender be content to bear part of the Borrowers Loss, as well as of his Gain.* 3. *If the Principal do miscarry without the Borrowers fault, the Lender will not only remit the Principal, but also lend him afresh*; which I think never any Usurer in the World did. So that here I will end with the Words of deep-learned *Powel*, (in his *Posit. pag.* 52.) *NO Writer that ever I could see, or hear of, ever allowed of USURY.* And presently after he explains his Saying: *There are many strong Poysons, which the learned Physicians can so qualifie, that a sick Person may take a Potion wherein some of the Poyson is: so holy men of God have done and do temper and qualifie the Usurers Poyson, that they make thereof a wholesom Medicine for many distressed Persons: For by their holy and religious Caveats and Lessons, they alter the quality of the Usury, and make it indeed no Usury at all, but a lawful kind of Trade and Dealing.* Thus he. Whereby it appears, that my Adversary has gotten no advantage at all by his Authors, (though Usurers mostly stand upon it, and some others) because their holy *Caveats* are not observed by them.

My

escription opposed, and my first answer to it.

Y next task will be to defend my fourth De- scription of Usury, viz. *That it is a most mon- thing,* wherein my examiner holds himself e concerned in, but only those Monsters which that he which takes but a mite for a 100 *l.* under the same Condemnation: whereunto I

a word or syllable of a mite taken for a 100 *l.* all my description: let the Reader peruse my Some famous men, indeed have mentioned a er account,and their words were quoted by me nine, and they doubtless will be able to give their words upon the great day of Accounts, ve named five in the 100 too, and made it he- mnable, as the *Wittenburge* Doctors, whom up- ints I have often quoted.

My Second Answer.

in a special manner, I brand some notoriously rs with monstrousness according to their de- ot exempt others: no more then both Fathers iters, besides the holy Prophets, as my book sheweth it: for therein I quote *Basil,* who ry in General, thus, *that it begets it self, and en it was by encrease:*

that because my Antagonist taketh but little I say to confirm my assertion, I will make my grow a little bigger by some addition to its am now upon encreasing, as thus: Declar-

onstrously encreasing thing *three wayes.* 1. In onster which is against nature, it swells and su- parts and members; there was of late years a orth in a Town, where I was Preacher, with rabunding parts and members in his infantile

---

ttenberg. * Monstrum est contra naturam. de Differ. Vocab. & donatus quoque, *And a* . * B. Jewel *in* 1 Thes. 4. *an ugly Beast.* * *A swelling Monster,* Suidas *in* Aristoph de Nubody and was called a *Monster*, and here was a * book written and published to the world. Answerably whereunto, Usury also may be called such a *Monster*, because against * nature its brought forth, and because the Usurer is all for double, that is for Principal and Use; And many times for other pleonasmes and excrescences and superaboundings also, not being contented with the single principal repaid, which is according to nature. As for advance money; and for bribes besides six in the 100. a bushel of Corn now and then, or something else; for some Usurers will first deny men to lend, pretending that they shall have occasion for their money to use it, but to do a man a pleasure they will let them have it, and so they look for somewhat for their Courtesie, besides their Use, and their Servants must have somewhat too, for the procuring of it.

2. In that, whereas the * dead cannot beget or bear * Children, the Usurer by his money will bring forth in a mon strous manner other money, tho the said money be a dead thing and doth not live, which is against nature, saith, *Peraldus*; so that Usury must needs be a monstrously encreasin thing.

3. In that against nature some Usurers will bring forth b their Usury hundreds, others thousands of Children, as it wer in a short time: one Writeth of some, that they know how, b a 100 pounds to gain forty or fifty pounds in a year; and wh knoweth not, saith he, that money continually put forth t Usury after ten in the 100. (as it was in his time) doth in se ven years almost double the principal, and in every seve years double the former Sum, so that a 100 pounds let out a

---

* *As I also desire in this Book to write of the Monste called Usury. Whereof Mr.* Smith *writeth thus, this word mo is like the sixth finger, which makes a monster because it is mo than should be p.* 95. *And as he, which first devised the breedi up Mules, in* Genesis, *joyned those things, which God would n have joyned, and so brought forth a Monster: so he that fi joyned gain with lending brought forth that Monster, called Usu* * *For in all Usury, a barren thing brings forth, saith a fam Doctor. Et Usuraria acquisitio est maxime contra naturam, c cit* Aristot. 1. Pol. c.7. *Et* Cicero *in* 3 Offic. *Est magis contra n turam quam mors.* * *Cum parere in rebus, quæ non vivu esse non habent, iste tamen vult nummus suos qui non vivu singulis diebus vel mensibus alios nummos parere, quod cont naturam est.* Peraldus De Avar. p. 66. * *As a great Doc calls Usury gains as well as my self.*

ter this rate, from three moneths to three moneths ariseth in seven years to almost 200. O monstrously encreasing Usury: There is another great Person, who has made the like Computation in a Tract of his presented to a Parliament in *England*, against Usury, whose words I will not now rehearse, but rather set down a little more of that, which the foresaid Author adds to the words even now mentioned, 'who would not sell his 'Lands and Goods, and all that he can spare, to raise a stock 'of money, that thereout he might by Usury reap so great and 'so certain a gain, if once in his Conscience he were assured, 'that Usury is lawful? Thus he, and as he saith this in General, so say I of my self in particular, that I would sell all that I have, and bring it to a sum of money and lend it out upon Usury too, as others do, if I were sure that Usury, which brings such a monstrous encrease were NO SIN: For then I should be freed from all care, trouble, charge, hazards of lives, taxes, reparations, which men that have Livings, and Lands are liable unto.

I add, and truly, truly, the world might well call us all, that will not put out our money upon fenory, FOOLS, and meer SOTS, that we will not do what lawfully we might do, to get such exceeding great gains.

Numb. 42. 4. To go on gradatim, higher and higher, it is a Monstrous encreasing thing, in that against nature, the Usurer by it (as barren as mony is) doth beget, not only hundreds and thousands, as his lending may be as so many Children in *infinitum*, even to infinite numbers, which is much more then I said yet, as thus:

Whereas a Debtor borroweth but Forty or Fifty pounds, he makes himself a debtor not only of so many, (in case he come not off with his payment) but no man is able to tell of how many, tho he pay but six in the 100. which because it may seem to be incredible, I will set down the words of a great Doctor instancing in ten Crowns borrowed, when money was lent out after ten in the 100. A borrower receiveth ten, or some such certain number of Crowns, and thereby maketh himself debtor not only of so many, but no man can say how many more if the borrower pay but two Crowns over, by the year, in one 100 years he shall pay for ten Crowns 200 Crowns: and yet shall he still remain debtor for the ten Crowns also.

And shortly after he saith further, that those ten Crowns may from Age to Age be only said to continue in the bank, as in some places it chanceth, and so within a 1000 years they make encrease of 2000 Crowns; add hereunto that in case the borrower do not pay his Usury in ten years, he is then debtor of twenty Crowns, of ten for the Principal and of other ten for the Usury, which the Usurer begetteth and ingendreth (as it were) to the intollerable loss to the borrower, and the excessive gain of himself, and yet these ten Crowns be not his own all this while, although he pick out so great advantage of them, yea, all this while they be no where at all, for in one moment they were * consumed and spent by him that borrowed them, and in place of them an idol is conceived which idol doth * remain refusedly, not any where in nature but in name and imagination : for its feigned, that the ten Crowns lie still in a certain bank, and there do beget little ones, which again have other little ones, and whereas all other things die and perish, and many beasts which nature made apt to encrease, by casualties prove barren, yet these ten Crowns, which by nature were barren, and in truth were spent, remain still so fruitful in the USURERS vain imagination, and in the borrowers most greivous pension, that if the world should stand for ever, they also should be immortal, and should neither die, nor ever become barren.

5. In that against the nature of lending he will needs grow rich and great, and yet so much as I have mentioned by lending, which ought not to be mercenary but free, for so all Nations and unbyassed Writers, Greeks, Latins, Jewes, Philosophers, Lawyers, Divines, and generally all Heathens, and Christians that have soundly Written of this subject; take that to be the true definition or description of loan, that it is to deliver to the borrower such things as are spent with the first natural and proper use thereof, with Bond to repay him so much again and so good again, and no more, as I have formerly shown it: And, 2. So Christ himself would have it, saying, *lend, looking for nothing again, Luke 6. 35.* Where note by the way, that Christ no where bids us to buy and sell, as men ordinarily use to do, or to follow the usual way of Merchandizing, because he knew that men were and would be of themselves, willing to do that, but to lend freely, which they are unwilling to do.

6. In that the Committant of Usury against the natural Use and end of money, which is a formost equality, doth introduce into the World a monstrous deformity, odness, and inequality, where let me discourse a little of the coming in and

* *Nor could he purchase with them.* * *Without Lands or Fields bought.*

using

using of money, and apply what I shall say concerning it, to the present matter of Usury, but before I go on with this subject, I will first premise the saying of a wise man concerning money, when money is given to loan (as in Usury it comes most times to pass) there is a special DEFORMITY also in that behalf: And now for a fuller handling of this matter of money, let me declare here, that money was first invented by the common consent of men, especially to serve mans necessity and commodity in chopping and changing things to and fro; for in the beginning he that lacked any thing, as for example, a new garment he went to another man, that had vestiments enough, and brought him such stuff whereof himself had store, as Cloth perhaps, or skins, or some like matter, to make an equal exchange between them both: So that thing for thing was exchanged: and that was the most simple and natural kind of Traffick between men: but experience declared that this at length was incommodious, and would not serve every mans turn, for sometimes he that had shoes, which I lacked, had also cloth and skins. as well as I, and then he was loth to take my cloth for his shooes, seeing that he had cloth enough of his own. For which cause wise men devised that some certain metal should serve the turn of all men, so that who so needed any stuffe, he should take such a kind of metal, or Coyn, to wit lead or leather, and at length brass, and for that he should receive of any other man whatsoever he needed. Thus metal was at the first esteemed by consent and delivered by weight: so that a pound of brass should be (for example) the price of a pair of shoes: And when it was found troublesome also, especially for them that went abroad to carry such weight of metal about them, and to stand long in weighing it, instead of a great deal of brass, a little Silver and less Gold was at length invented; yea, then it was also further devised, that a certain Coyn or print should be set upon Silver or Gold so that we should not need alwayes to weigh it, but that the very form should straight shew the value thereof; money therefore was made to serve all exchanges and to be the price of all other things, and to set forth a form of equality in the world, and not a deformity as Usury doth, together with a monstrous inequality, whereof I have spoken formerly, at present I will but add what a great * Doctor saith concerning this matter: it is utterly against the end for which either any other exchange or money it self was made; for it was

* *Doctor* Sand. *In his Treatise of Usury.*

made to bring all things to an equality, and to be, as it were a rule and measure, whereby the value of all things might be quickly known and easily counterpoised, but now Usurers make money to serve for the greatest inequality that can be devised of man, his words are too large to be inserted wholly.

A Reply to my fifth Description.

Num. 43. BUT *I must go onward* and see how the Champion goeth on

Mr. *Jelinger.* Fifthly, *A most cruelthing it is.*

For its alwayes biting, day and night, Winter and Summer. &c. *Reply,* (to omit his odd comparison, as not argumentative at all) it is great pity he had not been by the Parliament men, when they were passing the Act concerning Usury to have exempted at least the Nights and Lords days through the year from paying the Use: But doth not the Adventurer at Sea his gain go on too at the same rate, and he that Rents a Tenement; or Houses, do not Nights and Lords days and Winter come into computation with other times, for which they pay? had his arguing been his own, we should have counted it very weak and dregs, but he borroweth freely, and then makes a shew as if it were his own goods.

My Answer.

Whereunto I shall Answer thus.

1. Retortingly about the Parliament; that it's a great pity that he had not been with the Parliament men, when they made that famous * Act against Usury to advise them.

1. That they should not intitle it an Act against Usury because all men would see by that, that they are not for Usury.

2. That by no means they should use these words. FORASMUCH AS ALL USURY, BEING FORBIDDEN BY THE WORD OF GOD IS SIN AND DETESTABLE, mark, ALL USURY as I also say, for that would spoil the poor Usurer utterly, and make his gainful trade to decay irrecoverably.

2. Concerning adventuring and setting of ground and houses, I have this to say, that there is a vast difference between both these and Usury, because the former are not interdicted by the word of God, but the latter is, as I have already shewn, And 2. because they are no where in Scripture called Biting, as Usury is, and therefore cannot be said to bite night and day, Winter and Summer, Lords dayes and

Week days, as Usury doth, which is called *Morsura* in Hebrew נשקם. Some oppression may be thereby committed and so it may be called when it is so, but Usury properly so called cannot be, because that is otherwayes designed, as has been formerly ostended.

3. I answer, that whereas he tells the World, that I am a free borrower, &c. I am not ashamed of borrowing, because it is lawful, but he may be ashamed of lending, I mean upon Usury, because that is unlawful, *Deut.* 23. 19. but that is not all that I have to say. For I can sufficiently evidence it, that he is both a lender and borrower to himself, a borrower I mean, which freely borrowes of others, what they Write, and then makes a shew as if it were his own, to use his own words.

Where give me leave to add, that the same thing happened, when I read his Pamphlet, which happened when * Doctor *Fenton* (that Malleus or Hammer of Usurers) read a Manuscript for Usury, as this man is, he wondred where and whence he had it what he wrote, but afterward found it all in *Bullinger*; answerably whereunto, I wondred also whence he had his skill in the Oriental tongues, *Syriak*, *Arabick*, and *Persick* upon *Luk.* 6. 35. but soon after found the same in the *Polyglotte* which some body lent him.

Num. 44. 4. But I desire to come more closer to him, and to answer him more fully, because he relateth my words but slightly, and doth not answer that which is most material, but leaveth out that which maketh mostly against him, 'as namely that 'proof of mine which maketh it clear that Usury is alwayes 'biting, in that the Usurer is called in the Hebrew ננשיך a 'biting one, in the participle, because he is alwayes biting. O 'cruel biter! So that I am now resolved to shew more abundantly what a cruelly biting thing it is, *in two Respects.*

1. *In that* biting it wounds and thereby creates and *multiplieth cruel pain and sorrow.*

2. *Causeth many cruel and bitter Curses and Cursings.*

For the first; I shall make it evident how cruelly biting it wounds, paineth and puts to abundance of sorrow, four *sorts of sufferers: as namely.*

1. *The Usurer himself.*
2. *His Children, and Posterity.*
3. *The borrower.*
4. *The Poor and Common-wealth.*

1. *The Usurer himself*, because biting cruelly it wounds his Conscience: because he taketh it against the checks of his Conscience; as therein I appeal to his own evil and wound-

ed Conscience, which has caused a great and L
thor to let these very words drop from his Pen, *T
torment and assault his Conscience, that taketh Usury
Usury sads, and that sadness which cometh by its bit
ing, may well be resembled to* Abel *and* Cain. *Cain*
session, and *Abel* mourning and sorrow, I superadd
and sorrow doth then especially come upon the
he lieth upon his death bed, as I have read of dive
sadly they have ended their days, and what for
have said, before they died. And it cannot wel
because Usury is a birth called τόκος in Greek, b
pain trouble and sorrow as our Saviour tells us,
when she is in travail, has sorrow, John 16. 2
whereunto a poor Usurer must needs have sor
when he thinks he shall die ; because then that
vid, Psal. 15. 1. 5. *Lord, who shall dwell in th
that has not put his monney to Usury*, and that of
18. 12, 13, 36. *Has given forth upon Usury, and
ercase, shall he then live, he shall not live*, &c. *a*
ter this, therefore *I will Judge you, O house o
Judge you, every one according to his wayes*, (an
by the name, according to his Usurious wayes)
which when the poor wounded Usurer maketh
on, must needs exceedingly trouble his mind a
wounded Spirit, his Conscience telling him, th
shall be unmanned by death, he must forthwit
particular Judgment, and Answer for all the Usur
he had taken, and that at that Great day of the
ment he must appear again and be judged for
mination which is called Usury in Usury ; se
for it, these Verses the 13. *and* 14. *in Ezekiel*
tell the Usurer, that the Very *. *Sibyls* have
coming of the Usurer to Judgment, as I will
whose words are these,

——— ————— Ἠδὲ τοκισαὶ
Οἱ τόκον ἐκ τόκου συνα θροίζοντες
Then shall come before him Murderers, Adult

---

* Powel *in his posit.* p. 26. * *Where note
and is so called* quasi συνβουλὴ *after the* Æc
consiliis deorum, *as* Lactant. *has it.* l. 1. de
and that those Sibyls did foretel things divine affla
mirifick and divine inspiration, as Justin Mart. *i*
cum patrum, Sibyl, Orac. l. 2.

with the USURERS. So that this remembrance of both these Judgments cannot but make the poor Usurer lie down in sorrow, crying out and saying within himself: O woe is me that ever I was born to be an Usurer! for now, I must come to an account for every Penny, Shilling, Pound, and for all those hundreds of pounds which I have Usuriously taken, and after that my Soul must die, die, die, to all Eternity, and when Christ shall come to his General Judgment, my Soul and Body both will be cast into the lake that burns with fire and brimstone, which is the Second death, *Rev.* 21. 8. which I must die by vertue of the unerring word of God, who saith in express words of the Usurer, *he shall surely die his blood shall be upon him, Ezek.* 18. 13. And how! O how shall I be able to dwell in those everlasting burnings! *Esa.* 33. 14. O Eternity, how formidable is the very thought of thee! for when I have lain in that lake of fire so many thousand years, as there are hairs upon my head, piles of Grass in the coloured Fields, Sands on the Sea shore yet even then, it may be said, *now Eternity beginneth:* Ah poor Usurer think upon this long, long, long, duration of Eternity, how the thoughts of it will torment thee in the hour of death, and how thy cruelly biting Usury, and all thy bags and pounds of money which thou hast gotten by it, will not yield thee one dram or drop of comfort in that sad and sorrowful time.

Num. 46. 2. But I must be briefer next in my second branch, which concerns his Children and Posterity, Which it so cruelly, wounds, and hurts, as that commonly,

1. They die after him, I mean such as being led by his example follow the same trade, as it's written in *Ezek.* 18. 10, 12, 13. *If he beget a Son, that is a shedder of blood (as the Father is or was) and doth the like things,* &c. *and has given forth upon Usury, and hath taken encrease shall he then live? He shall not live,* &c. *he shall surely die,* I confess the Prophet speaketh of a Son, that is begotten of a Father that is no Usurer *verse* 8. but if that Son which is begotten of a Father which never put his money upon Usury, shall die, so that his Fathers righteousness cannot save him, then how much more shall the son of a wretched Usurer die, who lieth both under the guilt of his own Usury, which he has taken, and of his Fathers Usury, which he has taken, and should have restored together with his own, and did not:

So that I would not be the Son of such a Father for a world of Wealth: But I desire here chiefly, to aggravate the sin of a Father, which is an Usurer and cruelly bites, wounds, and hurts, yea * kills his Children, as * one saith, and that in two *Respects.*

1. In

1. *In that his * example maketh them Usurers.*

2. *In that the mony left them* is unto them the cause of eternal death, saith the same Author* : *Pliny* writeth of the Woolf ; that he brings forth blind Whelps, and so doth the Usurer commonly bring forth blind Children that cannot see what their Father left them, and then when the Father is gone to Hell for gathering, they follow after for spending.

2. But if this do not happen, because they will be no Usurers as their Father was, yet commonly the Usurers Children and Posterity lose, by one means or other, that which he has wretchedly gotten, and come to poverty ; his Goods being brought into the possession of others, for the relief of the Poor, according to *Prov.* 28. 8. *He that encreases his Riches by Usury and encrease, gathereth them for him that shall be merciful to the poor.*

Hemingius instances in one certain Usurer, who dwelt in *Chersoneso Cimbrica*, and grew exceeding rich by lending upon Usury, died, having abundance of wealth, and yet after his death, the children that he left behind him, fell into extream poverty : in so much, that a daughter of his was found to have not so much as a Coat to cover her nakedness : And innumerable examples and instances more might be given, and such as I have observed in my times of many rich Usurers Posterity, who have lost that Land, those Livings, those Estates, which their Fathers and Grandfathers have purchased with Usury money, and are now possessed by others, and others can and do testifie the same : Where let me mention but one godly and learned Minister more, who told me, that with his eyes, he saw a Widow, whose Husband was worth 12000 pounds gotten by Usury, beg a dish of Porridge, which affected him very much, because he had known them both in their Prosperity ; and that must needs cause sadness : So that Usury may well be assimilated to *Tyre* and *Sidon :* For *Tyre* is said to be the daughter of *Sidon*, and *Tyre* signifieth *Affliction* and *Sadness*, and *Sidon*, *Venation* or hunting, which

* Idem. *So that he deserves to be beaten and to suffer, which made* Diogenes *so beat a Father when his Son had committed a fault, because his Fathers example made him do what he did. Which* Crates *also did, as* Quintilian *asserts it.*

may

may fitly be applyed to Usury, which is a kind of hunting after wealth, and to Usurers, which are hunters after the Gain that comes by Usury; and then begets *Tyre*, that is much affliction to such as are begotten by them, and to their Posterity: So that I may well tell what a cruelly biting thing Usury is in respect of this hurt it doth to the Usurers Children and Posterity.

Numb. 48. 3. And doth it not cruelly bite, and biting wound, pain, hurt, and make sad necessitous † Borrowers? O yes, I appeal for it to you Borrowers, who are in the Usurers Books, do not you find it so? Doth not Usury, though it be but Six in the hundred make sad, yea almost break your hearts? doth it not make you wake and fetch many a deep sigh, when others sleep and take their rest? Do not Usurers arrest you, if you come not off to a day? and make you sell your Cattel, your Goods, and sometimes your fields or means to half price, or at least to your great loss?

Some I believe do not feel that which others feel for the present, but afterward they cannot chuse but feel it, so that divers Authors as *Pliny*, *Baldus* the Lawyer, *Powel Turner* compare the Usurers to the worm which is soft to a mans touch, but biteth deep and after a while will be felt to some purpose.

But I have a mind to name two Authors more. 'And '1. *Chrysostome*, even as leaven which is put into meal infecteth 'the whole lump and drawing it to it self, turns it into the na'ture of leaven: so when Usury enters into any mans estate it draweth his substance to it and turns it into debt.

2. '*Basil*, when the Usurer seems to have relieved a man, 'he casts him into a deeper want; and cruelly it hurts, wounds, and sads the poor and Commonwealth (to joyn them both) I begin first with the poor, whom he hurts and wounds grievously. How? the poor, some will say, is not the Usurer all for the poor, when he quoteth these Scriptures, *Exo.* 22. 25. *Lev.* 25. 36, 37. And would not have the poor oppressed by Usury, I know he is for the poor in words, but not in his practise: For he careth not what becomes of the poor,

† *Who for that cause is called in Hebrew* שיך *that is, bitten, even as for pain and dolour Usury is also called* τόκος, *which in it's primitive signification signifies a birth, next to which is the issue of it, namely dolour as* Ambros. *takes it.* lib. de Tob. 1. c. 12. * Chrysostom. 12. to. 3. *Where note again how far that holy man is from speaking against cruelly biting Usury only.*

when

when lending his money upon Usury, he maketh the borrower sell his Corn and ware the dearer to pay him his Usury, and to make benefit of it for himself, whereby the poor usually are bitten cruelly.

Num. 49. 2. The Commonwealth is so much bitten hurted and sadded by it, as that divers Commonwealths have banished and driven out all Usurers out of their Territories, Countries, and Cities: as *Scicily*, *Sparta*, and *Worms* that great imperial City *within* a mile of which I was born, who write this, and have seen six thousand Jews (as it was said) driven out for Usury, which examples, with the consideration of Usurers cruelty, has caused Dr. *Beard* to publish to the World this wish of his. *It is to be wished, that some would examine the Usurers Books, and make a bonefire; that some* Lucullus *would deliver* Europa *from that contagion, as the Romans did* Asia.

And now Secondly, I will speak both of the poor and Commonwealth together, and for both quote famous Bishop * *Downam*, whose words are, 'Usury is hurtful to the Commonwealth 'and especially to the Commonalty (whereby I understand the 'poorest sort) which payeth it, for whosoever thriveth by oc'cupying money borrowed upon Usury, he has pitched so the 'prize of his commodities, as that, besides a competent gain 'raised for the maintenance of himself and his charge, he al'so has gathered up an overplus, and tenth part for the Usu'rer: And thus by Usury the prices of all commodities are in'hanced, while the Sellers borrow upon Usury, if they will 'thrive must needs make the buyers to pay two shillings 'in the pound more then otherwise were sufficient, thus he.

I am necessitated to bring such Authors, because my Adversary maketh such a market man of me, as if none were like me, whereas now he may plainly see, that so great a man as this Bishop is, Writes after the same rate of markets, as I do, so that I shall leave him now to dispute it with great *Downam*, why he will busie himself so much about Market affairs, to make the Usurer a biter of the poor and commonwealth.

Lastly, I say, that Usury is a cruelly biting wounding sadding thing, because it causes most cruel and bitter cursing for what saith *Jeremiah*, *I have neither lent upon Usury, nor me have lent to me upon Usury, yet every one of them doth curse*

* B. *Downam* upon *Psal*, 15.

me, *Ch.* 15. 10. which has caused * Dr. *Luther* to say, *That the Usurer is the curse of God, and of the people*: where give me leave to declare. How he causes *three several curses*, for,

1. The poor do curse him, because, as I said, he is bitten through his occasion in Markets and Wares, which he buyes, and because he will lend no money to him though he be full of money: but only to the rich.

2. The necessitous borrower curseth him, because he must pay Use for his money, tho he neither buy an estate with it nor get by it, but only for bare need borroweth it; to free himself from an Arrest, or to save, and keep what he has, that it may not fall into * the Lords hand, or else to buy provision, when it is reasonable to maintain his Wife, Children, and Family: tho Christ has said expresly, *lend, looking for nothing again*, that is, *no Usury* for it, as expositors expound that place.

3. Both Fathers and Children, (which imitate their Fathers in the taking of Usurie, or else riotously do spend what their Father has wretchedly gotten by Usury) do curse one another in hell, when they are there, most bitterly and everlastingly: And there is a famous Writer who describeth their mutual cursing most pathetically thus, that in that infernal punishment Usurers and their Children will * curse one another, the Father saying, cursed art thou my Son, because for thy sake I am tormented in this flame; for I became an Usurer lest I should leave thee a begger, I gathered wealth that thou shouldst not be poor, and I was contented to be poor in grace, that thou mightest be rich in goods, and therefore am now poor in all things, but in torments: and the Son on the other side will say to the Father; nay rather, cursed art thou, O Father; because that thou gatheredst thy wealth with iniquity and leftest unto me with a curse which has consumed it, and destroyed my Soul; and now let the Usurer open his eyes and see what a cruelly biting sin Usury is, that he may leave it, and live, and not be cursed here and hereafter for ever, which God in mercy grant.

Num. 50. * *The Champions next work is to examine my inquiry*

---

* *Which occasioneth me to mention an expression of a godly man, which, as he told me, heard a pious man say, that it was pity but that mans tongue should rot in his mouth, who defends Usury.* * *Doctor* Williams *in his true Church*, p. 438.
* p. 16.

how

how Usury differs from other contracts and dealings, as interest, inter-usury, Shiploan, &c. *and to tell me.* 1. *That Regulated Usury has the same plea from reason, that either of these has. Take three definitions, saith he, which he mentioneth together: whatsoever is more then the principal* (saith Ambrose) *and all that a man takes over and above the money lent,* &c. *Take either of these definitions, without supplements, and you shall find, inter-usury, Interest, and Shiploan to be Usury, these being each somewhat above the principal: whereunto I answer,*

1. *That my three Definitions taken out of* Ambrose, *and the Council of* Agatha, &c. *tho short, yet make it evident in part what Usury is,* viz. an overplus beyond the principal; which cannot be denied, because God himself calls it *an increase, Ezek.* 18. 12. and to shew that they are not only against excessive, oppressive, griping Usury, but that also which my Adversary calls moderate; they add for example *five in the* 100. which also may serve to stop his mouth, for what he saith, that we must take these definitions without glosses, because this Council, which is chiefly alleadged by me, uses this gloss as others also from time to time have ἐξηγητικῶς used theirs, after their setting down of their short definitions, as for example, *Balsamon* in *M. M. p.* 43.

*Bolton, p.*45. Dr. *Fenton,* and *Turner* especially, *p.* 5. having thus briefly defined Usury, that it is a gain by a compact for loan, expoundeth his short definition by parts, saying there are five things belonging to Usury. 1. A Principal. 2. Lending. 3. Gain. 4. A chief purpose by lending to increase the stock. 5. A Covenant for that; but I desire to say a little more for the famous Council of *Agatha* which I mostly aim at for its Antiquity, and Authority, that some Translate it's words thus.

Given, or LENT FORTH: which maketh it's short definition more full and plain, and others also, for seeing that brevity breeds * obscurity, have therefore added *loan* in their short definitions expresly, as I will instance in one of the Ancient ones, who defineth Usury thus, *Usura est id, quod ex mutuo ultra sortem accipitur:* that is, Usury is that, (mark, *that*; (whatsoever it be) which is taken above the Principal for LOAN, whom the Modern Writers do follow.

---

* *As saith my old Master, that most learned Logician, Mr.* Hopsius *in his most excellent Logick* Dum brevis esse laboro, obscurus fio. * *Ludolphus* de vita Christi. *c.*49.

I add, that neither I nor my Brethren willbe confined to such short and somewhat imperfect definitions only, and therefore beware of, or give other fuller definitions for men to take their choice.

To close up this answer with God, I must send my Opponent to Gods own expositive way for condemning Usury in *Ezek*. 18. 12. he forthwith explaineth himself, and calls it ENCREASE, and more fully again glosseth upon it in *Deut*. 23. 19, 20. And much more fully ANY ENCREASE, *Ezek*. 18. 8. for which glossing and enlarging I send my Reader to that which I have written about it in my first Book against Usury, *p*. 37

2. These things premised, down totters what he inferreth, that we shall find in the said

3. Definitions, Inter-usury, and Shiploan, to be Usury too, these being each some gain above the Principal; because I hope that I have sufficiently proved, glossing in short distinctions to be admitted, tho by him causelesly they be oppugned.

Num. 51. More could I say, how he by him mentioned Inter-usury, and Shiploan, are not Usury properly so called, though in each somewhat be taken above the Principal, but that I shall defer to declare in its more proper place, only this I will mention here about Shiploan, that what is taken, is taken not so much for loan, as for hazard and adventuring.

3. As for those exacters *in Nehemiah* 5. I need not trouble my self about them: because that case will fall in the next when I come to answer him about Inter-usury, which next follows to be treated of: only this I will say for the present that his *thoughts*, that they came under some incommodity, cannot oblige me *to think so too*, and that therefore it is needless for me to answer him to satisfie him whether they might take Inter-usury, sufficient it is generally to assert, and to prove that damage, *alias* Interest, may be taken, in case a lender of money be really damaged by the borrowers not paying his money at the time appointed, and that according to the determination of a Judge, or Arbitrators, as I have formerly from the holy Scriptures shewn it.

Now 4*ly*. I will step forward, even step by step to trace my Antagonist, saying, that he will trace me in each of the forementioned definitions. Mr. *Jelinger, saith Inter-Usury is money received for an incommodity, &c. Reply: as if mans that lend money do not feel an incommodity too in the absence of their mony for moneths and years*, &c.

Whereunto I answer, that I cannot but take notice of his ignorance,

norance, out of which he so mistakes Inter-usury, as that he utterly confounds the incommodities which a Usurer may feel in the absence of his money for months, or years, and the incommodity which he that taketh Inter-usury doth feel, and for which so much money is by a Judge adjudged to him and for him: For so civilians define it, that it is interest cause, *an interest of a cause* * which consists in giving or doing.

Num. 52. 2. He wrongs me, saying, that I define it to be *money taken*, for I do not say so, nor name money, but an *incommodity* as also Civilians do.

In the next place the Opponent progresseth to interest properly so called: Mr. Jelinger: *Interest is money taken for the payment of money due to a day delayed or neglected: Reply.* It seemeth then for money delayed beyond the day of payment I may take interest, (whether the forfeiture of double bond he tells not) but for money lent, this side that day I may not take any thing, *salva conscientia.*

This is such discourse or reasoning as I understand not: I am sure such niceties have little foundation in Scripture, which he pleadeth to be his guide, when in any thing it seemeth to serve his turn; and here he brings in *Rivet*, as if he were on his side.

For Answer whereunto I say.

Num. 53. 1. That I do not tell whether a man may take the forfeiture of a double Bond to secure the Principal.

1. Because I together with many others and even such as are of his own side, do hold that in some cases I must be contented to lose the very Principal.

2. Because a man must be ruled in such a case by Judges and Arbitrators, as it has been formerly declared out of *Exod.* 21.22. And my second Answer is for the lawfulness of taking interest or damage after the not paying of money lent for a certain time nominated, that, tho such a thing is a discourse or reasoning which he understands not, how after the day of payment delayed, one may take interest, and this side the day he may not take any thing, yet others that understand * the Scriptures, which are for damage applicable to such delayes, as it has been proved, do understand such reasoning well enough, and therefore have left their sense wherein they harmo-

---

* Exod. 21. 22. *By which* Durham *who yet seemeth to be for some Usury) proveth damage also as my self in his treat upon his Command.*

ize with me, as I shall shew it, before I have done with my nswer.

As for *Rivet* by him quoted, I shall not concern my self to nswer what he saith, because he hath to do with *Tollet*, not ne.

He goes on and saith,

Ship loan, saith Mr. Jelinger, *is distinguished from Usury, for s much as that is upon adventuring upon a Ship Principal and ll, so as that if the Ship be lost all is lost.*

Reply, Seeing he sends us to Scripture for a proof of the awfulness of lending to the Rich for gain, let him prove from he same expresly, the lawfulness of his Ship loan, *&c.*

Whereunto I answer,

1. There is no express Scripture for Annuities neither, which yet are held lawful, because Annuities are new things, nd so adventuring is likewise, unless we will suppose that here were Adventurers, which adventured in *Solomons* Ships nd the Kings of *Tyrus*, which sailed to *Tarsis* for Gold, and hat therefore no express Scripture is to be expected.

2. That it is sufficient for us to know, that adventuring is ot interdicted, because men take such great gain, not for heir loan, but for their * hazard, which is so exceeding reat, and makes the gain of it so uncertain, whereas lending pon usury is certain,

3. That those which call the Gain of adventuring mony *Fœnus Nauticum*, Nautical Fenory, call it so not properly but quivocally, as a dead man, a man, and not Usury neither, but Fenory, because there is a difference betwixt Usury and Fenory, as some say, Fenory being a more milder name than Usury, as † *Pellican* would have it to be, whereof more hereof in liberal Usury, by some so called.

4. And whereas the Opponent mentioneth *Grotius* again, shall very little regard what he saith, because he is Heterodox, and therefore not much to be credited, as failing in other great points, and being deceived. Nor do his words much contradict that adventuring which I am for, as being a mixt contract, as himself calls it, mixt I say, of Parnership, which by all is held lawful, and of laying out so much money for so much gain, upon the safe return of such Ship having made a good and gainful Voyage, and not otherwise. So *Rivet* my ancient Friend differs but little in this;

* *Unde condictio certi pro eo datur*, Doctor *Freigerius* p. 333.
† *Pellic. in Comment. in Prov.* 28.

For, 1. He tels us, having spoken of trafficking between Party, and Party (under which cometh negotiating by Sea, in ships, and upon ships) that such a Contract is lawful so counted on both sides.

2. He saith, when such gain comes, something is *Given*; mark, given, (not as a mercenary Usury) but as a recompence to him that laid out the same, I add, upon a Ship For that is here in Question.

Lastly, I add, that I am not alone for this adventuring but many worthy Writers, besides me, are for the same als and give it their approbation; and

1. The * Doctors of the civil Law, who thus favour ably define it, that it is the gain of a Creditor, which h has for his mony credited to a Sailor for the danger of h mony which he takes upon himself; mark, for the dange even as I said even now for his hazard; where let it b noted withall, that the Civil-law stints this gain for h zard, which is most just, that it should be so cautioned.

2. Let me add blessed † *Bolton*, speaking of *twenty in t hundred by Sea*; There is great difference in the Merchan Negotiation, there is hazard, *&c.* Then speaking of the U surer, he saith, doth he bear any hazard? it is no part his meaning?

Where by the by, I must needs answer this Objectio why then is Usury called *sors* in Latin, that is, chance.

I answer, no otherwise then κατ' ἀντίφρασιν, that when men speaking one thing will understand the contrar as a Wood is called *lucus a non lucendo*, because it giveth n light, ; so Usury *sors*, or chance, *a non sortiendo*, because h hazards not]

3. And lastly Bishop || *Downam* (who is fullest) on more, because my Antagonist doth so vehemently urge r to prove ship-loane to be lawful by positive Scripture, whi is silent in it, because there was not in old time so mu traffick by Sea as now there is, and so consequently such a venturing upon ships, as far as we can perceive, unless v will guess it, as I said already, by *Solomon*'s and *Hiram*'s Navig tion: So that such a worthy, learned and pious man's Opi on, will afford as much light, and satisfaction in this case of a

---

* Dr. *Vult. in sua jurispr.* l. 1. C. 34 *de Naut. fen.* 2 D. 2. 4. C. 33. *Justin Const. sub. Tit.* 6. † Bolton Co *Usury* p. 43. *See Doctor* Fenton *also* p. 95. || *B.* Dow am. *upon* Psal. 15. 5.

venturi

venturing and maritime encrease. His words are these Maritime fenory *is a gain or allowance made for mony which is transported beyond the Seas, at the peril or hazard of the Creditor, contrary to the contract either of gainful Usury, or free Loan, and seemeth to draw near to partnership; after which words he sets down the manner of it; and brings in that most Godly and learned Lawyer* Hottoman, *approving and clearing it, by his distasting of* Gregories *words concerning it, and affirming, that where is hazard, there may be gain required at the due prize thereof: and then concludeth thus, and therefore adventuring Usury may be allowed*

I add, that I wish such Adventurers to be very cautious, that adventuring their money, they do not adventure and loose their darling Souls by excessive gain exacted, especially if a Voyage prove unprosperous, and by meerly pretended hazards.

Num. 55. *From Nautical Fenory he passes to liberal encrease.*

Mr. Jelinger, *Usury is different from liberal Encrease, in that it cometh unlooked for, and not the other*

Reply. What he quotes afterwards out of *Polanus* for another purpose, seems to thwart what he saith of the lawfulness of a gratuity, *mutatio debet esse gratuita absque lucri alicujus captatione.* Mr. *Jelinger* is forced to peece this sentence of *Polanus* with his own Interpretation, but to me it seems to condemn all talking of gratuities, and so makes work for ingratitude, which is no small piece of inhumanity, unless *Polanus* mean both one and the other with respect had to the poor.

For answer whereunto, I say,

1. That this Opponent by his, *it seems*, invalidates what he so inconsiderably asserts.

2. Let the Reader peruse *Polanus*, and then judge, whether it be for my purpose or no what he saith; his words are these: * *Usura lucratoria est furtum quod committitur cum quis lucrum accipit solius mutationis causa.* Lucratory or gainful Usury is Theft, when any receives gain only in lieu of lending; mark, only in lieu of lending; not denying, that something may be taken as given out of gratefulness; so that his words, without exaction and captation of gain or

* Polan. Syntagm. *Where, because* Polanus *is for me, let it be considered what a friend I have in him, he being stiled* Europ's *Ornament, and most eximious pattern of Holiness in* Clerks *lives.*

acceptation of a gift do not thwart what I say, because he explains himself, when he saith, that Vsury is gain taken *only in lieu of lending*, whereby room is left, and liberty given for taking of a free, unexacted, uncapitulated, unexpected gift, given as a gratuity due *ex officio gratitudinis*, by vertue of gratitude, which this Opponent need not press so much, as requisite out of *Cicero* and *Hesiodus*. For I together with my Brethren am for thankfulness, as much as he is, or any other can be.

2. As for his question about the poor, whether a rich Jew might take a gratuity of a poor Brother: I wonder why he will put forth such a question, when all without his questioning will grant, that the Rich should rather give to, then take from a poor Brother, both under the Law and Gospel.

3. To his assertion, that what is lawful for the Borrower to give, no doubt must be lawful for the lender to receive and then he may lawfully take encrease. For this gratuity is no other. *I answer* thus, that this is a fallacy of consequence: for it is as if a man should say, that it is lawful fo a Thief to take a mans purse, because as Divines say, it i lawful for a man to give to a Thief his purse to save his life for which he is thankful too, because he saves his life, so tha some have offered to give their purse and all that they hav to Theives to save their lives; I have done so my self, whe in the German Wars, I was beset by the Enemies Horse which threatned to pistol me in a Wood.

Where let it be remembred what *Polanus* said but now that Usury is Theft, when any receives gain only in lieu o lending, which mainly thwarts my Adversaries, saying tha the Lender may receive increase for his lending, for this gra tuity is no other.

Numb. 56. 4. As for his quoting of *Perkins*, that which th Debtor may give, having himself an honest gain besides, an no man any wayes endamaged, the Creditor may lawfully re ceive.

To that I answer,

1. That his words following shew his meaning, *viz.* Tha its convenient, that he that is benefitted by anothers mon should shew all possible thankfulness to him by whom he enriched, which I say likewise, yea farther, that the Lende may take what so cometh, I mean cometh unexpectedly.

2. I add that holy *Perkins* is so far from being against me as that in his Writing upon Christs Sermon upon the Mour he doth evidently declare to the World, that he is onl for recompencing and liberal Vsury, as that holy man M

* Bolt

* *Bolton* observes it also, who likewise, together with others, asserts the same thing, that liberal increase is lawful, saying,

Liberal Usury is only a gratuity, or free gift, which the Borrower finding himself much benefited by the Lenders courtesie, doth of his own accord, in testimony of his thankfulness, freely give to the Lender, though neither intended when he lent, nor expected any gain, much less covenanted for it.

And then saith further,

But in this case, although the Lender receive some allowance above the principal, yet he commits not Usury, because neither the contract, which he made, was lending for gain, neither is the over-plus, which he receiveth gain for, either covenanted or intended, or required for loan, but a gratuity or thankful courtesie, which may with a good Conscience be given and received from an able and willing giver.

With this worthy man will I joyn two more. And

1. *Bishop Downam*, who calls it a voluntary increase and free gift and gratuity, or reward, which the Borrower having gained by the money borrowed, voluntarily, and freely gives to the Lender in testimony of his thankfulness.

2. I will quote the words of the Author of that excellent Book called a brief Treatise of Usury.

Not only the taking of any thing above the principal, but also the looking for it doth make him guilty before God, who hopes or lookes for it by reason of the loan: but it is otherwise, if any man give or offer any thing not in respect of the loan, but to shew himself mindful of a good turn received. For that which is so offered may be lawfully taken without any Usury committed; so that there be no fraud used therein, but that the intent and conscience of the Receiver be upright, and free in that behalf, which last words cause me to subjoyn

3. Famous Doctor * *Chemnitius*, who writes thus, even just like Mr. *Perkins*, *If the Debtor have gained much by his borrowed money, or escaped a great loss, he is certainly obliged by the office of thankfulness, and mutual respect of Charity to antidotes, and retributions; for its truely said in the office of charity, that in the first place, we are bound to those of whom we acknowledge to have received a benefit. Nor doth the creditor sin if he take a gratuity. For the offices of charity and Usury differ one from another (just as I say also) but so by most slight occasions and pretexts are sought for Usury: For if either a compact or intention preceeds, so that the creditor would not have lent his mo-*

* Bolton *p.* 5, 4. † Downam *upon* Psal. 15. 5. || *Dr.* Chem. loc. com. de paup. *p.* 5. 8.

ney

ney, if he should not receive something above the principal, its certainly Usury, whatsoever name you call it by.

But here the Opponent oblatrates and fain would set my old friend *Rivet* and me by the ears, whose words by him quoted, tho they be somewhat large, yet are soon to be answered.

For 1. He brings *Syracides an Apochryphal* Author for his assistant, which invalidates and enfeebles altogether what he saith, and 2. Comes in with his *videtur, it seemeth*, which weakens his assertion also, as the Reader will see it presently, if he weigh in an even balance what *Rivet* brings for his proof, and what Anti-usurarians alledge for themselves, having the Canonical Scriptures on their side, when the defendants of Usury, as blessed *Bolton* tells them, cannot bring one Scripture rightly understood to make for them; if learned *Rivet* could have brought one, he would not have cited an Apochryphal.

3. I can name a greater man then *Rivet* is, who militates for me, *viz. great Beza*, whose words I will commit with *Rivets*, who insists on publick authority moderately prefixing a recompensation for which the Creditor may stipulate or come to a compact with the debtor, which *Beza* answers thus, as I said once already.

That Christian charity forbids to lend upon Usury, which notwithstanding, because many Magistrates do see, that in respect of traffick, and dealings among men they cannot simply forbid Usury. Therefore (which is the only thing which remains for them to do) they stint Usury; but may a man therefore with a good Conscience, LEND UPON USURY? *No* SURELY: thus this great and renowned author. Now whom shall a man believe? The Senior or Junior Author? The Greater or the Lesser? The more renowned or the less renowned? One that hath maintained a publick dispute against the Church of *Rome* before a great King and Queen, and the Peers and People of *France* in that great City of *Paris*, or him that hath not?

As for me I do and shall ever honour my great and old friend *Rivet*, who has been pleased to Write his great name and pious motto for me in my book of friends among other great and learned persons (which then were the luminaries of *Europe*) for a perpetual testimony of his favour and respect which he had for me, but yet I must needs prefer famous *Beza* before him, having lived in both † Universities, where both did flourish: because I have heard such extroardinary Enco-

* *See* Downam, *p.* 306. † Leyden *and* Geneva.

mium;

miums of that learned man *Beza* in the latter of these two Universities *Leyden* and *Genevah* I mean, which *Brightman calleth Harmageddon*, that is a Mountain of delight, according to *Rev*. 17.

Num. 57. Pardon me courteous Reader, that I do so expatiate, I cannot rule my self, when I come to speak of either of the now mentioned places, or persons, or both.

Now having said so much to answer great *Rivet*, my great friend, I am the less solicitous to answer so obscure an Antagonist as mine is; for what he saith deserveth no other answer then this, that whereas he saith, that the Creditor is bound not to hope or expect some recompence for his money lent, and by which he hath gained, is as much as to say, that the creditor is bound to hope or expect that the debtor will not prove an honest man, or do that which by the rules of gratitude he is obliged unto: Christ himself freeth me from so great an absurdity by his own words saying, *lend, hoping for* NOTHING *AGAIN*, or, FROM THENCE, and so do all these holy men whom I have cited, affirming, that in lending we must neither hope nor expect nor intend any gain by our lending, and that if we do, it is most certainly Usury, by what name soever men may call it (to use the very self same words of learned Dr. *Chemnitius*, which I formerly quoted.) But let us see what the Ch. saith farther,

Num.58. Mr. Jelinger, *Usury is differenced from letting and setting, because such things are (properly) not lent as Usury money is, but hired or put out to be occupied, as ground.* And why may you not as properly say such money put out is hired, or put out to be occupied. He knoweth what is commonly said in this case, and never solidly answered, &c.

Not solidly answered? who will say it, but one, who has not read the hundred part of what has been solidly written concerning this thing. As for my part, I shall answer him that saith so, presently and thus briefly. 1. That we may not properly say of money lent to Usury that is hired, because hiring and so setting and letting is lawful as being no where in Gods word prohibited, and condemned, but rather approved and by Gods Saints used, as it is to be seen, *Act*. 28.30. how *Paul* hired a house.

But lending and putting out money to Usury is unlawful interdicted and condemned by the law of God and man.

1. *By the law of God*, viz. *Deut*. 23. 19. *Exod*. 22. 25. *Luk*. 25. 35, 36. *Neh*. 5. 10. *Psal*. 15. 5. *Ezeck*. 18. 12, 13. and *ch*. 22. 12. *Luke* 6. 35. And many more, which I shall bring to condemn Usury, where let it be noted, what blessed

* *Bolton* quoting such places, saith to his adversaries now a-'gainst these many places condemning Usury, bring you so 'much as one to allow it: you are not able to bring one 'rightly understood: thus he, which words I also say to 'mine.

2. *By the † law of man*: where, tho I could be prolix to my hearts contentent, yet I will cite but one Act, which I did not quote yet, *viz. Queen † Elizabeth* which (tho some abuse it as making for Usury, because of ten in the 100, yet in truth it doth not so much as permit it, much less allow it) I say. 1. It doth not permit it, because it is an Act against Usury, and only restrains it.

2. *Much less allow it, calling it a sin, yea, and a detestable sin, and adding that all Usury is forbidden by the law of God.*

2. *I answer to his addition*, suppose a man hires a field worth 6 *l.* what matter is it whether he pay six pounds for the field, or for the money lent him, or, where is the oppression in the one more than in the other, or am I bound to lend him my money gratis, when I may my self buy the field field therewith, and so let it out to hire? *to this I answer* thus,

1. It is a matter, whether I pay six pound for the field, or for the money lent; because the one is for lending, Usury I mean, which excludes men out of heaven, to use the very words of Bishop *Sanders*, according to *Psal.* 15. 5. and which hath been from time to time counted theft, yea worse then other theft, as saith that other great and famous B. *Downam*, whereas they that bestow their money in a field to buy it, and then received rent for it, were never counted theeves, nor can be, because they do the thing that lawful is, and commended too in the word of God, as the vertuous woman in the Proverbs will serve for the proof of it, *for is she not commended for seeing a field and buying it, Prov.* 31. 16. *but where will you find any man or woman in all the Bible* commended for Usury, which is oppression, *Ezek.* 22. 12. *There is the * oppression, and extortion enquired after by the Ch. saying, where*

---

* *Not only the law of God but also Lawgivers and Philosophers have utterly condemned Usury.* Bodin de Rep. l. 5. c. 2. * *Bolt. in his Discourse.* * Anno 13. Elizab. c. 8. * *Bishop* Sanders on Rom. 13. 8, 9. * *Bishop* Downam on Psal. 15. 5. * *Because he has greedily gained, as Usurers use to do.* Ibidem.

is

is the oppression? so Nehem. 5. 7. *you exact Usury. He tells us farther, am I bound to lend him my money freely when I my self may buy the field therewith and so put it to hire? whereto I answer also thus.* O yes, the Champion must lend his money gratis freely: for so Christ will have it, as some render his words *Luk.* 6. 35. *lend freely.*

And because he goeth a step farther, telling us, that he might himself buy the field and put it out to hire, I ask him, and why will not you? seeing it is in your power to do so, and to keep your money as *Peter* said to *Ananias*, and bestow it your self, which is lawful? must we needs run and adventure upon things which are unlawful and prohibited, when we may safely employ our money by buying and purchasing, as the virtuous woman did? but I know where it sticks, when the Usurer lends his money he is sure of six in the 100. if he buy a field or living, lives may die, and then he is a looser, which he will not be if he buy Land that will not yield him six in the 100. he knoweth, for it is valued at five in the 100. and charges and taxes must be undergon, so that I have heard wise men say, that they can hardly make four at the 100. clear, which causeth the Usurer to put out his money to Usury rather, because then six in the 100. flows in without labour, without taxes, without charges, without repairs, and by this I suppose I have hit the Usurers right vein, which must be hit, if he shall be let blood duly and successively for the saving of his life and soul that he may not die as he is menaced, *Ezek* 18. 12, 13.

But it should seem he has some Physicians about him, which speak him fair and put him in some good hopes, that without this blood letting he may live, and therefore he tells me, *take reason from men that understand it.*

And so brings against me again *Rivet*, and *Windelin.*

Whereunto I answer. And so let him take reason from men that understand it, as well as his men do, and it may be a little better.

For, 1. *Rivet* cometh in again with his *non videtur, it seemeth not to be so*: but not with Scripture, which is sure: and saith positively *thou shalt not lend to thy brother upon Usury* (whether it be to buy a farm or field by the contract of Emphytensis, or any other thing to receive for it so much money or Corn yearly) *Deut.* 23. 19. where note, that this word Emphytensis makes for me not a little, for it is for ever as the Doctors in the Civil Laws tells us, so as that a certain rent must be forever paid for it, whereas things rise and fall, and changes happen and may happen to the great detriment and loss

loss of the occupier, which notwithstanding the lender or Usurer which lendeth the money, which buyeth this field, or living, by the contract of * *Emphytensis* must and will be paid whether he grow backhanded or no his six in the 100. which they count moderate Usury and profit.

2. *As for* Windelin, *who also is of the same mind, that it is* * *all one to buy a farm for an* 100 * Rixdollars, *or to lend so much to another, and to receive so much yearly for it, I wonder how he can be so confident as to assert such a thing*: Scripture he has not on his side, for that is against it, and so is reason: for what reason is there for it that the Usurer, who is loth to adventure his 100 *Rixdollars* by buying a farm for lives, which may die, or land, wherein he may be deceived, because of morgages or other conveiances, will lend those 100 *Rixdollars* to another, who must adventure upon all hazards to pay him six in the 100. which is the general and usual pension by the borrower to be paid, whether he win or loose; *is this* Windelins *perinde est?*

Num. 59. 2. Now take reason from men that understand it, *And*, 1. *From Lawyers.* 2. *Divines.*

1. *Lawyers*, and

1. *From* Dr. *Vulteius*, who

1. Maketh lending a * free contract, and setting and letting mercenary: See the † Margin

2. * Defineth location, and conduction, that is setting and letting and hiring thus, that it is a contract of consent, concerning a certain thing to be done, or used for a certain hire, which sheweth what a great difference this great *Civilian* puts between lending, which must be free, and location and conduction which is and may be mercenary.

2. From Dr. *Frigius*, who defines lending to be a contract, whereby a thing which is mine becomes thine, so as that the same thing, which consists in number weight and measure is

---

* *Emphytensis est contractus quo predium perpetuo fruendum alicui traditur, ut quam diu Domino pensionem, seu redituum canonem pro eo præstat, tamdiu neque hæredi ejus auferre id liceat.* Doctor Frigius *Rudim. Instit. p.* 335. * Which is 4 *s.* 6. *d.* * Dr. Vulteius *De Contr. Adjunctis l.* 1. *c.* 34. † *Contractuum quidam sunt gratuiti, quidam mercenarii: Gratuiti sunt, mutuum, Commodatum, promutuum: Cæteri mercenarii, & in his alii magis alii minus, magis ut locatio, conductio, minus reliqui.* * *Idem c.* 35. * Doctor Frigius, *p.* 335. * Bishop Downam *upon* Psal. 15.

not

not to be rendred: but that which is of the ſame nature, and quality, whereas in location and conduction, that is, in ſetting and letting, and giving, the ſame thing is rendred, as for example, the ſame horſe, houſe, field.

2. He alſo maketh ſetting and letting mercenary, which lending is not, ſo that his definition of location is this, it is an obligation of conſent for a certain thing to be done or uſed for hire.

2. *From four Divines.*

And, 2. *Biſhop* Downam.

Uſury is diſtinguiſhed from lawful location, or letting to hire, which is the rather to be obſerved, becauſe ſome imagine, that money and other things, which are lent upon Uſury, may as well be let as other things; and what ſay you to this Champion? is not this your opinion? but hear what this great man ſaith, who underſtands reaſon as well as you, or your two Authors, but he goeth farther this my great Author, as thus :

1. They differ ſaith he in the Subjects, Uſury is in thoſe things which are ſpent in the uſe, and conſiſt in quantity, ſtanding in number, weight, and meaſure.

Location is in ſuch things as are not ſpent in the uſe, neither ſtand in number, weight, and meaſure.

2. The ſubject of Uſury are ſuch things as have no fruitful uſe in themſelves, but the gain raiſed by it is to be imputed to the induſtry and skill of the employer.

The ſubjects of location have a fruitful uſe in themſelves naturally.

3. The uſe of things lent upon Uſury cannot be ſevered from the property and dominion.

In location the fruitful uſe may be ſevered and valued as land, houſes, &c.

4. In Uſury the borrower is bound not to reſtore the ſum but ſo much in quantity, or full value in the ſame kind without diminution or impair.

In location he that takes a thing to uſe is bound to reſtore the ſame particular, which for the moſt part is impaired and made worſe.

* Biſhop *Downam* upon *Pſal.* 15.

5. In mutuation the hazard wholly appertaineth to the borrower. For the very contract of mutuation includeth in it an obligation, binding the borrower that he shall restore the full value thereof at the day appointed, &c.

In location the thing if it shall miscarry without the fault of the hirer, belongeth to the letter and not to the hirer, because it came for his hire, *Exod.* 22. 14.

Thus by Scripture he proveth it, whereas my Adversary hath no Scripture on his side.

2. *From blessed* Bolton,

Whose words I shall set down but in part, because Bishop *Downam* hath some of the same things, with him.

The 1. *Difference between Usury and setting and letting* (saith he, *is this.* The land hath a fruitful use in it self answerable to rent: both without mans help, as in Meadows, Pastures, Woods, Mines, &c. as also in arable grounds, where the rent is proportioned, according to the fruitfulness thereof. But money being spent in the use thereof, the gain that is raised thereby is not the * fruit of the money, but of his skill and industry that employes it, and therefore must needs be uncertain. So thou demandest thy gains out of the fruit of his pains and industry, not out of the fruit of the money, &c. let the Reader himself read the rest.

2. They often instance in the letting of an house, saying, why may not a man as well take ten in a 100. for a year, as well as 10 *l.* for an house in some great City, which cost him an 100. *I answer*, the use of the house is habitation; and tho it be kept tenantable, yet it groweth worse, and towards ruine in the more substantial materials. But in money its otherwise, &c. see the rest in his own book, *p.* 27.

3 A thing that is hired if it perish without the default of the hirer it perishes to the owner. 1. Because he is the owner, 2. Because it went for the hire according to the equity of Gods law, *Exod.* 22. 15. thus he also proveth what he saith by Scripture, which the opponents two Authors do not. After all this he concludes thus.

But if there were nothing else its more then sufficient, that letting land to Tenants is not disallowed by Gods word, or any other learning in any time or Age. But lending for use is condemned by Gods book, and all other learning, and in all Ages, thus holy Bolton.

The 3. is holy * Greenham *who saith, Recompence is to to be made, where the thing is the worse for using (as in Location) But mony is not the worse for lending, therefore nothing is to be taken for lending of it.* † *Geminianus* also saith the same with these, in his *Summe fol.* 225. Now let the Reader judge and choose whom he will follow, the Ch. two Authors, or these whereof two give their opinion for law, and two being great and godly Divines, who together with the two commodating Legists understood reason as well as the Opponents two Authors; thus overmatched both by number and strength of reason, as their expressions shew it.

Num. 60. I should have differenced it also from commodating and society: But there is yet time for me to do it. And therefore I will begin with the first of these *viz. Commodating, which is as* || *Civilians define it, a contract whereby he to whom a thing is freely granted to be used, is bound to return the self same thing, which is not Usury:* as has been already ostended and shewn.

And its * *twofold.*

1. *Properly so called*, whereby a thing is given for a certain use and end, to be used, after which end it is to be returned and not before.

2. *Precarium* or *precarie is*, which is given to a man to be returned whensoever the Commodator pleaseth.

And the difference between the two kinds of lending is, that when I lend such a thing as is not spent ordinarily with the first use, the thing lent remaining still my own, as a house, or horse, it is called commodation, but when it is spent as Corn, and Wine, and Mony, it is alienated, and such a contract is called mutuation, whereby the property of the thing lent passeth from one to another, even to him that borroweth it, and good reason why. For all such things are so principally made of God for one certain use (as bread to be eaten, wine to be drunken) so as that the use differs not from the thing it self; because they cannot dure any longer when they are once used, but streight are consumed, and become either another thing, or at least another mans goods: Inconsideration whereof he that lendeth me such things, by the lending looseth the very propriety of them; for else I should spend another mans goods to his

---

* Greenham *alleadged by B.* Bolton p. 27. † Geminianus *l.* 8. 1. 78. || § *D.* 13. *C.* 23. *P.* 2. *Sent.* 4.
* *Doctor* Vult. jurispr. *l.* 1. *c.* 33.

injury;

injury; which is both against reason, and also against his will and intent: For as he would have me take the commodity of his Goods by using them: So would he not hinder himself therewithal. But if I should borrow a bushel of Wheat of another mans, and yet the same bushel of Wheat should still be his, I should either not use the Wheat at all in making bread thereof, or occupy it otherwise (and then it doth me no service) or else I should spend it being his, and thereby he should sustain farther loss than himself would agree to: For if I do spend another mans Goods by his consent, I am answerable unto him for them, no more than I should answer him his Oyle again, who should bid me throw it in the fire.

Num. 61. 2 *I come to Society, which* * Civilians *define thus. That it is a contract of consent concerning the having it by some in common*

And it is about either Things and Goods, or Doings.

1. *Things* by one or all Partners to be looked after, and that both in gain and loss.

And it lieth wholly in Negotiation, saith the Civil Law: And is two fold, First all Goods, and so is called general, or secondly some, and so is special.

2. *Doings in society, are pains, and the industey of partners.*

They have another distinction also, saying, that there is 1. *an accidental* 2. *conventional.*

But I desire to shew, as speedily as I may, how Usury and Society do differ.

In the Contract of partnership, as a learned † Author writeth of it, a man, having perhaps no skill in Merchandize, commits a stock of mony to another, being a Merchant or Tradesman (some name a Tucker) to the end, that he may employ the same in some lawful traffick, and covenants with him not only to be partner with him in a proportionable part of his gain, if it please God to make him a gainer, but also to pertake with him in the loss which without his default he shall sustain. And here, altho there be expectation of gain, yet there is no Usury: For in partnership the property of the mony is not transferred unto him that receiveth it, but remaineth in him which did deliver it, and at his hazard and peril it is employed; and therefore in partnership there is not so as much loane, and

---

* *Institut. de Societ.* l. 3. 26. 17. D. 2. 4. C. 37.
† *B.* Downam *upon* Psal. 15. 5.

much

much less Usury: For, as † *Molinæus* averreth it in partnership the subject of Usury ceaseth, *viz.* loan, for in loan the property is transferred to the Borrower, and with the property and hazard; so that if the Principal miscarry, it miscarrieth to the Borrower: It is safe to the Lender by the very contract of mutuation or lending, wherein the Borrower secureth the Lender by such security as the Lender thinketh sufficient, whether it be his Word, Bill, or Bond, or Pawn or Surety for the repayment of the Principal. In this contract of partnership he that delivereth his mony to the other, doth not covenant absolutely for the restitution of his principal, much less for gain; but conditionally, according to the event or success of the Negotiation, covenanting as well to be partaker of the loss as of the gain; but the contract of the free lending binds the Borrower by an absolute covenant to restore the principal; and the contract of Usury binds the Borrower by an absolute covenant not only to repay the principal, but also to yeeld the overplus covenanted for.

So that whether there be a covenant or intent of gain by loan, whether it be in the first act of lending, or afterwards in forbearing, it is USURY, saith that renowned Bishop, and contrarywise where the is neither a covenant, nor intent of gain in lending, or forbearing, there is no Usury; tho there be overplus or encrease received over and besides the Principal.

And this absolute Covenant (saith that renowned B.) is not an abuse besides the nature of this contract, as some have imagined, but as the absolute covenant of the restitution of the principal is included in the contract of mutuation, so the absolute covenant not only of repaying the principal, but also of paying Usury is included in the contract of actual, or, as they call it formal Usury: For if there be a covenant only in *eventum lucri*, to gain, if he gain, or have expectation of gain for loan, without any further covenant, but for the restitution of the principal, then is the former not formal Usury, tho it be mental, and actual in part, and the latter is but mental Usury and not then neither; if as on the one side there is a covenant of partaking gain, if there be gain; so on the other side, if there be a covenant of partaking loss, or as there is expectation of gain if the Borrower gain, so there be an unfeigned bearing part of the loss which the

* *In contractu Societatis cessat subjectum Usur.* & Molin.

Bor-

Borrower without his default ſhall ſuſtain. For then the former is the contract of partnerſhip, and the latter in reſpect of the outward act is the contract of lending, but in regard of the purpoſe of the heart,intending gain,where there is gain,and purpoſing to bear part of the loſs where there is loſs it is partnerſhip.

Thus much concerning the difference, which is between Uſury and Partnerſhip.

Num 62. In the next place the Ch. examineth Uſurie's age.

Mr. Jelinger 5. *How old is Uſury? What generation and kindred hath it? For its Father, quoteth he, it hath the Divel, whoſe work it is, being Murder. Reply.* Whether he that takes any thing above the principal from a perſon ſufficient be a Murderer, will admit an uſe of Addubitation, that is, none at all. *Whereunto I anſwer.*

1. That, whereas here he jeereth me for mentioning * ſometime ſuch an uſe of *Addubitation*, I would have him know, that I have this Addubitation matter from that famous and ſerious man P. RAMUS, who died in the *Pariſian* Maſſacre a glorious Martyr, and therefore is infinitely to be preferred before a Jeerer at godlineſs.

2. That I ſhall ſend him to renowned *Calvin* for an anſwer, ſaying upon 15. *Pſal.* 5. verſe, concerning Uſury which in *Ezeck.* 18. 12, 13. called Tarbit, encreaſe, that *Cato* did not without cauſe place committing of Uſury very neer in the ſame degree with Murther. Now why and wherefore they both, *Cato* and *Calvin* do thus make Uſury Murther, they will anſwer him at that great day, when both muſt be reſponſible for this name, which they have given to Uſury, animating me thereby to call it ſo too.

But the Devil was a metaphorical Uſurer from the beginning to Adam *and* Eve, *ſaith Mr.* Jelinger. Reply. *Strange arguing! My anſwer is, as ſtrange as he makes it,* † *better and abler men than he uſe it*, who alſo if they were now alive would ſtop his mouth, which now he opens againſt them and it: As for me it is enough to me that I have ‖ two ſuch ſeconds on my ſide as *Ambroſe* and *Auſtin* (which names he

---

* *In my ſeverally Printed Books.* † *With whom I could if I would joyn* HUGO *who attributeth to the* Devil *two Daughters, Avarice and Luxury beſides Uſury; in Gloſs in Teſtivet.* ‖ *But the two Authors by me cited may ſuffice.*

con-

conceals) who by all learned men will be preferred and beleived before him, and all his.

And I hope that these holy Fathers may very well make the Devil a metaphorical Usurer, as the defendants of Usury make that * metaphorical Usury in *Matt*. 25. Usury properly so called, quite contrary to Christs meaning, who called the well imploying of gifts and parts, and the spiritual gain gotten thereby *Usury*, as being like it. Where let the Reader give me leave by the by, to mention what a famous † Preacher in Print doth say concerning the metaphorical Usury *viz*. Because this text (*Thou ought to have put out my mony to the Exchangers, otherwise Table-mates, Campsores or Usurers, as some render the word, and then at my coming I should have received mine own with* USURY) has been urged by some to prove the lawfulness of Usury, aud that I have so opportunely met with this sin, so frequently practiced, so seldom preacht against; nay some that should tell *Juda* of his faults, and *Israel* of his transgession, *Esa*. 5. 8. 1. are such as the Prophet speaketh of, where the Prophet is very bitter against men looking after their own wages, every one for his own advantage, and for his own purpose, are practisers thereof themselves, so I shall not go far beyond the limits of the text, if I a little prosecute this sin. Thus learned Mr. *Turner* with whom my opponent must bear, if he hit him for one.

As for his saying, *Scriptura symbolica non est argumentum*, we that are against Usury do not deny it, but use it as well as he, in the interpreting of *Matt*. 25. 27. as even now it was shewn, so that he might have forborn to bring in || Christ as a metaphorical Usurer; only let, me add that the Arabick renders that expression with Usury *cum lucro suo with its gain, not Usury*,

As for the Mother and Sisters and Daughters, he counts it but froth of uncharitableness, and not worth spending time and Paper in, &c. but I would have him know that it is such froth (if I must needs call it as he calls it) as has been made use of by better men then himself, viz. *R. Turner* a late *Writer* and * St. *Basil*, an ancient one, who maketh

---

* *The Usury here in the text is taken metaphorically, as* Aquinas *observes, for spiritual thriftiness and the encrease of spiritual gifts and graces* 2. 2. q. 78. a. 1. † τραπεζίταις.

|| *Mr.* Turner *upon Matt.* 25. 27.

Τόκων πατέρας, the only * Fathers of Usury, *St.* Augustine *and* Ambrose *the devil, and* BORROWERS the only * MOTHERS, to bring forth this unnatural brood of Vipers, which eat through the entrals of their Mother, for so doth the borrower bring forth Usury to the Usurer, to the destruction of himself and family, saith my last Author.

Let my Adversary now disprove and check this great and holy Father, if he think it to be his best way, for using such a frothy comparison, and so others; to me it is enough, that I have such a Kingly father on my side, in this thing to free me from frothiness: and whether it be for my purpose, what I say, let these same holy men be consulted with, who agree with me in Usuries definition. *But he mislikes Usuries Sisters also,* Mrs. GREEDY *especially:* For so he adds, only a word to what he saith concerning Greedy, telling her Sister Usury still, we must not let our money lie idle.

Reply. I wonder how he finds Greediness in the inquiry it self, wherein there may be so much charitableness unto others, &c.

Whereunto I answer, 1. *That I find this greediness in Gods own word:* Ezek. 22. 21. *Thou hast taken Usury, and encrease, and hast greedily gained,* &c. see the place.

And I find it in those Authors, who make the Usurer a greedy Dog, as * *Basil,* yea, worse an old Dog, as Mr. *Trap.*

Num. 63. 2. And whereas he tells so much of the good, which the Usurer doth by his lending to such as redeem estates and purchase and buying for their families seasonably, &c. I will cite such learned and famous Authors, as will tell him the quite contrary, &c.

1. Plutarch *who compareth Usurers to Vultures, and Ravens, who pick out the guts of a mans belly.*

2. Cœlius Secundus, *who calls Usury a deadly and contagious Ague.*

---

* Powel *maketh the devil the chief, and principal cause of Usury.* * *As* Wit. *in his Commonwealth,* p. 291: *make covetousness Usuries Mother.* * *Accounting it doubtless but froth, tho other Writers as well as my self, and famous* Smith *by name, who saith, that bribery and simony are her Sisters goodly Sisters indeed.* Smith *in his.* 1. *Serm.* p. 73. * Basil *in* Ps. 15. * Mr. Trap *in* Prov. 28. * *Plut.* l. de non fœnerando. * *Cælius* secundum lect. Antiq. l. 12. c. 20.

3 B. Jewel

3. B. Jewel *who,* * *defines Usury as has been declared, tells us that Usury undoeth housholds, draweth dry hundreds, yea, thousands of people, and is the utter destruction of infinite families.*

Thus *B. Jewel*; now let the Ch. shake his boasts of the great good, which Usurers do, some good they may do sometimes, but that is not their chief aim, but their own gain, and nriching of themselves, whether the borrower win or loose, which caused *Leo the Great to say, what event soever betide the borrower, gain he or gain he not, the course of lending upon Usury is, EVIL and UNGODLY.*

3. And seeing the Champion doth ask me, whether I let my money lie idle by me, or whether I do well in so doing, &c.

I answer, that as my case stands now, I cannot have money lie idle by me, livings being brought so low by these dead times, but when I had any, I bestowed it in means, which now must maintain me and mine, and which is lawful. But, I perceive that the Champion is most of all displeased with and about Usuries two Daughters LOW and WOE, because he feareth that they will be chargeable unto him, charging him still, the one being able to bring a man low indeed: and the other crying continually, even day and night within; *woe, woe, woe*, to him that lendeth his money upon Usury, and encrease: *For he shall die, die, die to all eternity, and his blood shall be upon him, Ezek.*18.12.

His great mislike he discovereth *two wayes.*

1. Mr. *Jelinger, p.*19. Tells us, that in *Lev.* 25. 37. and *Deut.* 23. 19. over brother and money there is an accent put, which shews that, as Hebrecians say, the word must be sung with a low voice, because Usury afflicts and brings low.

Num: 65. *Reply*, to one that contended about a word 'twas replyed, that *Cæsars* fortune did not depend thereon, whatsoever this punctation or accent be, I hope that the souls eternal salvation doth not depend upon Criticisms, &c.

Whereunto I answer, that I do not by mentioning this, collocate or place mans eternal salvation in a dependance upon criticisms, but only make use of criticisms, as other divines do, who have Written whole Books, which they call Criticks, and which may serve to illustrate things, which appertain to life and salvation: where let it be remembred what the

---

* B. Jewel: *Serm. in* Thes. 4 6. * Leo 1 *Serm.* 6 de jejun. 10. Mensis, c. 3.

Hebrew Rabbies write concerning accents, as I quote them in my Usurer cast, *p. 6.*

2. He adds to shew his mislike and to disprove,me I confess, 'that it is the first time, that ever I heard, or read, that these 'books were marked out to be sung.

Whereunto I answer, that this very thing will disgrace him, more than any thing he wrote yet, for thus it is.

By this he bewrayeth his shameful and gross ignorance, even in Grammar principles, tho he be a Schoolmaster.

Hebrew Grammar principles, I mean, amongst which there is one (as the greatest of Hebrecians * *Buxtorf* my old friend and instructer has it, in his Grammatical treasure,) *usus accentuum triplex est; primus designat musicam sive rationem cantus apud Judæos, qui textum Biblicum non legunt sed cantillant, That is, there is a threefold use of accents: the first designates musick or the manner of singing among the Jews, who do not read but * sing the Bible text*, mark, he doth not say, that they sing the *Psalms*, but the text of the Bible, and so this book also.

So that, if this great Hebrecian were now alive, I should advise him to leave his teaching of his Schollars to Write, and to travel to the University of *Basil*, where I have been and taken this great mans advise about the Hebrew, and to learn of the same famous Hebrecian the Hebrew a little better, that he may write of Hebrew better himself than here he doth, to his foul disgrace I write it.

Num. 66. I should have said something concerning *Cæsar's* fortune by him mentioned, but that will and does come elsewhere to his confusion.

Chap. 5. *He is considering, saith the Champion, what reach Usury has*; and he grants it reaches very nigh over all the World. For

1. || The Jews who are scattered over the world are great Usurers.

2. Particularly it reacheth * to some great Scholars, as *Seneca*, and to some learned men in the Church in *Chrysostom's* time.

2. Some Princes and great Lords in *Germamy* do espouse it; some whereof were well served in the *German* warrs when they † lost their Usury mony.

---

* Buxtorf. *in suo Thesauro Grammat.* l. 1. c. 5. p. 33. † *I have heard them do so my self in their Synagogues.* || *Where he leaves out* Worms, Asia, Italy, Germany. * *By* Spinola *the Spanish general*

Re

Reply, What remarkable providence or wonder was it, if they smarted by those Wars, under which the Country groaned, and he adds: that at such times the good and bad are commonly involved under one common lot, or rather the former smart most, mark, the good smart most, speaking thus favourably of the Usurers by me mentioned: For Usurers will take one the others part: where before *I* go further, I must do right to *Seneca*, whom I fear I have injured, quoting the words of *Reynolds* concerning him, that he was the greatest Usurer that ever he read of: For since that time, I met with such passages of the said *Seneca* formerly cited, which will evince the contrary, and because he was one of the stoicks, which were so exceeding strict, as that they would speak most bitterly against all sorts of vices; and lastly, because divers Fathers, as * *Tertullian*, *Austin*, and *Jerome* write, that he was converted by *Paul*, and did for two years before his death withdraw himself from *Rome* to his Country house for his souls good. As for *Tacitus*, who saith, that, dying he called upon *Jupiter*, to that I answer, 1. That *Tacitus*, as it is observed in him, Writes many lies. 2. That some excuse him saying, that his words were misprinted, naming *Jovem* for *Jesum*.

Num. 67. Mr. *Jelinger*, it reaches also many great * professors of Godliness.

Reply, And yet all these censured by him to damnation too, without a particular repentance if they took but a mite above the principal.

Whereunto I answer, that I never pressed the taking of a mite as he has often charged me, for I do not think, that any ever took or gave a mite. Only I quoted others, very learned men, who use that expression to shew that whatsoever is taken above the principal by a compact explicite or implicite is Usury.

Num. 68. 2. That some such professors may profess that they know God, and deny him in their deeds, as those in Tit. 1. 16. *He adds*, Mr. *Jelinger*. I hear that some such are lately departed this life, and have left behind them their money lent upon Usury for their posterity. O sad! sad! for they have plunged thereby their poor Children into the same gulf of the damnable sin of Usury.

Num. 69. *Reply*. They are more beholding to him for his pity than for his charity: and why so sad? if according to his own casuistical divinity they do but ask forgiveness of the parties concerned, all is well.

* *That very ancient Father, who lived near to the Apostles time*

 Answer.

Answer. 1. That my casuistical divinity concerning forgiveness of restitution to be made is not now, as he maketh it, nor mine only; for I shall hereafter bring mine Authors for it, which are old and able enough to answer him, and to maintain what they and I assert in this matter, the Doctors which write upon the Canonical law especially.

2. That other grave, learned, and godly Divines also have their most pitiful and lamentable expressions concerning Usurers and their Children that imitate their Parents, whom I mean cursing one another in Hell: The words of one of them at present shall suffice.

In HELL, saith Mr. * *Smith* (who also defineth Usury as it is in the margin) the Usurer shall cry to his Children; You *were the cause of these torments: For lest you should be poor, I was an Usurer, and robbed others to leave riches to you; to whom the Children shall reply again (in hell) Nay cursed be you* † *Father; For you were the cause of our torments, for if you had not left us other mens goods, we had not kept other mens goods.* I add, and we had not been Usurers too, if you had not put out your mony upon Usury for us, to take up the same trade, and to do as you did, and therefore I may well say again. O sad! sad!

After all this the Champion cometh to examin my Reasons. *Mr.* Jelinger. *What Reasons has this Doctrine?*

Now we come to try his strength, and indeed he needs to have good Supporters to bear up such assertions as he has laid down. *&c.* *Answer*, I need not fear that I shall want supporters, I have at least thirty Arguments and Reasons more to come.

Mr. Jelinger. 1. *Reason because this Usury, which is here treated on is prohibited in both Testaments*

1. In the old, 2. in the new.

1. In the old, *Exod.* 22. 25. *Lev.* 25. 36, 37. *Deut.* 23. 19. *Reply.* 1. To these in general: It will be hard to proove his definition of Usury condemned by him from these or any other text in the old Testament.

Whereunto I answer.

1. That it will be no more hard for me to prove what I say;

* *Non inducit liberam remissionem* Joh. *Baptista in* Jus Can. † *Mr.* Smith, *like Doctor* Williams *formerly cited in his second Serm. upon Usury.* || Idem ibid. *Usury is that gain given by lending for the use of the thing lent, covenanting before with the Borrower to receive more than was borrowed.* * *Tho you were a great Professor.*

say, that this Usury, which here I treat of, is condemned in both Testaments and first in the old, then it has been for others before me,

Whole Councils have said the same. And

1. *The Council of Nice* has these words, because many Clergy men * following after filthy lucre out of covetousness, have forgotten the divine *Præcept*, which saith *Psal.* 15. 5. *he that hath not put his mony to Usury, turn Usurers, &c.* Mark, they call *David's* words a Divine Precept, which forbids Usury

2. So that great Council of *Paris* sets down this dreadful sentence: Among many and innumerable evils, whereby God is highly offended, there is extant one especially most execrable, and to God a detestable kind of Covetousness, whereby without doubt he is highly provoked to anger, because thereby men insult over his precepts, mark, Precepts and arguments of damnation are prepared, in that some Clergy-men, mark, Clergy-men, and some Laicks (note that too, because that some say that Ministers only are forbidden to become Usurers) take such most filthy gain *&c.* forgetting that PRECEPT, which saith *Thou shalt, not give thy mony to Usury, nor exact any encrease for thy fruits* &c. (mark, nothing above the principal) Any *Encrease* as it is in *Ezeck.* 18. 8. And again in another Chapter saith the same Council: For the Lord doth most horribly and minaciously prohibit Usury both in his *Legal* and *Prophetical Oracles* &c. And lest men should think, that they speak against oppressive Usury; they cite St. *Jerom.* defining Usury thus: some think that Usury is committed only in mony, which the Scripture, mark, Scripture foreseeing, *takes off all that, which is over and above the principal, that thou takest no more then thou gavest or lendest.* Lo, how this holy Council conspires against thee, O Usurer, and brings in Gods Word to condemn thee,as more fully yet it will appear by that which they say farther.

Of Usury not to be committed, &c. we have left us the *Oracles* of *Both Testaments* (just as I say, so say they, so that I am not alone) and the sayings of the Holy Fathers, which say, that they which follow after Usury shall not live nor dwell in the holy Hill, but rather because they have not been merciful, shall be punished, with that purple and covetous *Dives*; and

* *Council.* Nic. c. 18. † *Here let those many Clergy-men, and Ministers, which now are Usurers also, ponder these words of this holy Council,* || *Council.* Paris. l. 1. c. 53.

ſo ends that holy Council thus tragically, ſo ſad a Tragedy concerning Uſury, and Uſurers.

And therefore how dareſt thou, being a Miniſter, who above all men ſhouldeſt not be an Uſurer by this ſame Councils prohibition, live in this execrable ſin of Uſury, as it cals it, and thou alſo that art a private Chriſtian, how canſt thou read thoſe words without trembling? me thinks thy knees like *Belſhazers Dan.* 5. ſhould ſmite one againſt another, and thy guilty heart ſhould ake within thee, when thou peruſeſt ſuch dreadful expreſſions, uttered and thundred out, not by a deſpicable Miniſter, nor any other ſimple perſon, but ſo many Godly Fathers, and learned men againſt thee from the holy ſcriptures. But this is not all: For not only theſe ancient Councils and Divines, but latter ones alſo, and even an whole Univerſity of learned men, I mean, that already mentioned of *Wittenberg*, ſaith the ſame.

Whereas Uſurers are not only by a poſitive Law, but alſo by both *Old and alſo New Teſtament*, as in themſelves unlawful, are forbidden of God *&c.*

And then: But theſe are Uſurers, whoſoever by a compact take five in the hundred *&c.* I cut ſhort becauſe I made uſe of this determination above already.

Bleſſed *Bolton* * I ſhall quote laſt, tho he be not the leaſt, his words are, *But let us come to Scriptures, and dare you indeed* M. S. *ſtand to that tryal of that pure and heavenly touchſtone? Anſwerably whereunto I ſay to my Adverſary ſo too*; and dare you ſtand indeed to that ſame moſt ſure and heavenly touch-ſtone?

Conſider then theſe places, with the ſame holy Authors, even as I do alſo;

Exod. 22. 25. *Lev.* 25. 36. *Deut.* 23. 19. *Pſ.* 15. 5. *Ezek.* 18. 13. 7. and 22. 13. *Prov.* 10. 8. whereunto I now add, *Nehem.* 5. 10. *I pray you let us leave of this † Uſury.* Now *M. S.* againſt theſe many places condemning Uſury bring you ſo much as one to allow it. || How do you like this Champion?

Num. 71. Secondly The *Ch.* replyeth, that theſe texts

* *Where note that in the Hebrew Uſury is not called* בשך *biting but* משא *a burden as indeed it is, to cut off that cavil that only biting Uſury is forbidden in Scripture, and that the Defendants of Uſury ſay, that by* Maſhah *moderate Uſury is ſignified which alſo they hold to be allowed.* B D. P. 97. *contrary to this Scripture.*

† Bolton *ſpeaks it, not I.*

for-

forbid lending to the poor only upon Use either explicitely or implicitely.

I answer, No such matter: for 1. *Deut*. 23. 19. forbidds lending upon Usury to a brother, and so to the * rich, as well as the poor, because both are brethren; so B. *Jewel* expounds the place, and before him that most learned and most ancient Father † *Clemens Alexandrinus*, saying, The Law forbidds to lend upon Usury to your brother, under the name of brother, comprehending not him only which was born of the same Parents, but also who was of the same Tribe, † and of the same opinion, and partakers of the same Word: Now whom shall a man believe in the expression of the name brother? this Novice? or these far more abler Divines which I have cited? Let the Reader judge; considering withal how in the Chaldee there Uusury is not called נֶשֶׁךְ Biting but כנשא a burden, or oblivion as indeed it is.

2. Not only in *Deut*. but also in *Psal*. 15. 5. and *Ezeck*. 18. 12. 13. The poor are left out of purpose to prevent mistakes, as if only to the poor we were not to lend upon Usury.

3. If the law of Usury did only forbid men to lend to the poor upon Usury, and allow such lending to the rich, who will lend to poor decayed trades-men and others? so that such a law so to be understood would have proved to the hurt and ruin of such poor decayed persons.

3. He saith this law was *political*, and the Jews intrest was peculiarly heeded in it &c.

A. Soon said, but not so soon proved; I have on my side (besides Scripture, which makes it moral, reckning Usury still among the sins which are committed against the moral law, as *Ps*. 15. 3. 5. *Ezeck*. 18. 11, 12, 13. and *Ch* 22. 9. 10. 11. 12.) at least two most ancient, most renowned, most learned Fathers, Authors and Writers, who assert and prove it to be moral and not political. *viz*.

Origen. Clemens Alexandrine, *Gregory Nyssene*, St. *Basil*

---

* *B.* Jewel. † Clemens Alex. *From* l. 2. *formerly alleaged also. To both these may two more be added* 1. *Dr.* Taylor, *who in his progr. of Saints* p. 96. *saith about the poor, thus: Men are deceived in their distinctions; for God doth not distinguish in the case of Usury between Rich and Poor in* Israel, *but between Canaanites and Israelites. The word poor in* Exo. 22. 25. *doth not restrain the law, but is set down for example.*

St.

St. *Chris.* St. *Austin*, St. *Jerome*, *Tho. Aquinas*, *Dionysius Carthus*, *Gabriel*, *Biel*, *Lyra*, *Raynerus*, *Luther*, *Melanchton*, *Brenchius*, *Musculus*, *Chemnitius*, *Aretius*, *Hemingius*, *Wigandus*, *Zegedinus*, *Molanus*, *Viguerius Wolvius*, enough for the present.

Mr. Jelinger. 2. *It is forbidden in the new Testament*, Luke 6. 35. *lend freely, hoping for nothing again.*

Num. 72. *Reply.* There are several interpretations of this, that to me carry a greater probability, than that he pleads for: but if taken in his sense, I shall proove it will not reach the sense he driveth at; that is, to a prohibition of all Usury &c.

He driveth at 1. to a prohibition of all Usury &c

Whereunto I *Answer*, I know it well enough that there are several senses given of this place by several Authors: which notwithstanding in every sence they command the duty of free lending, saith famous * Bishop *Downam*, whereby it followeth, that all Usury properly so called is thereby forbidden, which I drive at, and shall demonstrate more and more before I have done.

But 1. If this text be understood of a free gift, saith the Ch. it quite spoils his market, and overthroweth his definition; and so there be those that understand those words without any wresting of them: and here he brings in the old translation, *Lend freely*, which maketh altogether for me, and *Psal.* 37. 21. which I do not deny, and then cites *Jeremiah Taylor*, the learned *Casuist*, whose words are, *give*, looking for nothing again, and *Deodate*, interpreting the words of a perpetual giving, and after him *Rivet*, affirming that Christ doth not immediately here speak of Usury &c. and *Spanhemius*, asserting the same of giving, all which quotations the inquisitive Reader may read over himself (because they are too large to be inserted) if my Adversary print them, or in his written papers, which he hath sent abroad, giving out far and near, that he hath confuted me. But my Answers for my self herein are these.

1. *Answer.* That he may well say thus doubtfully, by way of *if*; *if this Text be understood of a free gift*, viz. generally, because there are more that deny it than there are which assert it, as it will be made to appear.

Num. 73. 4. He names for himself, *Taylor*, *Deodate*, *Rivet*, *Spanhemius*.

1. *Taylor.* Whom to answer I shall commit † Doctor

---

* *B.* Downam *in Psal.* 15. † *Doctor* Taylor *in his progr. of Saints* p. 96. *with Bishop* Taylor.

1. *Taylor.*

Taylor. with B. *Taylor* , saying, in my behalf as much against Usury as a man can say, as namely, *Men deceive themselves in their distinctions in case of Usury. And yet farther, if learned men allow that Usury, which is commonly practiced, I oppose the word of God against them, and 2. A far greater number of late learned men , besides Fathers and School-men who do not. 3. if those Divines be Usurers themselves, then no wonder.* This by the by, to shew how much this great man is my friend in writing against Usury, as contrary to this place in hand.

2. To answer the words cited against me, I must needs confess that they are not to be misliked by a charitable giver, but that they cross lending I cannot see at all.

2. *Deodate* is another, which he quoteth against me, a man whose memory is precious to me, because I have heard him usually both preach and read his Divinity Lectures at *Genevah*, when I mansioned in that Academy, and know what a Godly life he did live, but why he should oppose him against me I wonder, seeing he requireth no other thing, but that we should lend with intent to loose whatsoever we lend, if our Neighbours wants do require it, &c. which no good man can mislike, yea, which I and my friends require also.

3. As for my ancient friend *Rivet* , he also doth not much cross me : For I shall easily grant, that as he saith, Christ doth not immediately forbid Usury by this Scripture ; but I add that consequently he doth, as *Beza* also, who is greater than *Rivet*, doth averr the same, as I have formerly shewn.

4. So my dear Cousin *Spanhemius* and I do not disagree so much as the Ch. pretends : For he doth not say that Usury is not to be understood in that place ; but that Christ in and by that place would have us to erogate our mony to the poor, when they need it, even them from whom we can have no hope to receive either gain or principal ; which sheweth that he understands Christ's words of lending properly so called, and not of giving properly so called. For when a thing is properly given, there can be no looking for either gain or principal : and besides, if my Cousin *Spanhemius* should confound one with the other as to make lending giving, and giving lending ; he cannot evince it by an un undeniable demonstration, that Christ meaneth Alms giving.

Lastly. Whatever his meaning then was, he is now on my side.

---

* *We must lend not only freely without gain, but also, tho it be to the loss of the mony lent.* Powel p. 4.

As

As for that place in the *Prov.* 19. 17. it doth not prove it, because that speaks of a metaphorical lending; and Christs words of that which is proper.

Num. 74. *But what doth Mr.* Jelinger say against this interpretation, saith the Ch.

Mr. *Jelinger*. It cannot be understood of giving, because giving to the poor is spoken of there distinctly from lending by Christ, who would not use a tautology.

Reply. And yet he can bring in God speaking a tautology within six lines after this passage. But by his leave it is no tautology; For what more common in Scripture than for the same thing to be laid out in various expressions &c. Here is the whole, that he hath to say to weaken that solid interpretation, or strengthen his own, what force or cogency it is, let it be considered.

I answer.

1. Do I bring in God as speaking a tautology? because I say he would not use a tautology? Here let the Reader judge in which of the six lines I say it.

2. I would have him know that this is not the whole that I have to say to weaken his Interpretation.

For 1. It cannot be that by lending must be understood giving, because lending is another thing, distinct from giving: For lending is a real contract whereby we deliver a thing consisting in quantity, so as that he which receives it is to return it in kind and not in its species.

So * *Civilians* define it.

And it is twofold. 1. *vera*, true. 2. *quasi*, as it were.

1. *True*, which is in the beginning by and by perfected by the tradition and reception of a thing.

2. *The other*, tho at first it was not, yet afterward is introduced, and that *two wayes. Either by man, or by law*, so the law sets it forth.

But giving is when a man bestoweth a thing upon another, with this intent, that he would presently have it become his that doth receive it, and never in any wise to be returned again to himself (whereas mony lent is to be returned)

---

* *Dr.* Vulceus *in sua Jurispr.* l. 1. c. 31. *And* Paulus *that great Lawyer writes the same.*

That we lend with a purpose to receive idem genus, *the same in kind. For if we receive again another thing, as Wine for Wheat, it is not* mutuum *or lending, saith he.*

So

So * Donariff *the Lawyer defines it*, where it will concern me to occur two objections.

The 1. *Objection is*, that some of my own friends call lending giving, as Dr. *S*. and others, which I answer thus.

I know some do, but they call it giving to loan to difference it from other giving; the one being a giving for a time, as for a half year or so, the other a perpetual to use my Adversaries own word.

Num. 75. To make this alittle more plain, I will add two things.

1. That the Lender can do no other then so give away what he lends, and that is to say, to make it his for a time to whom he lends it, as for that cause its also called in latin † *mutuum*, because of *mine* it becomes *thine*, the reason is because if it should not be his, but he should be forced to render the same mony in kind, and in the very same pieces which he has received, he cannot use it at all; seeing that by using it, he changes it, and puts it away from him: which has caused one to say, that when mony is delivered to be used by a man, its not possible that the Deliverer should remain still Lord and Owner of the said self same mony.

2. That the Lender will no other but give it, that is, alienate it, and make it his to whom its lent, because else the danger of loosing would be his; and this is the greatest ground of Usury saith he, in that men will not hazard at all their principal sum of mony (otherwise perchance they might have more gain, and that lawfully too, in the trade of merchandising, either by themselves or in fellowship together with others) but whiles they will by all means be sure of their principal, and will adventure nothing; they are doubtless of this mind, not to have it lost, and perish from them; but will have it made his own mony who borroweth it, (and so to give it, as it were, making it a *mutuum quasi*, as Civilians call a kind of lending, as I said even now) and to have him Debtor not of the very same again, but so much in quantity, so as that Usurers mony is still safe and cannot perish in that respect; For no general quantity doth ever perish, but only the particular things, which are within some

---

* Donariff. F. de donationibus et Donot F. de Reg. Jur. *and it is twofold* 1. mortis causa, *for deaths sake*. 2. inter vivos *among the living*. *Dr*. Fregius in suo pedagogo *p*. 226.

† *Mutuum quasi de meo tuum*.

Sic Calepinus, *Mutuum dicitur ab eo quod de meo tuum &c*.

certain place, or circumstance; and has not my Adversary well gotten by his giving?

Num. 76. *The second Objection is*, that the Scripture it self calls lending for gain giving in several places, as namely, *Lev.* 25. 27. *Thou shalt not give him thy money to Usury*, and *Ps.* 15. 5. He that giveth not his money to Usury, as some translations have it: and *Ezek.* 18. 13. *Has given forth upon Usury.*

Whereunto I answer first, we must not be so simple as to gather from thence that the Usurer practiceth the contract of giving properly so called, for as much as he intendeth for the return of every 100 *l.* and for six over and above: So that the Prophet *Ezekiel* notably addeth to giving taking, even taking of encrease, which sheweth what a GIVING is * meant, *viz.* such as carrieth taking again with it, and a returning again of the principal with an encrease, whereas in giving properly so called there is no returning.

2. *I answer*, that as the Opponent brings his four Authors, as making against me and being for him in the sense of GIVING, so I shall adduce more then four as able Divines as any of his, which really are for me (whereas his do but seem to be so) And, 1. Powel, *in that Christ saith, LEND; he bids not to give but he would have the principal restored.*

2. A learned professor of *Losanna*, called *Aretius*, whose 'words are these upon *Luke* 6. 35. which sentence all do not 'take aright, for there are which judge that the very principal 'is not to be recalled for, nor to be expected (which imply-'eth GIVING) whose sentence I do not approve.

For of gratuitous beneficence Christ had spoken before, *sed quod mox additur* δανείζετε, that he by and by adds lend, he speaks not of the same species now, but expresly of loan whether the pricipal be to be recalled, or not to be hoped for, it is not now lending, and Christ should not speak RIGHT (mark what he saith) lend, hoping for nothing *from thence*, but that should chearfully be granted to him, without hoping for any gain counting it sufficient for thee to receive the principal in its proper time and place, *&c.* Thus *Aretius.* [Unless some intervening cases require it to be otherwise as has been formerly shewn] which exegetically I add.

---

* *Aretius probl. Theolog. loc.* 50, p. 627. *With* Aretius *I may joyn* Powel *against giving upon* Luk. 6. 34. *If you lend to them of whom ye hope to receive*, supple non sortem, *supply, not the principal, else it would be a gift, not a loan.*

2. And

2. And doth not Saint *Jerome* render Christs saying, δανείζετε, in the same sense lend, not give, in his old version.

3. So all manner of Translations do they not so too, as namely.

1. *The* Ethiopick, *lend, not give.*
2. *The* Persick, *lend, uot give.*
3. *The* Syriack, *lend, not give.*
4. *The* Dutch. Leihel, *not give.*
5. *The* French *also.*
6. *The* English, *lend, not give.*

4. I add, the famous Author of the brief Treatise of Usury, who not only useth the same version *lend*, but also tells us, that to lend is to deliver presently to another man such stuff as is spent with the first natural and proper use thereof with a bond to have him repay so much and so good again. And thus the Greeks, and the Latines, the Jews, the Philosophers, the Lawyers, the Diviness and generally all the Heathens and Christians take that to be the nature and true definition or discription of loan: So that by this his saying he makes it to appear that lending here required is not giving, because in giving is nothing repay'd

5. With this Author I joyn *Gratian*, saying, that in lending I say *do, ut des, do ut facias*, I give thee that thou mayest give me, or I give thee that thou mayest do to me that, which is not so in perpetual giving: So that I wonder, when I consider what this Author and others write of Lending, how they can say that giving by Christ is meant.

4. And yet I have more to say: *viz*. That other places also of holy writ do evince it, that lending and not a perpetual giving away is meant by Christ, as namely

1. *Luke* 6. 30. And then *verse* 35. where Christ distinctly speaketh of giving first *v.* 30. and then of lending next, which sheweth what he meant when he said and lend, not

---

* *And Doctor* Vultius *the Lawyer whose* juris prudentiam *I have extracted aud learned by heart, I cannot ommit here, who, to avoid this mistake of giving, has changed the name* mutui datum, *into mutuation* l. 1. c. 31. *And* Phil. Melanchton *I must needs superadd in the Margin too, to second* Aretius. *Christ saith* Luk. 6. 35. *lend, looking for nothing again thereby, which saying should not be so perverted, or foolishly understood. Nor that one might reason thereby that the principal should not be rendred: For then it would be giving and not lending, in his* Annot. *upon* Matth.

lend

lend, *but and lend, requiring somewhat more* viz. lending also. 2. *v.* 34. Where lending is oned, from whence I gather, that lending an to be understood *verse* 35. also, as answering sinners, only with this difference, that in len not expect any thing from thence, as they do

3. *Deut.* 15, 8, 10, 11. If there be among y that is one that is decayed, not a begger, of c thren, (by an high passage) *&c.* Thou shalt him sufficient for his need, in that which he n is lending (and no giving) and lending requi and that, as Authors say, after the seventh yea it would be a meer *donation*, saith *Lyra*, w granted in so great a plenty after the seventh y after this lending in cometh *Giving* v. 10. *Thou* *him*, and thine heart shall not be grieved when t to him. Where note that giving is mentionec glish, and three times in Hebrew, and that sort, to enforce the Notableness of it.

4. Matt. 5. 42. *Give unto him that asketh that would Borrow of thee turn thou not away:* V comes in again, distingishing giving from lendi ring both, just in the same manner, as in *Luke*

Num, 77. 2. *But there is another interpretat* saith the Ch. which serves not his turn any former. *v.* 34. *If you lend to them of whom you what thanks have yee; for sinners also lend to si as much again.* This is not to be understood Use, but the like kindness again. *τὰ ἴσα aq* pose they should lend a horse to their Neighbo they expected to be befriended in the like ki stances in a sum of mony. Thus to do was yet Christ thinks it not enough for his Disciples lend not only to such as will lend to them agai the poor and necessitous, yea, to their enemi and pinched, from whom there was little groun equal favour again, and here he quotes *Groti* *Zanchie*, and the Æthiopick version.

For answer whereunto I *say;*

1. That the Ch. is much mistaken in this,

---

* *Tantundem quantum dedit, ut pate.* so much as was given or lent as the words fc *Piscator. in Loc.*

retation serves not my turn more than the
For this very verse maketh altogether for me;
rein are so just, that they will lend without
nothing but their own again, τ'α ἴσα that
in, as † Divines expound that expression,
ace saith a most learned Author, we that bear
rists name, and have undertaken an holy pro-
n how we ought to lend unto our needy bro-
her we ought to take Usury of him or no:
eaves out τα ἴσα but who can like it? This by

† *The Gospel makes these sinners* (Usurers)
sinners, when it saith sinners lend to sinners, to
again, but these to receive more :

makes for me besides, by the word LEND
ve formerly shewn; so that I cannot by any
is 34. *verse.*

and *Grotius* are mightily mistaken in a horse
|| commodating with lending: and the same
of a certain sort of Usurers, which call Usury
the name of a beast, answerably whereunto
cloak Usury by the name of a horse, making
operly so called, which is not but commoda-

same *Grotius* his saying, that the Usury Questi-
roperly belong to this place, I do not weigh
he is not only an erroneus Writer, but also
ast himself, that by most of the ancient Fa-
er of Usury is handled and spoken against by
said place; as learned *Pool* also treats of U-
pon the same, and sets down Usury, as meant
t place; where let the Reader choose whether
the Ch. and his *Grotius*, or to *Pool* and all o-

---

tuation we do not look to receive the same particular
modation, but τα ἴσα *so much æquivalent thereunto*
p. 228. † Powel. p. 50. || Trap. *upon* Prov.
* Luke 6. 35. † *Which is when a man lendeth*
oketh to have the same again in his own individu-
if I lend a horse, I look to have the same horse a-
nother: Whereas Mutuation is, when a man lend-
and looketh but to have his own again in the same
. 11.

most of the holy Fathers, besides our * cheifest Protestant Authors, who prove Usuries unlawfulness by *Luke* 6. 35. As for *Jansenius* I do not see why he should be brought against me, so *Zanche* both of them, extending Christs words to the ungrateful, and the poor, and enemies, and saying, that it doth not follow that we must not love those which love us because we are to love those which do not love us &c. For who of us reasons so? and besides, do not the greatest Anti Usurarians say the same, that is here said? I'le instance only in one now, We are to lend not only to our friends, kinsmen and brothers, but also unto strangers, , yea, and to our enemies, *Luke* 6. *Matt.* 5. Thus *Gabriel Powel.*

4. Nor doth the *Æthiopick* cross me at all, which the Ch foreseeing, maketh him speak so faintly, That it seemeth t intend this sence. Yea, I say farther, that the same Æthiopick version doth rather make for me, especially in the last words, not hoping for a retribution, which self sam thing I assert most stifly, that in lending there must be no r tribution expected, but if any thing comes thankfully, freel and unexpectedly, it may be received.

Num. 78. 3. *saith the* Ch. The word ἀπελπίζοντ; hoping for nothing again, has a quite contrary sense put on by the learned men who render it desparing or causing despair. This latter sense the *Syriack*, *Persick*, and *Arabic* versions favour.

1. *Siriack*, Do not frustrate the expectation of any. *Persick* do not make any desperate, because great is your ward. 3. The *Arabick*, do not frustrate any ones hope, w which versions he joyns *Spanhemius* and another Author sides, affirming, that Christ by these words would not ha us to cut off the hopes of any, considering the reward set fore us; *whereunto I answer.*

1. Suppose all these versions be yeelded unto, and wl his two Authors say, what hurt can it do to me, who that which I have red in Criticks and Grammarians, can see that ἀπελπίζειν signifieth so much as the versions his Authors would have it, and am not inscious of this t that if it were so, it doth not follow that the word signifi the same in this place too, and this only, and no other thi there being those, which put other constructions upon t place, as the *Æthiopian* and several other versions do, which hereafter.

---

* *As* Erasmus, Melanchton, Xistus, Betuleus.

2. I add, that one word overthrows all that these versions say, *viz.* that little word μηδὲν, nothing; if Christ had said; μηδένα *none*, as the Syrick hath perverted his words, than that had been something, to establish that sense, but seeing it s μηδὲν *nothing*, hoping for *nothing* and not for *none*; I do not see what sure footing they have for their sense and meaning if to it they stick, for what a strange sense is this causing nothing to despair: For it is μηδὲν

3. I observe how he would fain be counted a man skill'd n the Oriental tongues, but he may thank the Polyglott for t, which some good man let him see.

He goeth on and saith, some, as aforesaid, render it * departing intransitively, and brings in Dr. * *Hammond*, saying thers translate it, not any way loosing all manner of hopes, iz. of a just retribution: But to no purpose is this also; because

1. ἀπελπίζειν signifies to hope, which I and other likewise say.

2. Because I do not deny what he affirms, *viz.* that Christians should not be diffident, but expect God to be their remunerator: But that it only is meant how will any one prove it?

Num. 79. *Passing on he saith moreover*, passing by others, ou see how many favourable interpretations this place is capable of, and those more probable than his *nibil inde sperante*, hoping nothing from thence taken from the *Vulgar*, the mphasis being placed in the preposition ἀπὸ tho not (I nfess an emphasis as he places † elsewhere in the same preposition in the word ἀπελθὼν *Matt.* 13. 46. as it is in the iginal, that is, he overcame, namely himself.

Whereunto this is my answer.

1. How more probable are those other interpretations than ne? because they take μηδένα for μηδὲν which is rists own word, which is worse, than to expound and pael ἀπὸ with παρὰ as I do in the spiritual Merchant, for ich here he jeereth me, tho' he has no just cause, the nter after my correction misplacing these two prepositions my lines and in the margin both.

* which is a little better rendred, nothing desparing, because Chris and Lexicons tell us that ἀπελπίζειν signifies sometimes to aire, as Lucan shews it, l. 5. but not always. † In his spiritual chant p. 4. ‖ Because these two prepos. being paralell'd make

But suppose his reading be the best, saith the
hoping for nothing again from thence, by way of u
and yet not at all taking of gain for mony lent l
ned.

For proof hereof I shall give you Mr. *Mag*
the place.

To which quotation I answer, I have read h
find that that good man would have us to lenc
freely as that we should lend it but for as short
want it, and that, if the borrower do not rep
the lender cannot have it again in due time
nance, (to use his words) the Borrower tradi
year to year, it is not against this precept to
pence therefore; Mark *recompence*, let the Reac
words upon this place, for they are too large f
insert, so that what the *Ch*. saith here makes
me.

What he subverts as from himself, and fro
Rivet, concerning three sorts of People, doth
neither; For my * friends use to make such
so, without granting that we may expect,
Use of the third sort called the rich, becau
no such exception in this place by allowin
gain to the wealthy. This we grant that the
consider the Lender, and that he may lawfully
freely, and thankfully offer, as † *Trescabala*
Merchant did when the Lord *Cromwel* for
lent him; gave him one thousand six hundred

Num 80. But he quoteth Bishop *Hall* too ag
I much wonder at, how he can, because in t
he confutes him (such a great man he takes
can confute so learned a Bishop and so famous

But to answer more punctually I say, what Bis
is concerning a man that borrows to enrich hi
a wanton expence and for his pleasure, that
reason why you should vail your own just ac
ther man's excess, which is by him so warily
by vertue of this place *Luke* 6, 35. || No ju
be taken by his words: For the good Bishop
to such as he describes, we are not to lend at

---

* *Where note, that in our greek Grammer bot*
signify of *and* from † *See B.* Downam *upon* P
|| *As Mr.* Clerk *in the Lord* Cromwels *Life*
† G. Powel. *p.* 59.

borrow out of excess, and for their pleasure, which is his own expression, because much evil comess of it: and how much he was against Usury, I have formerly shown; so that it is not nor can be imagined, that in this saying of his he is for it; I add, that the Champion himself confesseth that the Bishops of *England*, of whom himself was one, *descrie all Usury*, I superadd that this famous Bishop was so great a friend unto me when as an exiled Minister I lived in *Exceter*, as I have else where declared and so continued, as that I am confident that he would not now become an enemy to me in this matter of Usury which he himself so much warreth against, as I also do: But of him more hereafter.

Num. 81. *To advance* yet one step higher in the consideration of the Text before me. The things Sinners are said here to do, are at least lawful, and I think commendable in their kind *&c.* and then there is a double mistake in these words of Mr. *Trap.* (by me quoted *p.* 4,) Let the Reader peruse them and my present Opponents Opposition made against them in his Pamphlet, and pretended confutation thereof, which is so tedious as that I am loath to insert them, but shall deal therewith as he dealeth with more than twenty nine lines of mine, which he doth not touch at all, but wholy passeth over.

Only thus much I shall briefly answer thereunto.

1. *That we all say the same with blessed* * Downam, that we may not so understand our Saviour Christ as tho he did forbid men to love their lovers, or to do good to those that have deserved well at their hands, or to lend to such of their friends and acquaintances as will restore what they have borrowed; for they that do not thus much are worse than the very sinners of whom Christ speaks: But he requires a higher degree of Christians to lend---not only them that love us, but also them which hate us, to lend not only to them who will repay, but also such of whom we connot hope to receive that which we lent: and in this very thing Bishop *Downam* and my poor self agree with learned *Zanchy*, by him quoted:

2. That he sheweth in this his habitual pride and arrogancy, in that he emboldeneth himself to shew this great Author his mistakes, himself being but a Novice.

3. That I shall desire the Reader once more to peruse the words of Mr. *Trap*, in his own writing upon *Prov.* 28. *p.* 20 *&c*. for that very writing is enough to answer for it self.

* *B.* Downam *upon* Ps. 15. 5.

As for me, I shall not undertake to answer to every thing that is excepted against those many Authors which I do quote, for that would run on in *infinitum:* Nor indeed doth he.

Only this I will add, 1. That they must needs be sinners, whom Christ calls sinners, tho they were not * sinners in that they did lend to their friends and kinsmen, *Luke* 6. unless they did lend for Usury, which Christ frees them from, saying, that they did lend only to have the like again, that is, the like sum again, which is lawful: Their fault was that they would go no farther, their lending to their friends not being enough.

2. That in very deed and without mistaking it may be asserted that Christ gave it in charge to his, to lend not expecting any gain or overplus for their loan; because he saith expresly, *lend, hoping for Nothing*; which an abler man than this Novice understands that *Luke* 6. 35. *lend*, looking for nothing again, in that Christ saith so, he commands that nothing should be exacted more than was lent.

Num. 82. I conclude as the *Ch.* Consider what I have answered: Yet I have two things more to say and superadd concerning the same text, *viz.*

1. That I have sufficient Supporters to sustain and to support my exposition [*hoping for nothing from thence*] which I have only toucht yet, but now intend to insist upon, because its a thing of great concernment.

For upon *two Accounts* this translation and sense is embraced.

1. Because ἀπελπίζειν is, a compound compounded of the * preposition ἀπὸ from and ἐλπίζω I hope, and signifies *hoping from thence, or from it.*

2. *Because I have at least fifteen famous Authors on my side* who render Christs words in that manner, *hope for nothing from thence* (*ab inde*) which I desire the Reader to take special notice of, because my adversary is not ashamed to tell this falshood, that this exposition and version, *hoping for nothing from thence*, I have taken from the vulgar, as if I had only the vulgar on my side for it, which would be but a weak sup-

---

* *Let this be well observed, that neither Mr.* Trap *nor I think them to be sinners for lending to receive* τὰ ἴσα *the like for quantity, or for courtisie; but only mention these sinners, to shew that Usurers are worse than they, because they lent to receive only the like, but Usurers more.* † *Two things more added which I have as to* Luke 6. 35.

port for me in so momentous a Subject.

Now my first Author I confess is St. *Jerome*, who has studied the Hebrew twenty years, and learned it of a Jew, and lived in *Judea* at *Bethlehem*, and therefore most able to translate the Bible; and also was so holy a man, as that he heard the Angels sing in the Wilderness, wherein he lived, as he calls God to witness for it, and appeared to St. *Austin*, being dead, and told him, (as Mr. *Brook* has it) what a glory he was in.

And 1. His translation is this, *Nihil inde sperantes*, hoping for Nothing from thence.

2. So *Beza*, *Nihil inde sperantes*, hoping for nothing from thence.

So † *Stephanus*, that admirable and most rare Græcian, *Nihil inde lucri sperantes*, hoping for no gain from thence.

4. So || *Aretius* , that famous and learned Professor of *Losanna*, *Nihil inde sperantes*, hoping for nothing from thence.

5. Yea, * *Zanchy also*, somtimes so reads it with this addition, *ob officium mutuationis*, for the duty of lending.

6. † So famous B. *Downam* so renders *Luke* 6. 35. *looking for nothing thence.*

7. That Renowned and ever honoured man || Dr. *Luther* in his Dutch version of the holy bible, so renders the same words of Christ, *Luke* 6, 35. in Dutch thus, *Leihel, das iter nights dafeir hottet*, that is lend hoping for nothing for it or from it:

Seconds enough for its poor weak creature, which writes these things, and had need of Supporters, having so many enemies, which would even eat him if they could, like bread:

But because I spake of fifteen famous Authors to be my seconds in this translation; I will therefore name four more, as namely , 1. *Erasmus Roterodamus*, 2. The *Tigurines*. 3. *Castalio*, 4. Mr. *Pool*, which makes the number of || eleven.

And then Secondly I have this to declare yet, that there

---

* Beza *in* Luke 6. 35. † Stephanus *in his Marginal notes.* || Aretius *p.* 627. * Zanchy *as one observes it in him.* † B. Downam *in* Luke 6. 35.|| *Dr.* Luther. *in* Luke 6. 35. * *Besides which eleven I can bring, four more who render the words thus, hoping for nothing thereby, as namely* Melanchton *in* Luke 6. 35. † Brentius *in* Luke 6. 35. || P. Cæsar *upon* Luke 6. 35. * *And the French Bible, which maketh up the number of fifteen.*

is one interpretation more, which is received by most, and will mainly sustain my fabrick, which I have superstructed or erected upon that famous place, *Luke* 6. 35. viz. *That Usury by this place is evidently prohibited,* tho it be not named, at least consequentially. For

1. *If our Neighbour be to be holpen without regard of recovering the stock,* as *Beza* asserts it; *then much more all Usury in contracts are by that place in* Luke 6. 35. *prohibited.*

2. Because Christ by that place commands free lending, which word free, by way of explanation added in some translations, the old especially, and by Bishop * *Sands* upon *Luke* 6. 35. *lend freely*

3. Because the word μηδὲν nothing, enforceth it:

4. The word *from thence* sheweth that from the loan we should hope for nothing.

5. Most Expositors and Writers have therefore with one consent expounded that place of *Usury* by name, as namely

1. The ancient Fathers for the most part have so handled, and understood that place, which is confessed by *Grotius* himself, that *a plerisque*---as hath been declared already.

2. And learned *Poole* in his *Syn.* upon *Luke* 6. 35. sets own this † expositinn first, as I hinted it formerly, *hoping for nothing, that is no Usury.*

3. So ‖ *Langius* in his *Polyanthea.*

4 Renowned Bishop *Downam* has this expression for it; that most expound that place *Luke* 6. 35. so, that I must lend without respect of my own profit, or without any expectation of any benefit or gain thereby. And

5. *Blessed* Bolton *affirms the same, saying, as they * most expound that place.* p. 25.

6. *But I must needs add the learned* G. Powel's *Syllogism.*

The Commandments of God are necessarily to be obeyed.
But God has commanded to lend looking for nothing, *Ergo*

---

* B. Sands *serm. upon* Luke 6. 35. *And again God saith lend freely, and look for nothing again,* Luke 6. 35. *But will the Usurer whose mony is his God, remit his intrest because of this? Thus he.* † *i. e.* Nullum fœnus *Mr.* Pool *in* Luke 6. 35. ‖ *Langius* in sua Polyan. *p.* 14. 25. * Powel *p.* 33. *And in his pract. Catechism. with whom I joyn the Phœnix of my Country* P. Melanchton *in suis Annot. in* Matt. *This is the proper sense and true interpretation of those words of Christ.* Luke 6. 35. *So lend, that you receive as much mony back again, and for the lending hope for no gain above the principal* * Downam p. 226.

And

And seventhly Renowned Dr. Hamond, who upon *Luke* 6. insists upon that place as much as any man, to prove by it the unlawfulness of Usury by comparing the septuagints greek interpretation of *Nehemiah* with the greek in the new Testament and the old, which are his own words ; I do not set down all his discourse, because it is too large high and deep for ordinary capacities : referring the learned to his whole most learned discourse against Usury upon the 6. of *Luke* 35.

8. To close up this interpretation, I am minded to alleage the forenamed most worthy * B. *Downam* once more,

In this sense all Authors almost that have in former times written against Usury understand this place so ; for according to this (which as I said before is the most common mark, the most common interpretation) all Usury, whether it be actual or mental, is by these words most plainly condemned: and whereas some of these latter times understand this Nothing of the principal, others affirm that you might as well put out the word lend, and say give (as my adversary would have it) because the contract of lending presupposes *both in the Lender an intent of alienating the principal, but for a time, and in the Borrower a covenant to restore after a time the principal.* Thus he ; Let *M. P.* consider what I have answered him upon this text, and if he return a solid answer hereto, he shall be *mihi secundus Apollo*, but that I expect not save *ad Græcas Calendas.*

*I have * done with his first Reason, his next followeth.* Saith he

2. *Reason.* Because the Usurer stands expresly condemned by Gods own mouth &c.

Num. 84. *This is easily granted, but with the foresaid limitations,* Who are those Usurers thus condemned? such as transgress Gods *political* Law, such as by griping Usury oppress the poor and indigent, of whom it is forbid to take Use.

I answer 1. Lo, how he maims my words with an &c. that the nervousness and weightiness thereof may not appear by my proofs *Ps.* 15. 5. *Ezek.* 18. 12, 13. and may not I serve

---

* *But I have not fully done with my first Reason : For I have one Text more from the new Testament* viz. 1 Cor. 6. 10. Extortioners shall not inherit the Kingdom of God, *which Extortioners by the Translators of the Bible are also translated Usurers in* Psal. 109. 11. *in Hebrew* נושה *and in the foresaid place* 1 Cor. 6. 11. *where also the Usurer is expresly named, instead of Extortioner by a certain translation which I have seen* thus.

him so too hereafter, by cutting short his words to make this treatise the shorter? Well, his example will make me do so.

2. It will be easily granted, that griping Usurers which oppress the poor and indigent will be damned, but not, that such only, tho such will receive the greater damnation; for as I prove my reason by *Ezek.* 18. 12. such also shall not live, but die, who take encrease, * any encrease or overplus as well as † Nesheck. The words are, *If he beget a Son-- that has given forth upon Usury, and has taken any encrease in Hebrew* תרבית Tarbith, *which the old Latin translation renders more than thou gavest*, Luke 25 36. *Thou shalt not take Usury of him, nor more than thou gavest, and* v. 27. *thou shalt not lend him thy mony upon Usury, nor thy Victuals for encrease*, that is, as || *Ambrose* reads it, receive more.

And again, this sentence excludes all encrease above the principal; The Septuagint also call *Tarbith* πλεονασμὸν *supradundantiam*, and others an augmentation; and so most Translators upon *Prov.* 28. 8. Encrease (and *Tremellius Leo Juda, Lavaterus, Vatablus, Pagninus, Mercerus, Fœnory*, as distinct from Usury, and which signifies a Child or thing begotten, *fœnus quasi fœtus*, because it is begotten, as it were, by the Usurer, and brought forth by the Borrower, and I add, that *Tarbith* is somtimes put before *Nesheck* encrease before Usury as *Prov.* 28. 8. to shew that Usury is not only biting, but encrease, any encrease also, and that in *Ezek.* 18. 12. all the old versions render encrease, *amplius*, somewhat more.

And what saith blessed * *Austin* ? 'If thou hast lent mo- 'ny to any man of whom thou lookest to receive more than 'thou gavest, whether it be Wheat, or Wine, or Oyle, or 'any thing else; if thou expectest to receive more than thou 'gavest, *Thou art an Usurer.* How doth the Usurer like this 'think yee? So St. † *Jerome*, speaking against Usury saith, 'thou must receive no more than thou didst give. So *Gra-*

---

* *Where note farther, that Nesheck it self also is, as* Gel. *tells us*, supreans illa pecunia, quæ ultra sortem repetitur *that mony which above the principal is required, or asked.* † Ambrose l. de Tol. c. 15. || Danæus *in sua* Eth. Christ. l. 2. c. 15. *et* 39. * *The* Septuagint. *upon* Prov. 28. 8. † *The marginal note upon* Prov. 28. 8. || *Which* Targam Jonathan *follows upon* Ezek. 18. 12. *putting Encrease before Usury.* * *The words of the version are, has given to Usury and taken more.* &c. † Augustin. || *Et* Hieron.

'*tian*

'*tian*, Whatsoever for loan is exacted above the principal, is
'Usury.

'But after all this I must needs subjoyn the words of the 'famous Writer *Danæus*, they that insist on the Hebrew hold 'that there is a great difference between the words *Tarbith* 'and *Nesheck* and so think that not all *Tarbith* is a Vice, but is 'sometimes allowed: But all *Nesheck* is forbidden that is, bi'ting; but this their distinction is to be taken off, and to be 'confuted; for both are mentioned together and condemned 'together. *Luke* 25. 36.

Num. 85. *Of Political laws* by him here mentioned I have spoken already.

He saith farther, as for his additional reasons I shall consider them according to their strength they have, but I see they must consist in giving of hard names &c. and in this Art no Quaker could have exceeded him, I mean in foul language.

Whereunto I answer, What doth he make then of other grave Writers, who give such names too: and especially and by name of * *G. Powel*, who saith, *an Usurer is a Thief, a ravenous Vultur, a Murderer, an Idolator, and like unto the Divel, who continually seeketh whom he may devour: For so the Usurer night and day still devoureth the Borrower.* Is he such a one too, whom no Quaker has exceeded, I mean in in foul language? And what will he say to the Authors of Usuries Arraignment his words? *These are hard speaches and comparisons I confess, and such as might make a man loath the very name of Usury; yet there have, wise, and learned men written against it: If they say*, that such names by such are intended or of right belong to oppressing Exactors, and greedy Cormorants; *I answer*, how can this be, when the same Author doth plainly declare what the Usurers are, upon whom he bestoweth such Liveries, and to whom he gives such names and what their Usury is. *viz.* all gain or encrease unlawfully exacted or hoped, for the very duty of lending above the principal.

Mr. Jelinger. *Num.* 86. *The Usurer is a biter, for his sin is Nesheck biting.*

Reply. Let what his friend Bishop *Andrew* saith on the same word, serve for an answer to this, who asserts from *Galen*,

* Gab, Powel p. 40. *And I am even ashamed to tell in English, what* Coprovicus *that great Mathematician calls him to* 5. p. † Powel p. 4. and 2. §

Ety-

Etymologiam esse testem fallacem, that Etymology is a deceiptful witness; *whereunto*

My answer 1. *is*, a poor and often repeated come off: For we all say the same.

2. And besides he doth me a kindness, saying, that such a worthy Bishop is my friend: *Whereunto I add*, that the rest of the learned and grave Brethren are also, by his own confession in that same thing my friends.

3. *I Reply*, that, because the Ch. saith so little against this strong Argument I will say the more for it, as namely, *that the Usurer is a biter; in that*

1. He bites holes in a mans Estate, biting, like a dog, yea, like an old dog, as a famous Writer calls him.

But here I must answer a Question, which will be proposed, whether all Usurers bite, yea, or no?

Whereunto I answer, that all, so as that a Usurer by a general name is called in the Hebrew נשיך a biter, and the borower נשיך the bitten; *which has caused Divines to deliver it for an undoubted truth that all Usury bites.*

2. I add only this, that all do not bite a like, but some more and deeper than others: For if they be griping Usurers, they will take not only above the principal, but also above the ordinary Usury of six in the hundred, and Use upon Use, and advance mony, and forfeiture, and arrest men, if they come not off at the the payment day, and make them sell their Goods to their great loss to pay them: But if they be more mild, they will content themselves with six in the hundred, and crave no more; which notwithstanding they bite holes still; tho lesser ones, like lesser dogs; but without are dogs, all dogs, *Rev.* 21. 8.

Num. 87. *Where I shall be necessitated to answer two Objections.*

Objection 1. *And* 1. *that those*, *which set and let make holes too:*

Whereunto I answer: That their holes are no Usury holes interdicted by God, it being lawful to take Rent, and not Use, as I have fully proved it already.

The 2. *Objection is*, When the Usurer sees himself thus condemned, he snarles and barks and saith; I am no Usurer, no biter, no dog; for I do not wrong or bite any body, but rather do much good with my mony, and the borrower tels me how much he is beholding to me.

Answer 1. Why then doth every one that knows thee to be a lender of mony for six in the hundred call thee an Usurer?

2. *And why doth the foresaid most famous Council of* Agatha call

call thee Usurer, if thou take but five in the hundred?

3. And why doth every body curse thee for thy lending upon Usury, as *Jerome* tells thee, if thou wrongest no body?

4. And why doth the *Politephnia* compare thee to an Asp, which tho it bites but softly, yet killeth finally: For so as he which is stung with an Asp dieth sleeping, so sweetly doth he consume himself which hath borrowed upon Usury.

5. And why doth the learned renowned and voluminous CALPEINE *say of thy lending upon Usury, that it is properly Usury?*

6. And why do the very Heathens say, that such lending as thine is upon Usury maketh the borrower thine enemy: as I will instance, but in one at present viz. *Plautus* who asserts it: So that I wonder how the Usurer can truly say that he doth much good with his mony, and that the borrower gives him thanks; happily with his mouth he may give him thanks--- when the same time he curses him in his heart, *Jer.* 15. 10. The Lord convince the poor Usurer by this: So I prayed for him the night before I penned it, and when I wrote it by day; and so I pray for him every day, saying, *moriatur Usurarius ne moriatur*, let the Usurer before he dieth, die to his sin, that he may not die for his sin: and so I shall end this Paragraph with this *clausula* or close; *Even so, Lord Jesus, turn him that he may be turned I humbly beseech thee.*

Num. 88. *The Usurer is an Exactor, or Extortioner.*

Reply. A man may require his due, I hope, and yet be no Exactor or Extortioner? *I answer,* a Spade may be called a Spade, and so the lender taking Use for his mony, which the Ch. calls his due, when it is not his due, it being utterly forbidden, may be called an Exactor, especially when the Scripture calls him so: Where, *Psal.* 10. 9, 11. *Let the Exactor or* * *Usurer catch all that he has*, as the words are rendred by all translations almost, except the English as I said formerly, and *Exo.* 22. 25. where the Usurer is called an Exactor also.

2. The *Ch.* addeth, he goes on and taking many times excessively more encrease then he ought to take.

Reply. Then be like some encrease he may or ought to

* *Meaning thereby the Usurer, B.* Downam *upon* Ps. 15. 5. *Idem ibid.* || *Thou shalt not be to him an Exactor, Hebr* כנשה Sicut Usurarius sive fœnerator; qui accipit augmentum. *as a Usurer that takes an augmentation.* Poole.

take

take such as take excessively more we call them Extortioners.

Answer. When I say more then they ought to take, my meaning is, more then they ought to take according to their own opinion, which is that they must take no more then the Law stinteth.

Num. 89. 3. *He is an unjust person.*

Reply. *What is not against the Rules of charity and equity cannot be unjust* &c.

I Answer. 1. *And how will he prove it that Usury is not?*

1. *Against charity*, which is * kind, whereas Usury is inhumane and unkind, as it appears by his unkind dealings and denyings of lending of the smallest sum of mony freely, which has caused an † eminent writer to let fall these words; Evident and lamentable experience teacheth that whereas in the dayes of our Fore-fathers, when Usury was counted a deadly sin, a poor man or a young couple might easily borrow of a rich man forty or twenty Nobles freely, and pay it again at convenient leisure, a man cannot borrow five shillings, no not twelve pence for a week, but he must pay an egge for Usury, thus he, and I found it so, when I could not have five shillings lent me by a great and rich Usurer.

And || *another* hath this saying, *Christian charity puts not forth to Usury.*

And * another counts that Usury is directly against charity.

So † *another, establish Usury, and the Rule of Love is quite overthrown.*

2. How can he demonstrate it that it is not against equity?

He quoteth here Jer. Taylor, *and* B. Hall, *and* Rivet, *for himself.*

But I answer.

1. That I shall cite for my self four Authors too. And. 1. || Dr. *Fenton*, and 2. B. *Babington*, and 3. *John Knewstub* together, saying, that Usury is against the equity of lending; forasmuch as the Usurer will be at no hazard in lending: But whether the borrower sink or swim, lose or win, he

---

* B. Downam *upon* Psal. 15. 5. *And I heard this very day when I wrote this, a friend tell me, that Usurers are observed to be the hard heartest and cruellest people in the world, and that himsel f found it so.* † Humfred *in vita* Juel. p. 282. || Hugo C. *in* Psal. 11. * Heming. Comment. *in* Luke 5. † *Dr.* Fenton *against Usury.* || Babington *Quest. and Answers upon the* Comm. p. 3. * John Knewstub § 8. *in* Exo 20.

'will

'will be no looser, but have both his gaine and use full home,

'The fourth is *R. Turner*,whose words are : So you see here 'is no equity, the Usurer receiveth gain without labour, clear 'gain without cost, certain gain without peril, out of the 'industery, the charges, the meer uncertainties of the bor-'rower, a cleanly Alchymist that can extract much Silver, 'and wast nothing in smoak,these are the kine of *Bashan* that 'feed upon the Commons.

2. But especially I shall alledge for my self the word of God it self, *Exo.* 22. 14. *If a man borrow ought of his Neighbour, and it be hurt, or else die, the owner thereof not being by, he shall surely make it good*, where it is clearly to be seen, that God in lending provides only that the lender should be no looser; for the borrower was but to make good that which he had received, but the Usurer will be sure to have not only his own again, but his use too, and is that equity?

As for his three Authors, and,

Num. 90. 1. *Taylor.* I do not see that he names Usury at all or contradicts me.

2. B. *Hall*, as he is my friend elsewhere in his writings, and was my great friend, when I came first into *England* by preaching a Sermon purposely for me and one *Exul* more at *Exeter* to stir up the Citizens to provide for us a competency, wherein he himself joyned with them, and after that was exceeding kind to me, and familiar with me in frequent Latin discourses; so in this point of Usury he is my very good friend too, holding with me, which has caused my Antagonist to quarrel with him too, for his agreeing with me: whereunto I add, that even in this my Adversaries citation he is for me, *being for a voluntary satisfaction*, mark, *a voluntary satisfaction*, which is no other then a gratuity by me and my brethren allowed.

3. So my old friend *Rivet* also is for gratuities, and stands upon the same terms that some others do, *viz.* that so far as our brother be not hurted by lending and equity be observed, it is not contrary to charity, nor to the law *&c.* which maketh nothing against me, who am for gratuities, and would have no body hurted, and therefore am so much against Usury, whereby men are so much hurted, and the Law of Equity so

* Roger Turner *in the Usurer's Plea.* p. 9.

So

so much violated, as even now it has been demonstrated, so that *Rivet* must needs have respect to such a kind of lending as actually doth no hurt to any, which when it can be made to appear, as by a free gratuity, in case the borrower be really and justly a gainer, it will be evidenced, and no man can contradict it or speak against it: 2. *I answer*, that Usury is called * unjust gain, and that there is so much injustice in Usury, as that God thereby makes it so unlawful.

4. And whereas the Ch. addeth, that Usury may plead a License from civil laws, *&c.* I do wonder how he can so soon forget what he said so lately, that he will not vindicate those that keep not within the bounds of Equity, when all the while he takes upon him to plead for Usury, and for Usurers from the Civil-laws, and that most wonderfully.

1. Because the Civil-laws are all for Equity, and Usurers are not *wrongfully*, because the Civil laws do not allow it, as by and by I will prove it. And that

1. By *Justinian* the Emperour, who saith expresly, that the Senate of *Rome* did not constitute use, and fruit in things, which in their using might be consumed; as Wine, Oyl, Corn, Cloths; next whereunto is mony numbred, *nec enim poterat*, for it could not do it, but in ground and houses, *&c.*

2. *Cajus* saith, it was not effected by the decree of the Senate that there be a proper use and fruit of mony, for natural reason could not be charged by the Senate.

3. *Baldus*, put the case, my brother make an Usurer his Heir, I may break his Testament, and by excluding him, be admitted my self, by complaint of a Testament made against Office or good Right.

4. And what saith a great Modern Doctor, *The civil wise men of* Rome *did not allow Usury, as a thing that did either naturally belong to the contract of lending, or else that might be annexed thereunto: But they permitted it otherwise, as also they permitted Fornication and Divorces.*

He superadds, *We expect that he answer what Mr.* Baxter *in his* Directory *has said to prove that some Usury is neither against Charity nor Justice.*

Whereunto I *answer* 1. That I have red Mr. *Baxter*, and say so too, that there is a Usury which is neither against

---

* Prov. 28. 8. *and* Ezek. 18. 8. *If a man be just and has not given forth upon Usury: Whereupon see* Tho. Aquin. 2. 919. *So the* Syriack *upon* Psal. 15. 5. † Cajus *in* pandect. ‖ Baldus *de Infam.* * *The Author of the brief* Treat. *of Usury.*

Charity

Charity nor Justice; as namely the liberal and recompensatory, and when Mr. *Baxter's* cautions are observed, which because by a * *Novation* they alter Usury, I like exceeding well for my part, but not one of a thousand observes: So s that Godly and famous man will do our Usurers, by all ien so called, no pleasure at all, because not one of a thousand observes them.

2. It is expected also that one or other of Usuries Defendants do answer Doctor *Pie* against Usury, which was never yet answered, and *Bolton*. Mr. *Jelinger* (he saith farther) ome make the Usurer an alienator of that which is other iens not his own.

Reply. The borrower hath no more right to the lenders iony and the use thereof, than the lender has to that icrease, which is now spoken against, yea not so much, &c.

I answer. 1. I thought he would have flatly denyed my sertion, but if he had, I should have brought *Calvin*, and mous B. *Hall* to make it good: For he saith expresly; He at by vertue of such translation, or contract, (as also he lls it) doth but in a mannerly and legal fashion (which is for t in the hundred) rob the borrower.

2. As for his right he stands so much upon, I wonder w he will prove it, by the Scripture, which must warrant it, d doth not, but rather disanulls it by its forbidding of Uy *Deut*. 23. 19. &c. The Laws and Compacts &c. are *ambe bis cocta*, and have been often by me answered already d therefore will save me some labour to refell the same ngs again.

3. What he saith of B. *Hall* is soon to be answered, for *Hall* speaketh but by way of *If* If, you can find a way ether by loan or sale (mark sale also) to adventure your ck, that may be free from all oppression (mark, all opssion) and extortion, and benificial to others as well as to ar selves, ye need not fear to walk in it; and who will

---

* *So called by Civilians.* † *I say* Calvin, *who writeth expresly n* Ezek. 18. St. Ambrose, Jerome, Austin, Bernard, B. Hall, *with famous Mr.* Smith *asserts the same, saying*, p. 1. *Christ expounding the Commandment which forbidds stealing h, lend freely, shewing that Usury, because she lends not free- is a kind of Theft, and the Usurers a kind of Theeves: For this exposition were not right.* So G. Powel, p. 40. *The ver is a* Theef, &c. *So* Barth. Westhinerus *in* Ps. 15. 5. *ry is Theft* &c.

gainsay it if such a thing may be? But where is that Usurer, which is free from all oppression and extortion, sith by the wo[r]d of God he is called an extortioner, as I proved it formerly? so that he cannot inherit the Kingdom of God, 1 *Cor*. 6. 9, 10 Which famous place makes alſo for me, becauſe the Uſurer is alſo called an Extortioner.

Num. 91. *Mr*. Jelinger 5. *The Uſurer is a covetous perſon*. *Reply*. To which *I anſwer* in the words of B. *Taylor*. Covetouſneſs is to be cured by the proper motives to Charity, and by the proper rules of Juſtice, which being ſecured, the arts of getting mony are not eaſily made criminal. *I anſwe[r]* 1. But how are they ſecured by a Uſurer, who as I prove[d] him to be, is ſo unjuſt, and uncharitable; and whoſe Uſur[y] is by great * Authors made a very ſpecies of Covetouſne[ſs] upon *Pſal*. 15. 5. So that by no means he can be ſaved ex cept he repent: Becauſe it is expreſly writen, that no cove tous perſon, which is an Idolator, has any inheritance in th[e] Kingdom of Chriſt and of God, *Epheſ*. 5. 5.

Mr. *Jelinger*. But he looketh for his gain at the half yea[r] end.

Reply. And why not as well as the Hireling for his wage[s] when due, and the Adventurer for his gain at the return [of] the Ship, or ſuch as have ſet out their Tenements, expe[ct] their Rent at their proper Seaſons? *Anſwer*, Becauſe the [U]ſurers gain is forbidden in the word of God *Deut*. 23. 19. *N[eh]*. 4. 10. *&c*. But the other contracts are not. The very He[a]thens allow Rent, and Uſe, and Fruits, for Lands and Te[ne]ments, as I proved out of *Cajus* in the *Pandects*, and Lan[d]lords may expect it; but the Uſurer cannot lawfully exp[ect] gain for his mony lent. God as well as the heathens be[ar] againſt it, *Luke* 6. 35. *But let us ſee what the Ch. ſaith ne[xt]*.

Mr. *Jelinger*. Uſurers ſeldom repent. *Reply*. They t[hat] exceed not the bounds of humanity and † equity, need [not] repent.

I anſwer, 1. That all Uſurers exceed both, hath been [ſuf]ficiently proved, because all Uſury bites more or leſs. [...]

---

* Pſal. 109. 11. *In moſt tranſlations*. † Theoderet *in* I[...] 15. *With whom I conjoyn* Wits, *ſaying in his* Politeuphni[a] 290. *Covetouſneſs looketh out Uſury, and Uſury nouriſheth* [Co]*vetouſneſs, and* p. 291. *Uſury is the Daughter of Covetou[ſneſs]*. *The ſubordinate cauſe of Uſury is Covetouſneſs* G. P. p. 9.

|| *Uſury is againſt all equity and Conſcience and reaſon*. Fo[...] p. 15. *And all Uſury bites* ibid.

2. *I add* that, because the Champion speaks so slightly and Pharisaically in answer to my charge, I will more fully shew it, how it cometh to pass that the Usurer so seldom repents, tho he have great need of it indeed: *and*

1. Usurers seldom repent, because of their hard * heartedness as being like Crocodiles (as † *Gabriel Powel* resembleth them) which if a Cart go over their backs, feel it not: for so Usurers are sensel ess, tho a most powerful Sermon with a most heavy load of || menaces and judgements, hanging over them, be preached against them, and go over them, which has caused Divines to let fall such passages concerning their hardness of heart and usual impenitency.

Their Consciences are cauterized as with a hot iron, there is such a thick skin grown over their hearts, that they will hardly be circumcised in this point, and this senslesness seems to proceed from these causes.

1. From the examples of others. 2. From a perverse affection, saith Mr. *Taylor*.

2. Usurers seldom repent because of restitution, for they are told by Gods word, that they must make restitution, *Neh.* 5. 11. *Restore I pray you*, &c. and by holy Writers which have Written against Usury in these last dayes also, according to the word of God that they must restore, I will name but three at present.

1. The Doctor which has penned the short treatise of Usury: when any man has committed Usury he is bound to make restitution, except, *&c.* whereof more in another place.

2. Mr. *Smith*, that you may not die in your sins, it is necessary to make restitution before you die, *&c.* sutable to that of *Austin*, sin is not remitted, unless that which is taken wrongfully, be restored.

3. * *Powel*, who saith. 1. It is not enough that the Usurer take no more Usury, but that he must restore that which he has taken. 2. That the heirs of an Usurer may not keep it in any case, what the Usurer has gotten, because it is none of theirs.

---

* *And* B. Downam *upon* Psal. 15. 5. *Usury has turned lending into an act of inhumanity and cruelty: and Usury is unequal and uncharitable.* † *As the wrath of God, and the subjection of goods to malediction.* G, P. p. 38. || *Usury doth harden the heart.* Downam *upon* Psal. 15. 5. * Rog. Turner p. 15. † *Mr.* Smith *in his second Sermon of Usury.* G. Powel. p. 68. *and so* Capel *in his Usury Book.*

4. * *Seminianus*, Who saith that those which back what i not theirs is kept back by Satan. And thus; O what a har saying is it to the Usurer, so as that he seldom repents, becau he saith in his heart, suppose I should give over this sin of V sury, what shall I be the better for it, unless I restore, and tha if I should do it, would undo me: so that very seldom w shall here of an Vsurer that repents, * and some † Minister and my Adversaries present answer and defending of Usur by his Pamphlet, is the ready way to make the Usurers repen tance yet rarer; (which is the sense and saying of good men unless it be timely prevented, which thing I am about to do partly by my appearing against Usury in general, and partl by facilitating the Usurers repentance, when I shall come t shew what the poor Usurer must do in that weighty case c restitution, as partly I have limited it already; and shall de clare in its proper place more fully. being seconded there by most learned and able Assistants, being both Divines an Lawyers.

In the next place I will trace my Antagonist in that which h saith for it.

Mr. Jelinger. *6. He is a Destroyer. 7. A Merciless pers 8. Doth not walk Honestly.*

Thus he hurleth these weighty things together, skipping ov twenty eight lines, and slighting them as much as he can: Fo he saith no more but this. *Reply.* Those intended again all persons he accounts Usurers are but the products of mistaken Zeal, or purblind rashness; so that I shall there fore relate those things, which he so slights and abbreviate to render them so considerable to all men as in themselve they are.

1. *The Vsurer is a Destroyer*; whereof I have spoken els where as well as here, as there was cause, which notwith standing I will now say a little more upon this new occasio and provocation given me, shewing more fully

1. *How he destroyeth himself and his.* 2. *others also.*

---

* *Vsurarij dumdum aliena retinent, a Diabolo retinentu* Seminianus l. 9. c. 90. † *For I hear Vsurers generally sa in discoursing with me, such an eminent Minister is so.* || *As i* Luther's *time it was defended and commended: For so he saith Vsury is commended with full mouth-- as a most reasonable trad without which the common-wealth cannot stand*--- Luth. d Usura.

1. *Himself and his.* 1. Himself by his covetousness drowning himself in perdition and destruction, 1 *Tim.* 6. 9 10. his Usury being to him as a *Gulph*, saith a * learned Writer, which devoureth souls; I add that a Malefactor may be said to cast away himself and is guilty of self-murder, as *Korah* and his Fellows, so the Usurer casts away himself.

2. He destroyes his, I mean his own issue and posterity, whereof I have spoken already, so that for the present I shall only add what * *Hemingius*, that famous forreign Divine relateth of a great Usurer of a mean place, dwelling in *Chersoneso Cymbrica*: This man grew exceeding rich by lending upon Usury, and died, leaving abundance of wealth, And yet after his death the children that he left behind him fell into extream poverty, insomuch that a daughter of his was found to have not so much as a whole Coat on her back to cover her nakedness, and was many times seen to do most base and servile work to get her living and yet could not keep her self thereby from beggery. So his other Daughter came to the like poverty, of whom hereafter.

2. *Others besides*, even 1. *Whole housholds*, as appeareth by that tragical Scripture, *Neh.* 5. 4, 5, 7. which caused that pious Bishop *Je el* to say, that it is utter destruction of infinite families; with whom doth simpathize the learned *G. Powel*, saying: As Serpents do sting and destroy the body with their poyson, so Usury DESTROYETH, biteth and devoureth a mans substance very speedily.

So *Sextus*, Usury like a whirlepool utterly wasteth the Commonwealth.

But I know not what the Usurer will say. How can man say ? There be those which have grown rich by my money, and gotten great estates by it, which objection that great Father * St. *Basil* answereth most notably thus. Thou wilt say unto me, that men have grown rich by Usury; *But I answer* that I suppose, more by that means have come to the gallows. Thou lookest to these and repeatest those that have grown rich by Usury: but thou namest not those which have

---

* *And is guilty of his own overthrow, the Lord having threatned, that he shall not dwell in his holy Hill*, Psalm 15. 5. Numb. 16. 38. † Sextus Decret. *apud Dr.* Wilson l. 92. || Hemingius Comm. in loc. 5. * Jo. Juel Sermon. *in* 1 Thes. 4. 6. G. Powel. *p.* 29. *and p.* ... * Sextus Dicret *Num.* 92. *Objection answered.* † Basil. Psal. 15.

grown desperate, and faint hearted, and have come to their end by Usury.

I shall close up this answer with great * Dr. *Wilsons* pretty narration concerning this thing. A man coming into a certain Church, and seeing it full of Images made of wax, demanded, what might be the cause of such an unwonted sight? answer was made, that those whom these images did represent, were certain persons, which in a time were saved from drowning, by calling upon our Lady. Nay then, quoth he again, where are the images of those, I pray you, that called upon onr Lady, and were drowned notwithstanding? So say I in this case, if any man will set before me the images of those which took up money upon Usury and grew rich thereby; I would demand on the other side, that he shew forth the hundreds and thousands of those who by that means have utterly been impoverished, and overthrown theirs own estate: they will be found a million for one, yea, to be without all comparison. Thus this great Divine.

2. Usurers destroy and ruine the Country or City wherein they live, which has caused Magistrates, Countries, Kingdoms, and Cities to suppress them and drive them out; so *Nehemiah* did put them down, *Ch.* 5. 7, 8, 9, *&c.* and *Sparta*, *Worms*, and others, because they said they were oppressed, *ruined* and consumed by them. For as great † *Luther* tells us, as a worm in an Apple, or Nut, consumeth all that is within, so an Usurer devoureth the substance of theCity by wonderful and secret means.

And what that great Presul ‖ *Downam* saith concerning this consuming ruining and destroying of Countries and Commonwealths, see his words upon *Psal.* 15. 5. *p.* 256. 257, 261. And therefore how can this destroyer be saved, unless he repent and come to be a Lamb of a Lion, and a harmless Sheep of a ravening Wolf, and do no more hurt or harm, nor destroy, as it is the property of all the Citizens of *Sion* (who shall dwell with God in his Heavenly mount *Sion*, where no Usurers ever will be admitted to take up their habitation, *Psal.* 15. 5.) I say again, it is the property of all the Citizens of *Sion, not to hurt nor to destroy in all Gods holy Mountain*, *Esa.* 65. 25. which is his Church saith *Haymo* that ancient Doctor and Bishop of *Halberstat*.

Num. 92. Mr. Jelinger, *he is a merciless person*, which saying

---

* *Dr.* Wilson *fol.* 189. † Luther *in* Decalog. ‖ *B.* D. *upon* Psal. 15. 5. ‡ Haymo *Episc.* Halberstatensis.

be-

because it is so slighted also, I will, for its dilatation declare how it cometh to pass that he is so merciless, &c.

1. Because he wanteth that charity which he should have.

2. Because he is of a Serpentine nature.

For the 1. I say, he wanteth charity, and my reason why I say so that the Usurer wanteth charity is this, because if he had that charity, which he boasteth of, he would not be an Usurer, for as much as charity is, 1. *Kind*, 1 Cor. 13. 4. *and he inhumane*, as by holy * Writers he is called, and unkind, 2. Seeketh not her own, *v.* 5. whereas he seeketh his own, as much as any man, if some will not believe me, I hope they will believe a far greater person, then my self, famous Bishop *Downam*, I mean, whose words I will here rehearse; lending was ordained of God to be a contract whereby the lender should seek the good of the borrower, without respect of his own profit, so far should he be from doing wrong therein, but the Usurer has made lending a contract, wherein he SEEKETH FOR his OWN GAIN NOT ONLY UNCHARITABLY without respect, of the borrowers either profit or loss, but also UNJUSTLY, seeking gain where he bears no hazard, and taking another mans goods without his good will. Thus he,* and yet farther he saith, and the Usurers sometimes do vaunt, how KINDLY they deal with their debtors in forbearing them from year to year, yet the truth is, the longer they forbear the greater is their gain, and tho they defer the borrowers misery, yet indeferring it they increase it. See the † Margin also, and let me add,

And therefore by some are not unfitly compared unto the greedy Cat, which, tho for a time she playeth with the silly Mouse, yet in the end she will be sure to devour it. But if that which I said, and that, which that Author even now told us, will not suffice to make good what was said of the Usurers unkindness, uncharitableness, and self seeking, contrary to 1 *Cor.* 13. 4. and so to make to make him a merciless

---

* *But* Basil *who saith Usury is an excessive Inhumanity. And yet farther he saith whatsoever becometh of the principal, whether it be lost by fire, or be taken away by Theevs, or miscarry by any other calamity, the Usurer by vertue of his Covenant is to demand his gain as well out of the loss of the Borrower as out of his gain.*

person I will subjoyn what others also write besides as namely 1. Renowned * Mr. *Smith.*

All the Commandments of God are fulfilled by LOVE *Rom.* 13. 1. Which Christ noteth, when he draweth all the Commandments to one Commandment, which is, *love God above all things and thy Neighbour as thy self, Mat.* 22 37. as if he should say, he which LOVES God will keep all the Commandments, which respect God, and he which loveth his Neighbour, will keep all the Commandments which respect his Neighbour, therefore to maintain love God forbiddeth all things which hinders this love, and amongst the rest here he forbiddeth Usury as one of her deadly enemies; FOR A MAN CANNOT LOVE and be an USURER (as I also said even now) because Usuries is a kind of cruelty, and a kind of persecution (O sad!) and therefore the want of love maketh Usurers; for if there were love there would be no Usury, no deceit, *&c.* but we should live in peace, and joy, and contentment, like the Angels.

Num. 93. Object. *If it be objected*, that he means oppressive Usurers and Usury?

Answ. *I answer*, that cannot be; because he saith, *p.* 96. *All Usury signifieth biting, to shew, that all Usury is unlawful.*

2. He defineth Usury thus, Usury is that gain, which is gotten by lending, for the use of the thing which a man lendeth, covenanting before with the borrower to receive more than was borrowed. And therefore saith he farther, * one calls the Usurer a legal Thief, because before he steals he tells the party how much he will steal, as tho he stole by Law, and so B. *Hall* calls him, as I have shewn it.

2. Another defining Usury, calleth it the contrary to Charity; for *Paul* saith, † Love seeketh not her own, therefore Usury is far from Love; but God is *Love*, 1 *John* 4. 8. Therefore Usury is far from God.

A || *Third saith*, at the beginning Usury is mild, but in the end its merciless.

Now 2. I come to my other Reason, why a Usurer is a merciless person, *viz. because he is of a serpentine nature*, the Hebrew word which signifies Usury, *viz.* נֶשֶׁךְ being derived from a verb, which often in Scripture is ascribed to

---

* Smith *in his first Sermon upon Usury* p. 95. † 1 Cor. 13. 5. || Powel p. 48.

the

the biting of SERPENTS, so that divers Writers have compared a Usurer to a SERPENT, as *Chrisostom*, *Powel*, and others, with whom I Joyn *Pagnine*, who calleth Usury the biting of a SERPENT, because the Usurer will shew no more mercy to a Borrower than a Serpent to a man, but kills him, there being such an Antipathy between it and man *Gen.* 3. 15.

So that a great Author which knew what he spake, might well say, *fænus interficit misericordiam*, Usury killeth mercy. And therefore how can the poor merciless Usurer be saved, except he repent, it being written expresly in Gods Book, he shall have *Judgment without mercy, that hath shewed no mercy*, Jam. 2. 13. Again I say, how can any enter into the Kingdom of God, who is so far from God, being so far from Love.

Num. 94. But here, the Usurer seeing himself thus condemned as a merciless and uncharitable person, will plead for himself thus: I a merciless and uncharitable person, who so supply my Neighbour's necessities upon all occasions with my mony, which is always ready for him to help him? *Whereunto* let first the Author of the imperfect work upon *Matthew* ascribed to St *Chrys.* Answer,

'Crist therefore commands us to lend, but not upon Usury: For he that lendeth upon Usury, at the first sight seemeth to relieve a mans necessity, but indeed casteth him into a greater necessity, he looseth him of one bond and bindeth him with more: Neither doth he lend for the Righteousness of God, but for his own gain: For the Usurers mony is like the biting of the † Asp; for even as he which is bitten of the Asp goeth to sleep, as if he were delighted, and through the pleasantness of his sleep dieth; so he which borroweth upon Usury is delighted for a time as one that had received a good turn, and so through the pleasure of the imagined benefit, he doth not perceive how he is taken Captive: For even as the poyson of the Asp secretly conveigheth it self into all members, corrupteth the whole body: So Usury dispersing it self through all the Borrowers Goods converteth them into Debt (so that he must needs feel it at last.)

I will Joyn *G. Powel* with him *p.* 48.

* *Author operis imp. in Matth. Attrib.* Chrys. Tom. 3. Tom. 12. in fine. † *Of which somewhat has been said formerly.*

The Usurer pleads Love, not for thy sake but for his own sake.

The Eight Argument against Usury. That he doth not walk honestly, he slights also, so that I shall go to bring it to that estimate which is due to it, and to free it from my Adversaries slighting by shewing again,

1. How plainly God himself speaketh of the Usurers dishonesty, saying thou hast taken Usury and Encrease *Ezek.* 22. 12. Mark, not only Usury called נשך: biting, but also Encrease, that is, more than thou lendest; and then *v.* 13. *Behold therefore I have smitten my hand against thy dishonest gain*, which maketh perspicuosly for what I say, that the Usurer doth not walk *honestly*.

2. Shewing how, next unto God, some of the wisest men that have, since Christ, and his Apostles, lived and flourished in the world have made the Usurer a dishonest person. *viz*.

1. * '*Calvin*, who saith it is more than rare that one and 'the same person should be both an honest man and an Usu-'rer.

2. † '*Luther*, one of the wisest and worthiest men in the 'world, agreeth with *Calvin* and by him is brought in.

3. A great and wise man indeed, even || *Cæsar* himself, that mighty and first Roman Emperour, of whom the said *Luther* writeth thus; *Cæsar* made an Edict that an Usurer should not be counted or adjudged in Law, for a good and honest man, as I cited him formerly. Now are all these, all these sayings of God and men also, as the Champion saith of mine, the products of mistaken zeal, or purblind rashness?

In short if this be so, as it is asserted and proved; then, how can the Usurer be saved, unless he become an honest man indeed? For as much as God has expresly said, that he has smitten, that is, will smite his hand *at his dishonest gain*, to shew his great displeasure against him for his dishonest Usurious gain, *verse* 13. so as that he must not look to inhabit that holy and heavenly Tabernacle, wherin none but honest men will dwell, who do not put out their mony to Usury *Psal.* 15. 1. 2. Which has caused a great † Author to say, that the Usury which is now practised is not allowed by any Godly man.

Num. 95. *In the next place he advanceth to my cloud of Saints*

* Calvin. *Epist. resp. de Usuris.* † Luther *de tax. Usura* Tom 7. || *Idem ibid.* * B. Downam Psal. 15. 5.

against *Usury, saying, I acknowledge, if that must needs be Gospel, which Councils, Fathers, and School-men, (I mean some of these) have determined, then he has the advantage :* but *we are come*, &c. Let the Reader peruse the rest of his words if he have them either in Print or Writing : For my Adversary has scattered them and sent abroad his Pamphlet (as I am told.) They are too large for me to transcribe, with his citations of *Spanhemius*, *Windelin*, *Zanchy*, and *Gerard* in Latin : and the truth is, he has shewn me the way which I must take by his skipping over sometimes thirty-three , and somtimes more lines of mine ; but yet I will do him so much right as to answer his most momentous responses, and quotations, which kindness he doth not shew to me, in that he neither answers my words, nor the sayings of my learned Authors, but passeth by many of them altogether.

Num. 96. My Answers. *Now my answers will follow at large upon and after a serious invocation of the name of God for a blessing first craved to be powered down from above upon my poor endeavours.*

1. *Answer* And First in general I say, that my Adversaries Reply to my cloud of Saints is so advantagious to me, as that what he saith, for the most part maketh most happily for me. For

1. Whereas he granteth that by the determination of Councils, Fathers, and School-men, I have the advantage ; doth not that make for me, that so many hundreds (because Councils consist of hundreds commonly) of such holy and learned men as the Fathers are for me ? As for his Addition, if that be Gospel, doth not hurt me, who do not equal what they say with the Gospel (as the Council of Trent asserts it) *that their traditions are to be accepted* pari pietatis *affectu, with the same pious affection* with the Scriptures, but only approve of what they say according to the Gospel, and for example, according to *Luke* 6. 35. *Lend, looking for nothing from thence*, as *Grotius*, his Author himself confesseth it , that *a plerisque* most ancient Fathers that place is so handled, and understood, as making against Usury : I will add one saying more which my Adversary hath concerning Fathers, and also doth exceedingly make for me, viz. *That they descry all taking of Use*, which maketh me to break out into this exclamation ; how happy then am I that have such Saints and so many on my side, and what a friend is my very Adversary to me by his own confession ? The like whereunto I may say of the deep learned Casuists , and School-men, one of which, *Aquinas* I mean , admired above all his fellow Scholasticks, for his transcendent learning.

2. In

1. In that he saith that the Fathers opinion *descrying all taking of Use for mony generally passed for currant among the School-men*, being backt too with the Authority of Councils: He thereby also pleads for me, as much as I can wish; because he saith now GENERALLY, having said before (I mean some of these) School-men, Councils, and Fathers immediately before mentioned) which sheweth how he contradicts himself, and is even forced by the evidence of Truth to averr, that Councils, Fathers, and School-men *are generally for me*, O advantage! advantage!

3. Wheras he adds, I think that *All taking Use for Mony* was never more exploded than under the present darkness of Popery: But since the time of Reformation, that hidden things have been brought to light, this among other things has been discerned to be an ERROR, which Addition also militates for me: For as much as

1. Learned and well read men can confute him presently, and shew him to be but a meer Babe and Idiote in the knowledge of Antiquity: For that with a sonourous and loud voice he declareth, how the holy Fathers before the grossest Popery came in, were as bitter and eager against Usury and did as much explode it, as ever the Papists did since, thinking (as the Ch. himself tells us) they could not run farr enough &c. but by discrying all taking of Use: which I am sure makes as much for me as I can desire.

3. This Addition militateth for me, in that he would make the world believe that since the times of Reformation this discrying of all taking of Use has been found an Error: Because wise and observing men are able to refell what he saith presently, and to shew that his opinion since the times of Reformation that hidden things have been brought to light, it among other things has been discovered to be not only an Error, but called Heresie: For no sooner did the light of the Gospel break out at *Wittemberg*, where *Luther* fixed his Theses against Popery; but theses also were disputed against all taking of Use in the same University (as I have already shewn it) and withal it has been asserted in the same positions to be plain Heresie, and that those which take any thing above the principal, are to be accounted Hereticks, which has been likewise so judged by others, * especially if any defend Usury; See my margin.

---

* Wilson *fol.* 144. Archidiaconus § 1. q. 1 Card. *de Usura.* † Martin *ab Alinserist* Enchirid. c. 17.

All

All which must needs make for me, and make the world see who is in an error, he and his, or I and mine, and who speaks true and lieth not, he, or I, and whom men may believe hereafter, him, or me;

Num. 97. 4. Whereas he boasteth so much of *Calvin*, *Bucer*, *Martyr*, *Zanchie*, *Rivet*, *Junius*, *Salmasius*, *Wallelius*, *Windeline*, *Hornbeck Spanhemius*, *Brentius*, &c.

That they are for a Regulated Usury, even that maketh for me also. How for you? O yes, it doth. For

1. The word which himself useth, calling Usury, which they are for, regulated Usury, is and can be no other but well cautioned Usury: For these men have their godly cautions, which I will name and set down fully hereafter, before I end this matter, and which so alter that which he calls Usury by a Novation (as they term it) as that it is not Usury † properly so called, but another kind of thing and contract: Where give me leave for the present to set down some few of their religious || Cautions.

1. They say that a man must take nothing but that which his *Debtor* can get by good and lawful means.

2. He may not take more than the gain, nay not all the gain, nor that part of the gain, which drinketh up the living of him that useth the mony.

3. He must sometimes be so far from taking gain, that he must not require the principal, if this *Debtor* by inevitable and just causes be brought behind hand, and it be also plain that he could not make, no not by great diligence any commodity of the mony borrowed: With * which cautions may be joyned the most excellent ones of *Fabricus*, and of reverend Mr. *Baxter* in his directions concerning Usury.

3. *Answer* 3. I say, that if these Authors should defend Usury properly so called (which I will not grant) it would be the same thing with their opinion of our Christian Sabbath, which they hold is to be observed not by a Divine but the Churches Institution, and not to be so strictly kept as we keep it, calling it Judaism, so that I have seen all manner of servile and worldly work done upon the Lords-day in the *Netherlands*, where the Ch Authors, as *Spanhemius*, *Rivet*, *Grotius*, *Ametius*, *Salmasius* and others lived and tolerated it: So in *Geneva*, I have seen them in Sermon time sit one over against another, selling their commodities, and to pas-

---

* G. Powel. *p.* 3. † *See Dr.* Hamond's *Practical Chatech. p.* 315. || *In my* 2. *part of this Book.*

sed

fed through them, not being then convinced of the unlawfullness of it, as many others also are not at present, no more than of Usuries sinfullnes; which discovery by the Ch. occasioned, makes very much for me.

4. *Answer.* 4. It causeth me to declare, how his transmarine Authors cannot agree among themselves, Lutherans and Calvinists, warring one against another by Paper battels about consubstantiation, the ubiquity of Christs body, and the five Articles, so much discussed abroad; and how the most obstinate Defendants of Usury cannot accord among themselves neither, † some holding a compact lawful, || others not, and some by Nesheck understanding the Lords rack-rent, others oppressive Usury, and some taking Tarbith to be moderate Usury, others not.

Now if they be thus divided about these things, holding that such and such among them be out therein, why may they not be out in that Usury it self, which they hold lawful, and doth not this make for me?

5. *Answer.* 5. It occasioneth me to mention a thing which few know or have heard of, *viz.* that there are some risen up beyond the Seas (where Usury is most defended and practised by some) I mean, *John de Abiah* and his companions, who say, that they are all out there (even the very Protestants they mean) and therefore have set up their own way which they aver to be the right way in a certain * Dutchie there, where they gained that famous and learned Virgin Lady, called *Anna Maria Schureman*, which is now dead, but before her death, has set forth a certain Latin book which I have seen and read. The name of it is *Electio melioris partis, the Election of the better part*, because her name is *Maria*, whereof I make this use. That if it should be so as they say, that they be so out beyond the Seas in other things, why may they not be out too in the thing called Usury?

Num. 98. 6. *I answer*, that I shall set down the responses and answers of my friends, which they have made to the alleadging of Authors for Usury, lest men should think, or say, that I only go to shift off those great and grave Di-

---

* *Of whom I hear that my opponent is one.* † *I mean some of his Neighbours and divers more who could be named.*

|| *Where they live together about Eighty of them Families and Persons, as one told me, who being very godly is acquainted with them.*

vines which seem to favour Usury, when they do not: And,

1. I'le recite the words of Bishop *Downam*. Not only Usurers themselves have found out many subtle distinctions and instances to justifie Usury: but also divers Divines have either spoken or written more wittily than truly in favour of Usury.

'2. Dr. *Taylor*, if learned men allow that Usury which 'commonly is practised, I oppose the word of God against 'them.

'3. Dr. *Slater*, if those Divines that are for Usury be 'Usurers themselves, then no wonder: if not, then to re'solve others they set down such cautions as make it no 'Usury.

'4. Dr. *Fenton* sheweth how those Authors, which are for 'Usury take what they write one of another, as an instance is 'given in a manuscript for Usury taken for a great part of it, 'out of *Bullinger*.

'5. *Gabriel Powel* answers this plea from some learned 'Divines who Write in defence of Usury, thus, as I said once 'before now.

'1. No Writer that ever I could see or hear of, ever allow'ed USURY.

'2. There are many strong poysons, which the learned 'Physitian can so qualifie, that a sick person may take a potion, 'wherein some of the poyson is.

'3. So holy and godly men have done and do temper and 'qualifie the Usurers poyson that they make hereof a whole'some medicine for many distressed persons.

'4. For by their holy and religious caveats and lessons they 'alter the qualities of the Usury and make it indeed no U'sury at all, but a lawful kind of trade and dealing: thus he, '*bis ac ter quod pulchrum est*.

6. *Answer*. Sixtly I shall answer thus. That whereas one of his Authors called *Windelin* sticks not to say, that *a plerisque modernis Theologis*, by most modern Divines &c. The question is affirmed *duabus observatis cautelis*, it will be proved, that contrary to truth two things are asserted by him.

1. That *a plerisque* by most modern Divines, the question is affirmed (for Usury.) 2. That but two cautions only are to be observed.

---

* G. Powel 52. 53.

Fo:

For the first I ſhall prove it to be contrary to truth, by ſuch Authors as may be believed before his *Windelin*, as being free from Uſury and ſo unbiaſſed, whereas many I will not ſay all, beyond-Seamen are tainted by and with Fœnory: And

1. I ſhall cite again famous Dr. *Slater*, whoſe words theſe are: If learned men allow that which is commonly practiſed (Uſury he meaneth) A far greater number of late learned Divines, beſides Fathers and Scholaſticks do not. Now let Engliſh-men chuſe whom they will believe, their own Engliſh Doctor, or this Forraign *Windelin*.

2. With him I ſhall joyn the moſt renowned and moſt learned Biſhop * *Downam*, who firſt tells us that he could add unto Scripture-proofs, the teſtimonies of all wiſe and learned men, (mark, all wiſe and learned men, who have lived until our age, mark again, *until our age*, becauſe ſome falſly ſay, that now in our age Uſury is not ſo ſpoken againſt as it was, and that I only, and one or two more, are ſo much againſt it) The Philoſophers, tho Heathens, have written and ſpoken againſt it, the Fathers of the Church have with one conſent comdemned it, even to the Pit of Hell.

Num. 99. 2. He adds, The Godly learned Divines of this age, and namely of this our Church, do for the moſt part inveigh againſt it; thoſe few that ſeem to defend Uſury do in ſubſtance differ little from the reſt, erring eſpecially in this, that under the odious name of Uſury, they defend and maintain a lawful contract of partnerſhip.

3. || So the Author of the Conviction of Uſury. By the Church of England Uſury is ſimply and generally prohibited.

4. I will procure the moſt confident ſaying of famous ALCIATES concerning the infinite multitude of Uſuries enemies.

Totus mundus militat pro nobis, the whole world militates for us, as I quoted him formerly.

And well he might ſay ſo, for, beſides the holy Scriptures, and ancient Councils already ſo much ſpoken of, and the holy thers, which with one conſent have condemned it to the pit of Hell, as ſaith that great B. *Downam*, and the ſharp

* B. Downam *upon* Pſal 15. 5. † *The Author of the Conviction of Uſury in his Dedic. Epiſt.* || Council. *Arelatenſe. Agat. Terraconenſe. Nicenum. Eliebertinum, Turonenſe, Lateran. Laod. Pariſ.* * Downam *in* Pſ. 15.

ſighted

slighted Schoolmen, who, tho corrupt in many things else, yet herein do, as he saith well, retain the doctrine of the Primitive Church, I say, besides all these a world of modern Divines are of our side, blessed be God, *viz.* the British Divines, Bishops, and Churches, as even now it was proved, and by name *Bishop Jewel*, *Bishop Babington*, *Bishop Sands*, *Bishop Downame*, *Bishop Hall*, *Bishop Lake*, *Bishop King*, *Arch-Bishop Usher*, *Bishop Andrew*, *Doctor Wilson*, *Doct. Beard*, *Doct. Slater*, *Doct. Smith*, *Doct. Taylor*, *Doct. Kimbus*, *Doct. Pie*, *Doct. Web*, *Doct. Fenton*, *Doct. Wilkinson*, *Ainsworth*, *Fr. Whidden* the Elder, *Mr. Hirn*, *Mr. Saunderson*, *Cartwright*, *Swinock*, *Ambrose*, *Turner*, *Mr. Pool*, *Mr. Udal*, *Mr. Bolton*, *Mr. Smith*, *Mr. Adams*, *Lightfoot*, *Nosworthy*, *Hakins*, all of them being famous *English* Divines, to whom I may add *Mr. Dod. Mr. Capel*, *Mr Whately*, *Doct. Sutton*, *Mr. Bains*, *Mr. Greenham*, *Rogers* of *Dedham*: After whom in came Forreign Writers, *viz. Doct. Luther*, *Melanchton*, *Zuinglius*, *Doct. Paræus*, *Beza*, *Erasmus*, *Doct. Chemnitius*, *Doct. Didericus*, *Doct. Mordesius*, *Doct. Welleus*, *Doct. Ludder*, *a Civilian*, *Hottomannus*, *Camerarius*, *Lipsius*, *Oecolampadius*, Brentius, *Musculus*, *Aretius*, *Piscatus*, *Ursinus*, *Pomerianus*, *Doct. Saunder*, *Doct. Vulteius*, *Doct.* Frechius, *P. Fagius*, *Hen. Stephanus*, *Magdenbergenses*, *Pastores Manseldenses*, *Postores Gallici*, *Urbanus*, *Rhegius*, *Justus Jonas*, *Cuiatius*, *Calepinus*, *Albertus* Blankenberg, *Phil. Cæsar*, *Kekermannus*, * who saith, that almost all but reformed Divines hold Usury to be a sin *Langius*: where Note what a huge number here is, to his small number, which he musters up being about two, so that he cannot by any arithmetical skill he has, make it good that most Moderns are on his side: and so let him go with his vain boast, and boast of it to those, who know nothing, or but little of this matter by reading or experience; wise and well read men and such as have been abroad in the World, and have eyes in their heads, will not believe him, but rather those learned men which I have named.

2. So for his two cautions only, let me shew how contradictory to truth it is what his Author *VVindelin* saith, for I can cite against him far greater Writers than he is, who recken up many more: One I have already † named, and another I shall mention now, who numbers up seven more, as

1. That a man must not be a professed Usurer.

* *Keckerman* in his *Oeconomicks*, *c.* 7. † B. *Downam* upon *Ps.* 15. *p.* 274.

2. That gain be not required of men, whc do borrow for the supply of their necessity.

3. That they do not require it of him whic gain, unless he be a gainer.

4. That he which lendeth for gain must n no gain, but also must be content to bear borrowers loss; if without his own defau looser.

5. That the end of this lending must be cl the lender is bound to seek the borrowers goo own (and who doth so?)

6. That in this contract he respect the gc the borrower, but also of the Commonwealth that he require not so much gain as the party lawful means.

1. That this lending, be answerable to natu is to be judged of not by mens practice, bu God: so that here five times two.

I add what a famous Author Writeth of suc

Now how far Usury differs from this kin our common Vsurer will not confess, woful teacheth.

Num. 101. 6. About *Perkins*, *Mayer*, *Vines*, have given an account formerly, to which acc reader; and *Gataker*, I must likewise reckon am Divines which are here likewise named, beca Write to the same effect.

As for his fate (not to name it) to that I an

1. *That this fate* has infatuate him so as his will he did shew me the greatest friends such learned men, as those, whom he nar in this point of Vsury, acknowledging then side, and so consequently by name *Bishop J* a man was he) *Bishop Downam*, *Bishop Hall*, I *Bishop King*, *Bishop Lake*, *Bishop Andrews*, *Bisho* all the rest.

2. It infatuated him so, as to mix cer are no foundation things, with Vsury, whic and death, even life and death Eternal, *zek.* 18. 12, 13.

3. It infatuated him so, as that he takes

herewith beyond-Sea Divines are * charged, *viz.* that ıey are against the strict keeping of the Sabbath, which I ın testifie by sight, and to lay it to their doors, who will ɔt, as I suppose own it, because in Divine truth the anciıt Council, whereof the *Parisian* is one, which is as strict ɾr the keeping of the Christian Sabbath, as any of us in ngland; For they take more than ordinary notice of the ıdgments of God, (like the practice of Piety) shewn upon ıe Prophaners of it, by fire from Heaven, which has burnt ıem; and did charge the Emperour then reigning, to see ıe said Sabbaths strictly kept; so that I was much taken ith it when I read it.

8. *Answer.* Eightly to his insisting upon Emperours, *I anver*, that I have already cleared up that, shewing, how the *Civil-laws* and those pious Emperours hold with me, and *ıstinian* especially, whose very words I have cited: and as ɾ the sum beyond which no use must be taken, that is no ore than our English Parliaments have done, which have scried all Usury as a detestable sin and interdicted by the ord of God. viz. *Jac.* 13. and *Eliz.* 13. *C.* 8.

9. *Answer.* Ninthly Concerning *C. Molinæus* the Lawyer, have this to say 1. That I put against him *Hottoman*, that r more famous and pious Lawyer too, who, as I have already evidenced it in this book, is on my side.

2. That *Molinæus* has many frivolous and strange things because he is no Divine) but a Lawyer about publicans ecially.

Which doth very much disparage him: But I will say no ore of him but this, that he is held to be the first Defenunt of Usury, and not *Calvin* (as some have said of him) for ey know not what to make of that holy man *Calvin*, because of his bitter sayings against Usury by me quoted, and s holy cautions which make that Usury which he is for, no sury.

I am the larger in this answer to Authors, because those uthors which they do so objectate, are their cheif Pillar

---

* *In which charge I for my part must needs except the Author the* Heydelberg *Catechism, because he is as strict as a man ay be in his pressing the most strict observation of that holy day.*
Leges Civiles si bene sunt constitutæ nihil quidem præcipiunt od Deus prohibuerit, et nihil prohibent quod Deus præceperit. ɛza *Annot. in Mat.* || Hottomanus *in suo lib. de Usur.*
* Molinæus *de public.* &c.

which their defence of Usury relieth upon: as as it is observed by wiser men than my self, of whom at present I will quote but one, *viz.* the learned and most famous *Bishop* * *Downam.*

'And because the judgements of those learned men, who 'do not seem to condemn all Usury, are of such force with 'Usurers, that they seem to build their practise upon their 'authority, I will also take this hold from them, and out of 'their Writings manifestly demonstrate before their eyes 'that the Usury which is practised in the world is not al-'lowed of any godly Divine: thus he, and so he goeth on 'to prove it, and if so, what shelter have our poor Usurer 'then, both Ministers and people, having neither Scripture nor 'good men on their side.

10. *Answer. Num.* 102. *Tenthly*, I answer to that which he saith of the reformed Churches.

1. God forbid, that they should be all guilty of that damnable sin of Usury: for I was born beyond Seas, and know the tenents of my brethren, and fellow Divines there, how far some hold some Vsury improperly so called lawful with such cautions, as even now I named, which our Vsurers here do not observe, God knows I leave them to the Judge of quick and dead, I am no Judge, but only declare the Judgement of God against all unrighteousness and all Vsury properly so called, and usually here practised, as himself also doth, *Psa.* 15. 18.

Eleventhly, I answer to what he saith about † *Luther*, that he was more moderate in his latter Writings in his opinion concerning Vsury, which he partly names, as quoted by my old friend *Rivet*, thus.

1. That I can see no allowing of Vsury properly so called in all that he saith, but that he would have Vsury stinted by the Magistrates, advised by Divines and Lavvyers, conceding and yielding to a Nobleman four, to a Marchant eight, to others, six Florens or Guilders in the 100. vvhich has been || proposed long before him, as || one vvho vvas himself a lavv-maker asserts it, saying, (to confute * *C. Molinæus* who falsly affirms that the *Civil* Law allowes of Vsury) that the law doth not allow it as good, but permit as evil for the avoiding of greater incon-

* B. *Downam* upon *Psa.* 15. 5. † *The Eleventh Answer about* Luther. || B. *Downam* upon *Psa.* 15. *p.* 268. * *I say fal ly he saith it, that the* Civil *Law allows it, because in the* Novellis, *so called, it forbids it utterly.*

veniencie

'veniences; and then he shews, how the law stints the Merchants Usury at eight, and the Noblemans and Gentlemans at four, and the Usury, of other men at six in the 100. so that *Luther* did no more then the Bishops in *England* do in Parliament, stinting Usury at *six in the* 100. together with the Lords Temporal and the Commons, which notwithstanding *they descry all taking of Use*, as the Champion saith, *and together with the whole Parliament call it a detestable sin and forbidden by the word of God, and call their act an act against Usury*, Answerably, whereunto *Luther* might be for a stinting of Usury and Usurers, that they might not take above the foresaid sum, and yet be like our Parliament as bitter again Usury, as in his Writings he shews himself to be * exhorting Ministers to be bitter against it, and I could never read in any Author, that he did reclaim or repent (as *Austin*, and others have done) of what he had so bitterly Written, but on the contrary I see that all Divines and Authors, that since him wrote against Usury, cite him against Usury, as a chief enemy to it, nor is there any likelyhood for it, if we consider how he could not, but be a headman and chief approver of it in the *Wittenberg* theses or positions against Usury, as the chief Doctor and Professor in that famous University.

Num. 103 *My Adversary next progresseth to my last reason*, which is, and what should the Usurer do in Heaven. &c.

And I dare say no books written against Usury. *Whereunto I answer*, but such that wrote against it are doubtless there, as *Moses*, *David*, *Jeremiah*, *Ezekiel*, *Cyprian*, *Lactantius*, *Basil*, *Ambrose*, *Austin*, *Chrysostome*, &c.

As for his jeering at me, that it is well that Mr. Jelinger *is not Key-keeper, and that this he takes to be one of his Antelucane Meditations, I am so well used to it by his * often jeering, as that I do no more regard it than the dirt under my feet, it being but dirt coming out of a foul mouth, and a dirty pen.*

Nor have I cause to be troubled at it, especially at the least, about my rising before day to meditate and to pray, because I use to pray then as fervently as I may for his and other Usurers conversion, and find that God hears his poor servants prayers then poured out, and converts poor Usurers souls, whose gain is of more value to me, than if I should win the whole world, and which are comming in still. *Wherein I desire to imitate a certain holy man*, 'who, meeting with the

* *The Author of the conviction of Usury quotes him for it*, p. 170.
* *For a very Nautulus he is.*

'Emperour his Enemy, asking him whither he was going, 'returned this answer, I am going to pray for thee and thy 'Empire: Semblably whereunto, if an Usurer being mine Enemy, should ask me what I am going to do, when I rise mornings before day, I should tell him as I now tell this my Adversary, I am going to pray for thee, and thy poor soul, that it may dwell in Gods holy hill, and not go to hell, there to burn, burn, burn to all eternity.

Num. 104. *I thought to have superseded*, and ended here the confirmation of my Doctrine by Reasons, but because my bitter Adversary doth so exceedingly slight my four last Arguments especially, therefore I will superadd four arguments more, which I am sure will be strong enough. And

The First is that Usury is the Evil of Evils.

1. *Transcendentally*, as *Solomon's* song is called the song of songs, because of its transcendentalness, as I shew in my Rose of *Sharon*; so this great Evil called Usury, may well be called the Evil of Evils, as transcending other Evils, and being * in it self not only simply evil, but exceeding evil, even like mans deceitful heart, desperately evil, and wicked, *Jer.* 17. 29. and deceitful above thousands of other things, so as that for that cause it is called not only deceitful, but even deceit it self, yea deceits in the plural תככים from תכך *Prov.* 29. 13. because as a great † Writer observeth it, Usury is never without deceits, so that commonly by the man of deceits in that place foresaid, *Prov.* 29. 13. is understood the Usurer, as also by τόκος, which is Usuries Greek name, is understood deceit, as being derived from the Hebrew תוך.

Whereby it appeareth what a great transcendent evil Usury is, being so deceitful and desperately wicked, for its being deceit it self, yea deceits.

2. *It is the evil of evils*, as it is the cause of all manner of evils, *viz.*

1. *Grief*, For which cause also its called τόκος in Greek, because it is as it were the monstrous and unnatural breed of what is borrowed, and causeth such great grief in the

---

* *Which I know my Cousin* Spanhemius *denieth without any sufficient proof of his denial, alleadging only* Deut. 23. 19. *concerning the Stranger, so often and so substantially answered: See his words,* Ps. 27. 14. † *M. P. p.* 30. || *Bishop* Downam *upon* Psal. 15. * *The effects of Usury are, poverty, grief, death.* G. P. p. 29.

heart

heart of the borrower, as is answerable to the pains of Child birth: and so in Latin it is call *fænus quasi fætus* a brood, as *Nonius Marcellinus*, and others aver it; some add to grief *poverty and death*.

2. It is the evil of evils, as it is the cause of many other sins, as

1. *Theft*. 2. *Murder* which two great sins Authors so bring within the Circle and Compass of Usury, as to make them not only kinds, but also issues of it, and it self there upon a breaking of both the sixth and eight Commandements, and so consequently both theft and murder: See the Margin.

3. *As Idolatry*, because the Usurer is a covetous man, as has been demonstrated, and covetousness is idolatry, *Eph*. 5. 5. So *Cyprian*, *Basil*, and others.

4. *Oppression*. See *Ezek*. 18. 12, 13. Where oppression and Usury are joyned: because, if the Usurer be not paid, according to his time, he will trouble and arrest the needy borrower, and make him sell his goods to his loss, as by such as have been sufferers in that case, I have been informed: but yet I will not charge all Usurers, with this alike, but only such as are so cruel, as the holy fathers have done likewise; at present I will name but one of them, viz. * *St. Chrysostome*, who for this cause calls Usury a pestiferous womb, because it brings forth such pestiferous brats: with which holy Father I will joyn a great King of *England*, who said, that he heard it spoken in the Court of *France*, that Usury is the root of all evil, as well it might be said so, because of the love of money, which the Usurer so dearly loveth, and which the sacred Scripture it self calls the root of all evil, *Tim*. 8. 10. And therefore how can he who liveth in so great an evil, live in the heavenly Tabernacle with the greatest good, which is God blessed for ever, it being expresly Written, *Lord who shall dwell in thy Tabernacle, he that has not put his money to Usury*, Ps. 15. 1, 5.

Num. 105. 2. Usurers * for the most part are convicted of the evil of Usury in their own Consciences, and therefore living and dying in that sin, they cannot be saved.

To prove this, that * great disputant against Usury useth this Syllogism, in *Celarent*, *ab impossibili*, from that which is im-

---

* *For the Usurer is even a Thief and a Robber, saith* Calvin *upon* Ezeck. 18. * *And the Usurer is a Murderer saith* Mr. Powel, p. 40. * *Low what a livery and language these two great and godly men bestow upon Usurers.* * *Chrys. in Matth. hom.* 57. * *I cannot say all.* * Gabr. Powel.

possible: It is impossible that faith and an evil conscience should at the same instant be joyned together in the same man.

All Usurers have an evil conscience.

Ergo. No Usurer having an evil conscience hath faith, and so consequently has no faith, and so its impossible for them that wittingly and willingly persevere in that sin to be saved. Thus he.

I add, For without faith it is impossible to please God, *Heb.* 11.6.

But to prove that the common Usurer standeth convicted in his conscience of the evil of Usury I shall bring and adhibit twelve *Mediums*.

1. Because there is a light, even the light of nature, or the * law of nature Written in his heart, *Rom.* 2. 15. flushing as one useth that expression, into their consciences, and so illightening them as that needs they must be convinced by it, and come to see the evil of that cursed sin of Usury, as when a light shineth in a dark place, to use blessed *Peters* own words, 2 *Pet.* 1. 19. that which there is amiss must needs be seen and discerned by it: and the place it self must also be illuminated by it. So that, I dare upon that account ask any Usurer, whether that light which is in his conscience do not so far illighten him, as that he cannot but see and know that his practice is a sin. Observe what I say, I do not ask thee now, Usurer, whether Usury be an evil: for that happily thou wilt grant, understanding Vsury in thine own sense, and equivocating with me, as my Adversary doth: but whether thy practice of taking Vse by a compact, whether it be six in the 100 or less be not a sin and evil thing in thee? here let thy guilty conscience answer.

2. Because people generally say of thee behind thy back, that thou art an Vsurer, though thou takest but six in the 100. and thou canst not but know it, and hear of it by others; and *vox populi, vox Dei: the voice of the people when it* speaketh according to the word of God, condemning Vsury, as *Ezek.* 18. 12, 13. *is the voice of God:* and I believe that doth much convince thee.

3. *Yea,* do not some cast it in thy dish, and tell thee to thy face, that thou art an Vsurer, though thou takest *but six in the 100 or five?* I am sure I am told so by some, that

---

* *Which Divines say is meant by the law written in the heart,* Rom. 2 15. † *Joh. Wigandus, Syntag. part.* 1. *col.* 45.

have

have heard it with their ears, and say that they have told thee so to thy face.

4. The Usurer will not be known to be an Usurer. The * *Magdeburge* Centuries tell us of a Usurer, who, living in a certain place and lending his money upon Usury, did charge his borrowers by no means to tell of him that there was such a one in that place; but what befel him, when it was known, I shall not mention here; another time and place being fitter for it to be told: thus Usurers will not have the World know it that they are such.

5. The Usurer will colour and cloak his Usury by some other contract.

6. Usurers will not by any means call themselves by that name, as other men will call themselves Merchants, or Husbandmen, *&c.* according to their callings, but Usurers will not do so, being Conscious to themselves of the evil of their employment.

7. Usurers are convinced of the evil and baseness of Usury, because if one should call any of them by that odious name, Sir Usurer, as others are called by their Names and Titles, *Sir John*, *Sir Henry*, *&c.* he would be very angry with him, and tell him, Sir my Name is not Sir Usurer, but a lender of money?

8. The Usurer will not call his Usury by that name neither, but Usance, interest, consideration, the Rent of my money, *&c.* being ashamed to call it so, which also evinceth his conviction.

9. Usurers will not only deny it, that they are Usurers, but some of them, as ‖ one saith, swear deeply that they are none.

10. Some Usurers will take a certain note, as it is reported in Print, or as some call them, Letters Patents, Consined with the borrowers hand, in which he shall make it known unto all men by these present that the Usurer has lent him freely and without any mention of encrease.

11. I am confident that if a question should be made by a Godly Minister in his Pulpit whether there be any Usurer there, because he would willingly speak to him, not one would answer to the question that he is an Usurer, though forty should be there: and that which confirmeth me herein, is this, because I have read of a certain Preacher, * who knowing that

* *Magdeburge Cent.* † *M. M.* p. 107. ‖ *Id. ibid.*
* *John Bromyard summa prædict. Tit. Usura.*

there

there were many Vsurers among his Auditory, broke out in his Sermon into asking of the question, whether there were an Vsurer there? whenevery man held his peace, he demanded again, whether there were a Scavenger there? One rising up, and answering for himself said, yea, here is one, and I am that one; the Preacher thereupon infers this invective against Vsurers, behold, you may see hereby how vile a thing Vsury is, for this man answers for himself in the defence of his filthy employment, Vsurers are ashamed to answer for theirs, and thus they are convicted in their own Consciences.

12. And may I not bring in at last *St. Austins* testimony too, saying, how detestable a thing it is to lend money upon Vsury how odious and how execrable, I suppose Vsurers themselve are not ignorant of. So then upon and after all this I may wel end here, with that dreadful saying of another learned Author so then the Vsurers sin willingly, and of set purpose they follow a practice contrary to the light of their own conscience *&c.* I add.

3. The Vsurer is, as it is to be feared, not only convicted but also condemned of himself in his own conscience: for ther is, as it were, a Court kept, and there is accusing, witnessing and condemning, according to *Rom.* 2. 15. *Their Conscience al bearing witness, and their thoughts mean while accusing, or else ex cusing one another.* In which respect * some have called consc ence forum, a Court, a Consistory, because in it men are co vented, and convicted, and condemned upon witnessing and a cusing passed, so that, even as an Heretick is condemned of hin self, because with an evil conscience, or against his conscien he sinneth wilfully, and of purpose, as * *Calvin* expounds t place, so I am afraid, it may be said of Vsurers, that in the sinning they are condemned of themselves, because witting and willingly they follow a practice contrary to the check a touch, and light of their own conscience, did I say, I am afrai I know I did: but I can tell you, there is † one who saith p sitively from that place in *Tit.* 3. 11. that they are damned themselves, being counted by learned men to be Heretic And there is a famous Doctor called *Doctor Beard*, who Wr eth of a certain Vsurer, who being condemned of hims made his last Will and Testament: as word for word it is

* *August.* in *Ps.* 36. † *M. P.* 35. || *Phil. Greg. The* * *Tho. Langius de vita Christ. tom.* 3. † *John Calvin Inst. l.* c. 10 *Sect.* 3. || *Idem* in *Tit.* 3 11. *M.* P. p. 35. * *Doct* Beard *in his Theater.*

down in the end of this Book. the *Part*.4. *Num*.18.

Num. 106. *My fourth additional Argument is.*

That the Usurer is an enemy to God and man.

1. *To God, and that,* 1. *Because he rebelleth against him by yielding and using all the faculties of his soul and members of his body, as Weapons of unrighteousness against him, that* I *may use the great Apostles words, Rom.*6.19.

And, 1. The faculties and powers of his soul, as for instance 1. *His mind* he uses against God to Usury, minding his Goddess and great *Diana*, Usury, I mean, more then God, who is seldome and little in his thoughts : for if he were, he would not be an Usurer. 2. *His will*, in that he will be an Usurer, tho God will not have him to be one, *Neh*.5.10. 3. *His love*, loving his Usury money more than God, like a covetous wretch, as he is, who will needs be rich, 1 *Tim*,6.9,10. and like an Idolater, as he is also, according to that famous saying of *Lactantius*, whatsoever a man loveth more than God, that is his God.

2. So the members of his body, as namely,

1. *His eyes* he yields as weapons of unrighteousness against God, by his most earnest looking after, and for his Usury money from half year to half year contrary to *Luk*.6.35. *Lend, looking for nothing from it again*. 2. *His tongue* he useth as a weapon of unrighteousness against God, by his enticing young rich heirs (as *Basil* describes him) and others, to borrow money of him upon Usury. 3. *His hands* he useth to take Usury money therewith, according to *Ezeck*.18.12,13. *He has taken Usury and encrease where* † *Calvin* note: *That God, to cut of cavils, joineth both names, and condemns all accession to the principal*. 4. His feet he employeth as Weapons of unrighteousness against God. by his running after covetousness. For what else is his Usury but covetousness, as has been abundantly declared? at present I will cite but one great friend of mine, *viz*. Great || *Luther*, who may be instar omnium, *instead of all*: saying, *expresly*, that Usury is covetousness, his words are, Usura est detestabilis avaritia. *Usurie is detestable covetousness*, mark, covetousness it self it is, and detestable covetousness after which the Usurers feet so run, see *Ezek*. 33.31. where running may be extended to feet too, by which the heart runs as well as by its thoughts.

2. The Usurer is an enemy to God, in that no kind of people, as * one saith notably, think worse of God then Danists,

---

* *Lactant*. † *Calvin* in *Pentat*. *p*. 355. || *Luther de taxanda Usur. to*. 7. * *Nullum de Deo hominum genus pejus sentiunt quam Danistarum*. Roger Turner, *p*.10.

that is, Uſurers; for they ſlight and vilipend his providence, ſo, as that they of all others will leaſt truſt him. The Mariner looketh after the wind, which way it bloweth, and prayeth to God that it may blow fair for him, and ſo doth the Wimſter, and ſo doth the Miller that hath a Wind-mill: but the Uſurer thinks that he hath leaſt need to ſay his prayers ſo, let the Wind blow Eaſt, Weſt, North, or South, its all one to him: his Mill, I mean, his Uſury Mill grinds for him ſtill, I will not ſay Corn, but the face of the borrower; his fanning, ſifting, and Wimbing of that which is in the borrowers purſe and barns go on, he taking the ſubſtance which he has, and leaving the chaff, which is nothing, and an empty purſe to him.

2. The Uſurer is an enemy to man too, and to a world of men, even as a worm is to a round fair Apple, eating it out and ſpoiling it.

So is the Uſurer by his Uſury to this round and fair World, I mean the men that are in the World, by eating out and ſpoiling ſo many men and houſholds with his moſt ſharp teeth.

And the multitude of Uſurers is like ſo many *locuſts*, which are called in the Hebrew tongue from the ſame verb, that Vſury is called תלביה *viz.* רבה to multiply, becauſe locuſts * multiply as Vſury doth, and did a great deal of miſchief in *Egypt*, as it is to be ſeen in *Exo.* 10.15. anſwerably whereunto Vſurers do a World of hurt in the World to a World of men, eating up men which borrow of them like bread, as it is † Written of ſome, *they eat up my people like bread* which is applied by a || great Writer to the Vſurer thus: the Vſurer is a ſoft beaſt at the firſt to handle, but in continuance of time the hardneſs of his teeth will eat a man up, fleſh and bone, if he have not a ſpecial care to ſhun him: with this learned || Author who maketh the Vſurer *a man eater*, I ſhall joyn two or three more, whereof,

1. 'Bleſſed * *Bolton* ſhall be one, who maketh him a Canni-
' bal alſo, ſaying if Vſury find a man rich, yet it bringeth with
'it a pair of CANNIBAL chops and many cruel teeth to eat
' out, *&c.*

2. The great *Luther, who calls the Vſurer the blood ſucker of the people*, as alſo † one more calls him ſo ſaying, *as the Ivy culleth and claſpeth the Oak, as a lover, but thereby it groweth up and overtops the Oak, and ſucks up the juice and ſap of*

ארבה *Locuſta, quia eſt ſpecies multa.* Pagnin. *in* Lexic.
* *Pſal.* 14.4. † *G. P.* p. 48. *in his poſit.* || Bolton *in his Diſcourſe concerning Vſury.* * Luther. † G. Powel, p. 48.

Oak

Oak, that it cannot thrive nor prosper, such a blood sucker is an Usurer, saith he, and besides him * one more, *these (Usurers) are cursed flies, suckers of mens sap, the drinkers of their blood.* So *Adams* saith the same.

3. *That grand enemy of Usury Bishop* Downam, who saith, *wise men, when they have considered not only the wrong, which is done to particular men, but also the manifold inconveniences and mischiefs, which come to the common-wealth by Usury, they have confidently affirmed, that Usurers are worse then theives and that it were better for the common-wealth that there should be a thousand theives in it, then an hundred Usurers*; what a remarkable passage this is against poor Usurers, coming from so great a Prelate.

4. *Cato* who speaks very near to the same effect, that whereas by the twelve Tables, it was ordained, that if any Usurer should take above *one in the hundred*, he should be punished fourfold, whereas a Thief was to be punished but twofold, whereby we may gather how much they esteemed a Usurer to be worse than a Thief.

5. || St. *Chrysostome*, who did not doubt to say that the Usurer is to be esteemed, AS A COMMON ENEMY TO ALL MEN. All which if it be so that the Usurer is such an enemy to God and man, how can he dwell with God in his Kingdom? will an earthly King suffer enemies to be in his Kingdom with him therein to live? no, no, he will have them slain and dye rather: So God, for so, he saith, *But those mine enemies bring hither and slay them before me*, *Luk.*19.27. and lest men should say that this concerns not Usurers at all, but others, and that therefore he will not have them dye, he speaks more plainly in *Ezek.* 18. 12, 13. concerning the Usurer, who has taken Usury and encrease, *any encrease* verse 8. *shall he live? he shall not live, his blood shall be upon him*, and being asked by the holy Prophet *David, Lord, who shall abide in thy Tabernacle, who shall dwell in thy holy hill? he returneth this answer, he that putteth not out his money to Usury*; and is not this as clear as the Sun, who dareth slight it?

---

* Roger Turner *in his plea answered*, p. 15. † *Bishop* Downam *in* Psal. 15. 5. || Chrysostome *cited by Bishop* Downam, *p.* 261.

Num. 108. But here I must answer two Contradictions. One concerning my Authors mostly, and me in part. The other mostly me, and my Authors in part.

The First Contradiction. To begin with the first, some hereupon will say, your men whom you quoted even now, are too harsh, too bitter, too severe against the poor Usurer, giving him such language, and taking up such comparisons against him, and making an enemy to God and all men: One would think that such wise, learned, holy, and grave men should not have such hard thoughts of him in their hearts, nor divulge such sayings against him to the world with their pens, the world speaking hard enough of him already; and we wonder why you will mention them.

Whereunto I thus answer in their behalf;

1. That God himself giveth the like language to all the Wicked, * whereof these are some, saying, that they are † *Dogs*, || *Sows*, * *Asps*, † *Vipers*, || *a generation of Vipers*, yea, * *Divels*, and *the Children of the Devil*, and the Usurer a biter like a Dog, and therefore why should any man blame them, for saying what God saith, and calling them what God calleth them, biters?

2. As God maketh them so bad, to make them better, so they.

3. That they do but speak the truth and do not belie them, calling a spade, a spade.

The second Contradiction.

4. As for me, I am but the Eccho of these men, and mention their bitter sayings, because I look upon them as wise, learned, and Godly men (Christians I mean) whom one may safely make use of, and without any disparagement, and because I would have the World to see how I am not the only man, who dealeth so hardly with the poor Usurer, as to give him such language now and then, but that others, being my betters by far have given him the same or the like before me: but of this much has been said formerly, and therefore I shall say the less now.

Num. 109. 2. The second Contradiction concerning me most-

ly, and my Authors in part is this, (as methinks I hear it whiſpered.)

If theſe reaſons, which you have given us, be the beſt you can ſhew, and in that, which out of Authors you have quoted to us, your ſtrength be ſuppoſed by you to lie, as it ſeemeth ſo to us, becauſe you reckon up ſo many, you might well have ſuperſeded, ſat ſtill, and not troubled the world with your Uſury Books: For we look for ſtrength of reaſon and not for railings, of which your Writings and Sayings and theirs are full.

1. Anſwer, *Whereunto I anſwer thus.*

1. That I and my Aſſiſtants (called Authors) need not to be aſhamed of what we hold forth, becauſe we let all the world ſee it at home in *England* and out of *England* beyond the Seas, where many of my Authors like flowers did flouriſh in Gods Eden, and ſhine, like Starrs in the Firmament, as *Luther*, and * *Zwinglius*, who preacht the Goſpel before *Luther* in a place called *Clarona*, and many † others formerly named; and as for my poor labours lately publiſhed, and the Uſurer caſt by name, (I can produce a Letter written to me from the Belgick Orbe concerning both ſome of the Miniſters themſelves, and many private perſons too. So that I do not regard what ſome may ſay againſt me, and againſt my brethren, which agree with me in this point of Uſury, and are a numerous company; nor do I count my labour badly beſtowed, and I hope withal that no judicious Reader will ſay ſo, that if the reaſons, arguments, and ſayings, which I and my friends uſe and have uſed againſt Uſury to make it damnable, are ſo ſimple and weak, as that I might well have ſuperſeded and forborn to trouble the world therewith; ignoramus's may ſay it, but true learned men will not.

Not to ſay much of and for my reaſons, ſure I am, that ſome of my Authors eſpecially, have ſhewn as much reaſon as men can, being admirable Logicians, ſo as that they touched their mediums in unanſwerable ſyllogiſms, *Dictick* and *Apodictick*, fetcht from all manner of Logical terms, internal

---

* Keyſerberg, Cruciger, Weſſelius, Capito, Wittenvachius.

† *Monſieur* Hotton *my learned* Brother *in law makes it out in his* Concordia, *reports it.* || *Of whom my friend being a Stationer Writes thus: Our Citizens (which underſtand Engliſh) are much taken with your book (wherein the Uſurer caſt is concerned): and our Miniſters ſtill come to me to know whether I have any more of the ſame Authors labours, thus he.*

and

and external and consequences, and from comparatis, or comparisons, definitions, and divisions, and *ab impossibili*, from that which is impossible, and from testimonies both divine and humane, and did with much exactness make use of *Barbara*, *Celarent*, *Darii*, that is Logical Figures, so called, whom also I did trace as near as I could all along, being backt by them still, tho not in syllogisms (for that, if need be, I reserve for a peculiar Latin Treatise syllogistically penned against Usury) yet by Logical mediums, as also the holy Fathers, Schoolmen, and other Writers by me cited do, without railing, without jeering, without slandering, seriously, soberly, satisfactorily: which is not so to be seen and observed in my Adversary, and his Second. For I do not remember that I met with one syllogism in any one of them, they supposing that αὐτὸς ἔφα was enough for them.

---

* *Who is best skilled in jeering and knows how to do it artificially. Only one made a syllogism since this his book was penned and gave it to me in* Witten, *which I will answer next in a proper place.*

THE

THE THIRD PART OF THIS BOOK now followeth.

Containing Objections made by Usurers in the 6th: *and* 7th: *Chapters of my first* Book, *and replyes put to my Answers thereunto, by my cheif Opponent; and my several Answers to his Replies.*

Num: 1. I now advance to the Vindication of my answers put to the objections made by Usurers, in Usuries behalf.

The first Objection is, Biting is in your text condemned: I am no biter, *ergo*, I am not concerned in this matter, the Psalm speaks of *Neshech* that is biting.

His answer is, every Usurie biteth naturally, either actually, or, potentially, directly, or consequentially.

Reply. Let *Spanhemius* answer him; whereunto I answer. Here let the Learned Reader read *Spanhemius* in his Dub. Evangel. p. 870. For to no end it is to set down his Latin words, as the Champion does, because unlearned men cannot understand him.

And because he would have *Spanhemius* to answer me, I will say the same to him. Let another grave Author answer both *Spanhemius* and him, and first the learned *Christophorus Cartwright*, * late Minister in the famous City of *York*, whose words 'are. 1. It is falsely supposed, that *Neshech* only denotes one 'Certain Kind of Usurie, as if there were some Usury not bit-'ing (as *Spanhemius asserts* it giving instances) whereas it sets

* *Christophorus Cart-wright upon Psal:* 15.

'forth the Nature of all Usurie (to wit) that it doth bite and
'take away something with it.

2. To exclude this Cavil, As *Calvin* also, who is greater than *Spanhemius*) * observes it, in divers places, where Usurie is called *Nesheck*, biting, is condemned, there *Tarbith*, which signifies increase is condemned also, as the Notation of the word, and the Interpretation of it in all Languages does shew: *Salmasius* himself, tho a patron of Usurie, grants *Nesheck*, that is, biting, and *Tarbith*, encrease, to be *Synonymaes* and to signifie the same thing in divers respects; In respect of the Borrower, whom it bites, and in respect of the Lender, who is encreased by it. And my Country man *Mollerus upon the* 15. *Psal:* can make nothing else of *Neshech*, here, but the takeing of any thing above the Principle in respect of loan.

2: I add, That as *Spanhemius* speaks of An ti-Usurarians; that they say, and doe not prove; so the same may be said of him here, and most times and so do his associates; For how will he prove it, that none is bitten, when the borrower payeth his Usurie money; suppose he deal in Merchandizing, as he saith, or buy in Provisions, how will he prove it, I say, that neither the poor nor Common wealth is bitten, if himself be not, which is very rare; but hereof more hereafter.

3: This only I will graunt, that all are nor bitten alike, nor presently feel it alike, some are bitten more, some less, as by several sorts of Dogs greater and lesser, for Usurers are compared to Dogs by diverse Divines, and by Mr. *Bolton*, and Mr. *Trap* by name, as it hath been formerly shewn. I say again, that some bite more, as those in *Nehemiah* did, and as we read of others that did so, and more too as a certain Author writes, that the Jews Usurie has been so abominable as that what I have red of it, is incredible. And † *Graftus* writes, that in the 47. year of *Henry* the 3*d*. 500. Jews were slain by the Citizens of *London*, because one Jew would have forced a Christian to pay more than two pence a week for twenty shillings, and such a like thing I have heard of a wretched woman living in a City near unto me, and various instances more might be given.

* *To be looked upon as but a weak one; as pious and learned Mr.* Capel *proves him to be, in the matter of Usurie, in his* App. conc. Usurie. *As he is no Divine, so his judgement is not very great in matters Divine* saith he. *So* Thomas Hall *in his touchs. of long hair* p. 12. *shews him to be out in saying that no where in Scripture long hair in men is condemned, contrarie to Ezech.* 44. 21. * Graftus *in Chron: suis.*

But

But then there be others who take less, some, 4. some 5. some 6, in the 100. And this I know, and can say upon experience and observation, that even such as have paied but six, have bin so bitten (tho less than others) as that they, that came to look after their Estates, when they were deceased, were glad to sell their Land and Lease, which they had bought to pay debts, which, paying Usurie still, they had Contracted.

Num. 2. But *my cheif Adversarie* goes on, and jeers at my proofs, from the Market, and from *B: Jewel*, as the Reader may see, that will not count it tedious to read his jeering expressions; saing, that I speak like a man that understands the Market, and write *Stilo veteri*; after the old Stile, whereunto I answer:

1. That it is well known, to all my Neighbours how little I have to do with Markets, desireing to live like *Jeromie* 15: 10: and studying as hard as a man can both day and night; what I write of Markets I take from *B: Jewel* and * Mr. *Bolton*, let him blame them if he can justly; as for his expressions of the old stile, I shall quickly stop his mouth for that, telling him, that all that which he can make of my saying is that when men pay but six instead of 8. or 10. in the hundred, that there is the less biting, but biting there is, say I, and my friends; as when the Borrower taketh up 400 *l.* and buyeth Land worth 20 *l. per. annum*, he biteth the Borrower, who must pay the Usurer 24 l. and cannot make 20 *l.* free, all out-going discharged: and still he rises actually or potentially. *The Reply which is made, is but a lame one*; the Suppositions which he makes, signifie but little; for when shall one meet with such a bargain that he tells of, and some bodie else did before him, I mean a bargain upon which is so much timber, that in a short time he is able to make up his 400*l.* which cost him; such purchases are *Rara avis* rare Birds.

What he writes of me is to jeer and to disgrace me, as his manner is, so to do all along, is a meer storie and false report. I add, however things be carried, the Usurer bites the Borrower potentially, because he may loose many waies, which notwithstanding he will have the six in the hundred, whether he win or loose, sink or swim, and whether there be timber upon the Barton, or not.

And tho he bring my Coosin *Spanhemius* again to be his second in Latin, which I will not set down here, because the

* *With whom I joyn famous* Capel: *in his* App: *to Usurie* p. 289.

Vulgar do not underſtand it, yet will not that help him in any wiſe, becauſe he imputeth all the Miſchief that is done by ſuch as have the Uſurer's mony, to the borrowers, whereas the poor borrower muſt needs make up his Uſury mony, which he is to pay to the Uſurer by ſelling his things, if he be a Seller, as that he may both ſatisfie the Uſurer, and live too himſelf by his trading, which cauſes biting, wherein I will not excuſe the Borrower neither, if he do oppreſs any, being ſore preſſed by his neceſſity which may be great, but rather ſhal tell him with that great Apoſtle, that the Lord is an avenger of ſuch wrongs, 1. *Theſ:* 4. 5. Which Vengance doubtleſs will reach the Uſurer alſo, who by his Uſurie is the cauſe of ſuch things in the firſt place.

But here ſaith Mr. *Jelinger*, the Uſurer will reply that ſome other Contracts, as by buying, ſelling, ſetting, a man may be bitten and wronged too.

Reply. And I add, that *B: Hall* makes theſe the worſt of Uſurers. Whereunto I anſwer.

1. I plainly ſee, that this man would fain ſet Biſhop *Hall my old Friend* (as himſelf calls him) and Mr. *Bolton*, and me by the ears to make ſport for him; but I truſt he will never be able do it as long as his head is hot; for, 1. That good Biſhop hath already ſhewn his Enmity againſt Uſurie ſufficiently, which hath ſo netled this man, as, that it made him forget himſelf ſo much as to offer to confute him as his Pamphlet ſhews it

2. And I am alſo as apt to run down ſuch as oppreſs men in buying, ſetting and ſelling, as much as the ſaid honeſt Biſhop

But let us go on, as he goes on, ſaying what does Mr. *Jelinger* ſay to the aforeſaid objection? So it may fall out, but herein lieth the difference, that thoſe foreſaid contracts are in themſelves lawful, but Uſury is in it ſelf unlawful.

Reply. This is τὸ ἐν ἀρχῇ and ſome of his Fathers that condemned Uſe as unlawful, do alſo condemn Merchandiſing for gains ſake, as *Chryſoſt.* ſo *Caſſiodorus*, and Biſhop *Hall*: *Whereto I anſwer.*

1. That he needs not make a *petitio principii* of that which has been ſufficiently demonſtrated.

2. That if *Chryſoſtom* and *Caſſiodorus* ſhould be againſt all Merchandizing, which I know they are not, and are not because God is not againſt it, with whom ſuch men will not fight; but I ſay if they ſhould be, I ſhould reject them, as being to be beleived no further, than they prove what they ſay

* *Mr. B.* p. 49.

by the Word of God, which in this case they cannot do, because the Word commends honest Merchandizing, and Merchants; for else what means that which is said and storied of the Vertuous Woman, *Pro.* 31. and *Lydia a seller of purple and yet a worshipper of God, Acts* 16. 14. So that Bishop *Hall*, whom he alledges does not hold Merchandizing unlawful, as also I believe, that that Holy Man *Chrysostome* neither would or durst hold it unlawful in it self; but only spake against Merchants, as likely they were in his time,and as he found them,to be most of them very unjust,oppressive and dishonest in their dealings, as Riches in the word are called *the unrighteous Mammon*, by Christ himself, not because that all Riches are so, as being unrighteously gotten; but because commonly and by most they are so gotten; otherwise it would follow, that he spake against *Abraham, Lot*, and *Job*, and their wealth as unjustly gotten, which cannot be said of these holy men, See *Luke* 16. 9. 11.

Numb. 4. But let us see what he saith next. Lending must be free, *Luke* 6. 35. It being reckoned among the liberal Contracts.

Reply. This seems to be one of the great mistakes, that runs through his and Mr. *Bolton*'s discourse; That all lending or laying out of mony to supply anothers occasions must needs be free &c. *VVhereunto I answer.*

1. Little strength can be put into a saying, which begins with *It seemeth*; an expression often used by him and his Authors, which sheweth their feebleness.

2. And so it is well for me, that he joyns Mr. *Bolton* and me, shewing thereby that I am not alone in this assertion, That lending must be free; where I could heap up Authors both Divines and Civilians asserting the Law, but sufficient it is that Christ himself hath said, as some Translations have it, *Lend freely, Luke* 6. 35.

3. As he referreth the Reader to that which he had said already, so do I both for *Luke* 6. 35, and for calling lending by an other name, concerning which last particular thing I intend to say more hereafter.

Object: 2: Mr. *Jelinger*. The Law against Usurie is *Political*, concerning the *Jews* only and not us, therefore we cannot be condemned for it.

Mr. *Jelinger*,this is a Fallacy,and the contrary cannot be sufficiently proved: Let us see his proofs. 1. The Prophets enumerate Usurie among the transgressions of the Moral law,*Ezek*: 18: 8: 15: *Jer:* 15: 10: and so doth this *Psalm* 15: 5: *Reply*, as for *Jer.* 15: 10: It makes little for his purpose. *A.* Nor do I make any great matter of it here, but upon an other account

I shall make something of it. That which is asserted of *Ezek.* 18. that it contains only Morals, may admit of an use of *Addubitation*, thereby he jeers me; because *I* did in my last Book often mention such an Use of Addubitation, which I have learned from a better man than he is, *Viz.* of that glorious Martyr *Peter Ramus*, who dyed for Christ in the *Parisian* Massacre, and hath it in his Works; and there he goeth on, and saith, *It seemeth to me* there are Judicials and Ceremonials too, expressed and referred to, *&c.*

A 1. *It seems* he saith doubtingly. 2. But suppose it were so, there be Scriptures for certain wherein Usury is placed among Morals only, as *Psal.* 15. *Ezek.* 22. 7, 8, 9. As Bishop * *Downam* also hath observed it; saying, There remains the last Testimony if such Exceptions can be taken: For here is no mention made either of the Poor, as if it were committed against them alone, or of the detaining a pledge, as if Usury were matched therewith; for it is matched with murder, Idolatry, incest, and other such abominations; neither is it in this place, so subject to oppression, as a species thereof, but generally and simply it is condemned as a grievous abomination. So then this place will hold it, to shew that Usury is reckoned among moral Evils, to make it self a moral Evil. As for the places by him quoted, *Lev.* 15. 14, 18, 35 and 36. and *Acts* 15. 29. *to them I have this to say.* 1. That he infeebles again what he saith, by this *It seems.*

2. That as one Sun is sufficient to give light to the whole World, so that one place in *Ezek.* 22. is sufficient to give light to all the rest, to all them that went before, and comes in after such a manner, purposely to shew what a moral Evil it is, being so placed among moral Evils only, to take off the Cavils of Usuries Champions.

3. That his Assertion is false in *Levit.* 25. wherein Usury is forbidden, *ver.* 35, 36. placed as he saith, in the midst of political Laws, there are no other Laws mentioned but such in that Chapter. For there are mentioned, *ver.* 17. these moral Laws, *You shall not oppress one another, that is one, but thou shalt fear the Lord thy God, that is another*, and the same is repeated to convince this bold and impudent Assertor with a Witness, *ver.* 43. *Thou shalt fear thy God*, and one moral more there is in the same verse: *Thou shalt not rule over him* (namely a Servant there mentioned) *with rigour*; who therefore can believe a man that will say so, as he saith when it is not so; this ut-

* *Bishop Downam upon Psal.* 15.

terly

terly cracks a mans credit, and puts men *upon a Use of Addubitation* ſure enough in a matter of ſuch concernment as is the preſent Controverſie; about the Law of Uſury, whether it be Political or Moral.

4. From that place, *Acts* 15. 29. Where Fornication is placed amongCeremonials it doth not therefore follow that as Fornication is reckoned among Ceremonials, and yet it ſelf is a moral Tranſgreſſion; ſo Uſury may be reckoned among Morals and yet be Political,this I ſay doth not follow. 1. Becauſe theſe Ceremonials there mentioned, were to be obſerved only for a time; as we ſee that they are not now obſerved; becauſe there is no ſuch reaſon for it now as there was then, when the Chriſtians lived among the Jews, who were highly offended by ſuch things as are there prohibited for a Seaſon, whereas Uſury is a ſin for ever prohibited, being a moral Tranſgreſſion as has been partly proved, and ſhall by and by yet be more proved.

Num. 5. 5. And becauſe he brings his Authors aſſerting the Law of Uſury to be political, as *Calvin*, *Hughes*, *Rivet*.

I'le alledge Authors too, and I trow a goodly company of Famous and Learned Men indeed: *Viz*. Beſides Doctor *Fenton* and the many famous Biſhops of *England*, St. *Baſil*, St. *Chryſoſtome*, *Clemens Alexandrinus*, *Origen*, *Gregory Niſcene*, *Ambroſe*, *Ciprian*, *Auſtin*, *Hieronimus*, *Thomas Aquinas*, *Peter Lombard*, *Dionyſius*, *Carthuſianus*, *Gabriel Biel*, *Lyra*, *Rainerus*, *Aquileius*, *Luther*, *Melanchton*, *Brentius*, *Muſculus*, *Themnitius*, *Aretius*, *Hemingius*, *VVigandius*, *Zegedinus*, *Molarcus*, *Viguerius*, *VVolvius*, (and many more) to which names formerly named, I ſhall add the Names and very Words of many more very worthy men; as namely Mr. *Moſ's* firſt, who ſaith in his conviction of Uſury, *I ſee no reaſon why thoſe precepts of* Moſes *concerning Uſury ſhould not be reckoned among the judicial, and not amongſt the moral Laws; for ſure I am moſt learned men of all Ages, and of all kinds have numbred them among the morals.*

2. Mr. *Powel* frames this ſyllogiſm for the morality of the Law againſt Vſury, in *Barbara*, from *Exod.* 22. 25. *You ſhall not oppreſs him with Uſury, Oppreſſion is a breach of the moral Law; Uſury is oppreſſion*, Ergo *Uſury is a breach of the moral Law*, p. 43.

3. The Learned and famous Biſhop *Downam* proves the morality of it from *Luke* 6. 35. *Lend, loking for nothing from thence*, and ſo I cheifly prove it from thence.

4. *Great Baſil* tells us, that therefore it is moral, becauſe Uſury is reckoned ἐν μεγίστοις κακῶν, the greateſt of Evils: *Ezek.* 22. His words in full are theſe ἐν μεγίστοις κακῶν τίτεται τόκον λαβεῖν καὶ πλεονάσμον, he places Uſury and encreaſe

 among

among the greatest of Evils, therefore it must needs of it self be a Moral Evil, and a great one too; with which Authors I joyn the learned *Capel* in the * Margin.

5. And now to answer his Authors, what are those few to so many, say I, as was said of the *Loaves*, what are these few among so many: He names 3. *or* 4. and I name 29. and could name many more, and how inconsiderable is their authority all things considered. For to begin with *Rivet*. He tells what might be the causes why the *Jews* might not lend to their Brethren upon Usurie, but proves it not that they were the causes, and besides Christ in the 6, of *Luke* 35. Overthrows all that he saith, and *Hughes* saith, and *Calvin* saith. But a little more of Mr. *Hughes* first that he was too short in so great a matter, and wants Scripture for what he saith; and 2. I know the time (for we were Ministers together in one and the same Parish) when he was bitter enough against Usury, and others there are who can tell and satisfie, how he kept them from the Lords Supper for Usurie.

As for *Calvin*, I confess he was a glorious Sun in the Firmament of Christs Church, and one whom I admire and reverence as much as any one Protestant writer; but this must be confessed withall, that he is but a man, and therefore may err as well as other men, and doth err in the Doctrine of the Christian * Sabbath; and therefore is to be commended for this, that *in the Doctrine of Usurie, holding it to be forbidden by a political law, he would have no man take his Opinion for an Edict; as his words do declare it, whereby he requireth that no man should stand upon his judgment for a full and absolute Determination of this Controversie.*

Whereupon a great Author makes this Inference; that unjustly Mr. Calvin *is cited as a Patron of their unlawful party.* So that I have no reason or cause to be of his Judgement, whilest he himself would not have me stick to it. *Rivet* is also for me;

---

* Capel. *of Usurie.* p, 267. *Neither can the law against Usurie be thought to be Judicial (Otherwise Political) law of* Moses. *For such laws as such, are known only by some intelligence from the Books of* Moses: *But Heathens of all sorts, who never once heard of* Moses *his writings have with one voice cried sin upon Usurie, and shame upon Usurers (Poets, Orators, Historians, Philosophers, all) they have condemned by the light of Nature: and therfore it could not be a Political law of* Moses. *Besides we have it forbidden in the New Testament when judicials were out of date, lend, looking for nothing again. Luke* 6. 35. *so* Capel. † Calvin. *Epist. respons. de Usuris.*

for

for he is against Injury in the place by the Champion quoted; and so am I, and so against Usurie, which is an Injury.

6: And why should not the Laws of Usurie be reputed for Moral, as well as those which concern incest, of which no Divine ever doubted but that they ought to abide perpetual as precepts of the Moral law? For if it be objected that the laws of Usurie have received some exceptions (whereof hereafter) it is most evident that the laws of Incest have received exceptions, and dispensations too. In the Law one Brother was permitted, yea commanded to raise up Seed unto another, *Deut:* 25. Contrary to *Lev: 18: 16: Thou shalt not discover the shame of thy brother's wife.* Yea in the beginning of the World when the Moral law was written in Mans heart.

Cain married his Sister 4 *Gen:* 17: I say his Sister, because he could marry no other, there being no other woman in the world but his Mother which he could not marry, and his own Sisters of whom *Josephus* * writes, that there were also Daughters born to *Adam* and *Eve*. And if it be objected that there was an absolute necessitie for it; I answer, that there was no such absolute necessity for the brother, but now mentioned, to raise up seed to his Brother; because the Children of *Israel* did multiply exceedingly unto several hundred thousands; and besides I say there was no simple or absolute necessity for *Cain* neither, but a necessity only ex hypothesi or Supposition as Logicians speak; for what necessity could compel God to Create only *Adam* and one *Eve*, when he might have many women of many ribs, he having abundance of spirit. *Mal:* 2: 15: Thus I reason a Pari, from the comparison of this Equality. The laws of Incest are Moral and yet have received Exceptions, and why not then may not the laws against Usury? Tho they received exceptions semblably whereto we instance in Moral laws against Murder, and Theft, which received exceptions in *Abraham*; and *Israels* Case, of which hereafter.

This for the present may suffice to stop my Adversaries mouth, and to answer *Spanhemius*, and others who stand so much upon Exceptions to prove that the law against Usurie is not Moral but Political: † Only one thing more I will add in the Margin.

* Joseph *Antiq. Jud.* l. 1. c. 3. † *The very Atheists, which now call themselves Theists, confess that the Scripture is against Usurie, and make a great matter of it: so that their Confuters have no other way to answer them but that it is against it, by a Political law, which they little regard; because they cannot prove it. More I could say of these Theists about Usurie, but this may now suffice.*

7: Sup-

7: Suppose it were Political, yet doth the Equitie of it hold still.

8: It is true, that a Political tolleration is annexed to the law as an Appendix, which doth not therefore make the law against Usurie Political, but leaves it in its morality, even as the tolleration of Incest, leaves the Moral law against Incest, in its morality as perpetually to be observed and even now under the Gospel by name, as is evident from the Incestuous. 1 *Cor:* 5: 1.

9. Yea, even my very Adversaries concession strengthened by Doctor *Taylor*, *Rivet* and *Spankemius* makes for me, saying, that tho Usurie among the *Jews* were immediately and directly against a Judicial law; yet it might be Moral secondarily. I must not be an Usurer; because this follows, that I must not be an Usurer, because Usurie is a Moral Evil, at least secondarily. And thus Usurers strangle themselves by their own distinctions, and that especially in the great and weighty controversie of, and about the Morality of the law of Usurie; whereabout I have been the longer and larger, because the Objection is a cheif one, intending to be briefer in my Answers to the rest.

10: In answer to that there is an Usurie, which the Champion saith is directly and immediately a Moral Evil; let Bishop *Downam*'s Sylogism and Inference upon it be seen upon the 15: *Psal.* 5. I cannot now enlarge being bent to abridge.

3. The very law of Nature is against it. Reply. I grant if ment of biting and oppressive Usurie, &c.

Num: 6. 1. Lo, how he does, *ad nauseam usque*, repeat his thread bare and near worn out distinction; between biting and toothless Usurie, and if there were an Usurie which is a harmless thing and wants teeth, a distinction which he hath not from God but men; his new men which have coyned it: and * which as a learneder man than he is, Doctor *Rainold* I mean writes, is but a meer flam. For where doth God distinguish so; let us look to his principal law against Usurie, in *Deut.* 23. 19. Where he gives Usurie two names; the one is *Nesheck* the other *Tarbith*:, (which *Salmasius* himself, as was formerly shown, Calls synonymaes, and which without any distinguishing between biting and toothless Usurie, God makes both damnable, and unlawful, and sinful, 18: *Ezek:* 12, 13. I say abominable, because of encrease, saying. *Hath he taken Usurie, or Encrease* † *shall he then live, he shall dye*;

* Dr. Rainold *in his B: of Divorce* p. 8. † *He shall not enter Heaven, who taketh more then he gave, saith Dr: Sanders*

tho

tho he take but *increase*. 2: Unlawful and sinful both because, else it could not be damnable.

2. As I say it is against the Law of Nature, so greater Christian men than my self, say it: and not onely say it, but also syllogistically prove it: I will now name great * *Melanchton*, the Phœnix of *Germany*, whose syllogistical Arguments do prove that Usury is against the Law of Nature, are these;

'It is unlawful to exact money where there is no exchange 'for any thing, (that is when for nothing we exact mony).

'An Usurer keeping his Stock doth exact Usury for nothing; 'because his stock is whole, but only in respect of lending.

Therefore to exact Usurie is unlawful; thus he goes to the Law of Nature.

2: A thing by nature barren, is not to be used as if it were fruitful.

But money is by nature barren, Ergo.

3: The price should not be ware: ergo, *money should not be ware.*

The Antecedents proof. Because at what time the prior is made ware, there doth always something above the price come to the Usurer, whereby for nothing something is gotten, and an inequality is done; so a few Usurers bring the wealth of many Cities to themselves; For the exchanges cannot be continual when no Equality is observed.

Num: 7: Now to exercise Usurie is contrary to Nature; it is forbidden by antient Laws and godly Preachings. Thus my Author *Melanchton*.

Yea, eminently great Heathen men say the same *viz*:

1: *Great* † Plutarch, *who saith. The Usurers also mock at the laws of Nature, just as some of our Christian mockers do, which affirm that of nothing nothing can be gotten.*

2: The very Heathens find therefore two great faults in Usurie committed against Nature. The first is, *That the Usurer will make a barren thing (as money) to bring forth, as it were Children; that is to say, as a wise man saith, pence and shillings. 2: That he exacts Usurie so long, that at the last the debtor payeth Usurie not only for the principal sum, but also for the use of it.*

3: As for *Cicero* and *Proculus* by my Adversarie cited and named, tho he would make them mine enemies, yet are they my constant and faithful friends still. 1. *Cicero*, || whom I

---

* Melanchton *in Epist. Philoso. morum. Anno* 1542.
† Plutarch *quod non oporteat fœnorari.* || *Cicero, Offic.*

read all over in my youth and extracted; and who I am sure is as much against the Usurer as my self, as by these his words it appears, that he brings in *Cato* thus, *That being asked what it was to lend out mony upou Usury; he answered it is no better than to kill a man; which* (as saith a great *Author) Tully *rehearses in the dispraise of Usury*; nor doth this *Tully*, in the words by the Champion quoted, make against me at all.

Nor 2. The words of † *Proculus*; who that I may let men see how he is for me: holds thus, *If I give or deliver to thee ten to make thee debtor for eleven.* Proculus *thinks, saith* Ulpian, *that no more can be certainly demanded than ten, his reason is, for an obligation cannot be made touching a thing, but so far forth as it is delivered*, and in the very words against me alledged, he saith no more, than I can say my self for my self, *viz.* that is *Dolus Malus*, for a man takes to make gain of anothers loss, where the word signifieth all that which is repugnant to all natural right and equity, as Usury doth; which is contrary to natural right and equity. Here hear what Wise-men say, *That if I deliver ten pounds to my neighbour with this intent that he shall pay me the same ten pounds, and also ten shillings more by the year, so long as he keeps it, and I either take or in my heart look for the ten shillings as my debt, I do injury and sin against the command of God, who forbids me not only to steal, but also to covet another mans goods*, saith Doctor *Sanders*, who also fully proves it, that Usury is against the Law of Nature, and that Wise men and Lawyers, whereof *Proculus* is a cheif one, confess Usury to be against nature, and so against Right or *Natural Equity*, which I have formerly proved sufficiently.

I end with ||*Aristotle*, who saith expresly, *The Traffick of Usury is worthily hated; because it seeketh gains upon the penny; and seeks not for that which mony was invented: for mony was invented to make exchanges withal, but Usury exchanges not, but encreaseth the penny, whereof also it took its name in Greek. Now those things which are begotten, are like to them by which they are begotten; In Usury mony brings forth mony, wherefore that kind of gaining is especially against Nature.*

Num. 8. And so I have by Authors and Reasons made it evident, how Usury is against Nature and natural Equity, and how it is an injury, and how well *Proculus* and I do agree, and so I will go no further.

The Second Reply is, that God permitted his people to lend

---

*Mr. *Mosf.* † *In Pandict. de pactis l.* 5. *&* *l.* 11. || *Arist. l.* 1. *p.* 60. *Polit.*

upon

upon Usury to a Stranger, and that therefore the Law against Usury is Political, for if Moral, how could they lend to a Stranger. *Deut.* 22. 19.

Answ. Some say one thing, some another, I for my part shall cut short what I have to say, and go to that most notable and emphatical expression, *Deut.* 23. 19, 20. לנכר, *unto that Stranger thou mayest lend upon Usury*, the Canaanite, namely, whom it was lawful to kill, so blessed *Ambrose : Reply*, A bad shift is better than none, and so forth, let the Reader read the rest of my Book, *pag.* 33. and in his Pamphlet, which he hath sent abroad, and is either printed or like to be, *pag.* 57, 58. till he comes to Mr. *Bolton pag.* 59. and take and peruse also my several || Answers, which I shall give: As 1. to the sayings of my Opponent; to be seen in his Book, and to his Authors: And whereas he saith, that a bad shift is better than none, and so forth; I answer, that I hope I shall make a shift, (but no bad shift) to make good what I say and said concerning the Stranger, that it is the Canaanite, and that this saying is a better mans shift than either he or I, *Viz.* St. * *Ambrose*'s, whose words I'le now set down a little more at large; that he may not say it is the same which I said already, because I say more; St. *Ambrose*'s words at large are these, (for I have read him all over long ago and therefore can quote more yet out of him) as namely, *Perhaps you will say, it is written thou shalt lend upon Usury to a Stranger,* &c. *who then was the stranger but the Amalekite, but the Amorite, but the Enemies of the People of God? There exact Usury whom thou desirest to hurt worthily, against whom thou goest to make war lawfully, on him thou mayest impose Usury lawfully, whom thou canst not easily overcome by war, on him thou mayst easily wreak thy self by Usury : Take Usury of him whom thou mayest kill, against whom there is a right to wage War, against them there is a right to take Usury.* Let me add learned †*Capels* words, *Some plead for Usury, that it is not unlawful, for that God did permit it to the Stranger, if it were permitted indifferently to all and every Stranger, than there were some colour for it. But it is onely to the Stranger, that is to the Strangers of those cursed Nations, whom they were bound to bite and to eat out, and if this permission were not looked upon as a punishment, why is it denyed to a Brother,* Deut. 23. 18. *were it a favour then of all they*

|| *Et videatur etiam Testatus in Deut.* 23. 19. p. 217. * *Ambrose de Tob.* l. c. 11. † *Rich. Capel in his Appendix of Usury, added to his* Tentations. *With whom may be joyned Ainsworth saying the same.*

should

should have been permitted to lend unto their Brethren. I add lastly we are forbidden to lend to a Brother, and now all Christians are Bretheren, and therefore we must not lend to any Christian upon Usury as Usurers do.

Now let all true English hearts judge and choose, whom they will follow, this Novice or *Calvin*, who || thinks, that by the Stranger are meant all the Nations and Countries adjacent to *Palestina* or *Ægypt*, *Syria*, the Isles of the Sea, and such like, or this learned and holy man *Ambrose*, who was so transcendently godly and able a Divine and Preacher, as that the most pious Emperour *Theodosius* said of him, that there was but one such Bishop in the whole World.

2. But lest men should say that I must not think to carry it by Authors only, and by this mans greatness, we look for strength of Reason. I will go to Reason, and rip up this matter of the Stranger, so far as that the unbiassed Reader shall be constrained to confess, that the truth is on my side. And first I will go to the Hebrew word, which is לַנָּכְרִי, and signifies not every Stranger,* which is not an Israelite by birth, or on him that was either *Ger*, גר, that, *Advena*, a Proselite, dwelling among the Jews, who tho he was a Stranger by birth, yet was a Brother by religion, or † *Toshab* תושב, *Inquilinus*, one that was a Stranger by birth, but lived freindly among them; though not circumcised, as appears by *Exod.* 12. 43, 45, 48. usury was not to be imposed, *Lev.* 25, 35. but only on him that was *Nocre*, *Extraneus* or *Hostis*, an Enemy, see *Obadiah ver.* 11. *Lam.* 15. 2. as formerly I mention the same thing, and in this sense may be meant any alien, or especially the Canaanite; but doubtless we may more rightly understand the Canaanite for these reasons.

1. Because as I said already, the word in the Hebrew is not לְנָכְרִי, but לַנָּכְרִי, that Stranger, that is observed not only by me, but by far greater and abler men than I am, as namely by those two famous men * *Junius* and *Tremellius*, who translate that Text thus, *Extraneo isti*, *That Stranger*, that is to the relicks of the Canaanites; What can be plainer? So the famous Bishop † *Downam*; observes it, saying as I, the words are not *lenecro*, but *lanecro*, *the Stranger*. And so that learned Man Mr. *Moss*, saying, I am sure *Junius* and *Tremellius* so understand the place, for they translate it to the Stranger. And one

---

|| *Calvin in his* 134 *Sermon in Deut.* 2. 3. * *As Bishop Downam saith upon* 15 Psal. 5. † *Qui diu habitavit in aliquo loco* Pagnin. * *Jun. & Trem. in loc.* † *Bishop Downam* 12 Psal. 15.

saith,

faith, to this ſtranger as if even by it he did point at him. So Dr. * *Taylor*, the word is not *lenecro* but *lanecro the ſtranger*. So *Capel*.

2. Becauſe this ſtranger was appointed to deſtruction *Deut.* 7. 2. *Thou ſhalt ſmite them and utterly conſume them:* So alſo *Joſ.* 9. 2. *It was certainly told thy Servanns how that the Lord thy God commanded his ſervant* Moſes, *to deſtroy all the Inhabitants of the Land from before you, meaning the ſeaven Nations*, Deut. 1. 3.

Which very reaſons the two forenamed great men, *Junius* and *Tremellius* alſo give as well as I; their words are ſet down expreſly thus,after they had rendred theText thus, to this ſtranger, that is, theſe *remainders. Illas enim Deus exitio deſtinaverat. For them he had ordained to deſtruction.*

3. This ſtranger was to be † conſumed by little and little. *Deut.* 7. 22.

Whereupon † one Gloſſeth thus, and becauſe he ſaw that Uſurie was a means even to EAT *them up, (by little and little) he permitted Uſurie.*

4. And it could not be any other ſtranger and every other ſtranger,becauſeGod is juſt and will not deſtroy a righteousNation *Gen.*20. 4. But thoſe *Canaanites* and Nations ſpoken of *Deut.* 7. 1. had greatly and greviouſly ſinned againſt God, and his people, as namely the Amorites, *Gen.* 15: 10. Compared with *Deut.*7.1. and ſo the reſt of thoſe Nations,did all conſpire againſt *Iſrael*, (which we do not read of the *Syrians*, *Egyptians*, and Iſles ſpoken of by *Calvin*: That they be the ſtranger) *Joſ.* 10. 1, 2. *The* Hittite *and the* Amorite, *the* Hivite *and the* Jebuſite, *the* Cananite, *the* Perizite, *gathered themſelves together to fight with* Joſhua *and with* Iſrael *with one accord*; *the Hebrew is with* One *Mouth.* פה אחד Crying, down with *Iſrael*, down with them, we will certainly and utterly conſume them, and eat them up; ſo that it was juſt with God that they ſhould be conſumed and even eaten up, partly by Warr, and partly by Uſurie as St. *Ambroſe* hath it; but I muſt needs deſire men to parallel this place in *Joſhua* with *Deut:* 7: 1. Where thoſe 'ſame Nations and one more called the *Girgaſhites* and their 'Neighbours too, are named *viz*. The *Amorites* and the *Ca-* '*nanites*, and the *Perizites*, and the *Hivites* and the *Jebuſhites*, 'ſeaven Nations in all with the *Girgaſhites*, and ordained to deſtruction to be conſumed by little and little, and eaten up

---

* *Doctor Taylor in his Progreſs of Saints.* † *Pool in Deut.* 23. 19: *Mr.* Moſs.

which is a thing very remarkable for the proving of my subject matter.

5: And besides, these Nations were so near as that they would be a great snare to the *Jews* by their Idols, if they should not be utterly consumed by the sword and Usury. *Vers* 4. Wherein God himself gives this reason, why they should consume them, and make no marriages with them, even because of their Gods and Images. So that no wonder it is, that besides me, and the aforesaid men, and other grave and great Divines have been of the same opinion, that I am of, concerning this stranger; as Namely *Petrus* * *Tagius*; who writes that there are those which are of this opinion, that the Usurie here spoken of was granted to the *Jews*, to be exercised only upon those seven Nations, all whose Goods (whereby Usurie comes in) God had given to *Israel*; so that by this grant they might take Usurie of them.

Num: 10. *6:* Nor can other Nations which were farther of, be understood with any likelyhood; because of securities and conveyances, which must be made and given in Usuries case, which cannot be done when men live far asunder in Isles, to use *Calvin*'s expression; for how can men with any convenience or security of the Principal, not to speak of any Use, send out of *England* into *France*, or *Germany*, and indeed who doth so?

7: But suppose it were so as they say, that we are to understand every stranger, yet has my Adversary not gotten the day, for his saying and exception of lending to a *Stranger* is but a † permission of a lesser evil to avoid a greater, saith famous || *Lyra:* God was contented to suffer the Jews to take Usury of a Stranger, lest being covetously minded they should exercise that tyranny towards their own Brethren, and lest for want of gain they should have refused to lend to any, and so let their mony lie and rust, which is a great evil also, as it is mentioned by St. *James*, your gold and Silver is cankered, *James* 5. 3.

Now this lending upon Usury was permissive only for a time and not to indure for ever, appears from this, that *Galatinus* reports, as I have once before now, said it out of the Jewish *Talmud* that it was the Judgment of the Jewish Rabbins, That in that place in *Psal.* 15, 5. *He hath not given his mony to Usury.*

* *The Martyr digged up to be burnt.* † *Or a thing permitted to the Jewes by priviledge, as their spoiling of the Ægyptions was, Zeppeon.* || *Lyra in Exo.* 22, & *in Deut*, 33. 19.

God

God did not *only* forbid Usurie to the *Jews*, but also towards him that was a *Gentile*, and what saith St. *Jerome:* it is said in *Deut*; 23: 19. *Thou shalt not lend to thy brother upon Usurie:* In *the beginning of the Law, Usurie is only forbidden to be taken of their brethren* in the *Prophet* Ezech. 18: 12, 13. *It is forbidden towards all*, * *A* sentence so excellent, as that it deserves to be repeated again and again, yea to be engraven with letters of Gold upon a Pillar of Marble.

8: But I must needs *confess*, that this law is imperative also, and not permissive only, tho so for a time: *Thou shalt lend to a Stranger*, even as he saith *Thou shalt destroy this Stranger. Deut:* 7: 1: In which respect God is both an Indulgent Father, and a severe Judge, and a Legislator; an Indulgent Father, by his permitting of Usurie to his Children for their benifit, and a severe Judge and Legislator, in respect of the Stranger, whom he will have consumed by Usurie; saying, *thou shalt lend unto that Stranger, upon Usurie*, and so kill him.

9: And let it be noted, That we † grant the law of Usurie to be Political, in regard of its Appendix: Unto a Stranger thou mayest lend upon Usurie: Tho in it self it is and hath been proved to be Moral: So that || *Chemnitius* also might well say, that God in the old Testament, showeth himself to be a Divine and Legislator, which I also shall presume to say after this fashion; that he sheweth himself to be a Divine by forbidding Usurie, and a Legislator or Politician, by granting liberty to his people to lend to the Stranger.

10: And I cannot but wonder why the Patrons of Usurie, are so earnest for this Stranger, which will do them no good at all upon three accounts. For 1: Are we not all brethren; as many of us as are Christians and no Strangers, and so consequently ought not to lend one to another, by vertue of that famous place concerning Brethren and the Stranger. (2.) It doth so plainly appear by the aforesaid arguments, that that Stranger is the *Cannanite*, and those Nations, which are worn so, as that all Usurie is now absolutely forbidden towards all, without any exception of any, as *Psal:* 15. 5 *Pro* 8. *Ezech:* 18: 12, 13: and 22: Which is confessed by the *Jews* themselves, *Rabbi Solomon* (as *Lyra* reports it in *Exo:* 22: 25.) *Denies it to be lawful for a* Jew *to take Usurie of a Stranger, and the Hebrew Gloss saith the same.*

Num: 11. 11: Even that which they so much urge as an

---

* *Hieron: in* Esech: 18. † *lex de extraneo est politica:* Walæus *in* Deut: 23: 19. || Chemnitius: *loc. com. de paup.*

Exception, that Usurie is permitted to a stranger makes against them; For if it were lawful in it self, it had not need to be permitted; as the putting away a mans Innocent Wife, being in it self and simply evil, was notwithstanding permitted to the *Jews*.

12: And whereas * *Ames* and *Spanhemius* and others of his Authors presume, to prove the immorality of the Law against Usurie by the Stranger thus. That if it were Moral, and simply and in it self Evil; it would not be allowed to a stranger: I answer, that the exception of a stranger doth no more upon the Law against Usurie not to be Moral, and Usurie not to be unlawful in it self; than allowance of Manslaughter in time of War doth prove the law forbidding of Murder to be Judicial. For although the law condemning Usurie be Moral, yet as all the Commands of God, so it is to be understood with this Limitation, unless God otherwise determine, it is a Moral law, which forbids Theft as well as Usurie, which is Theft too, yet if God by his special Prerogative and Warrant will have the *Israelites* to spoyl the *Egyptians*, they may lawfully do it; if the Lord bid *Abraham* to kill his only Son, he may and must do it, and so it is an Usurers Case here.

But some will say that these are extraordinary Cases; I answer, so is this matter of this stranger.

13: But I had almost forgotten one thing which is, that whereas Usurers Champion tells me that what I say is but a bad shift, I must tell him that it is such a shift as hath made one of Usuries defendant so bold as to wrest the very Scripture, saying, that *lancecro* is put for *lenecro*, as not being able to bear the weight of such a mighty Argument which is taken from that noble Hebrew Expression, *this stranger pointed at* viz. the *Cannanite*, which is Scripture, and no humane invention.

14: In answer to a saying of his, that my proof overthroweth it self; I shall tell him that it doth not; if I may explain my self that I mean the *Cannanite* Unconverted, and not continuing an Enemy; for a *Cannanite* might live among the *Jews*, Civilly and Friendly: and his case was altered then, as Divines do shew it, he going under the name of a Proselite at large.

14: His saying *p.* 57. Concerning lending to an *Egyptian*, a stranger, and that lending to him is not against the Law of Nature, to me is strange, because it is an extraordinarie Excep-

* *Quoted by the* Ch: p: 59.

tion

tion, that he is lent unto *Ames*, which he makes his second here, I have answered in my second Answer.

Num: 12: 15. To his other Authors I shall answer; 1: Severally 2: Jointly.

1: Severally, and to pass by *Ames* whom I answered in my 2: Answers.

1: I shall answer a few words to his Grotius, that he does not very excellently, well and fully clear the point as the Champion saith, for 1: The Anti-usurarians do not place the strengh of their Opinion, in a permissive right of fact only, and cheifly, but in other more weighty grounds and reasons, besides given in my Answers premised. Nor doth he speak true, affirming that all the *Rabbines* do otherwise understand that which is said of the Stranger then the Anti-usurarians do. For I have clearly proved the contrary by * *Rabbi Solomon.* (out of *Lyra*) who denieth it to be lawful, for a *Jew* to take Usurie of a stranger, and the Hebrew Gloss which understands that. 15 *Psal:* 5. *Has not given his mony to Usurie thus:* No not to a Gentile, (saith he.) And as for *Josephus* and *Philo*; he doth not tell us what both say, so that I should be loath to trust to what he saith: and especialy of the Text that it will not bear the sense by me and others given, when as the quite contrary hath been even now most clearly proved: To end what I have to say of him, I wonder how *Grotius* can make it good that Christ hath left no Prescript for us in this thing, when the quite contrary can be proved by *Luke* 6 35.

But I desire to say a little more about *Josephus* and *Philo*, tho he say but little, and can say but little, I perceive by him † *Philo* lived in Christs time, and I am sure could not see his *Jews* lend upon Usurie to strangers, which were either *Romans* or *Samaritans*; not to *Romans*, because I have formerly shewn it they were against it. Not to *Samaritans*; because it is written, *the Jews have no dealings with the Samaritans*, which were of all Nations. *John* 4: 9. 2 *Kings* 17: 24: 29. and *Josephus* lived shortly after, when *Tiberius* and *Cajus*, had put down Usurie; so as that the *Jews* durst not lend to strangers, nor do we read that they did, and besides, *Josephus* in the mane I am sure is for me; for thus he writeth. *We have a Law among us, that the lender shall take no Usurie*; makeing no mention at all of brother, or stranger.

---

* *Besides whom, others are of the same Opinion, saith Dr.* Willet. † *By whom* Conscience *is called a* Court *or* Consistorie, *wherein Usurie is condemned saith a learned* Writer.

Num: 13. 16: I thought to have ended here, but because the Champion hath a little more to say, I will be saying a little more too, he saith *p.* 58: think on it again, what an unlikely storie it is, that they might lend to those Nations whom they were bound utterly to destroy, and charged to make no Covenant with them, and so forth. *whereunto I answer.* 1. God foreknew that they would not do as he would have them, being a stifnecked people, but would let them live among them, and make Covenants with them, in Marriages and otherwise; and that (to instance in what *Grotius* mentions) that they and their posteritie would be employed by them to do them service, and therefore seeing they would needs have them live among them and make Covenants with them; he lets them indeed make covenants with them by Usurie, Contracts, having reserved to himself his Royal Prerogative to dispence with his Moral laws at his pleasure. And then 2: I say that, that which *Grotius* saith, that the command of Extirpation was perticular to the men of that Generation will not hold, because that long after *Moses*, and when that generation called *THIS* present *STRANGER*, so * pointed at, was dead, as *Moses* also was in *Joshua*'s time, and the Judges time after *Joshua* they were extirpated, and to be extirpated still by little and little, and by degrees till they were worn out, as it clearly appears from *Judg*: 1: 2, 3: 4: 5.

3: And that they were *to eat them up*, consume, destroy, and kill them, and so by Usurie, even gradually is clear to me by this. Because Usurie is Murder, † *Calvin* himself makes it Murder. Yea God himself makes it Murder. Where? *Lev:*. 25: 35. Where God speaking of a stranger sojourning as a Friend, friendly among his people, that they should take no Usurie of him: adds *That he may live with thee*, as if he should say; for else *You kill him*: This is by the by. And

17: Whereas the Champion adds: For a farther proof take a Parallel place, *Deut:* 16: 2, 3.

And what doth he make of it? a mighty Matter, for there is in the Hebrew as Emphatical a with stranger as that which Mr. *Jelinger* translates That Brother. And whoever did make it so Emphatical besides him; as Mr. *Jelinger*'s is made by many famous Writers by him named? But to the matter.

---

* *Extraneo isti. Poole in* Deut: 23: 19. *Ubi addit, which tho it be unlawful saith he, yet has God by the power of his supreme dominion granted and thereby made lawful (for this stranger)* B.

† Calvin *in* Psal. 15: 5.

What

What can he make of it? *and yet I think none understands it barely of the* Cananite; *I reply thus.* That is the same *Cananite*, because other Nations did not so live among them as they did.

18: As for *Diodate*, whom he brings in to confirm what he saith, to that I answer, I have heard him many times read his Divinitie Lectures, and preach too: but never did I hear him plead for * Usurie, or for this Stranger, or Foreigner; and as for this place by him quoted, he doth not so much as mention a *Cananite*, or the word of a *Stranger*; but in general *Israel* and *Proselite*. See the † Margin also. So that I cannot see, or any one else I think, what the Champion has gotten by his jeering of me; and by speaking so much for *any stranger*: and I add, that he hath rather made himself like unto those few || *Rabbines* which plead for any stranger and by that for Coveteousness and Usurie, that it is lawful for *Jews* to take Usurie of Christians as of strangers; for so do Usurers and many defendants of Usurie, take Usurie of their brethren and fellow Christians, which the very *Jews* will not take of their brethren.

Num: 14: *And now the Champion goes to confute that famous and holy man Mr.* Bolton; *saying I shall make bold,* (*bold sure enough*) *to look into Mr.* Bolton, *to see what he replies to this Objection, takeing from the Lords permitting them to lend to strangers* &c. *wherunto I answer.* 1: That I do perswade my self that, if that great man were now a live, he would disdain it as much to answer this sawcy young man, as Mr. *Hughes*, to one *M. E.* and other such, and therefore that I may not be so weak as to offer to defend such a man as Mr. *Bolton* is, of whom it may well be said as *John* 9: 21. *He is of age and able to speak for himself, and to defend himself.* Let the Reader but read both, and he will soon see that this Novice hath not spoken right of this thing, as the Lords Servant *Bolton*; whose * memorie is and will be blessed, when the name of that man who defends Usurie will be Cursed *Jer:* 15 10.

2: I add that this godly and learned man *Bolton* is so esteemed, by learned and godly men; as that * one of above fourscore, being a great writer himself, and an able Preacher, did say to me,

---

* *Yea* Diodate *my friend saith expresly upon* Luke 6: 35. *Lend, without any respect to your selves to expect a recompence.* † *Of whom grave Authors give out this report.* || p: 59. * *Who also gave me ample thanks for my Usurer Cast, even as another great Divine did likewise.*

that if but Mr. *Bolton* had written against Usurie it were enough.

3: I say that this reverend man was so highly favoured of God, and so well visited by Jesus Christ his Son, as that he could tell his Parishoners, coming to visit him, when he lay upon his death bed: *I am as full of Christ as my heart can hold.* So that any honest Reader will infinitely rather beleive what he saith in this Usurie matter, then one that cannot tell us of such an experience of Christs love, and I do verily beleive, that the end of this mans present assaulting of this grave, godly and gratious man, will prove like *M. S.* assaulting him; who by challenging Mr. *Bolton*, thrust himself upon the greatest infelicity of War, as first to be disarmed, and afterwards to be killed in the field with his own Weapon, for we hear no more of *M. S.*

Only this I must super-add, that divers things which this Champion goes to confute, are answered in my 17 Answers premised, and that I count it an honour to have such a worthy Champion in this War, in which this defendant of Usurie would fain overthrow me, if he could, yea, thinks that he hath overthrown, confuted and fully answered him and me, as it appeareth by his brags in the close of this digression, which is this *Diversion may serve* to evidence, that Mr. *Bolton* is not unanswerable. But I resume to answer Mr. *Bolton* in Mr. *Jelinger*. And is not this a Champion indeed, that can so bravely wage war against so great a warrior against Usuries Army, and not me only?

Num. 15 3. *Object.* Doth not Christ allow of Usurie when he saith, *Matt.* 25. 27. *Thou oughtest to have put my mony to Usurie.* His Answer is; The words are part of a Parable, and Symbolick Scripture is not Argumentative. *Reply.* I hope he will grant from hence, that Christ is at Metaphorical Usurer *&c. whereunto I have answered already* but he proceeds, saying, that he never thought much strength to lie in that text for Usurie. Whereunto I answer 1. He grants me as much as I can desire; and 2. Makes his Doctor * *A*

* *Against whose single judgment I oppose the joint judgment of the godly Ministers of* France, *who in a French Treatise against dancing.* p. 131, *Couple Usurie with dancing, and say, that those laws in* Matt. 11. 16. *and* Luke 15. 25. *proves no more the sinfullness of Dancing than the words in* Matt. 25. 17. *concerning Usurie, do prove the lawfullness of Usurie. And the* Geneva *Professors and Ministers of their French Annotations approve the said place in* Mat. 25. 17. *they likewise exspresly that not thereby approve of Usurie.*

mesius

nesius, who stands upon that place, a weak man not to be trusted unto very much in this Usurie matter. Whereunto

3. Ile add this only, because some of the vulgar sort of Usurers insist much upon the word Usurie, used in that Text, that the Arabick leaves out that word Usurie, and in the room of it renders the words thus, *cum lucro suo.* With its gain, and that the antient Fathers did call their very Preaching Usurie: and 3. that *Ames* himself makes it only *probable that Christ meant Usurie there as we understand it in comon speech.*

And 4. That Expositors understand grace even to be employed and the yealding good works and gifts.

5. Usurie by God is forbidden to the Poor only; but lending to the Rich is lawful &c.

* *I answer*, this is a very specious plea, I confess, but yet I hope through mercy to overthrow it.

1. The most wise God foreseeing how some would abuse poor people, leave out the poor in the repetition of his laws *Deut.* 23. 29. *Thou shalt not lend to Usurie to thy Brother.* And is not the rich our brother too? *Reply.* I commend his after sight in finding out such an answer as this, it shewing his skill in secrets &c,

For answer whereunto I say that, tho he deals jeeringly with me, I will deal seriously with him, and tell him, that if it be a fault in me to tell of Gods foresight here; he is guilty of the same fault in his Pamphlet, making use of the same foresight as I do here † and that a wiser man than he or I used the like Expression; see the || Margin.

2. That I make rich and poor alike in this; that they are Brothers and not as he feigns, that I do, for I know as well as he that there is a vast difference between rich and poor in respect of their outward Estates, and so grant that we are not to lend to the rich, for them to oppress others in bargaining, as he alleadges my words, and so with heart and good will subscribe to *Solomons* words *Pro.* 22. 16. And again I confess that I make them alike in this, that we must not lend to either upon Usurie, because God hath no where in all the Bible allowed Usurie, to be taken and exacted of the rich, if the Champion can

---

* Orig. Hom. 3. *in* Psal. 31. Dionis. *in* Psal. 15. Theophil. *in* Matt. 25. *Mr.* Jelinger. † *God, foreseeing in his wisdom how men would cavil at the word* Nesheck, *hath properly exspressed his meaning by the Exegetical word* Votarbith Doctor Fenton.

ſhew me any, let him. Which has cauſed * *Toſtatus* alſo to ſay as I do, ſee my Margin for it.

Num. 17. 3. Whereas he Adds. But to ſhew further that the man is out in his reckoning, and that God did leave out the *Poor* in the repetition of the law concerning lending upon any ſuch account, you ſhall find expreſs mention made in the buſineſs of lending in this ſame Book *Deut.* 15 7, 8, &c.

I anſwer 1. That it is enough for me; that in his Repititional lawes, and in the chiefeſt concerning Uſurie he leaves out the poor, one ſuch great Sun is ſufficient to give light to this great thing, and that very place *Deut.* 15. 7, 8. Which I have formerly alleadged for my ſelf as making for me, and Biſhop *Downams* concerning the ſame place may be ſeen *p.* 279. And to come nearer home, that expreſſion in *Deut.* 23. 19. *concerning victuals* makes not for him; ſo as to conclude that the poor is intended, as having moſt need of borrowing *Victuals*, becauſe it is added *Uſurie*: Of any thing that is lent upon *Uſurie*. And the word *Victuals*, by others is rendred *fruges*, or *frumentum*, Corn, which people of good faſhion borrow too. And laſtly that place in † 18 *Ezech.* 17. Will not ſerve his turn neither, becauſe; *The taking of the hand from the Poor* is one thing, and the taking of Uſurie and increaſe is another, tho joyned together in one verſe, even as *Luke* 21. 34. Surfetting, and Drunkenneſs, and Cares; where Surfetting is one thing, Drunkenneſs another, Cares another and not the ſame, and ſee alſo *Heb.* 13. 4. *Whoremongers and Adulterers God will Judge.* And 2. I anſwer, and do not men uſually rather give then lend victuals and bread to poor people?

3. Neither *Zanchie* nor *Rivet* do his buſineſs; for neither of them prove what they ſay, but only confine the Text, in *Deut.* 23. 14, ſo as he does, to victuals, only leaving out Corn and Bread, which are as I ſaid, is and may be lent to ſuch as is well to paſs, and is alſo to be underſtood (as greater men than themſelves are) avouch it, *viz. Great Auſtin twiſe* and great Dr. *Themnitius*, who has examined and confuted the great Council of *Trent*, and great Dr. *Sanders*, and others.

---

* *In hæc verba, abſque uſura id quo indiget commodabis, dicit* p. 218. *Non ſolum pauperi, ſed etiam Diviti. Not only to the poor but alſo to the rich thou ſhalt lend. Sic* Toſtatus. *So* Capel. *in his* App. p. 292. *Nor can they ſhew a place where Uſurie is granted to a rich man.* † *And in the* 12. *verſe, the poor comes in with* Violence, *with the Pledge, and with Idols before Uſurie comes in.*

4. Where-

4. Whereas he Adds. The law ſaith, *Thou ſhalt not lend to thy Brother, that is waxen poor with thee. i. e.* Saith Mr. *Jelinger* in his Comment upon it; Thou ſhalt not lend to the poor or rich upon Uſury. This is a Comment indeed. *My Reply is this.* That he wrongs me in it, Biſhop *Jewel* in his Comment upon that place, couples rich and poor, ſo ſaying: *He is thy Brother, whether he is rich or poor.*

My words are theſe upon *Deut.* 23. 19 Mark, *Brother*, and is not the rich thy brother too (who can deny it) I pray tell thou, who doſt ſo ſtoutly defend thy Uſury, and hear what learned Biſhop *Jewel* even now ſaith in this Caſe, and which this Champion fathers upon me, as if I ſhould ſay, as he ſaith, upon the law, which as he tels us ſaith, thou ſhalt not lend upon Uſury to thy brother, which is waxen poor with thee, when I ſpeak upon *Deut.* 23. 19. and is this fair dealing?

2. He wrongs me, leaving out here near 80. lines untoucht, and unanſwered in *p.* 35, 36, 37. So that he gives me juſt cauſe to deal with him ſo too.

3. And beſides, becauſe he puts me ſo to it to defend my ſelf, as well as I may in this weighty matter, ſo overskipping what St. *Baſil*, *Lira*, and Biſhop *Jewel* ſay, I will now ſay a little more than I thought to ſay, to anſwer more fully to his preceding Replies. And firſt, That, tho in places by him named, expreſs mention is made of the poor, yet in others (beſides *Deut.* 25. 15.) as namely in *Pſal.* 15. *Prov.* 20. 8. *Ezek.* 22. 12. and *Luke* 6. 35. there is noted.

2. That it is confeſſed by * *Joſephus*, that the *Jews* have a law, as I ſaid once already, that the lender ſhall take no Uſury, making no exception of the poor at all.

3. And why ſhould thoſe places which mention the poor rather reſtrain the other which make mention of them, than the other, which make no mention of them ſhould enlarge them which name them, eſpecially if we conſider, that thoſe places which mention not the poor were the latter written, and that Divines have a Rule; which ſaith, that latter books were written ſomewhat to this purpoſe, that they might be Interpreters and Expoſitors of the former.

Where Note, how I go to work to ſtop gaps and mouths by this rule, and by an obſervation of mine too, that the *Pſalms* and ſo the 15. and *Ezekiel* eſpecially *thoſe* 2. and the *Proverbs*, and *Luke* 6. 35. Were written after thoſe which men-

* Joſephus *contra A. vion.*

tion

tion the poor; so that now I do not only stand upon *Deut.* 23. 19. where mention is made of Victualls, which some of the Church great Authors so much stand upon, which I wonder at, that wise men should do so; I say again, I do not only Insist on that, but to cut off all other Cavils whatsoever, upon others also.

4, I say farther, that there is great reason for it, why there should be so often mention made of the poor; because 1. That shews what care God takes of the poor, even as he doth for Orphans, and Widdows also and Strangers. And 2. because they are so much and so often oppressed by the men of this wicked world; where let me recite the words of the famous Doctor * *Chemnitius* to second me.

Wheras, *(saith he) in some certain Testimonies of Scripture concerning Usury, there is mention made of the poor by name, that is done for the same reason for which in the sixt and eight Commandments the Widdows, Orphans, and poor folks are commonly recited by name, that no injury should be offered unto them; yet it follows not from thence that an injury may be done to married persons, to mighty men, to rich men &c.* is no sin; Even so it is in the Case of Usury.

Num. 19. 5. And that it may more fully appear, who is meant by the brother in *Deut.* 23. 19. I will at present name two great men more, to ballance his lesser, who tell us, what that brother is.

The first shall be that foresaid great and antient Father, † *Clemens Alexandrine*, who lived near to the Apostles time, and saith, *The law forbids to lend to Usury to our brother* under the Name of a Brother, Comprehending not only him which was born of the same Parents, but him also which was of the same Tribe, and of the same Opinion, and partaker of the same word. I must repeat his words, because the Chapter repeats his.

2. Great || *Aquinas* upon *Deut.* 23. 19. *We ought to count every man to be a Brother.*

3. *Dr.* Sanders. *The Carnal* Jews *had certain Infidels to their enemies, whom as they might kill, so might they oppress them with Usury; but now seing every man is both our neighbour and our Brother, we may not take Usury of any man at all.*

5. And, because they stand much upon a needy brother and decayed, I will set down here, the words of Renowned

* Chemnit. *Loc. Summum de paupert.* a. 6. † Clemens Alexand. *Strom.* l. 2. Tho. || Aquinas. *part.* 3. *q.* 79 *a* 1.

Bishop

Bishop *Downam*, *The signification of a needy brother is not to be restrained to them which are of base condition, but is to be extended to all those who, being of good callings, are come behind hand, or faln into need, not having means of their own to supply their wants;* I add, *and such are many which Usurers lend unto. The Bishop goes on and saith, for if men have means of their own, they ought not to borrow, which makes against those vile wretches, which will borrow and lend the samd mony again to profit, for* 8. *in the* 100. *themselves paying but* 6. *which is oppression.*

Num. 20. 6. I hope the *Ch.* will let me note also the 3. expressions by him noted *Levit.* 25. 35, 36. concerning the poor and decayed brother, and the reason therunto annexed, as namely, this that he which is called our brother and poor, is also called one faln in decay, mark, a decayed brother not a begger, which must be relieved by Alms; but back handed, as a Gentleman, or Farmer, by borrowing and other mishaps may come so to be, and yet have Land or Lease, as those in *Nehemiah*, of whom next.

2. That of such a one we must not take any thing above the Principal, for so the words run, *of such a one thou shalt not take more then thou didst deliver, as some Translations render the same, whereupon a great* Author *saith, Hear whom we are forbidden to bite, we are now forbidden to take any more than was delivered unto him; for he that takes one Penny more than he delivered; wrings and bites him as much as that Penny comes too.*

3. And upon the 36. *verse* containing the reason, Note what may be the meaning of it; *that he may live with thee;* as if he should say, for else how can he live? Usury will kill him, if thou take Usury of him, therefore take no Usury of thy decayed brother.

7. The several other laws which he speaks of in the same 68. *page*, are not at all against me, nor for him, because the laws for the poor are not denied.

8. But as I said, let him prove by any place of Scripture in all the Bible that because we must not lend to the poor upon Usury, therefore we may lend upon Usury to the rich; let him shew the place.

9. And here, because he takes his advantages by Authors which he cites, as holding it lawful to lend upon Usury to the rich, because we may not to the poor.

I will take advantages also, and match his Authors with Authors far exceeding his for age and Renown.

As Namely 1. of the Old Holy Fathers and of our modern Writers.

1. Saint

1. Saint *Austin* by * some called the wisest man in his time, is against all Usury without any exception of Usury taken by the rich.

2. And Saint † *Basil*, who was such a holy and self denying man, as that he gave all that he had to the poor, and being a bitter enemy to Usurers, describes them thus: *Usurers go thus to work, to entice rich young heirs; they employ their own Creatures to understand their domestick affairs, and necessities, They tell them there is such a Barton to be sold, and an ample house, they extol its revenews, perswade them to buy it; They answer that they have no mony to buy it; Thereupon they offer their own, saying, use it as your own; you will pay us of the incomes of the same Barton; They pretend to other mens land to entice the young Gentleman to spoil him of his own. Thus holy Antiquity has been against lending upon Usury to the rich, and so are and have been our best new writers,* viz.

1. Famous Bishop Jewel, *as* Humphries *has it, writes thus, what manner of Logick is this, a man may not take Usury of the poor*; ergo *he may take Usury of the rich*, non sequitur: *It follows not in art, let us see the like in other examples,* Solomon *saith,* Prov. 22. 22. Rob not the poor because he is poor, (*just as I say so saith he*) *shall I thence conclude, therefore I may rob the rich, because he is rich; so when* Moses *saith lend not to the poor upon Usury; doth it therefore follow, Therefore I may lend upon Usury to the rich, nothing less, it carries no Consequecne at all.*

2. *Bishop* || Downam Deuter. 23. 19. *There is no mention made of the poor, but* all Usury *is forbidden towards any, either* Israelite *or* Proselite, *or as* Clemens Alexandrine *speaks*, ὁμιόφυλον ἢ ὁμιο νυομιενα *and in this general sence including both rich and poor, the learned among the* Jews *have so understood this law, where note that here is now Antiquity and Authority.*

3. Mos. *If the law of lending to the poor without Usury, should Infer the lawfullness of lending to the rich upon Usury; then it is evident that Gods intendment in those laws for the benefit of the poor, should rather prove a hurt and hindrance unto them. For who will lend to the poor for nothing, that might lawfully lend to the rich for* Usury?

4. Tostatus. * *Not only to the poor, but also to the rich thou shalt lend without Usury.*

---

* Humfr. *in vita Jewelli.* p. 221. † Downam *upon* Psal. 15. || Tostatus *in* Deut,

5. Powel

5. Powel *Answers that Objection from* Exo. 22. 25. Lev. 28, 35. *For not lending to the poor upon Usury thus*, ergo, *we may lend to the rich, This is no good Consequence. The law saith* Deut. 27. 24. *Cursed is he that smiteth his Neighbour secretly*, ergo *it is lawful to smite him openly.*

6. † Capel. *No opression is like to this to oppress a poor man; yet I hope it is a sin to oppress the rich because he is rich.*

Num. 22. In the next place let us go on with him to *Nehemiah:* and what were those Usurers which *Nehemiah* so condemns for Usury, were they not such as lent to them that had Lands, Vineyards *&c.*

Reply. Whether they were to be called poor or no, it seems they were for the time Necessitous and much straitned, they would not else have morgaged their lands to buy Corn and things necessary for a livelyhood, nor have suffered their Sons and Daughters to have been brought into bondage: Here I consult *Rivet. &c.* and then to answer once for all, let it be considered, whether the case were not extraordinary *&c.*

Whereunto I answer 1. That his reply is a poor come of, because, tho they were necessitous yet were they landed, and landed even then, when they borrowed, for their land they morgaged when they borrowed *vers.* 3. *and then others come which said, we have borrowed mony for the Kings tribute, and that upon our lands and vineyards*; *Mark* 1. *our lands and vineyards in the Plural,* which may imply that they had much land some of them, if not all, tho morgaged.

2. *Our,* because the propriety was theirs in the land tho morgaged.

3. We borrowed mony *upon our lands and vineyards vers.* 4. Note, they which did not morgage, borrowed and took up mony upon their lands, binding them to the Usurers, as many Necessitous landed men do now, and therefore where is the *Ch.* now?

O saith he, *Rivet* is of my side. *Reply*, but you cite him in Latin, and I do not mean to translate him for you, so that he can do the vulgar no good; but if he were Enlished, it would be the same, for he is not against me, who say, as he saith, even the very same that we should lend freely to the necessitons, which those Usurers in *Nehemiah* would not do, but would have Use of such Necessitons, landed men, which our Usurers also will have.

---

* Powel p. 42. *mihi* p. 218. † Capel, *in his App. conc. Usury* p. 292.

Num.

Num. 23. *But* he has one shift more, that the Case in *Nehemiah* was extraordinary, and how was it extraordinary? it is as if Ordinary Christians should be prest to praying seven times a day, because *David* said so often he would pray, or to require of every one solemn prayers three times a day because * *Daniel* did so, all which makes against him, because neither the one nor the other is such an extraordinary business, because there have been of late times those, which have prayed six times a day usually, as blessed *Bolton*, † witness his life; and as for *Daniel*, of him it is said that he prayed three times, || *as he did aforetime*, *Dan.* 6, 10. So that by these very examples he makes the Case in *Nehemiah*, but an ordinary thing, but me he aims at, in all those extraordinory things, which he speaks of, to disgrace me, and make me a spectacle to men and Angels, and a sign and wonder in *Israel*, and the Drunkards song; for so he goes on with his extraordinary things and wonders, as to rise at midnight, or before day because I desire to do so, as *David* did, and my Saviour did, who rose a great while before day and prayed *Mark* 1. 35. me, me, he has an aim unto, I say, as being the man of his indignation, because I cry down his great *Diana* for so he goes on; some such extraordinary Zeal has prompted this Author to exhort his readers in Prayer, to reach forth their arms as high as they can, or to fall all along upon the ground in prayer in their own houses and in their several rooms, where they are wont to poor out their prayers, because he was wont to do so himself; these being gestures becoming none but persons of a Giant like affections &c. And the like affection induced him to will every ordinary Christian to resolve thus; fasting and humiliation days I will keep by the same divine power to the Lord my God at least once a month, and before the Sacrament of the Lords Supper, and when there is great need, and at other times also; but where to find an example for this (as for some afore) I know not, unless it be taken from the *Pharisees* that fasted twice a week &c. Whereunto I answer. Loe, how *Ismael*-like he mocks me, and also Censures both

---

* *To which devotions he might have aded the great devotion of the* Eunuchs, *which to go to* Jerusalem *to worship, went* 4000 *miles as Doctor* Cave *computeth it in his lives of the Fathers.*

† Bagshaw *in his life.*

|| *which sheweth that it was his ordinary practice.*

me

me and all the godly ones that fast so, pray so, resolve so, as others before them have done. But I hope to come of with honour after all his disgracing jeers and cruel mockings, so called *Hebr.* 11. 36.) cast after me, with the help of my God, whom I serve, and do resolve to serve day and night.

And 1. the reaching forth of the hand or arm in challenging God to make his promises good; I have from those worthy men Doctor † *Abbot*, and Mr *Bolton*, who in his Direct. for right comforting afflicted Consciences, writes of one *Sprot* who did so, when he died. *S*ee the || Margin for it.

Now let the *Ch.* go and challenge Mr. *Bolton* and Doctor *Abbot* why they would write so.

2. For often praying and lying on the ground and upon the face, I have from *Abraham Gen.* 17. 3. from *David*, yea from * *Christ* himself who so fell upon the ground, and prayed: from all the Elders of *Israel* who so fell upon their faces before the Lord, joyning with *Joshua* in that posture praying, as you may see *Jos.* verse 7. Alas O Lord God *&c.* And from *Moses Numb.* 14 5. *Then* Moses *and* Aaron *fell on their faces before all the assembly of the Congregation of the Children of* Israel*:* and from that good people * in 2. *Mach.* 10. 4. and from † a certain holy Minister whom his wife, which was an excellent woman often has found by night lying on the ground, weeping and wrestling with God, even in cold winter nights, (as saith my Author) and from that wonderfull Minister P. *S.* in S. p. *page* 37. who by a Convert of his was found by night lying in a garden upon the ground, and praying so earnestly as that God sent an Hoast of Angels to him to bring him an answer from the Lord, which made him cry out and say, O what am I, being Dust and Ashes, that the holy Ministring Spirits should be sent to deliver a message and an answer to my prayers. Let the *Ch.* now go, and jeer these holy Ministers,

---

* *His words at full are these* George Sprat *Notary in* Aimouth *at his death said thus to Christ, Thou hast left me this comfort in thy word,* Matt. 11. 28. *come unto me all* &c. *And Lord I am heavy loaden with my sins, I am ready to sink even into Hell without thou in mercy put out thine hand and deliver me; and with that thrust out one of his hands, and reaching it as high as he could, with a loud voyce and strained, cried I challenge thee by thy promise, which thou hast made, that thou perform it unto me. Thus this great Doctor reports this.* † Matt. 26. 39. *he fell upon his face.* || *Which also fell down flat before the Lord.*

† *in* S. F. p. 24,

which

which care not for him, being above him in endless glorie: But let me tell my Readers, that I do not * press all this upon any, tho I mention it, and tho I desire to imitate such pious souls my self.

3. For resolving to fast monthly, or weekly, I have (besides *Matt.* 9. 15. *Then shall they fast*, and the 2. *Cor.* 11 27. *In fasting often*) this ground when it pleased God to reveal his Son to me in *Germany*, and I returned home from a Sermon after joy unspeakable, I resolved to fast twice a week, and therefore dare not do otherwise, and as for others I force none, but only advise men so to do, even as I do not force any to rise before day, tho I desire to do so; And to say a little more of fasting, I can bring against this Champions cruel mockings, and censurings, great † *Calvin*, who did fast Ten years together, abstaining from meat till Even, and spending his time in Preaching, Praying, reading, and writing, which is more than once a week, and therefore by my great friend Doctor *Rivet* is so extold, as that he brings in a great Jesuit for it, saying, that *Calvin* was *Un Grand jeuneur*, in french, that is a great faster, and will the *Ch.* say that he was a Pharisee too?

And besides, I know a godly Minister living not far from me, who fasts every week, as well as my self, and is highly applauded and commended for it, and by no body accounted a Pharisee; Unless he be so looked upon by him that accounts me so: || see the Margin also.

Well, this I will say now last of all, concerning all this that I meet with such comfort, such delight, such joy, such expe-

* *For I know that our acceptable service consists not in external gestures, and in serving God within, as that Author* Potho Pruniculis *well inculcates* lib. 5. *de dono Dei. Intus Deo offertur omne Deo acceptabile munus.* † *In my twelfth* Resolut. *set down in my Resolution Table,* || *With whom I may joyn the Lord* Harrington, *who was a great and Renowned Father too, fasting not only monthly before the Sacrament, but other days likewise.* Clark. *in his life* p. 60. 61. *So* Picus Mirandula, *who was such a great Faster too, as his Nephew, and* Boesardus *in his* Bibliotheca *reports.* * *I add that if this man had but read* Ferbis, *and* Figurius, *extolling a Cousin of* Cardinal Baronius *fasting and praying three days together, when he was irresistably moved to discover a Plot for which he had received Commission from the Pope to all Popish Kings and Princes for the extirpating of the Reformed Religion, he would not have jeered me for this Fasting so.*

riences

riences of Christs love; such gyantlike affections, as he jeeringly calls them; as that if the whole world were turned into a lump of gold, and I might have it, if I would give over such practises, I would utterly reject it; and I trust in God, that I shall never give them over, during my natural life, for all the jeers and censures of any scoffing Ismaelite, because of that sweetness and joy which I find and feel therein. So help me, O my God.

But I desire now to return to *Nehemiah* (from whence the *Ch.* hath drawn me by his cruel mockings) fetcht and forcably drawn in by the hair, because he is not willing to hear much of him.

And that which I have to say of him is this;

1. That he is such an eye sore to Usurers, and their Defendents, as that they have attempted to make him an Usurer too, falsly rendring the holy Scripture thus, as Bishop * *Downam* sets down their wrested Translation thus, *So the Author of the English Treatise reads* ver. 10. *For even I, my Brethren and my servants did lend them upon Usury, mony and corn.* O dreadful, to prove the lawfulness of Usury by the Example of *Nehemiah*, which makes me exclaim, Good Lord, what man will not do to uphold cursed Usury, they will wrest thy holy Scripture for it; and falsly translate it: well thus Usurers abuse Scripture it self, as in *lenecro* for *lanecro*, so in this also to make *Nehemiah*, that bitter enemy to all Usury an Usurer too, even as they will needs make me a Usurer too, who never lent one pound or peny upon Usury in all my life time.

Numb. 26. And because the *Ch.* would fain set him against me, by saying that they had mortgaged their Estates, and suffered their Sons and Daughters to be brought into Bondage, &c. to make them poor, therefore I will now let him see, that he is one of the best Friends that I have, because he furnishes me with so many mighty arguments against Usurers and Usury, as I shall now set down.

For first tho he tells of Mortgages and bondage of the borrowers Sons and Daughters, yet still he makes them owners of their Lands, as I have shewn already; and as for the bondage, we know, that mens Sons may be in bondage, being taken by Turks and other Foes, when their Parents are landed men, but want money to redeem them, and cannot be called poor.

2. He forbids Usury expresly and absolutely, without ex-

* Bishop Downam upon Psal. 15. p. 215.

 cepting

cepting the Rich, saying, *I pray you, let us leave off this Usury* ver. 10.

3. He saith to the Nobles, rebuking them, *you exact Usury every one of his Brother*, ver. 7. without naming rich or poor but Brother only, which might not be poor, and calling Us[ury] exacting, to denote the cruelty of it.

4. *He shook his lap, and said, so God shake out every man from his house, and from his labour, that performes not this promise which was that they would do as he had said, let us leave off thi[s] Usury*, ver. 10. *O dreadful, this methinks should make Usurer[s] tremble for fear, lest they be shaken out of all too.*

5. *It is not good that you do*, he saith further to them, to shew that Usury is an evil, and therefore unlawful.

6. He tells them, *Ought ye not to walk in the fear of our God* intimating by it, that Usurers do not fear God, *ver. 9.*

7. Adding, *because of the reproach of the Heathen our enemies* he shews what, a reproachful thing Usury is, because Gods enemies reproach such for it, as profess themselves to be th[e] people of God, and yet will be Usurers.

8. He calls Usury, נשא *a Burden*, because it is a Burden t[o] the Borrower indeed, and to defeat that Cavil, which Usurer[s] use, pretending they are no Usurers, because they are no bi[t]ting Oppressors, and that the Usury in the 15 *Psalm* condemne[d] and so in other Scriptures, is *Neshecк*, which has caused a de[fendent] of Usury to write a little Book, called *called the execu[tion] of Neshecк*, that is *biting*, which, because the Spirit of th[e] Lord foreknew *Nehemiah* must call Usury נשא, *a burden*, an[d] not *Neshecк biting*. to cut of that new distinction between bi[t]ting and toothless Usury, and that after *Moses*, and after *Davi[d]* and after *Solomon*, and that after *Ezekiel*, and the rest of th[e] more ancient pen-men of the Scripture, which is very remar[]kable.

Num. 27. 9. ' He commands the Usurers to make restitut[i]'on, and they promise him to do as he had said, and add w[e] ' will require nothing of them, as thou hast said, *ver.* 1[2] ' *Mark* 1. *we will require* NOTHING. 2. *as thou hast said*, whic[h] shews that he would have them take nothing, because the[y] say expresly, *as thou hast said*, see also, ver. 10. *let us leave o[ff] this Usury*, as if he should say this taking of more then was len[t] as this verse makes it evident; besides many other Scriptures So they agree then both, even *Nehemiah* and the Usurers upo[n] NOTHING to be usuriously given, or taken for mony lent,

* *Usura agros & prædia onerat intolerabili exactione*, Aretius.

if they had seen or heard the words of Christ, when he spake them, *Luke* 6. 35. *Lend, hoping for nothing from thence*; which makes as much for me also as any thing I have yet said of *Nehemiah*, only let me add by the by, that those Usurers as bad as they were, yet are not so bad as Usurers are now, for they made restitution, even a full restitution of lands, and monies, and other things, which they had taken, *ver.* 12. which our Christian Usurers will not do.

10. And here because I am faln upon restitution, I will say a little more about it, *Viz* That after restitution made of their Lands, Vineyards, Houses, Mony, Corn, Oile, they were landed men indeed, not only *de jure*, of Right, but also *de facto, really and indeed*, and so consequently well to pass indeed, which notwithstanding the said Usurers would require NOTHING of them, as *Nehemiah* has said; O how plainly therefore *Nehemiah* is for me. O what a friend he is to me among so many enemies, that are against me!

11. But yet lastly I will be so courteous to the Christian lender, as to grant that it is all the reason in the world, that the rich, which has well gotten by his mony, should be thankful, and let the honest lender have part of his honest gain, and that he may lawfully take, when it comes freely and unexpectedly offered and given to him, as I have formerly shewn, so that at present I will only add what a worthy Author saith to the same effect. 'But it is otherwise if any Man give or offer any thing 'not in respect of the loan, but to shew himself mindful of a 'good return received, for that which is so offered may be 'lawfully taken without any usury committed, *&c.* So that 'there be no fraud used therein, but the intent and Conscience 'of the Receiver be upright and free in that behalf.

But let us go on with the Champion.

1. *What Mr.* Jelinger *saith is a fallacy.*

Whereunto I answer, so both his replies avail nothing; Not that to the 1. *Fallacy*, because what he saith, that the Usury in Scripture is forbidden only with respect to the poor, is false, as has been shewn.

So that concerning the Rich he lacks proof;

And so is his reply to the fallacy of Consequence, for as much as it has been by me sufficiently proved, that all Usury properly so called is a moral evil, and against the Law of * Nature, *and whereas he saith*, that I do prudently leave out the reason why the poor should not be robbed, because he is poor; *I answer*, that I left

* *As Tostatus asserts it in* Deut. 23. p. 318.

out

out, because I saw there was no reason why I should enlarge my self upon it, as a thing making against me, when it doth not, for I hold with old Mr. * *Diodate*, whom he quotes upon it, only this I add, that as he saith of Robbery, that, as it is forbidden to all, so is Usury, as it hath been proved out of *Deut.* 23. 19. where that which is moral in that Law, runs thus, *Thou shalt not lend to thy Brother* (mark Brother, whether he be rich or poor) *upon usury.*

And what he quotes out of *Rivet* availeth him nothing neither, because *Rivet* takes this for an absolute verity, that the things mentioned by the English Bishops, and by him opposed are in themselves evil, (which is not denied) but as for Usury that is not so, when that which he names last, Usury mean, is as much in it self evil as the former, as it has been convincingly demonstrated: The whole sentence taken out of *Rivet* I shall not write, because it is set down in Latin, and do not owe the *Ch.* so much service as to translate it.

He tells us from *Deut.* 23. 19. That the Stranger is excepted and not the Rich, whereas, if God would have granted lawful to lend to the Rich, there had been a fit place t be named as wel as the Stranger: His reply is, *What shall I ca it but sauciness*, &c. *Answer*, Not such sauciness as that of h Brethren, which wrest the Scriptures, and put *lenecro* for *lan cro* in this same place now in hand, *Deut.* 23. 19. and *none f nothing* in Christs own saying, *lend looking for nothing* from thenc *Luke* 6. 35. which is sauciness indeed, yea, the highest inju offered to Christ: But in my Saying, how can there be any sa ciness or injury, when God might have so easily done it, b would not, because there was no need, no more than the was for Christ to say *lend without Usury*, when he spake plai ly saying, *lend hoping for nothing.*

Numb. 29. 2. *Usurers reply*, Divers Presbyterian Ministe allow of use taken from the rich.

1. *Answer*, I have named several before, and divers othe might be named, *Rivet* names several, *Zanchy* saith their nur ber is almost infinite. *Windeline* affirms, it is held by mc moderne Divines, &c. even by *B. Hall*, the Pillar he leans c fails him, and so forth: *Whereunto I answer*,

1. That I also have named several before; and more I w name now to ballance, yea, to outballance his; which m thinks speaks either *too little*, or *too fast*. *Too little*, as nami but a few, or not relating what they say, or *speak too fast*; h

---

* *Who also holds with me in* Deut, 23. 19.

when one of them saith their number is almost infinite: for which *almost* I will not blame him, because I know what else I should have said; and so when *Windeline* affirms it; as held by most modern Divines, which I much wonder at, if he mean Usury properly so called; for my friends will tell him, and prove the contrary, as for example, * *Dr. Fenton, that famous* London *Minister*, who writes thus of Usury.

A practice, which has no approbation of God in Scripture, nor any Church that is, or ever was upon the face of the Earth.

And Mr. † Gabriel Powel, *No Writer, that either I could see or hear of, ever allowed of Usury.*

So Keckerman, *All the Greek and Latin Fathers, and almost all our Reformed Divines hold Usury to be a Sin.*

And to answer *Windelines* brags especially, *viz.* It is held by Lawyers and moral Philosophers, † that learned *Oxford* Scholar *Powel* saith thus, *Philosophers have condemned it, Poets have exclaimed against it, the Civil Law forbids lending upon Usury, by the* || *Canon Law also it is forbidden.*

Now let the Reader chuse, which he will believe an English Scholar which is his Country man, or this Stranger.

So the renowned Bishop *Downam*, which saith this of our English Divines, in answer to the Champion about Episcopal Divines. *The godly learned Divines of this Age, and namely of this our Church, do for the most part inveigh against Usury; those few among us, that seem to defend Usury, do in substance differ little from the rest, erring especially in this, that under the odious name of Usury, they defend and maintain a lawful contract of partnership*, thus he. I quote him again, being urged to it by this mans repetitions.

Numb. 30. I add *Alciates*, who speaking of Usuries Opposites has this expression, *Totus Mundus militat pro nobis: The whole world militates and wars for us*; meaning those that are against Usury, as well he might say so; for besides the holy Scriptures, all the ancient Fathers have abhorred and written against it, saith the foresaid * *Powel*, and the ancient Councils are against it, School-

* *Dr. Fenton*, p. 259. *Whom* Filburn *by his catches at some of his sayings is not able to confute, as the learned Reader may easily see it.* † *Gabriel Powel* p, 52. || *Where the Words of the famous* Jer. Taylor *in his* Ductor Dub 1. 196. *is remembred,* The Church forbids Usury, and in this Case the Canon Laws are to be preferred. * *Gabriel Powel*, p. 52. *With whom joyn* R. Capel, p. 202. *The best and best learned of our Prelatical, and anti-Prelatical Divines have taken good and great pains, to prove Usury to be a thing utterly unlawful.*

men

men and Casuists against it, and modern Divines against it; and the learned Bishops of *England* against it; as the Champion himself in his Pamphlet confesseth it. As for *Geneva* and the *Helvetians*, they are of *Calvins* mind, who was so wary in his opinion, as that he would not determine any thing absolutely concerning it; but only cautioned it, and so doing made it partenership; so that his boasting of *Geneva* (which I know better than he) out of B. *Andrews* my friend, will do him no good. As for the Germans my Country men, they have a * Commissary, which takes up mony, and deals with it at *Franckfort* Marts, and gives part of the gain, which is gained by it but as for Usury properly so called, none dares to defend it, but a great many of their Divines have written and are against it whom I have formerly named, as namely Doctor *Luther*, *Melancthon*, *Brentius*, *Musculus*, *Philip Cæsar*, Dr. *Didericus*, *Heminigius*, *Mordesius*, *Mollerus*, *Aretius* of *Helvetia*, *Universitas Wittenbergensis*, *Hottomannus*, Doctor *Luder*, Dr. *Pareus*, Dr. *Vulteius Ursin*, the Preachers of *Mansfield*, *Albertus* Blankenberg. *Conradus Paulus* Brunswicensis, *Justus Jonas*, *Wellerus*, *Pomerianus*, of all which some are Lutherans, others Calvinists †.

As for || *Abulensis*, who hath written more Volumes upon the Bible than any man, him my Adversary only names, but I do own him as one of my chief Friends; for he writes against all Usury: *All modes of Usury are unlawful. And Usury is to be understood according to all its modes, when namely any thing determinated is taken above the Principal* p. 516.

And in Deut. 23. 19. he saith, *p.* 317. *It was permitted unto the Jews to lend upon Usury for the hardness of their hearts, as Bill of Divorce, because if they might have lent upon Usury, they might either not have lent at all, or stollen*: This makes for me. And as for the Heathens, by him and his friends clamed to be for them: I do deny it, because I am sure that the chief ones among them are for me, As *Cicero*, *Plautus*, *Plutarch*, *Columella*, *Aristotle*, *Plato*, *Lucanus*, *Ausonius*, *Cato*, *Proculus*, *Ulpian*, &c For the proof of my assertion, I will set down some of their assertions: * Cicero *saith, such things are to be blemished which are odious, as namely that of Usurers, and* † Columella *saith, that*

---

* *Which I will not have understood of all but many: having already granted it, that some in simplicity follow* Absolom, *and took a kind of Usury, which they should not, out of ignorance.* † *The Gallick Ministers in a French Treatise against* Dancing, p. 131. So *in their Annotations upon* Mat. 25. 27. || Abulensis *in* Levit. 25. *&* Deut. 23. 19. * Cicero *de Offic. l.* 1. † Collumella *de re rust. l.* 1.

Usury

Usury is odious even unto them which it seems to help. And * Plautus *saith, There is no worse kind of men this day to deal with, than the Usurers.* *Hugo Grotius*, I do not value at all, because of his unsoundness; that he tells of Schoolmen to be for usury I wonder at; because my Cozin *Spanheimus* himself takes it for granted they are Anti-usurarians.

What he saith of all the men, by him supposed to be for usury, that I deem them to be damned, he wrongs me in that; for I take them, that are truely godly among them, to be such as will be truely glorious Saints in heaven, and such as here are far enough from that cursed usury, which is practised among us, as allowing no other usury, but that which is recompensatious, and liberal, and by godly cautions become another kind of thing, *viz.* Partnership. What he faintly speaks of my Country men the Dutch, is not so, for what saith *Aretius*, *One shall often hear these words come from cordial men (in* Helvetia, *which is in* Germany, *where he lived) that those usurary Instruments are one time to be corrected as the Popes* Bulls: (which sheweth how weary the German Divines are of usury) nor would friends be wanting, if but an apt *Adis* or *Lycurgus*, or *Cato* did appear once.

Num. 31. But my work is not fully done, for I cannot but find fault with the quoting of his Authors, because he only mentions men but not their words; and therefore I will now name some of our best Divines, and recite their very words at large, that the World may see how false it is, what some of his men say; that most modern Divines are for usury; and the English too.

And I will begin with *Perkins*, who saith (as I and my friends do defining usury) *Usury is a gain by covenant above the principal, only for loan and recompence of the lending of it.*

2. I will name *Adams*, who saith, *The Usurer is a man made out in wax, his Pater Noster is a Pawn, his Creed is the Condition of his Obligation, his Religion is all Religion, a binding of others, and a binding himself to the Devil: Infinite colours, mitigations, evasions are invented to countenance on Earth, Heaven exploded usury; God shall then frustrate all, when he shall pour out wrath his upon the naked Conscience.*

2. † *Rogers* of *Weatherfield*, *That common dealing for ten in the hundred, or nine, or eight, or any such like. Note ANY, without*

---

v *Movestella.* * *Plautus*, † *Aret. de usura.* || *Perkins upon 2. Com.* * *Adams in his Works*, p. 55. † *Rogers of Weatherfield.*

consideration of the Common-wealth is utterly to be condemned, which if well considered, will soon answer all conscionable men about the question of Usury and Oppression, and he addes that there is no use of them in the Church, and the Christian Common-wealth.

4. Mr. || *Dod* (and O what a man is that man, even one of a thousand) *Usury is not a Calling appointed by God, but a humane invention devised by Worldly men to gain filthy lucre to themselves, whereby they live of the sweat of other mens brows.*

5. Mr. * Wheatly, *Usury is a notorious injustice, where a man makes a gain of lending, and binds the Party borrowing without consideration of his gain or loss to pay the principal with advantage.* And again he saith, *Christians must serve one another in love and not serve themselves in self love, both which principles are directly contrary the trade of the Usurer, for he makes sure to himself to have a part only and infallibly in the profit, and therefore serves himself only, and not at all his brother, and therefore the Usurer is set among those, that cannot dwell in the Mountain of God:* (Just as I say in my Doctrine, so saith he) which he should not be, were he not unjust.

6. Dr. † Sutton, *There is no Sin be it never so prodigious and foul, but his Master has a plea for it, Usury has;* Deut. 23. 19. *unto a Stranger thou mayest lend : Mark this thou Usurer, who defendest thy filthy Usury by this.*

And yet further he saith, *Those that live by Usury let them remember this, my heart trembles to think what calling these men have, my Soul mourns how they glorifie God in them : O Usurer, do thou tremble and mourn too, as this great Doctor doth.*

7. Mr. || *Sanderson*, that great *Oxford* Scholar saith, *The Texts of Scripture are so express, and the grounds of reason so strong against all Usury, that when I weigh these on the one side, and on the other side how nothing all that is, which I yet saw, or heard,* [and he could not but have read much, being a Batchelour in Divinity in *Oxford*] *alleadged to the contrary, I cannot find charity enough to absolve ANY kind of Usury from being a Sin : And of the Usurer he tells how bitterly he is inveighed against by Heathens, how universally hated by all men.*

8. That great and famous Arch-Bishop *Usher*'s opinion, and condemnation of Usury, is to be seen in the front of this Book.

And I have in readiness other learned Men, and even a

---

* *Mr.* Wheatly *in his Caveat to the Covetous.* p. 71. † *Dr.* Sutton *in his Lectures.* || Sanderson *upon* 1 Cor. 7. 24.

Cloud

Cloud of British Divines more, but I shall forbear to name them now for brevities sake, and onely perswade all true English hearts to hearken to those their own holy Countrymen, which they have either heard or read, or can read in their own English Tongue, rather then look after, and unto such others as are cited to them in the Latin Tongue, which the Learned only understand, considering that this Usury matter concerns the Salvation of their Souls, which as that foresaid holy man *Usher* tells them should not be adventured upon wild Discourses, and subtle Distinctions, as being more worth than all the World.

9. Mr. * *Udal* saith. 'That it is as clear in the Word, that 'usury is a Sin, as that Christ came into the World to save 'Sinners.

Dr. † *Fenton*, p. 154. 'An absolute contract for mony lent 'for 10. 9. 8. or 6. in the hundred, *N.B.* 6. in the 100. is without 'warrant or authority, even among those Divines, who upon sifting and examining this point, have concluded most favourably for the Vsurer: *And this he saith also*, Ah poor 'Soul whether wilt thou turn thy self for succour, when thy 'best friends forsake thee? How dost thou think to die a Christian, if thou live an Vsurer. Here consider, Dear Reader, what those few inconsiderable Ministers are in our Country, being compared with such holy and learned Doctors.

Numb. 32. But I have a great mind to return again to that famous saying of *Alciates*, *That the whole World militates for us, and war against bloudy usury*, as well he might, if we farther consider what a world of men and countries there are against the same hateful usury; as namely those under the Mahometan Empire, which the Great Turk saith is half the World, because *Mahomets* Law is against usury in his † Alcoran, as *Azoara*, the || Centuries, and Bishop * *Downam* assert it, his words are *Even* Mahomet *and his Alcoran has forbidden ALL USURY.* O wonderful the very cruel Turks abhor usury, all usury, and shall Christians redeemed with Christs precious blood practice it?

Again, The Papists also condemn usury, all usury, insomuch as that the Pope of *Rome* doth every month excommunicate all Vsurers, as one also of our Ministers, Mr. † *Turner* affirms it: And O what a World of Countries there are under

* *Old Mr.* Vdal *in his Obed. to the Gospel.* 2. *Sermon.* † *Azoar.* || *Magdeburg. Cent.* 7. * Downam *upon Psal.* 15. † *Mr.* Turner *against Usury.*

Popish

Popish Kings and Princes? where let it be thought upon too, what great Scholars the Casuists and School-men are, which have most learnedly and profoundly written against deservedly abominated usury, though in other things are out, are so as that yet they could not be carried away with this foul error of usuries lawfulness, but rather joyn with those, which war with their pens and tongues against that Enemy of Mankind, Usury, as it is justly called; fighting against it also as well as they. See *Lorinus* upon *Psal.* 15. and shall Protestants fight for it? O for shame, for shame, let it be no longer reported, as the aforesaid Jesuite *Lorinus* relates it of Calvinists and Reformed Writers, that they write and are for unlawful Usury.

What the Champion saith of Bishop *Andrew* my friend too, I do not regard at all; for I know what a Book he has written. *Quod Usura licita est illicita*, that even lawful usury (so counted by some) is unlawful.

12. But I have not yet done with *Alciates*, who saith that all the World fights for us, that fight against that sin which is an abhorring to all flesh; for what saith *Jeremy* 15. 16. (that I may end with Gods word) *I have neither lent upon usury, nor men have lent to me on usury, yet every one of them doth curse me.* Mark, EVERY ONE, and may not I well say that, well might *Alciates* say, that all the World fights for us against the Usurer, seeing every one hates an Usurer: O sad man that every one hates and curseth thee: Should not this, if there were nothing else against thee, make thee leave that hateful dreadful Sin? Now let every body that reads all this, consider who has most on his side; whether the Champion and his few Authors, or *Alciates* my friend. As for me I stand upon this most; that I have God and his holy Prophets on my side, whereas he and they have not one, but only a little handful risen of late since *Carolus Molnæus* the Lawyer, their first Founder, whose Followers are not for them neither, as they think; having and proposing such cautions and limitations, as scarce any Usurer by report, does observe, so as that my cozin *Spanhemius*, on whom the Champion and other Defendents of usury do most quote has wisely left them to their ingenious confession formerly mentioned.

Now in what case is the poor Champion then here. Readers, what think ye? Doth he not stand like butter in the Sun? How doth he look think you in this sad defeat, whereby his men in whom he trusted, and his own arms too are taken away from him, being over run and over-matched by the holy Prophets first, and a multitude of men besides, holy Fathers I mean, and modern Authors, yea Turks, and Papists too, falling upon him, and his poor, by him defended Vsurers. O sad, I say once more, though he mislikes it, for so he discourses himself (he cannot choose poor man) saying of his men that are for regulated usury, What shall we think is become of all these men? Damned doubtless for their usury, O sad! *I answer*, No, no, I cannot think so; for they most of them, I hope, are safe, and they and we that are against all usury shall meet in glory, because of their godly cautions, vvhich makes that usury, vvhich is supposed to be but partnership, or some such like harmless Contract.

Numb. 33. *As for the burden*, which every man shall bear at that great day, vvhen he thinks mine vvill be the greater for my uncharitable censure of my professing brethren.

To that I answer, I need not fear it because I do not condemn my professing Brethren, as appeareth by my preceding vvords, but let him look to it, that looks and is for משא *Vsury* I mean so called, because it is a *Burden*, vvhich sinks the Vsurer into hell, for he must die, *Ezech.* 12, 13. and be buried too in that bottomless pit, as I shall ostend and shevv hereafter, God vvilling in my next printing.

Numb. 34. The Champion goes yet further and saith, I vvonder at his confident expressions, *&c.* Time vvas vvhen he vvas far from such confidence, nay I vvondered saith he hovv others could sing so merrily in their Congregations beyond the Seas, *Luthers* hymns, vvhich are so full of confidential expressions, vvhen I durst not, nor could sing so vvith them, unless I would lie?

Whereunto I answer,

I bless God, that it vvas so vvith me then; for then God did prepare and fit my troubled Soul for ensuing joyes, vvhich vvere after such troubles of mind so great and glorious, as that I vvent home one day from a good Sermon preached in the country, vvhere *Luthers* confidential Hymns vvere sung, into the City vvhere then I resided, in a triumph.

The Champion goes on (but very confusedly) and saith, seeing he sends us so often to the Council of *Nice*, I vvish he vvould read and vveigh, vvhat the learned Author of the naked Truth has vvritten of Councils, and of this in especial, *&c.*

Whereunto I answer, I have read the Author of the *Naked Truth*, and vvish he had vvritten more discreetly; for not to speak of other things, he goeth to bring preaching in contempt, by his going to vvork; advising such to preach as are

not

not called to it: If he had advised them to instruct those which are committed to their charge, by Catechizing, *&c.* I, and many others should have liked it better. But,

2. I wish the Champion had read *Beza*, a better man than his Author, who saith, *that the Sun never beheld a more divine meeting since the Apostles time, than the Council of* Nice.

3. *I wish he had read** Bolton *concerning it, for he would have told him that those* 318 *Fathers which met in that Council, were the learnedest and greatest Divines in the whole Christian World.* And I add, that there were those in it, who had lost their eyes for Christ, whose holes the great *Constantine* kissed, and this Novice will go to confute this grave, learned, and holy Council: O Sawciness! Sawciness most base and abominable.

4. Methinks he should have learned more wit and modesty of pious † *Calvin*, which he takes to be his Tutor, and speaks after another better rate of this famous *Council*, as namely thus. I do embrace those Ancient Councils, the *Nicene*, the *Constantinopolitan*, the *Ephesian*, the *Chalcedonian:* Mark how he embraced, not slighted, this sacred Synod.

5. When I first saw this mans boldness and sawciness in this thing, I wondred; but when I considered how sometimes a young contemptible Scold, will scold, if she be a little provoked, with one of the best and antientest women in a Town or City; I ceased wondring: Let the Reader apply it. This old Council is against Usury, and therefore this young Champion picks a quarrel against it, and scolds with it, God forgive him. As for me, I bless God for so holy and glorious an Assembly, so happily met after so long and sad a time of persecution which preceded it, and for its condemning of Usury.

|| 3. *Reply*, We must not make more sins than God makes. I confess it, saith he, but does God make lending to the Rich no sin? where is that place, shew it if you can?

Reply, That is not needful, let him shew some proof against it, *&c.* *I answer*, 1. In so great a matter which concerns the Souls salvation, it is needful. 2. I will make a Syllogism of the *Ch.* Reply thus.

Those things which God has not forbidden, we may safely do without hurt of Conscience.

To take Usury of Rich Men God has not forbidden.

Therefore of them lawfully without hurt of Conscience, we may exact Usury for our lending.

---

* *Bolton, p.* 4. † Calvin *in his Institutions.* || Mr. *Jeling.*

My

My Answer is, I deny the Minor; for it is plainly said, *Luke* 6. 35. *Lend, looking for nothing thereby.* If they be rich men they have no need to borrow, and yet we ought to shew our charity to all if need require, but if rich men out of covetousness, and to maintain pride and filthy prodigality, will borrow, and others lend to them upon usury, both of them offend; of which thing * *Pomerianus* speaks thus. *The Borrower asks for his filthy pleasure, and the Lender lends for unlawful lucre, this lending is not friendship but enmity, far differing from honest contracts, because Usury is contrary to Nature; for it takes away equality, and brings one party to extreme beggery, &c.*

† Dr. *Tayler* goeth this way to work to answer this matter about the rich, *Some Divines have undertaken the defence to lend to the Rich, which he answers thus.* 1. *The Moral Law forbids all Usury.* 2. *Never any Divine that ever I could see or hear of, ever allowed Usury, but with such cautions as alter the case of Usury, and maketh it indeed no Usury at all; just as I said before, what the Ch. saith concerning civil Contracts, needs proving and clearing.*

Numb. 35. I have been somewhat long about this matter concerning the Rich, and Authors, because it is a chief thing, but hereafter I must and shall be briefer.

|| *M. J. Obj.* 5. I shew charity to my Neighbour, by my Loan he preserveth his Estate, &c. I answer,

1. Charity is kind, but Usury is cruel. *Reply, Dictum sed non probatum.* The thing is plain and undeniable, being every days experience, &c. And must we not believe what our eyes see, and ears are so often witnesses unto? This hold he cannot keep, therefore he adds,

2. Charity should be free in lending, *Luke* 6. 35. *Reply,* So Charity should be free in giving too, where it is most conspicuous, &c. both require due Objects.

To both I answer thus.

1. *To the first:* That we have eyes too, to see how many Families are ruin'd by Usury and quite undone; and I do ap-

---

* Pomerianus *in suo comment. in Deut.* † Dr. Taylor *in his progress of Saints, with whom I will joyn the famous* Richard Capel *of Usury, p.* 292. *shew a place that it was granted to put money to a rich Jew or to a rich Christian, else all they say is as much as nothing. See also what follows, p.* 293. *and* Greenham *p.* 41. *To the Poor give freely, they use to say, of the Rich take usury, the Lord was never the Author of this distinction.*

peal

peal for it to the Country, whether they have not seen divers of their Neighbours put from house and home by and for Usury, and so we have heard the cry of those which have been quite spoiled by Usury: I for my part can truly say it, with these ears of mine I have heard it, &c. which has caused famous Dr. *Wilkinson* to cry out in his debt book; of many thousands it has been the ruine in our Nation.

2. *To the Second I answer*: I shall easily grant, and have granted, that Charity should be free in GIVING, to use his own phrase, that is, we should freely bestow a gratuity upon the courteous lender, if we be gainers.

|| *Obj.* 6. I will never be perswaded that God will damn that man who doth as he would be done to, it being Christs command, *Mat.* 7. 12.

I would be willing to pay, &c.

Ans. 1: Nor will I be perswaded that the Usurer would be willing by an absolute free will.

Reply. I believe so too, if any would so far befriend him as to lend him freely to purchase a bargain. *Whereunto I Reply*, 1. That to the Q. which he proposes here, of what Right Reason dictates; as namely, that it is reasonable for me that have borrowed an hundred pounds to enlarge the Estate which I already have, or to drive a Trade to get gain, that he should have a due proportion of the gains, &c.

I answer, That I say so too as he, that it is reasonable the Lender should have a proportionable gratuity, or that the Borrower should part Stakes with the Lender, and let him be a partner of his new Purchase or Profit, gotten by Negotiation. For I am all for Partnership, but not for forbidden Usury, so that my advice still is, that if a Rich Man will needs purchase more means, he agree with the Lender to let him have his proportionable part in the purchase, for there is no reason for it that he should have all the profit of his money, and the Lender none: Let them divide, and so let neither the Lender in this purchase offend God by Usury, nor the Borrower by Ingratitude, but rather forbear to purchase.

† *He adds*, Would he be willing with an absolute and free will to pay interest, if he were in many a borrowers case?

Reply, I think so too, but this will not do his work, &c. *Whereto I answer*, that this hath been answered already; his second Answer takes that for granted which is still in question,

* Dr. Wilkinson *in his Debt Book*. || Mr. Jel. † Num. 36.

and

and therefore I pass on and shall look into the Rule laid down by our Lord Christ, of doing as we would be done too, which is the Rule of all civil Trading and Commerce: and here he brings in B. *Tayler* and *Zanchy* in Latin, and *Rivet* in Latin, and B. *Hall*, and Mr. *Burton*, and *Cicero*, and *Grotius* and *Rivet* again, and all the three last in Latin.

To all which I answer thus.

1. That I have examined all that he and his Authors say, and find that what they say doth not cross me, for they make it unreasonable that another should get by me, and I loose by him, but he should have part of my gain, and I do yield to it, though I cannot yield to Usury, because God will not yield to it, as men may see, *Nehem.* 5. 10. *Luke* 6 35.

2. That I cannot mislike my old friend *Rivet* especially, whose expressions are very considerable, as namely, "That he "is for a *Recompensation*, which they call Recompensatory Usu-"ry, and hold lawful, and is for a participation twice which "makes way for Partnership, which I do exceedingly approve "of, and am glad for, but not a word he has for VSVRY. And I insist upon him the rather, because the *Ch.* saith, that he answers more fully than the rest; granting that they do not answer fully though they are many: His Latin I do not translate because I am not bound to it.

3. *I answer*, that the Assemblies words do not hurt me neither, for they are very harmless, and I can safely say the same, that those commands require the lawful procuring and furthering of the wealth and outward estate of our selves and theirs, and besides the Assembly doth so much befriend me, as that it defines Usury just as I and my Friends do, and what can I desire more?

* After all this the *Ch.* comes in very confusedly with some remarks, formerly by him omitted; which therefore I shall slight as he me.

1. *Reply*, That Usury is not named by Christ, *Luke* 6. 35. nor any where in the New Testament, *&c.*

† 1. *Answer*, Nor is Sodomy committed with a Beast.

Reply, The Reason is not the same, this Sin being of rarer practice, *&c.*

Whereunto I answer, Though it be never so rarely practised, yet might it have been named as well as those sins, *Rom.* 1. 26, 27. committed by men with men, by women with women, which also are to be abhorred, without any ones crying out fie, fie, upon *Paul*, who names them.

---

* *Num.* 38. † *M.* 7.

2. But

2. But if this Sodomy be such an abhorred sin, as that I should not have named it, then I hope I may instance in divers others which are not so: as namely, Biting Vsury by them so called, Polygamy, High-Treason, nor the prophanation of the Christian Sabbath, which Vsurers Defendants and Vsurers are very much guilty of in *Holland* and *High Germany*, where let me alledge what Dr. *Pye* saith, which has never yet been confuted, as * *Bolton* tells us the same, that many other breaches also of the Moral Law are not forbidden in the New Testamenr, tho' they be in the Old; as for example, all degrees of Incest save one, Removing of our Neighbours Land-mark, and the prophanation of the Sabbath.

2. *Answer*, Other famous Writers shall resolve them.

Reply, I have said enough to take off this before.

A. And so have I, and so Mr. *Trap*, and therefore I will let it go, and say no more but this: That whereas Reply is made to what I said, Vsury was suppressed by the *twelve Tables*, and by *Tiberius Caius*, and *Vespasian*, &c. that my reason is but weak, I hope I shall make it strong enough by and by. And

1. *Bishop Hall* my friend (as the Champion himself calls him) who makes it strong enough, for he reports it from approved Authors.

2. By *Alexander* of *Alexandria*, who goes to the very time, when *Tiberius* did suppress Vsury, *viz.* in the latter part of his Reign, and that Vsury was so effectually suppressed by him, as that it is supposed that it was not practised in *Judæa*.

3. By *Bishop Downam*, to make up a threefold cord which is not easily broken.

4. I shall make my Reason and all the rest that goes with it, strong enough by other Emperours also; as *Leo*, who utterly suppressed it, as † Mr. *Poole* and others affirm it, and by *Justinian*, as the *corpus juris* makes it good, and *Charles* the Fifth at *Augusta* in *Germany*.

5. I add, And whereas the *Ch.* makes a matter of it, that I make such a halt between *Claudius* and *Vespasian*, I answer, that it might perk up again as often as it did, and so be put down from time to time.

6. About *Seneca* I have this to say, that I was misled by one, who made him so great an Vsurer, from which Aspersion I have since freed him.

N. 35. *But* the Champion Replyes here, did the twelve Tables,

---

* *Who also was never yet confuted, saith*, R. Capel. p. 288.
† Poole *upon* Luke 6.

or

Tables, or these Emperors reach *Judea*, that it was needless there to preach against it. *&c.* and doth he not consider that Christ in his Gospel delivered rules not only for the present, but also for after times of his Church?

Whereunto I answer, That doubtless the twelve Tables, and Emperours Edicts reached *Judea* also, yea all the conquered World, for *Luke* 2. 1. *It is said, that there went out a Decree from* Cæsar Augustus, *that all the World should be taxed*; and did not *Pilate* in the dayes of *Tiberius*, govern in *Judea* by the Roman *Law*, so as that Christ was judged and condemned by it; and *Paul* examined and committed by it afterward; thus in general: And of Usury in particular, it is said by Authors, as it was said before, that usury was not practised in *Judea*, as it must needs be so, for to whom should they lend? to their Brethren the Jews they durst not, because of *Deut.* 23. 19. To the Romans they durst not, because of *Tiberius*, who had interdicted it.

As for after times Christs law in *Luke* 6. 35. was and is sufficient to suppress usury at any time, but to be more plain, is not the Scripture plain against usury, both in the Old Testament and also in the New, the Usurers deny it; yet can we sufficiently prove it; partly by the forequoted place, Luk. 6. 35. *lend hoping for nothing from thence*, and partly from other Scriptures; namely by a necessary consequence, as thus, *we must not be covetous*, *Luke* 12, 15. and therefore not lend upon usury, for that by most Expositors upon *Psal.* 15. 5. is counted covetousness. See *Mollerus, upon Psal.* 15. Again we are forbidden to steal, *Matth.* 19. 18. and usury is accounted theft by most Authors, and Writers, and we must not wrong one another in bargaining, 1 *Thes.* 4, 5, 6. and usury is wronging, because it is biting, so that by a consequence it follows, that we must not be Usurers.

And to be more plain yet, * Some translate that place in 1 *Cor.* 5. 11. expresly and even by name, *Usurers*, and not Extortioners, which may be made yet farther good by *Psal.* 109, 11. Where the *Extortioner* by † most Translations is rendred Usurer, *let the Usurer take his substance.* Now if these || Translations be in the right, in what case is the poor Usurer then? being named by his very name Usurer in the very new Testament, as I can shew it, and in *Psal.* 109. 11. also. So that the Usurer is thereby caught and condemned, which way soever.

* *Edm. Binny*, † *The English excepted.* || *Both Translations I mean*: Psal. 109. 11. *and* 1 Cor. 6. 10.

Numb. 40. 2. What needs so much ado about the prohibiting of Usury by Name in the New Testament; seeing that many other great and damnable sins forbidden in the Old Testament, are omitted also, and not named in the New, *viz.* besides the Christian Sabbath, Oppression condemned, *Ezek.* 18. 12 *Bribery*, *Job* 15. 34. *Esa.* 33. 15. Going after Wizards, *Lev.* 20. 6. cursing Father or Mother, *ver.* 9. a mans lying with his Sister, his Fathers Daughter or his Mothers, *v.* 17: with his Mothers Sister or his Fathers, *v.* 19. or with his Uncles Wife, *v.* 20. So marrying with the Fathers Wife, *Lev.* 18. 10. thy Sons Daughter or Daughters Daughter, *v.* 10. thy Fathers Sister, *v.* 12. thy Daughter in Law, *v.* 15. all which are not named in the New Testament, as also the worst kind of Usury, called griping Usury by the Patrons of Usury, and vexing the Stranger, *Exod.* 22. 21. and afflicting any Widow or Fatherless Child, *v.* 22: and lending to the poor upon Usury, *v:* 25. So that if any, hereafter shall presume to lend upon Usury, saying that he may because it is not by name forbidden by Christ and his Apostles; it will be as if one should plead that a man may venture upon any of the horrid Incests even now named, and lie with his Fathers Wife, *&c:* and curse his Father, and oppress his Brother, and afflict Widows and the Fatherless, because such horrible sins are not forbidden in the New Testament.

But I have not yet done with this great thing, but I shall say yet farther, that whereas he saith, that what I say is weak, I answer him thus: Not so weak as what he saith, in that

1. He saith forth and back, blaming me for saying, that the all-wise God, foreseeing that men would abuse the mentioning of the poor in the Law of Usury, in *Deut.* 23: 19. left out the poor, and yet saying the like here, *and will he not allow the same all-wise God the like foresight here, as to foresee, that Usury if it were suppressed for the present, would perk up again, and therefore there was need of severe rebukes in the Gospel, which is easily answered thus.* That by the places even now named, it is by necessary consequence, and even by name, as some render the Apostles words, prohibited and condemned, and that the like may be said of *Poligamy*, which some even of late and in print, would have perk up again, and so of the prophanation of the Sabbath, which though it was suppressed in *Nehemiah*'s time, yet in our time perks up again as much as ever especially in these Countries where Usurers swarm, and the defendants of Usury do wink at it, as in some part of the *Netherlands*, where it was formerly suppressed, and in the *Palatinate*

wher-

where by * *Ursin* and † *Pareus* it was written down.

I add, Nor is my saying so weak, as many are which, one of Usuries great friends has in a Manuscript of his, since published in part by one of Usuries enemies, || who of thirty two Reasons of his for Usury, could find but seven that looked like a Reason, and were also, being as weak as water, overcome by and by, and confuted.

Num. 41. But the *Ch.* thinks that the case is not the same now, since regulated Usury came in; and adds, that some wiser Emperors coming after, did not absolutely forbid, but limit Usury, instancing in *Alexander*, *Severus*, and *Antoninus Pius*, which practised it as I taught him. Whereunto,

I answer thus:

1. That it it true, the case is altered from taking no Usury to take six in the hundred, which they call regulated Usury, but should rather call stinted.

2. That the said Emperors seeing a necessity of tolerating some Usury to help many which could borrow no mony, because men would not lend freely, being hard hearted, would lend themselves mony at such an easie rate as theirs was.

Num. 42. *Mr. Jel. Obj.* 7. The Laws of Men and even Christians, the Civil Law, the Canon Law and Statute Law do all allow of Usury; and do you think they would if all Usurers should be damned as you say?

His first Answer denyes the assertion, *viz.* that those Laws allow of Usury, they do but tollerate, permit, and restrain it, for some civil good to avoid greater evils.

Reply, Greater evils! what greater than the damnation of so many millions of Souls? Neither can I be perswaded, *&c.*

For answer whereunto, I say,

1. That he confounds temporal evils with eternal, not meant.

2. That what great evils soever the damnation of many millions of Souls be, yet so it is, that Usurers let them be never so many, must die, that is, be damned, by vertue of *Ezek.* 18. 12, 13. as Divines expound that place: I will name but one or two, and 1: * Dr. *Sanders* upon that place, *he shall not live*, that is, *he shall not enjoy heaven:* And † Bishop *Downam* from that place speaks to the Usurer thus. *Thou Usurer takest increase*,

---

* Dr. Fenton. † *Bishop* Downam: || *For* Paræus *published* *Ursin's books, wherein he wrote against Usury, and so approved of his writing against it, as* Clerk *asserts it.* * Dr. S. *p.* 7. † Downam *upon Psal.* 15.

and therefore thou shalt, if thou continuest in this *TERNALLY.*

3. As for his assertion that the Law not or tollerates, but allows Usury, because men may that Laws prescribe; *I answer*, that it cannot l because the Title of the Law is, *An Act against* ' seconded by *Beza*, saying as I said once already vil Laws themselves do not ALLOW, No, i tradicting the *Ch.* to his very face] but rather which they do ONLY TOLERATE, fo by the wickedness of men.

2: I answer, That the use of mony is not to l Law, as Use; but as a debt upon another accou it is, that the Usurer has his Use added to the which thing he is highly condemned by Author

The third fault in Usurers is, saith one, ' \ ' the penalty of the Law, they colour the matte ' write in their Bills of debt, one to have bor ' of them, when it is not so much: And again l ' can be no obligation of Usury, no not so much ' Law in the contract of Lending; and Usury ca ' vered by force of lending, * but another way

3. All that which he tells of Law-makers pov Contracts, alledging *Grotius* and *Luther's* ἐπιι *Beza* answers in a few words, saying: '*The only* '*mains for Magistrates to do is, they stint Usur* '*totters all that the* Ch. *said for allowing.*

4. I cannot but highly commend *Rivet* for so ings, *viz. That the Magistrate is not to be blame ending of strife he doth for a yearly Rent grant a (as is done in these Provinces) for mony by the thereby to reward them, which intimates a gratuit ry, and disarms the Champion.*

Num. 43. And because some will hardly belie Law does not allow of Usury, I will once more i of Parliament, *viz. Jacobi* 21. An Act against \ vided that no words in this Law contained shal or expounded to allow the practice of Usury in gion or Conscience, a dreadful Thunderbolt from ed King, and a wise Parliament. 2. And *Eliz.* as all Usury being forbidden by the word of God, testable, O sad again! that that worthy Parliam

---

* *And so the Pandects hold it.*

prove such a bitter enemy to the poor Vsurer! but so it is, who can help it?

6. I say that a simple construction it is, that some weak defendants of Vsury do make of those words, (as Dr. *Fenton* reports it) all Vsury, which is forbidden by the Word of God, when the Law never said so, *but being forbidden by the Law of God*; which shews what simpletons they are several of them, who defend weakly guarded Vsury.

7. And because some will say, why then doth the Law tollerate Vsury, if it be the damning sin of so many millions of Souls? I answer, 1. That therefore it will not own the practice of it in point of Conscience, as it saith. Nor 2. Does it more than *Moses* did in the case of Divorces, which Divines instance in, and *Beza* by name, clearing Godly Magistrates in this thing thus; *by reason of the wickedness of men, they are compelled only to moderate* (mark *moderate*, not allow or defend) *many things else, and then adding, as in Usury, which many Magistrates are compelled to permit, because they see that it cannot be utterly abolished.*

8. And forasmuch as some think that the Law allows of Vsury, because if a man takes but six of the hundred, the Law has nothing to say against him; *I answer*, that it doth not follow from that, that it allows of Vsury, because it condemns all Vsury as sin and detestable, but only this may be said, and is said by great Divines about it, that it remits the punishment which is to be inflicted on such as take more.

2. Yea so far is the Law from allowing, and favouring Vsury in the least, as that if an Vsurer offend but in the least clause of the Law, he is punished for it: As for example, if he take his mony but a day before it is due, he suffers for it upon complaint made; so if he taketh any thing above the flint. I will give two Instances for it.

1. † A Borrower came before the day of payment, desiring the Vsurer to take his mony and use, because he dwelt a great way off, whereupon he took it, but the Borrower procured a treble mischief.

2. And || one lent two hundred pounds to two men for a year, the day being past, they brought the mony, and use, and a Gown for a free gift, which he took; but how these two men were served, is too tedious here to relate.

9. But desiring to be more full yet, and shew how far the Law is, and has been from time to time, from countenancing and al-

* Beza *in Mat.* 19. † *The death of Usury, p.* 23. || Ibid.

lowing heaven exploded Vsury, I will give forth a rehearsal of *Englands* Laws against Vsury, in the days of * *Edward the Third*, the cognisance of the Vsurer deceased was allotted to the *King*, *in King* † Henry *the Seconds time:* Also all the Chattels and Moveables which the Vsurer deceased, had, were to be taken for the use of the King, *in King* || Henry *the Sevenths time:* All usurarious Contracts were made void and of none effect, and by another, Vsurers were punished with the forfeiture of the moiety put forth by the Vsurer. *In* * Henry *the Eighths time*, those that took above ten in the hundred, were punished with the forfeiture of treble, and of the goods put forth to Vsury; the which Act saith the Parliament assembled in the Reign of † *Edward the Sixth*, was not meant for the maintenance & ALLOWANCE of Vsury, as by the Title and Preamble of the same Act it plainly appeareth. Then in comes *Edward the Sixth*, a Protestant King, in whose time, by an Act of Parliament, were condemned all kinds of VSURY, and measures of Vsury, and it was confirmed, that Vsury is BY THE WORD OF GOD VTTERLY PROHIBITED AS A VICE MOST ODIOVS AND DETESTABLE. This was done since the Reformation, not in Poperies time. After him in Q. || *Elizabeths* time Vsury was stinted, because of necessity, and a relaxation was thought upon by reason of Vsurers breaking out into their wicked ways and courses which they took up.

Num. 44. Mr. Jel. What he says of the Civil Law makes nothing to his purpose, but rather against him; since it declareth that a mediocrity may be found out between a Lender and Borrower. But more fully

I answer this, shewing him by and by how it makes for me. * *Philip Cæsar* a German Divine writes thus: 'I can say with a 'good conscience in this place, that travelling by that notable 'Lawyer, Dr. *Ludder*'s house, to the Earl of *Mansfield*, being 'sent for; he shewed me many Books of Lawyers most excel'lent and learned, written against Vsury; (and that is one hun'dred years ago) which, saith he, will in the day of Judgment 'condemn the Patrons of Vsury. O dreadful, dreadful again!

2. The Civil Law, I say, (which I have read all over as big as it is) is divided as it were into three parts.

---

* *Anno* 3. *c.* 5. † *Anno* 11. *c.* 8. || *Anno* 37. *c.* 9. * *Anno* 5. *&* 6. † *Edw. c.* 20. || *Anno* 13. *c.* 6. * *Philip Cæsar*, *pag.* 20.

The

The first contains those Laws which were made before the Roman State became a Monarchy, and with them those which were made after, from the time of *Julius Cæsar* unto *Constantine the Great*, and are called *Pandecks*.

The second contains those which were made from *Constantines* time to *Justinian* the Emperour, and those are called the *Codex* or *Code*.

The third contains those Laws which were made by *Justinian* the Emperour, also called *Novellæ* and *Authenticæ*, or Novels and Authenticks: Now before the Authenticks, Usury was sometimes wholly prohibited, and sometimes stinted, but at last by the Novels which abrogate the former Laws, it was and is altogether forbidden; for *Justinian* among other decrees enacted this also. *We decree, That the holy Ecclesiastical Canons, which were published and confirmed by the* * *four holy Councils*, that is, *by the Council of* Nice *consisting of three hundred and eighteen Bishops, by the Council of* Constantinople, *consisting of an hundred and fifty learned Fathers, by the Councel of* Ephesus, *and by the Council of* Calcedon, *shall have the power and place of Laws:* So that thereby Usury is prohibited, condemned, and put down in the world, as being condemned by the Council of *Nice*, which the said Imperial Decree in the first place nameth, establisheth, and sets up for Law: Whereupon it is that my Adversary cannot abide that holy Council, because it and its holy three hundred and eighteen Fathers are against Usury, and because its Canon against Usury was made a standing Law by this excellent and learned Christian Emperour through the world. O brave Council!

2. For *Canon-Law*, the Doctors, saith he, use this Argument, That one inferior Law cannot take off the Law of a Superior: His answer whereunto has been answered before now.

3 *Statute Law*, *Jac.* 21. Provided, *That no words in this Law shall be construed or expounded, to allow the practice of it in point of Religion or Conscience.* Reply, *Allow it then they do civil Converse, neither is it fit the Parliament should take it upon them to determinate things as lawful or unlawful in the Court of Conscience.*

Whereunto I answer, 1. Let a better man than he here speak, they slander the Laws, who say they allow of Usury.

2. I see he would fain quarrel with the Parliament too as well as with me, because it makes it unlawful by the word of

* *Which* Calvin *also alloweth.* † *See* Dr. Jer. Taylor *in duel, dubit: l.* 3: c. 3.

God,

God, but what God saith and the Parliament saith, that all Usury is unlawful and sin, being forbidden by the Word, will stand for truth, when his Carkass shall rot as other mens.

3. What he saith all along till he comes to the question, whether, if a man sell a Commodity and allows time for payment, he be bound to sell it as cheap, as if he had sold it for ready mony, *p.* 85. I suppose I have already answered it as far as need required it in my preceding lines; only this I will add about Law.

1. That I cannot by any thing said by the *Ch.* be convinced, that the Laws are bitter against oppressive Usury, because the Parliament saith expresly, *That all Usury is sin.*

2. That any one may see how angry he is with the Civil Law too, calling it *uncivil*, because it is against him and his Usurers, but *vana sine viribus ira.*

3. That the Emperour *Leo* is against Usury too, makes for me who am against all Usury as he is, and that I have formerly proved it, that the first Christians neither did, nor durst lend upon Usury, by Authors which are a little more Authentick than his *Grotius.*

4. I confess that by the *Code* it appears, as I said before, that sometimes Usury has been stinted, and sometimes wholly prohibited, and till by *Justinian* it was quite put down in the * Novels.

5. I observe also, how much he is displeased with Ecclesiastick and Canon Laws, depriving Usurers of the Sacrament, saying, that this began under a degenerated antiquity; when as I can tell him, that my Colleague Mr. *Huish*, whom he cites as his friend, has kept Usurers from the Sacrament also, under the Reformation, even lately; as I intimated it formerly upon another account.

6. What he saith to undermine *Randulphs de Glandevils* Authority, (whereby he proves that Usury is committed, when a man, having lent any thing consisting upon number, weight, or measure, takes any thing over and above the Loan) bringing in his Oxen in a jeer, I look upon as a mere shift and frivolous answer; because there is a difference between things mutuated and commodated, as it has been formerly manifested.

7. Now to the Question I will answer for all, (though I may chuse, because it concerns not the matter in hand which is Usury)

* *Grounded upon the Council of* Nice, *which* Constantine the Great *who was present at it, also approved.*

sury) that there is a great discrepancy between lending upon Usury, and taking something for wanting my mony and staying for it till the time be come for which I lent it, and selling the thing the dearer for staying a year till I can be paid: For doubtless that is lawful, because Selling is a lawful Contract; and I am one that lives by selling if I be a Merchant. And if I want it so long I cannot trade with it, but am forced to borrow, it may be, and there are hazards in it besides; as Bishop *Taylor* well mentions it: so as that I may lose it by mens death or otherwise; whereas lending upon Usury is illicite and forbidden, and not so hazardous neither, because the Usurer will make all as sure as a man can by sufficient Sureties besides the Borrower, and by Morgages, Pawns, Extents, and but from half year to half year; and by changing Sureties. Only this I will super-add, that the Seller may sell the dearer for giving so long time as a year is, yet he must not sell too dear, for there is a conscience to be made of all such things; because we must not wrong one another in bargaining. 1 *Thess.* 4. 5. 6.

And because else we commit some kind of Usury too, as divers do assert it; I will name but one at present, *viz*: *Augustinus*, who saith expresly: *He that selleth dearer than the just price of things requires, commits Usury.*

Num. 46. I could name and alledge Bishop *Hall* too, but he has been quoted already:

Mr. Jel. Obj. 8. *Divers modern Divines allow of Usury, if it do not exceed the Sum appointed by Law, and be moderate, &c.*

I answer, I know some few do so. *Reply*, I doubt not there be many more than he knows of; I have spoken of this before, *&c.* *Answer.* And so have I, and therefore let that serve for him and his *Grotius* also.

He saith, He has brought many witnesses already, and threatneth to bring many more against the poor condemned Usurers burying.

Reply, But I desire in the behalf of the poor Usurer, that he may have a fair Tryal, before he be condemned, and dead before he be buried; and when dead and buried, he that prophesieth what great things Prince *Rupert* was destinated to from Eternity, cannot foretel whether the Usurer may have a Resurrection, *&c.* *Whereunto I answer*,

1. Here the Reader may see how this Champion loves the poor condemned Usurer, for lo, how he begs for him that he may have a fair Tryal; so as that a man cannot chuse but grant him his request, and promise him as fair a Tryal as possibly he can desire, because he begs so pitifully: And the truth is, I intended it before he begged it, that the poor Wretch should

have

have as fair a Tryal and Proceeding as any man whatſoever: For my purpoſe is to invite, beſides the holy * Prophets, whole Councils, even thirteen at leaſt, conſiſting of hundreds, and hundreds of godly Fathers, and an incredible number of other ſingle Doctors and Writers, old and new; (able to make two Armies) to paſs their direful Sentences upon the Uſurer in order to his condemnation, and after condemnation to his Grave, called the Pit of Hell; which notwithſtanding I promiſe, profeſs, and declare withal before hand, that he may, yea ſhall have a Reſurrection, by my fourth Book of his Reſurrection, in caſe he will be ruled and repent; for I ſhall but threatningly bury him, that room may be left for his joyful Reſurrection; which God in mercy grant unto him.

2. Lo how he jeers me again, and far greater ones than my poor ſelf, about *Prince Rupert*, of whom a great Writer (whoſe Book I have ſeen and read, being dedicated to the ſame Moſt Illuſtrious Prince, Son to the late Pious King of *Bohemia*, my Gracious Lord) has this Prophecy; That he was deſtinated to great Atchievements from Eternity, which alſo was fulfilled in part (not to ſpeak of Land-Fights) when he was Lord Admiral of two great and formidable Fleets, the Engliſh and French upon the Britiſh Seas, and gallantly reſcued the Engliſh, and repulſed their Adverſaries †. If, not to write here of ſome late moſt remarkable deeds which, by Report, he did, now the *Ch:* hath a mind to go on with his jeering and ſcoffing, let him take his belly full of it, but let him take heed withal, for God will not be mocked.

As for his eighteen men, that are ſaid to be for Uſury, and have been anſwered by *R. Bolton*, he might have ſaved that labour, and have Reprinted but only Mr. *Bolton*, but if he have a mind to try his ſtrength, I ſhould deſire him to anſwer Dr. *Rivet* upon the Q. written ſince Mr. *Bolton*; alſo what Mr. *Baxter* writes of this Subject in his late *Chr. Direct*. *Whereunto I anſwer*.

---

* *One of which called* Ezekiel, *ch.* 18. 12, 13. *ſaith expreſly*, Shall he live? He ſhall not live, he ſhall ſurely die: *which very words, as all men may ſee, ſtrike the poor Uſurer down dead to the ground, yea, under ground, even into hell.*

† *Wherewith I ſhall joyn part of a Poem called* Rupertiſmus, *concerning this valiant Prince, by one* C. p. 158.

Ingredients of his vertue threat the Beads,
Of Cæſar's *Acts, Great* Pompey's, *and the* Suedes:
And 'tis a Bracelet for a Rupert's *Hand,*
By which that vaſt Triumvirate is ſpan'd.

1. That

1. That this makes for me also, for if what I have written be Mr. *Bolton's*, then he fights all this while against Mr. *Bolton*, and I go free and may sit still: As for *Rivet*, he never troubled me being still my friend, and why should I trouble my self about him? But let him try his strength upon Dr. *Pye* against Usury, which was never yet confuted.

Or if he be too old for him, upon that Learned Man, *viz*. *Christophorus Cartwright* late Minister in *York*, who wrote a Treatise against Usury since *Bolton* too, about twenty years ago. As for Mr. *Baxter*, I have read what he says in his *Directory* about Usury, and like his cautions so well, as that we two need not fall out about this matter, because the said cautions practised, free him from Usury, making for Partnership.

Num. 47: *Mr. Jel*. Bishop *Jewel*, But what speak I of the ancient Fathers? 'There was never any Religion, nor Sect, 'nor Profession of Men nor State, but they have misliked it. *Reply*, May it not be said concerning all those, there have been some of them that have approved of it by their practise or pleading.

I answer, 1. Who be they that have pleaded for it? Some indeed have practised it among the corrupt Clergy Men, and for that the Council of *Nice*, and other succeeding Councils have made Canons against them, that they might be removed and punished: And St. *Chrysostom*, and St. *Austin*, and others, have written most sharply against them, but never did any of the holy Fathers, whom I read or could hear of by others, plead for Usury.

2. Nor is it to be proved by *Grotius* substantially, that *Leo* was the first Emperour that did forbid all Usury, and that the first Christians did practise Usury for four in the hundred; for I have proved the contrary before now by substantial Authors, *viz*. Bishop *Hall*, and *Alex. ab Alex*. and others, that *Tiberius* and *Caius* did put down Usury before *Leo*, yea by *Luther* himself, how the very first Emperour *Julius Cæsar* was against Usury, and proved how the first Christians did not at all practise it; so then I leave it to true English Hearts to chuse, whether they will believe their own English Divines, Bishop *Jewel*, Bishop *Hall*, Bishop *Downam*, and such like; or this Stranger *Grotius*.

3. But see the boldness of this man, who also will confute and affront *Englands* Jewel,* who was a sufferer and exil'd man

* *And was a Prophet too that foretold* Q. Mary's *death and his own too unto a precise day*, Clerk p. 320: *and said of Usury by him so cryed down, if I be deceived in it, thou Lord hast deceived me:*

in my Country, and there had time and opportunity to converse, and to confer with German Divines, about Usury at full, and is extol'd to the Sky by *Peter Martyr* for his Apology, and was as great a Scholar and Antiquary, as ever *England* bred, Great *Usher* excepted; and has as famously confuted Popery, as that his Confutation of *H.* is to be procured to be read in every Parish Church.

4. As for the fifteen hundred years for which Bishop *Jewel* saith, Usury was not defended by the ancient; I would have him to know, that not he only, but two or three great Divines more have asserted the same; let him bring but one Ancient Father or Dr. (*Maniches* the Heretick excepted) who has defended Usury as now it is practised: I challenge him now to do it if he can, even as Bishop *Jewel* challenged the Papists to prove their Religion and Opinions to have been maintained in such first Centuries as he named.

Of his sophistical representing of Bishop *Jewel's* words I forbear to speak, let Readers note it.

Num. 48. *Mr. Jel.* Bishop *Hall*, Nature teaches that mettals are not a thing capable of superfœtation.

Reply, I shall consider more distinctly what is here said.

Whereunto I answer.

1. This Champion having beaten, overcome, and confuted, as he supposeth, renowned Bishop *Jewel*, thinks to beat Bishop *Hall* too, out of *Mars* field, by several assaults made upon him which sheweth his peremptoriness, sawciness, and impudence, yet more abundantly, that he will offer to confute such a great famous man as Bishop *Hall* was, who as one said, was able to keep a better man than he to wait upon him, and whom King *James* sent to the Synod of *Dort* against the Remonstrants, and whose most excellent Books have been translated partly into Dutch, as upon my knowledge I told him, and partly into French, as one born in *France* lately informed me.

So that if that most pious and learned Man were now alive, he would disdain to answer such a Novice, which makes me to do here as in blessed *Bolton's* case, for I do not see how I can presume to defend such an able Bishop, who has fought so well for himself against his Adversaries when he lived, and in this matter of Usury has done so well, and therefore is well able to defend himself without my poor help, his words being of that weight, as that of themselves they are able to defend themselves, and being seconded also by what *Aristotle* of old, and Bishop *Downam*, and Dr. *Sanders* of late, have written to the same effect: And this I must needs add, that whilst he lives, he will never be able to overthrow what these three and others

have

have ſaid and proved of moneys barrenneſs in and *of it ſelf*; if any profit comes of it, it comes from and by the induſtry of him that employeth it, and not by it; whereas ground ſet brings graſs of it ſelf, and Trees fruit of themſelves, *Gen.* 1. 11.

As for that great Dr. * *Pareus* my ancient friend, under whom I lived in the Vniverſity of *Heydelberg* in the *Palatinate*, where God took him away to himſelf before that City was taken, as he took St. *Auſtin* from *Hippo* before it was taken; him alſo he ſerves no better than the foreſaid three great perſons, becauſe he is againſt Uſury too, labouring to defeat him by *Hornbeck*, though he be not able to do it, becauſe *Pareus* will be believed before him, being a far greater and more able Writer, and one of a thouſand, whom God did remarkably own upon his death bed, in that calling for Pen and Paper, he wrote theſe confidential words when his ſpeech was gone: *This Catharre has taken away my ſpeech, but ſhall never take away my faith and love to Chriſt*: which very words were related in his Funeral Sermon, which I heard my ſelf being at his Burying; all which I relate the rather, becauſe he was a chief man in the New Army riſen up againſt Uſury, which has moved queſtionleſs this Champion to riſe up againſt him, and to get † *Hornbecks* help to defeat him, and to ſhew what a man he is that can confute theſe four mighty men.

To that which he ſaith of me, that if I ſhould be put to prove the whole, if any be a Thief or Uſurer, 1 *or.* 6. 10. I ſhould have a hard Task of it; I muſt now tell him, not ſo hard as he ſuppoſes, for VSVRERS are named expreſly by ſome in their Tranſlations in the ſame place, as I formerly ſhewed.

Num. 49. Mr. Jel. *I will ſet down the Theſes of* Wittemberg *againſt Uſury, a little after* Luther *was riſen.*

Reply, 1. It could not be expected that men lately come out of Popery, ſhould on a ſudden ſhake off all the errors held in that Church, *&c.*

2. And *Luther* himſelf became more moderate, *&c.*

Whereunto I anſwer, 1. As he leaves out the words of that Univerſities *Theſes* or Poſitions, becauſe they do extremely make againſt him, ſo ſhall I leave out the many words which

---

* *I add, that the ſame great* Pareus *was ſo graced with the Spirit of Prophecying too, as that ſeeing three Moons over the City of* Heydelberg, *foretold its taking, and the troubles of* Germany *as a Prophet.* † *Who layeth the fault of* Iſrael's *not coming in upon Chriſtian Magiſtrates, which* Pareus *layeth upon Uſurers.*

he useth here, and *Rivet* too, because they cited in Latin, and so I will only 1. Shew the occasion of those *Wittemburg* Positions again Usury so famously known; as I have it of a certain German * Divine, who lived neer *Wittemburg* in *Saxony*, and informs me by his writing against Usury; that the said *Theses* were affixed in *Wittemburg*, disputed and approved when *Mordesius* proceeded Doctor in Divinity, and that *Luther* himself was a strong condemner of Usury.

2. I will refel what he saith that it could not be expected, &c. after this manner: When *Luther* had set up his positions against the Popes Indulgence, spread by *Terdius*, then *Mordesius* set forth his *Theses* against Usury at *Wittemburg*, that both Popery and Usury might fall together: And to let men see that it was not only in the beginning of the Reformation, but afterward also, and ever since to our present time, the ablest Wits and holiest of men, both Ministers and Writers, have with one voice cryed down that loud crying sin of Usury. So that it is a mere and vain boast that most modern Divines, Lawyers, and Moralists have received the opinion favouring moderate Usury; for all that which those Divines so much talked of, I do say is, that men must use such and such cautions, which are eight or nine, and make that which some call Usury no Usury, whereupon what he saith of *Gesner* and *Windelin*, Professor of the School (not University) of *Anhalt* and of † *Tubinghen* an obscure University to my knowledge, in the Dutchy of *Wittenburg*, where I have been my self also, and of *Wollebius* whom I have heard often preach and read his Latin Divinity Lectures in the University of *Basil*, but never any one for Usury, and who has written his worthy Name and Motto, as my friend, in my Book of Friends: So that all that which here this Champion saith, will stand him in no stead, because he is none of them that follow their godly cautions, as I understand. And because twice in his Pamphlet he tells of *Luther*, that at last he became more moderate, he must prove substantially, which will be a hard task for him to do: For other great Divines make light of it, and Dr. *Fenton* especially, and one more; so that still he is quoted by all Antiusurarians as a bitter enemy to Usury, which would be very injurious to him, if he had recanted.

Num. 50. Mr. *Jel. I am ashamed*, quoth he, to see and read how our || Adversaries the Papists, who scorn to appear for Usury

* Philip Cæsar. † *Which pious and renowned* Polanus *left being infected with dangerous Tenents, as* Clerk *relates it.*

|| Lorinus *upon Psal.* 15.

cast

cast it into our teeth, that the * Calvinists allow Usury, &c.

And will you be such Calvinists and Hereticks?

Reply, The man is become as one of them, &c.

I answer, 1. How can he be as one of them, who even now called the Papists our Adversaries, though not in the doctrine of Usury, wherein we agree as we do in the Doctrine of the Trinity.

2. As for that which my Friend Dr. *Rivet* tells of the Popes publick banks, and of *Scotus* and *Maldonate*, that they speak as much in effect as the Calvinists; what is that to me, who know what limitations and cautions they have, and how they are for money given as an instrument of *Negotiation*? Mark that, as *Maldonate* speaks, and that they are for damage, as *Scotus* saith, but not for use.

3. I am not bound to justifie all that any holds or writes, concerning Usury; if he defends what is true, I assent, and am for that truth, if not, I leave him; as also then I do when Papists defend Theft in any person, or any sin committed with the eye, or any other evil, as many such things one may meet with in *Tolet* and in the *Enchiridium* of *Navarra*, and in *Sa*, *Filiutius*, and *Escobar*, Jesuits.

4. But this is most certain that the Scholasticks, the Canonists, and the Casuists, are generally against all Usury, by * *Spanhemius* own confession; for these are his own words, *The Schoolmen, the Canonists, the Casuists decisions we do not regard.*

And † again he saith, A wonder it is, that they do so anxiously and scrupulously proscribe ALL USURY, even moderate ones too, though circumscribed with due cautions, &c.

Num. 51. Whom shall one believe now, Him or the *Ch.*

Mr. Jel. *Will these few Divines bear you out at the Tribunal of Christ?*

Reply, These few Divines (how few soever) have been famous for learning, and men of known integrity, and their reasons so strong, &c.

Whereunto I answer, 1. Who denies it that several are so?

2. But who knows not this too, that they have their great errors too, about and against the morality of the Christian Sabbath some, and others being *Lutherans*, erring in their doctrine of Consubstantiation, and the ubiquity of Christs body.

But 3. I will say a little more of that which he speaks but little of. Will those few Divines bear you out before Christs Tribunal? *viz.* 1. That I say so, because they will leave him there

* Spanhemius *in Dub. Evang.* † *Idem ibid.*

saving

saving themselves by their godly cautions. 2. That in this very thing I have a great Dr. and famous *London* Minister, Dr. *Fenton* for my Second, his words to the Usurer are these.

Alas poor Soul, whither wilt thou turn thy self for succour, when thy friends forsake thee? What wilt thou plead for thy self when thou comest before the Eternal Judge upon thy Trial? This methinks should make the Champion's and every Usurers heart to tremble.

4. As for his saying, that the practice of his regulated Usury is under the allowance of publick laws; to that I have answered formerly proving the contrary, whereunto I will now add again the saying of the foresaid great Dr. *Fenton, viz. An absolute contract for* 10, 9, 8, or 6, *in the* 100, *is without warrant or Authority even among those Divines which have most favourably concluded for thee: Observe 6 in the* 100.

Lastly, To his additions, these be some of his men, some bad Papists he means, which will rise in judgment against our Usurers. *I answer*,

1. He wrongs me if he says that these be the only men which I mean, when I say that they would rise in judgment against the Usurers: No verily, I do not honour those men so much who are very scrupulous in the matter of Usury, and yet are for Whoredom and other grievous sins; but I mean those Schoolmen, Canonists, Casuists, and learned Doctors, which are both against all Usury and all other vices too, will rise in Judgment.

2. And I can name one who nameth the foresaid men, *viz. Philip Cæsar*, that eximious Saxonian Divine, who said the same of the very Papists by name, about an hundred years ago, (for his Book against Usury was printed, *Anno* 1578.) and his words are these, *The Papists will condemn our Patrons of Usury in the day of Judgment.* Which he said after he had read their Books, and the Lawyers Books against Usury, which he met with in Dr. *Ludder*'s house, as he was going to the Earl of *Mansfield*.

Num. 52. Mr. Jel. *Divers modern Divines are against the strict keeping of the Christian Sabbath.*

Reply, Yea, and these many of his Divines that have pleaded against all Usury. *I answer*, where and which are they? let him name them.

But saith he, we will grant it, that it is their sin though not the sin of Usury, yet we censure them not as damned for this sin, &c. *Whereunto my answer is*,

1. Nor do I damn them, because damnation is not denounced against them as against Usury, *Ezek.* 18, 12, 13. *Psal:* 15. 1, 5.

But

But 2. The morality of the Christian Sabbath denyed, is alledged to shew, that as those Divines are out in the Sabbath, so they may be in Usury.

3. Though I dare not say that they are damned, yet I will be bold to say that God has most severely punished the prophaners of his Sabbath in this life, with fire from heaven and otherwise too, as the Practise of Piety and Council of *Paris* tells us; so that by such dreadful examples in *England* and elsewhere shewn, I for my part being newly come from *Geneva* and *Holland*, *&c.* where I saw the Lords day most horribly polluted, was mightily convinced, and to the strict keeping of the Lords holy day induced; as also by the reading of the most rare writings of the Bishops, Doctors, and godly Ministers of *England* I was fully made to see the unlawfulness and odiousness of Usury, and so began to preach about thirty years ago in a Town called *Kingsbridge*, to all the Country round about, coming to my Lecture, which weekly I there preached upon *Psal.* 15.5. the substance whereof with several enlargements is contained in my *Usurer cast*; which upon the earnest intreaty and approbation of some of my brethren and others, I publilhed, and am now defending, but I must hasten onward.

Num. 53. Mr. Jes. *Is it not the best way, where two ways meet the one doubtful and the other sure and safe, to chuse the best?*

Reply, If he had followed this Rule, he would not have condemned the guiltless, let him read *Psal.* 15. 3. *whereunto I answer.*

1. Is it guiltless for a man to commit murder, for so *Calvin* himself makes Usury to be, upon the same *Psal.* 15. 5. and *Cato* too, a meer Pagan, by *Calvin* quoted upon the same Psalm?

And again, Is a man guiltless that commits Theft, as Usury is called also by a number of learned men, of whom I will cite but one, *viz.* * Dr. *Williams*, who speaking of Usury, saith expresly, *This Theft transcends all other Thefts*, and proves it; *and here I could bring in a world of Divines writing upon the eighth Commandment, and making Usury Theft, which also proves the morality of Usuries prohibition, as another time, and in another place, if God permit, I shall shew, and have partly shewn in my Preface to the Reader.*

Num. 54. *But saith the Champion*, let him hear Mr. *Baxter* and *Calvin*, and then he sends me to my friend (as he calls him) Bishop *Hall*, and to *Grotius*, and so ends with his own

* Dr. Williams *in his true Church.*

 bravado;

bravado , *whereunto I shall briefly answer,*

1. That Mr. *Baxter* speaks not a word here, for that Usury which is commonly practised in *England*; but in the same Directory sends us very wisely to larger Volumes, wherein I desire to follow him,* approving withal of his godly cautions so much, and so of his * other most excellent Books, as that this man shall not make me, by all his malice he has against me, fall out with such a man.

2. As for *Calvin*, he leaves me to my liberty elsewhere, and would not have me tied to his judgment, as I have formerly shewn.

3. And Bishop *Hall* is not against me neither in his sayings, that if we can find a way [mark if] free from oppression and extortion (as Partnership is, when we lend with a condition that the Borrower and we will divide the purchase equally, and be partners in loss and gain) we may take that way.

4. As for *Grotius*, I will say as *Spanhemius* concerning Schoolmen; *I do not regard the Schoolmen, &c.* so I do not heed much what he saith, as long as we do not reach farther than God reaches, who is not only against *Neshech*, but also against *Tarbith, any increase, Ezek.* 18. 8. Note *any increase.*

5. Nor do his words clear the point, or satisfactorily answer the thing mentioned about the two *ways*, a doubtful and dangerous, and a sure and safe, concerning which I shall say more before I end, shewing them plainly to every ones eye.

Num. 55. *Mr. Jel. seventh answer*, Those very Divines which you lean upon, will be but a broken reed to you in this respect; because they use so many limitations as scarce any Usurer in the whole world doth observe, and at last make it no Usury at all, I mean as it is commonly practised.

Reply, It may be presumed then in his account, that there is some Usury lawful, &c.

Whereunto I answer, [passing by many of his words to be read in his Pamphlet, as he doth by mine, thirty three lines at a time and more] *after this manner.*

1. That what I say in this case, many other greater Divines than he and my self say likewise.

And 1. Dr. *Fenton*, as I have shewn already.

2. Bishop *Downam* having rehearsed nine cautions, prescribed by those Divines which are for some Usury, concludes thus. *These cautious men must observe, or else they may not build their practise upon the Authority of godly learned men, who have by these and*

---

* Spanhem. *in dub. Evang.*

such like conditions so qualified Usury, as that when they are observed, there is no Usury, or at least no actual Usury committed.

3. Mr. Bolton, Divines *pretended for Usury deal with it as the Apothecary with Poyson, working and tempering it with so many cautions and conditions, that in the end they make it no Usury at all.*

2. What he saith of other contracts and failings committed therein, and of preaching and praying, and infirmities and swervings from the rule of Gods Word, will not answer what is said of cautions not observed, to make that which God calls Usury no Usury; for the contracts by him mentioned are lawful, and preaching and praying lawful and commanded, but Usury is a thing unlawful and prohibited.

3. Nor does *Gee* take him off, nor justifie what he saith, as not saying one word for Usury.

4. Nor will the Casuists by their *dolus malus* help him, for they are against his Usury altogether, as I have proved it.

5. And because he saith that it may be presumed that I account some Usury lawful, I will now tell him what Usury I hold lawful, *viz.* that which Divines call *Recompensatory*, of which *Gabriel Biel* speaks thus. *Usury is taken sometimes very largely, for any thing which is taken in lending above the principal, and so all Usury is not unlawful; for voluntary thankfulness has been proved lawful formerly.*

Num. 56. *Of* * *Weems*, The Primitive Church ordained that no man should eat or drink with Usurers, nor fetch fire from them, *&c.*

Reply, I hope Mr. *Jelinger* doth not practise by this rule, and if all other among us should be bound to it, I know not what work it would make, especially in Cities and Towns, *whereunto I answer,*

1. See its parallel, in 1 *Cor.* 5. 11 *if any man that is called a Brother be a fornicator or extortioner, (and so consequently an Usurer)* &c. *with such a one no not to eat.*

2. Let it be noted, how this grave Author's Speech by this his Inferior is slighted, and though it be the more momentous, because it shews how odious Usury was in the Primitive Churches eyes.

3. Let him know that as he slights what *Weemes* relates of the Primitive Christians, so I do and shall slight what he cursorily speaks till he comes to Orphans and Widows, and by name *Luther*'s being become more moderate, and of the *Wittemberg Theses*, because I have sufficiently spoken of the same things formerly, whereunto may be added what he saith about the dissent which he conceives to be among the Anti-usurarians,

who to my best knowledge do agree in the main matter and form of Usury, so as that he cannot justly upbraid them with and for any notable difference in their opinions: So for the matter of Covenants and Bills and Bonds, put forth to answer what I said to a Reply by him made, because he comes so fillily off with, as I THINK Mr. *Baxter* saith, and *as I remember*, HE SAITH too, so in Tenements, making the Usurer like one that hath a Tenant, which the Usurer is not. I slightly pass over that too, and in like manner I take little notice of his words about a silent consent, as if it were hatching some secret mischief, which some are very well acquainted with, because malice dictates, and calumnies uttereth what he saith; but the truth is, as he saith, some are too well acquainted with secret mischief.

As for *Amesius*, by him quoted, he doth not trouble me, nor can, because he proves nothing; so what he saith of my Saying by him set down, that he understands it not, signifies nothing to me, because others do, of whom I have asked; but enough and enough said to so little of matter.

*Num.*57. *Mr.Jel.* 9. I am a Widow saith one, I am an Orphan saith another, and God knoweth that some cannot employ their money as some, *&c. whereunto I answer*, that now being past those things, which I valued as little as he valued Reverend Mr. *Weemes*'s Report, and come to more serious matters about Orphans and Widows, I intend to be more serious also, and large withal. And

1. I say, If God did intend to exempt the Fatherless and Widows, he would have said something of them, when he named Usury and them together.

Reply, Whether Widows or Orphans in *Israel* might take Usury of any, I shall not stand here to enquire; but as to the poor and the indigent, *&c.* And then I wonder at Mr. *Bolton* here, *&c. whereunto I answer.*

Here he has a fling again at that worthy man, because he cannot abide his Writing against his *Diana*, even as his Adversary *M. S.* could not abide his preaching against his Usury; so that I will let them two battle together a while, and return to mine own defence.

Mr. *Jel.* The sum of his second Answer. They should rather trust God, *&c.*

Reply, Here it is taken for granted what is in debate, God has taken care for them, but this should not take them from using due diligence, and from all lawful means within their power for a subsistence.

A. But is Usury a lawful way? who will say it that it is, but an Vsurer, though he cannot prove it?

Num. 59. Mr. *Jel.* As for them that put out their money to Vsury, and say what will become of them else, if we do not put it out for them, *I return this answer*; they should rather ask what will become of them that have no money left them?

Reply, Though they that have Wives must be as if they had none, and so consequently those that have money as if they had none; yet this must be understood of affection and not otherways, for these that have Estates must be as those that have Estates, and those that have money must improve their money for their livelihood.

I answer, But how? by Vsury? God forbid; for God forbids it: Let *Grotius* moderate between us, saith he.

I answer, A Godly Moderator! I do not intend to yield to his Moderatorship, for he is a man that can err and I am sure doth, even God shall be a Moderator for me and my friends, who cannot err, and gives no toleration for Orphans and Widows: But if it be fit for me to hearken to men too, I will hearken to men that are sound and Orthodox, and will not be for Sabbath breaking and loosness, and wink at Sports used on Gods holy day; and I will quote but three at present, *viz.*

* 1. Philip Cæsar, *Seeing Vsury is contrary to the word of God, and against the faith which we should repose in him, and therefore no doubt it is unlawful for Orphans and Widows to use the same.* And again he saith, *What a wonderful company of Widows and Fatherless is there, which having nothing of their own yet are sustained?* And yet farther, *Let these which are their Guardians and Keepers of their money, if any come to them, buy ground, and the Revenues thereof let them bestow on their maintenance the same money; or if that cannot be done, he that will convert it to his own use, and distribute to their sustenance, doth like an honest man, &c.*

† 2. Gabriel Powel, *If Vsury be in it self evil and condemned by the word of God, then it cannot be good in any*, Rom. 3. 8. it is said, *We must not do evil that good may come of it, therefore we must not relieve Orphans and Widows by Vsury.*

|| 3. Mr. Moss, *In the days of King* Edward, *men being more careful to provide for the poor than now, the Orphans were well and sufficiently provided for, even when Vsury was altogether and utterly forbidden.*

---

* *Philip Cæsar, p.* 55. † *Gabriel Powel, p.* 55. || Mr. *Moss.*

What Grotius *saith*, that Christ has not left a peculiar precept of this thing, signifies nothing to me; seeing we have his mind plainly set down in general, *Luke* 6. 35. my supposed case he slights, *p.* 100. and therefore I slight him, and what he saith.

Num. 59. Mr. *Jel. Obj.* 10. God knoweth that I cannot live else, because I do not know how to employ my money otherwise. *I answer*,

1. Are there no other ways in the world to live by, but Usury?

Reply, *Let* Mr. Baxter *answer this*. As for them that say it may be as well improved otherwise, they are unexperienced men. To this, 1: Let St. *Chrysostom* answer. 2. *Spanhemius*. 3. *My self for my self.*

1. Let Great *Chrysostom* answer Great Mr. *Baxter*, *Chrysostom*, I say, who being so great an Archbishop, residing in so great a City as *Constantinople*, the Metropolis of the World whereof he was Archbishop, and so one that must needs have had great experience, his words are: *Are there no other ways of living justly to be found? Is there not Husbandry and Tillage to be taken in hand?* With whom

2. I joyn Great *Spanhemius*, who after he had disputed for a kind of Usury (as I shewed once already) a good while, at last broke out into this confession, as I said before now. *It must needs be confessed, that it is far better for thee to bestow thy money either in Husbandry, or Merchandizing, or any other honest way to increase thine Estate, than to lend it upon Usury.* Shewing how men may employ their money otherwise than in Usuries way, and to my knowledg he was a very experienced man, which I can speak, because he was related to me and we lived together at *Genevah* first, from whence he removed into *Holland* to *Leyden*, and I into *England*, where he has been a considerable time also; so that having been in so many Countries, as *High Germany*, part of *Italy*, and in *France* also, and *Holland*, he could not be a * Stranger to the worlds affairs, but one that could write from his great and manifold experiences, what a man may do with his money without Usury.

3. As for me, though I must confess that I am one of the meanest Ministers, yet some small experience I have gotten by my being in so many Countries, Kingdoms, and Universities as I have been in, in my time; wherein I have seen and observed

* *Which caused many Nobles to make use of his advice in Civil Affairs.* Clerk *in his Life*, *p.* 501.

what

what use men make of their mony; so that upon request I wrote and intend hereafter (when my other Vsury Books promised by me shall come forth) to Publish very many ways whereby men may lawfully and without Vsury employ their mony, besides the ways of, at least, ten great and learned men more, leaving men to chuse either any of their ways or of mine, as they please; hoping that if my poor experience be not sufficient, theirs will make up what is wanting in mine.

Num. 60. Mr. *Jel.* How do they live that have no mony to lend? Whereunto his Reply is not worth the mentioning, it is so short and inconsiderable.

Mr. *Jel.* How do they live in those Countries where Vsury is not known, in the *Indies. &c.*

Reply, There too Gold and Silver are not currant money, no wonder then that Vsury there is not exercised in the loan thereof: We have heard of Nations that have had no Houses but Tents, but what is that to us that have Houses? *VVhereunto I answer.*

1. That the Gold and Silver there was not coyned as it was here in former times, yet it may be now since the Spaniards arrival, and so plentiful Gold has been there, as that an Indian King had his house full of it, and was slain by the Spaniards for it; and likely it is that they deal by way of Exchange, as now also they do, and it may be they would deal now and have dealt formerly in a way of Vsury, if they had not thought it to be against Nature, as indeed it is.

As for the Tents by him spoken of, they signifie nothing; for they served instead of Houses, as in the Patriarchs time, *Gen.* 18. 1. and *Heb.* 11. 9.

Mr. *Jel.* From *Chrysostom, &c.* I need not trouble my self about him any more, having spoken enough of him already even now.

And as for the hazard which the Champion takes an occasion to speak of, bringing *Grotius* again with him, and Dr. *Tayler* to bear him company, of that I have spoken at full, so of *Chrysostom* speaking against Merchandising.

Num. 61. Mr. *Jel. Obj.* 11. I lend for pities sake, and do good with my money, *&c.*

I answer, Dost thou good with thy money? Thou dost but furnish many men with sinews to do mischief, to oppress others in bargaining, and forestalling, *&c.*

Reply, If this be said of all that lend, it is a notorious 'calumny.

Answer 1. 'He cannot but see that I speak not of all, because 'I speak of many.

 2. As

2. *As for his occasionally*, it makes against him too, for we must not give men an occasion to do evil.

3. *And whereas he saith*, that *such ill accidents may befal giving too*; *I answer*, It's true, but then there is not an occasion lawfully given as by unlawful Usury, but taken by lawful giving.

Mr. Jel. Nay many Families and men are undone by Usury, or at least so entangled, oppressed, and put down, as that, *&c.*

I answer, True, they may thank themselves partly, and the Usurer chiefly, who by and for his filthy usury brought them to so much misery and mischief.

Mr. Jel. But the Borrower gives thanks and is glad.

I answer, Being forced, he gives that and is glad, because he is necessitated to go to the Usurer.

Reply, If the necessity be of Nature's making, and he borrow that he may live, and Traffick here, lending ought to be free.

I answer, Here now is something to be commended, and I say still that there is no reason for it, that a Purchaser growing rich by my money, should not freely and thankfully make me a partaker of his free gain, which thing Divines call a gratuity, which may be taken.

Num. 62. *Mr. Jel.* But being forced, he gives thanks.

Reply, Who forced him? Nothing but his own convenience drew him to it, and I pray may not a man gain by the money he pays me reasonable use for? And if so, then he owes me thanks for the moneys he has gained by means of mine, and then *Demosthenes* will tell him, *&c.*

I answer, His convenience sometimes may, but commonly necessity makes me to borrow money. 2. He might get and not get. 3. He is bound to give thanks, not use. As for *Demosthenes*, he is for me, calling and making Usury odious, and the Usurers Name odious; for he would have a man so wary in his dealings, as that he may not get the odious name of an Usurer, as his words do shew it.

THE

THE

FOURTH PART

OF THIS

TREATISE,

CONTAINING

The Eighth and Ninth Chapters of the Usurer Cast; *and four Additional Objections answered, and Replies put thereunto, answered also; and the Nine Chapters Applications by Exhortations prosecuted, and several Additions,* viz. *Of a Citation, A Narrative, and the Usurers last Will.*

1. *Num.* 1. *Mr. Jel.* ADditional Objection. 1. Vsurers plead, that Countreys and Kingdoms cannot subsist without Vsury.

I answer, It is false; for did not *Israels* subsist without Vsury?

Reply, *It is likely they did not, seeing they might lend to Strangers, &c.*

I answer, 1. The Stranger was the Canaanite, or seven Nations, which were about them, not of them.

2. The Ch. himself weakneth what he saith by his, *it is likely*, which shews that he is not sure of what he saith, as indeed he could not well be, because the holy Fathers and new Writers also say, that in *David's*, and the succeeding Ages and Prophets time, that political exception of the Stranger ceased to be in force as I formerly proved it.

Mr. Jel. And happy was the State of *Germany* before it knew Vsury, &c.

Reply,

Reply, And ſo it might be before it knew Printing and Guns, but was Vſury the cauſe of theſe miſchiefs it groans under? Not, I dare ſay, not that regulated Vſury which is here pleaded for.

I anſwer, 1. Lo how he leaves out *Sicily* and *Sparta* and *Egidius* his Common-wealth, becauſe all three make againſt him.

2. And becauſe he tells of Printing (invented by a good man called *Gottenberg*) I will ſay a little more of it, as namely, that I wonder that he brings in ſuch a good thing, invented by a man whoſe name imports goodneſs, becauſe it is derived in the Dutch Tongue from *Got*, in Engliſh *God*) with ſuch a bad buſineſs as Vſury is: I call Printing a good thing, to which I and others that Print are much beholding; becauſe much good is done by us in it to many poor Souls which are converted by it from that abominable ſin of Vſury, and many other enormous vices, but for Guns he hits right, for they were invented by one *Berehtold Swartz*, which Dutch word *Swartz* ſignifies black, as invented by a black man, who may well be called an inventor of a black Art, producing black, ſad, and dreadful effects, even the killing and deſtroying of poor men after a fearful manner, and ſo conſequently well befitting Vſury, which in Hebrew ſignifieth alſo hoſtile weapons, *Iſa*. 22. 8. *Pſal*. 78. 9. and befitting alſo the Vſurer himſelf, who fights as it were, by his Vſury, with Guns and hoſtile weapons which kill many; for which cauſe Vſury by *Calvin* is made as bad as murther; ſo that it might well be ſaid that *Germany* was happy before thoſe Guns called Vſuries came in, becauſe ſo many thouſands have been killed and deſtroyed thereby in my time, during the wars which were there then, and ſince I came away; or rather was perſecuted away for Religions ſake, by the Papiſts, who have burnt and deſtroyed many Towns, beſides a number of men.

3. *As for moderate Vſury*, which with him is ſix in the hundred, let him prove that ſuch Vſury is lawful, and that *Germany* is not unhappy for ſuch a kind of Vſury, yea for leſs; for there they pay but five in the hundred to my knowledge, and yet poor Souls what do they ſuffer for it, and have ſuffered? * Aretius *tells us, that* Germany *learned the evil of it by the Ruſtican War, and foretold what would follow it.*

4. As he ſaith, that where Merchandizing is, there muſt be lending; ſo ſay I, but not upon Terreſtrial Vſury, there is no need of it; becauſe there may be adventuring, which is held

---

* *Aretius de Vſura.*

lawful

lawful, and is most practised in *Holland*. To answer him for that too, because I can say a little more of *Holland*, having been there, than he who was never there; The King of *Bohemia* (in whose Court I have been when he resided there) adventured upon the Sea his money, and by adventuring the Hollanders have gotten their wealth, and not by Usury, which has made the King of *Spain* poor.

5. The Words of *Grotius* by him cited in Latin, I do not intend to translate for him to answer him, because they deserve it not; nor does he answer all that my Authors say, and why should I answer all his?

Num. 2. *Mr. Jel.* 3. I grant there is a necessity which, not God has brought upon Kingdoms, but mens sins, &c.

Reply. And are not some of these sins found on the borrowers part? &c.

I answer, 1. Lo how here he cuts off my many words indeed, because as I am apt to think, he is afraid of the Egyptian Lice and Frogs, and Locusts, which God sent as a just Plague upon the Egyptians for their hard-heartedness. Semblably whereunto, B. *Babington* and I say, that God brings the Usurers upon a Nation and People for their sins, *viz.* Hard-heartedness, Prodigality, Lavishness, Luxury, Drunkenness, Pride, Lasciviousness, and suffers them to enter into mens houses and fields morgaged, &c. Where Note, that he cuts off thirty three lines, that men may not see by his Writing what at large I say in this place especially, which also will cause me to serve him so too; only this I will add, that I will not excuse Borrowers, for many deserve to be blamed very much, for spending their borrowed money very idly and lavishly, in drinking, vvhoring, and playing at Cards and Dice, and such like unlavvful vvays, vvhereof the Usurer commonly is the cause, because he lends to such as he should not lend unto for filthy lucres sake: Where let me add the vvords of that grave and learned Helvetian Writer, * *Aretius*, Professor of *Losanna* in *Helvetia*, vvhich is vvell knovvn to me. *By Usury*, saith he, *Men are called away from their labours*, and abuse and spend their borrovved money in compotations and drunkenness, and other acts of idleness.

Num. 3. *Mr. Jel.* 2. *Obj. Addit.* Divines themselves vvhich speak against Usury, allovv of divers sorts of Usury, as Shipfenory, Recompensatory Usury.

I answer, I vvish that some had abstained from such expressions, there being other fitter names to be given them, as Ad-

* *Aretius de Usuris.*

venturing money, Damage, a free thankfulness, *&c.*

Reply, Usury by its usage has gotten an ill name, he saith, it is the name that frights people, *&c.* And so he citeth *Spanhemius* and *Calvin* in Latin, which I will not translate, having enough else to do, but thus much I will say,

1 Usury has gotten an ill name sure enough, and that deservedly, it being such an odious thing, because the Usurer will have his six in the hunred, and sometimes more, whether the borrower win or lose.

As for *Calvin* s word and wish, I will go a little farther with him, saying, *It were to be wished that ALL USURY, yea and the very name of it were banished out of the world: And again, I say with* Calvin, *we must always hold that it is scarce possible that he which takes Usury should not wrong his Brother, and yet farther, I will say with the same godly man* Calvin, *that it can hardly be that an Usurer may be found in the world, which is not given to unjust and filthy Lucre.* Thus far *Calvin* and I agree, for all the Champions endeavour to set us at variance.

As for my Cousin *Spanhemius* by him here cited in Latin too, I wonder why he will quote him any more, seeing he has after his writing for some Usury several leaves, given up Usuries cause, so that he and I are now agreed.

Num. 4. Mr, Jel. 3. Addit. Obj. Why may not I get by my money as well as others by their ground, *&c.*

Answ. Because the one is expresly forbidden, but not the other.

Reply, So is the Usury of Victuals, *&c.*

But the Question still is, whether universally?

Answ. That all this hath been answered sufficiently.

Mr. Jelinger Answers farther, Lending is a liberal Contract, whereas setting and selling is mercenary.

Reply, Why may not Lending be mercenary too?

I answer, 1. That our Masters and * Doctors in the Civil Law, whereunto such Contracts properly do appertain, do teach us so.

2. And because he will say this is but mens saying, I add, that our Great Master Christ himself makes lending freely, saying, *Lend freely*, as some Translations have it, *Luke 6. 35.*

And 3. *I answer*, that all that which the Champion here saith till we come to *p.* 107. has been so largely answered formerly, as that his *Grotius* with his limitations, cannot confute

---

* *Et artifici perito in sua arte credendum.* Shoppius *in sua Logica.*

and

and overthrow it, I am confident, appealing to the Reader for it.

And whereas the Champion saith, that I have given but a lame account of *Exod.* 22. 14, 15. I answer thereunto, that he comes off but with a lame Charge, wherewith he charges me, because he cannot make it good; and therefore betakes himself to a new, being gone of a sudden.

Num. 5. *Mr. Jel.* Of no greater force against Usury is what he adds, and according to the Law of man also, which saith, that the Commodary is not bound to a fortuitous case, or accident, unless he have bound himself.

Whereas to money lent, the Borrower stands to all hazards, and the Usurer to none.

Reply, But has not the Borrower bound himself too? And does not the Lender stand to no hazard? Even the same that a Seller does, that gives days of payment: Whereof Bishop *Hall* makes mention. But I desire to answer more fully, And,

1. That it is the Borrowers misery that he must be so bound to a wretched Usurer for unlawful Use, and the Usurers sin that he binds men to all hazards, and to pay forbidden Usury too. And

2. To the Usurers hazard let Dr. *Luther* answer: And yet will not the Usurer take upon him any adventure or hazard. Whereunto another great * Author adds this, *Will any man say that the Usurer adventureth, or meaneth to adventure, or thinketh that he doth adventure the Principal? No assuredly, for because he will not adventure, he will never lend upon Usury to a man that is not sufficient. No Usurer will lend to a poor man, saith* † Plutarch, *nor he will not lend to a rich man for two years, but with new Sureties, for fear, I trow, that he or they will be undone in few years by Usury, and so not being able to pay he should lose his advantage.* Thus he, *I superadd, yea from half year to half year Usurers bind now, and put in extents into their Usury Writings and Bonds, whereas those that sell to a day never make this so sure, and therefore are at great hazards.* So that Bishop *Hall* here can do the Champion but little good, nor Bishop *Taylor*: But of this I have spoken already sufficiently.

Num. 6. But I find him mistaken, saith the Ch. concerning the account he gives of the Law of man, concerning the Commodary; if *Grotius* speaks true.

Whereunto I answer, I will set down the very words of the

---

* Mos.. † Plutarch *de non foen.*

Law.

Law, for then I cannot be mistaken. The words are, *The Commodary is not bound to a fortuitous case, unless he have bound himself to ballance his* Grotius, whom himself thinks not to be very sure, because he saith, if *Grotius* speaks true, I will ballance a surer, *viz.* blessed *Bolton*, who saith as I say, *A thing that is hired, if it perish without the default of the hirers, it perishes to the owner.*

1. *Because he is the owner.*

2. *Because it went for the hire according to Gods Law, Exod.* 22. 15. See the * Margin also.

Now let all true English Hearts chuse again whom they will listen unto, this *Grotius* who whom they never read or heard of before now, and who is one of them that are against the strict keeping of the Christian Sabbath, and therefore unsound in Doctrine and in practice, differing from them in their godly practises; or to that sound and holy man, Mr. *Bolton*, whom they do and can read in their Mother tongue, most learnedly writing against Usury, (even as others also do) and of other excellent Subjects tending to Godliness, and made a most godly end; † and to whose pious Soul mine also desires to go when it goeth hence, that as we have warred together here against execrable Usury, so we may live together hereafter, and be Crowned together with the Crown of Glory.

Num, 7. But I see this Adversary would have me answer to thirteen Questions, to which bold and sawcy proposal I shall say thus much.

That as Christ said once when he was asked, *By what Authority dost thou these things? Matth.* 21. 23. 24. So I will ask him but five Questions also, to which if he answer me solidly, I will answer such of his questions as are worth the answering next, thinking it necessary and fit to answer but one of the thirteen now.

The First of my Questions is, How this Champion can justifie the putting out of his money upon Usury, without any allowance of any express Scripture, making it lawful for him so to do?

---

* *Videatur etiam* Tostatus *in Exod.* 22. *p.* 419. *de Commodatario & in* *l.* 3, 4. *& in Digest. de regul.* *in l. contr.* *de Actionibus & obligat. l.* 1. §. 15. *qui &* Foroneus *apud* Isidor. Eth. cap. 18. Foroneus *inquam de hac re qui primus Iræcis leges dedit, & pauco tempore ante Israelitarum exitum ex Ægypto fuerat ut id asserit.* August. de Civ. Dei, l. 18. † *To use the words of* Diavelarius *in his* Alt. Damasc. & Rob. Brussius, *anima mea cum*

The

The Second Question is, Whether he have ever made any restitution of all the mony which he has taken for the use and loan of his money, since he first began to be a lender upon Usury?

The Third Question, Whether his Conscience doth not check and smite him, when he receives his Usury Money of such and such? He knows whom I mean.

The Fourth Question, By what Scripture he will prove the lawfulness of his moderate Usury by him maintained? Seeing that not only *Nesheck*, biting, but *Tarbith*, that is any increase, is by the word of God forbidden as a sin, as a Great Parliament of *England* declares it, saying: *That all Usury being forbidden by the word of God, is sin and detestable, &c.*

The Fifth Question, Whether he that does not observe the godly cautions prescribed by godly Divines, may be excused and escape in that great day, by *Jam.* 3. 2. *In many things we offend all.*

As for that one Question, which at present I will only answer, is the very first.

Whether I have made restitution of three pounds for money put into a Tradesmans hands.

Whereunto I answer, That I have no need to make such restitution, because I never lent to a Tradesman or any man else in the whole world, any money upon Usury; God is my witness, let any prove it if they can. I add, that this hath been sufficiently sifted already by those which have heard of it, for I have proffered before many witnesses to a person which gave out such a report, a great sum of money, if he could make it appear that ever I lent to any person upon Usury in all my life, but it could never yet be proved.

And no new thing it is for the Servants of God to be so used, *Athanasius* for Writing against the *Arrians*, was accused and charged with murther and uncleanness: *Calvin* for Writing and standing against Popery, had a Book written against him by *Bolsecus* an Apostate, charging him with Sodomy. So *Luther* in his life time had most hainous things laid to his charge in Print; and one of the Champions Friends whom I forbear to name, and Mr. *Moss*, for writing against Usury, was said to be an Usurer himself, as he writes himself: Yea *Nehemiah* himself, who was such a notable enemy to all Usury, has been made an Usurer himself by some Usurers Translations, as out of Bishop *Downam* I have proved it: So that no wonder it is that *Satan* that old Lyar, playeth his old Game of Lying against me the least of all Gods slandered, belied, reviled Servants also, after my laborious Writing and setting my self against his

great

great Idol, which he has set up in the World, Vsury I mean, the Vsurers Great *Diana*, but confident I am, that my God, whose Truth I am vindicating, will deliver me and clear mine innocency gratiously, To whom alone be all Honour and Glory.

Num.9.And now I have no more to do, but to Exhort and to Pray,

1. *To Exhort.* And

1. My Brethren in the Ministry, that

1. They themselves above all men should abstain from that great and grievous sin of Vsury, * because by their practice and example, so many thousand Souls are led and drawn down to hell, when they see them which should shew them the way to Heaven and Salvation, † shew them the way to Hell and Destruction by their taking of *Neshech* and *Tarbith*, Vsury and Increase, contrary to Gods own Inhibition. For what do they say when I and others do Preach and Print against that odious sin? If Vsury were such a damnable sin as some make it, such and such a Minister (naming thee that art a lender upon Vsury, by thy very name) would not lend his money after that manner. Whereupon, saith one, I know where he lends so much to such a one, who pays him according to the usual rate; nay saith another, I had hundreds of such a Minister, and because I paid but five in the hundred, he vvas not contented because I paid not six, when of another, who though he vvas a Vsurer too, yet let me have it for three in the hundred. Thus they talk of Ministers, vvhich caused a Godly Minister in discoursing vvith me about it, to say to me, that he did ever hate Vsury, and would not take any though never so little, if he might gain the World, because of the bad example which a Minister gives to others: And again he said, Many of our Ministers now turn Vsurers, and their Hearers turn after them, making that the cause of it, why there are so many Vsurers now; whereas some years ago, men counted Vsury to be so odious a thing as that few would venture upon it.

Num, 10. The consideration whereof impels me therefore to beseech you, dear Brethren, for the Lords sake, and for your own dear Souls sake, and for the sake of those precious Souls which Christ has redeemed with his own blood, and are committed to your care and charge, and guided and led by

---

* *Which caused a famous Writer to say, we Ministers are to be blamed for many of the exorbitancies of our people, because of our example we harden them in their sin.* † *I mean those Ministers only which are Vsurers.*

your

your * example, that you will not have any hand at all in Usuries filthy and abominable trade and occupation, by lending your money as many do upon Usury, as being most deeply charged by that faithful and pious Servant of God, *Nehemiah* 5. 10. *I pray you let us leave off this Usury.* He doth not call Usury *Neshech*, *biting*, as if biting and oppressive Usury were unlawful only; but משא a burden, because Usury is a burden indeed, as poor Borrowers find it and feel it, though they pay but six in the hundred, when out of their Estates they must pay ten, twenty, or thirty pounds for Usury by the year, which to my knowledge has undone many who have been forced to sell their Means.

I am the more earnest in this, because Priests and Clergy men in all Ages have been ever spoken against and censured for Usury, if they were guilty of it; it being thought to be a thing above all other men, most unbeseeming and unbecoming them: I will instance only,

1. In the Jews, among whom as *Lira* Writes, their Priests might not so much as lend to strangers, though others could. And

2. In the holy Council of *Nice*, (besides which I could nominate many more) which did most severely censure such Clergymen as were Usurers.

And 3. I will quote *Gregory* the Great, who saith expresly, *That they are not to be ordained for the Ministry, who are convicted that they have taken Usury:* Which saying of his is also cited in the Decretals.

Num. 10. 2. And I must yet farther desire all godly Ministers, to joyn with their Brethren which are against all Usury, and cry it down as they do, hearkning to that learned Dr. † *Welleius* thus Writing. *Teachers and Pastors are to be admonished, that vehemently in their Sermons, they inveigh against Usury, and that they lay before men the threats of God, and shew them how horrible a Monster an Usurer is, which is worse than any Thief, Robber, or Murderer.* I add, and that they will imitate therein *Moses*, that man of God, and *Ezekiel*, and *Nehemiah*, who so cryed Usury down in their time, and all the holy Councils and Fathers in their time, and *Luther* who did the like in his

---

* *Even as they are led by the examples of their Magistrates, being always apt to receive either good or bad impressions, according to their deportment, as* Tamberlain *told* Axalla. Clerk p. 218.

† Dr. Welleius *upon Psal.* 15.

time, * exhorting Professors in Universities to read it down in their Lectures, Ministers in their Pulpits to preach it down, and Schoolmasters in their Schools to teach their Scholars to hate it from their youth up, and when they are grown up to labour every where to put it down. But I must go yet farther, endeared Brethren, beseeching you that you will go and joyn to throw it down, as that holy, incomparable, and wonderful man, Archbishop *Usher*, did go to put it down in his *Body of Divinity*, seven times Printed, *p.* 300. where he saith as I said once already, *That it is a most wicked and unlawful contract*, &c. *which if we live and die in without Repentance, we are excluded out of the Kingdom of Heaven*, which he proveth by *Psal.* 15. 1, 5. *Ezek.* 18. 12. *Ch.* 22.

Again, I must desire you to joyn with the famous and most learned Bishop *Jewel*, the Jewel of *England*, and the Renowned Bishop *Downam*, and that mirror of all manner of Learning, Bishop *Andrews*, of whom a very able Divine gave me very lately this Character; that he was the learnedst man that ever *England* had, and who has written, as I said formerly, a Book purposely to shew that even *Usura licita est illicita*; and for his excellency in all manner of Learning, is extolled by great *Spanhemius* himself, in his *Evangelical Doubts*, and by Name in his *Dispute of Usury*: So that you need not to be ashamed to Preach and to press this great and noble Truth of Usuries unlawfulness, which has been preached, published, proved, and maintained by such Worthies: Nor should you count it needless, because the whole World is concerned in it, especially upon the account of Trades, wherein men commonly make Usury their Standard, and because those many thousand, thousand Souls which are in the World, and are more worth than all the world, *Matth.* 16. 26. (and are blindfoldedly led into that grievous sin by commoness and † example and ignorance,) should be made to know what it is, and how unlawful and execrable it is in the sight of God and good men, and how damnable, that they may not be unexpectedly and suddenly cast into that formidable Lake (which burneth with fire and brimstone) for this very sin of Usury, which God in mercy prevent, by giving them true and speedy Repentance.

Well, methinks I cannot but hope that many good Ministers

---

* *Which I mention twice because it is so notable.* † *When they see Ministers practice it, whose sin therefore is the greater?* As Salvian, quo sublimior prærogativa eo major culpa. De Gub. Dei. l. 4.

will

will hearken to good counsel, and cry down this great and grievous evil, as their Predecessors have done heretofore, because some are and have been awakened of late already, and begin to Preach it down very much, saying as I am told, that whereas some speak against Ceremonies as evil, they do that which is worse, by lending their money upon usury, and defending it against the express Word of God, which in plain terms forbids it; and I have heard of one noted Minister especially, whose Son is a Learned Bishop, that to make that odious sin of Usury yet more odious, he called it *that whelping of money*, as he was Preaching a worthy Knights Funeral Sermon, before a great company of Hearers, saying in the commendation of that eminent Knight, that he was no Usurer, for he could never abide that whelping of money.

Whereunto he added, Pardon me for using this expression, it was his own when he lived, that he could never abide it, and therefore he never lent any of his money upon Usury: For the certainty of which remarkable Report, I did ask the Preacher himself being in his Company very lately, and he owned it; so that I say again, that to be hoped it is, that more Ministers will follow, which that it may prove so, is the prayer of him that has written these Lines; wishing that he might write them with his Blood and *not with Ink*, if it would please God, and he might do any poor Soul good thereby, and free it from that bloody sin of Usury, called Murder, even by *Calvin* himself and many others. And wishing farther, that the Great God, which hates and forbids both *Nesheck* and *Tarbith*, Usury and all Increase, would be pleased to write the same which is written in *Deut.* 23. 19. and hereto, with his own Finger as with the Pen of a Diamond, *Jer.* 17. 1. in mens hearts, putting the point of it upon their hearts, and especially the hearts of those that practice Usury and defend it, their hearts being made truly penitent and deeply sensible by himself, that being disswaded they may *wholly forbear all Usury*, as himself would have them to do, *Ezek.* 18. 8.

Most Great God, *Fulfil this thy Servants Vote, and hear him graciously, for the sake of thy Son, who is also against that mercenary kind of lending, called Usury, saying: Lend freely, hoping for nothing from thence*, Luke 6. 35. Amen, So be it.

And so I have done with Ministers first.

2. AND You, Gentlemen, whatsoever you do, do not put your money to usury; for you have Estates to live by comfortably, and if that which you have be not enough, you may buy more, and you have no need at all to live by Vsury, as many others plead that they must, because they have no Lands, but Moneys only to employ for their maintenance. Oh that you would hearken unto me in this! Oh that you would do as other great ones, even Heathens have done, those great Emperours *Tiberius* and others I mean, who would rather lend freely to others to prevent Vsurers, than to be Vsurers themselves.

Oh let not these Heathens rise up in Judgment against you.

3. And you Old Men, who have one Foot in the Grave already, do not take up that cursed Practice of Vsury, because Age doth disenable you from following a lawful Calling, lest with both Feet you be made to go into Hell, when Christ comes to Judge the World in Righteousness, and to adjudge Vsurers to everlasting destruction for their unrighteousness, and for despising and disobeying his righteous Commandment, *Luke* 6. 35. *Lend, hoping for nothing from thence*.

4. So you Young Men, do not you live in that great sin of sins, for as that great Apostle wrote of you, 1 *John* 2. 14. so do I say to you, *You are strong*; and can employ your selves and your strength in lawful Callings, Trades, and ways of Living, and have no need to take up such a lazy Trade as this of Vsury is, which even a poor Heathen calls *Quæstuosam segnitiem*, a *gainful laziness*: You may take an example from other young ones, which since my first Book against Vsury came out, did promise me faithfully that themselves would come out of that detestable sin, intreating me to direct them in it, which also I did.

5. To Orphans and Widows I say, O let not those to whom God all-gracious has made such gracious promises, and for whom he hath made a special Law to secure them, become Transgressors of the very next Law to it, *Exod.* 22. 22, 23. Nor let them for whom he takes such special care by his Providence, be so ungracious and ungrateful as to mistrust him, that he will not provide lawful ways and means for them, whereby their portion and moneys may be employed for their maintenance, and support, and let them not provide for themselves Vsury

Bags, therein to put their Usury money for their sustenance, for fear lest they put it in Bags that have holes; and will not hold their dishonest gain long; God smiting at it with his fist, as he has menaced it, in *Ezek.* 22: 13. and so their money perish and they too with it for ever.

I add, Orphans are coming into the world, Widows, who intend to continue, are looked upon as going out of the world, and shall these two Ages which above all other ought to be made heavenly, the one for Innocency, the other for Devotion, be stained with Usury? Christ is *Alpha* and *Omega* unto us, the first and the last, the beginning and the end; and shall the *Alpha* of our Nonage, and the *Omega* of our Dotage, be dedicated to Usury? Christ calls himself by the name of the first Letter in the Alphabet, that Children may learn Christ so soon as they are able to know their Letters; and shall we suffer our Children to be died in the Wool of their Infancy, with the Scarlet Sin of Usury? And will our Widows be tinctured so too? God forbid.

O that poor Orphans and Fatherless Children would all do as some of them have promised me, that they would leave that filthy sin of Usury from henceforth, being convinced by my *Usurer cast*, and never more have to do with it, desiring me to shew them a way whereby they may lawfully and without Usury employ their money, which I promised and did: *The Lord give a blessing to it:* And what I say of and to Orphans, I say to Widows also.

O that you also would do as that Ministers Widow, which having read and well considered what is written in the said *Usurer cast*, left that detestable sin of Usury, and made a full and free restitution.

Num. 13. 6. To such as profess Godliness and bear the name of Good People, I shall speak next: O do not you embark with that sort of people which are called Usurers (forsooth) in the same brittle and dangerous Vessel called Usury, lest together with them you also be cast away in the Sea of Wrath, called Hell, otherwise the very Pit of Hell, to which Usurers and their Usury are condemned of old by the Scriptures, *Ezek.* 18. 12. by Councils, by the holy Fathers, * By Schoolmen, and all sorts of wise and holy Writers, as one has made it † good,

* B. Down. *in Psal.* 15. † Idem ibid. *The Schoolmen retain the Doctrine of the Primitive Church about Usury: and deep learned men they are, for I have heard them read their learned Lectures in the Sorbone of* Paris.

whose words I will relate. *The Philosophers, the Heathens, have written and spoken against Usury, and will you Christians practise it,* say I? *The Fathers of the Church have with one consent condemned it,* saith the same great Author; yet farther I add, *And will you do what these holy men (who have lived so holily and so angelically, as that they heard some of them the Angels sing) condemn to the bottomless Pit, preferring what some young Divines tell you, before the grave and Scriptural Sayings of those Aged Saints?*

And let this be minded by you too, what hurt you do to many other poor Souls by your practice: For what do they say of you? If Usury were so bad as some make it, what will become of such and such, who I am sure have as good Souls to God, as those which prate and preach so much against it?

Ah poor Professors, you did not think upon this it may be heretofore, but now give your minds to it, and say as * *David, What have these Sheep done?* So what have those poor silly creatures, whom we draw in by our example, done to us, that we should bring so much evil upon them? And so though ignorant and silly creatures do offend in this kind of harm, by bringing one another into the same condemnation by their example, yet do not you so go to Hell with those whom they draw to bear them company.

Again, Let this be thought upon by ye, my Brethren, that if you shall refuse to leave and shun that filthy sin of Usury, you will make all men that know you to live in that sin, say of you, that you have but a form of Godliness, and deny the power thereof, as it is said that some shall do in the latter days, 2 *Tim.* 3. 1. *Because no truly pious man will defile himself* (as saith *Lactantius,* that ancient Latin Father) *with that iniquity.*

And therefore for the Lords sake, do not cast in your Lot among the Lots of Usury-mongers, whose sin is Lottery, unlawful Lottery, because their Principal is called *sors,* that is, *Lottery,* whence comes Usury, which therefore well may be called Lottery. I say again, do not cast in your Lot, your Portions, your Money among and with theirs, lest though you seem to win, you || lose your immortal Souls, and heaven it self for ever, as every one doth who liveth and dieth in the sin of

---

* *Psal.* 4. 17. † Lactantius. || *Which what an extreme folly and desperate madness it is, for Usury, which is not the tenth part of a mans money, to cast away his Soul; which thou oughtest not to hazard for the gain of the whole World.* See Matth. 16. 26.

Vſury, though he get by it a little painted earth, ſee *Pſal.* 15. 1, 5.

The Lord awaken poor deluded Souls, that they may depart from the Uſurers Tents, and from that foul deſtroying ſin of USURY, before they depart out of this preſent World, being deprived of the uſe of Light and Life, and before the decree be gone forth againſt them, that they ſhall die the ſecond death, which is burning, burning, burning in a Lake of Fire for ever and ever. See *Ezek.* 18. 12, 13. *Rev.* 21. 8.

Num. 14. 7. And Laſtly, What I ſay to thoſe which even now I named, I ſay to all: O let them all leave that horrid ſin of Uſury, and hate it and ſhun it like a biting Serpent: For a * Serpent it is and has been called before I was born, as I have formerly ſhewn it. And let this be alſo taken into conſideration, (for conſideration is here allowed, which if Vſury be meant it is prohibited) that it will be your wiſdom to chuſe the ſafeſt; for vvhich advice I vvill name ſix great Divines at preſent, vvho ſay it.

1. † *Antoninus*, It is a Maxim in Lavv, ſaith he, that in doubtful caſes vve muſt take the ſafeſt vvay.

2. || *Alciates*, When it is a doubt or queſtion, vvhether a thing be a ſin or no, it is to be held that it is a ſin, becauſe that it is the ſafeſt opinion. So he,

3. * Dr. Hammond, *In matters of this Nature, I conceive it to be our duty to take the ſafeſt courſe.*

4. † So Archbiſhop Vſher, *It will be our beſt way to take the ſureſt courſe, which is wholly to forbid it (ſpeaking of Vſury.)*

5. || So pious Mr. Francis Whidden ſaith the ſame, *In doubtful things take the ſureſt and ſafeſt way:* Inſtancing in this.

Which 2. Manuduceth and brings me to the Figure mentioned and promiſed in the ſaid Title Page, and here ſet out and repreſented in the next Page, for a Chriſtian Traveller to make his choice of one of the vvays lying before him in the ſaid Figure, vvhich novv immediately follovvs.

---

* *By* Pagnine *and others, morſura ſerpentis.* † *Antoninus ſum. part* 1. *num.* 1. *tit.* 20. *de regul. juris.* || *Andreas Alciates, reſponſ. l.* 1. *concil,* 3. *cap.* 24. * Dr. Ham. *in his Pract. Cat.* † *Archbiſhop* Vſher *in his Body of Divinity, p.* 300. || *Mr.* Fr. Whidden *the Elder, in his* Topaz. p. 85. *So* Mr. Noſvvorthy.

A FIGURE.

Of Two Ways; One Safe leading to Heaven, the Other a Dangerous and Deadly, leading to Hell.

The Safe Way is not to lend upon Usury, according to Psal. 15. 5.

The Dangerous and Deadly is lending upon Usury, as Ezekiel *represents it, ch.* 18. 12, 13. *whereby a Christian Traveller is put and left to chuse one.*

A Wide Gate, and coming in, *Mat.* 7. 13.

The Right Hand Rosie Hedg.

The dangerous and deadly vvay is a broad vvay called Vsury, hedged in with tvvo pleasant easie hedges, one at the right hand the other at the left; and having at his Entry a very wide Gate, *Mat.* 7. 13. and ugly Devils called Murtherers, walking in it, and the lake of fire, *Rev.* 21. 8. at the end of it, into which the Devils called murderers do cast Vsurers, that walk in it, therein to burn and die to all eternity, according to *Ezekiel's* words: *He hath given forth upon Usury and hath taken increase, shall he then live? he shall not live he shall surely dye, ch.* 18. 12, 13.

The Left Hand Rosie Hedg.

Here chuse Christian Traveller thy way, and take either the left hand and dangerous way, if thou darest adventure among Devils & murderers which will surely cast thee into the lake of fire, in case thou walk in the way of Vsury, therein to suffer the vengeance of eternal fire, or the right way which (thogh a narrow way) yet is safe being without Vsury, and full of holy Angels which will conduct thee into Gods holy hill call'd heaven there to dwell to all eternity, in that 15 *Ps.* of that sweet Singer of *Israel.* Or thus, *Judg thou therefore which is the safest wa,* saith reverend Mr. Fr. Whiddon *in his* Topaz. p. 86. *The Lord of heaven and earth direct thee into this way, inclining thy heart unto it.* Amen. So be it.

A little Gate, *Matth.* 7. 13.

The Right Hand Thorny Hedg.

The safe way is the narrow way, *Mat.* 7. 14. without Vsury, shewn by holy *David Psal.* 15. 5. in these words, *Lord, who shall dwell in thy holy hill? He that puts not his money to Usury:* being hedged in with two thorny hedges, one at the right hand the other at the left hand, and having a very strait gate to it, *Mat.* 7. 14. and the holy Angels meeting those that walk in it, and Heaven at the end of it.

The Left Hand Thorny Hedg.

Num.

Num: 16. A Citation annexed.

WHich citeth all the Commitants of that odious sin of Usury, to answer for themselves before Jesus Christ, (who hath said, lend, hoping for nothing from thence (*Luke* 6. 35.) at that great and terrible day, when *Moses*, and *David*, and *Jeremiah*, and *Ezekiel*, and *Nehemiah* will appear against them, and stand with great boldness before them, to bear witness against them; together with very many Antient Councils, and a Multitude of particular Fathers, which have most bitterly written against them; and a numberless Company of School Divines, Casuists, * Civilians and a world of Protestant Writers and Preachers, Lutheran, and reformed, Danish, Polandish, Dutch, French, Scottish, Irish, English, Helvetian, Belgick, besides Heathenish Poets, Orators, Philosophers, Historians; and when *Mahomet* himself also whom his *Alcaron* is against Usury and forbids it, and with his blinded Mahometants will arise against Usurers, and testify against them: As the Lord Jesus Christ tells us that the men of *Ninive* † will rise against that generation, which then lived and heard him, and saw his wonders and would not repent, *Mat.* 12. 41. Even as that sad Generation of Usurers which hearing him in his Ministers saying, *let us leave off this Usury. Nehemiah* 5. 10. And will not repent tho guilty of a sin which is called *Sodomy in nature*, *by great* || *Divines*. I add, and when the Jews also themselves, which from time to time have been great Usurers, yet will rise against the Christian Usurers, otherwise * *baptized* Jews, because they will not lend to their brethren, which are Jews, and they, being Christians, would lend to their Christian brethren upon Usury and condemn them, O sad! sad! sad!

Thus that faithful Martyr and Witness of Jesus Christ, *John*

---

* *The civil Lawyers and Papists, which have written so much against Usury, will condemn the Patrons of Usury in the day of Judgment.* Phil. Cæsar. p. 20. † *With whom we may joyn other Heathens too, which do abhor Usury, tho they never heard Christ speak against it, but their Philosophers only by whose witness their Pains in Hell shall be encreased, which in so great a light of the Gospel have remained impenitent.* P. Cæsar p. 35. || Hugo. Comm. *in* Psal. 15.

Huss

Huss who was burnt at *Costnich* for Religion, cited *the Council of Costnich*, which condemned him; saying, *after a hundred years hence ye shall answer God and me*; which fell out accordingly, when one hundred years after great *Luther* rose against the Pope as he did the same time rise against all the Usurers of the world by his writing that famous Book *De Taxanda Usura*, of Taxing Usury, answerably thereunto, I am risen also now, to tax Usury, and Usurers in and by those Books which I have written, and shall write against the same; and do tell Usurers to their faces, by this Citation, that they must and shall answer; I will not say an hundred years hence, but very shortly, because the end of the world and that great day are at hand, and *the Judge stands at the door*, ready to judge them: Answer, I say they must; those learned and great men, which in great numbers have spoken, written and testified against them, and their wicked and ungodly trade of Usury, and me also the unworthiest of all the Lords servants, who have written several books against them, and Preached at least fifteen Sermons besides at a publick Lecture in a certain Town called *Kings-Bridge*, to reclaim them, but could not work upon them (some few excepted, which were then converted by Gods blessing) and do now tell them, that they must prepare themselves as well as they can; if they will needs stand it out to defend that detestible sin of Usury, as a great Parliament of *England* calls it, and that they bring with them their strong reasons, Papers, and Writings, if they think they will be able to endure that terrible fire, which will devour before that formidable Judge, who will judge them and me, and thereby put an end to this great Controversy which is between them and his Godly servants; which together with my dispiseable self will make their appearance against them, and with great animosity testify against them, whereunto shall be added no more than this. And who, being a wretched Usurer, whom his own † Conscience has before hand accused and condemned, even in this world, and abide his coming; and with his Usury bills and bonds stand before him and that devouring fire. Oh dreadful! dreadful! dreadful! Oh that these poor deluded Creatures, whom we call Usurers would hearken to this, and be perswaded; would burn their Usury books and

† *Which divers learned Writers do therefore call Forum or a Court wherein Men are Convented, accused, condemned.* Philo. Gregor, Theol. Langius *in* Justin *Martyr.*

Papers,

Papers : As a certain Minister did cause to Order his Usury Papers to be burnt after his decease (as one of his neer Relations told me) Execrating Usury, would not live one half hour longer in that evil of Evils ! would listen no more to their former Leaders, which misled them, and trust no further to their nice discourses, and subtile distinctions (as that renowned * Lord Primate of *Ireland* Arsh-Bishop *Usher* calls them) as they tender the Salvation of their immortal souls, and would be ruled by the unerring word of God , which prohibits all Usury, properly so called, *Deut.* 23. 19. And sheweth what it is, even any Usurious increase, *Ezek.* 18. 8. Which cuts in pieces all frivolous Effugies, Shifts, and distinctions used by the Defendants, of shameless and opprobrious Usury. The Lord my God awaken them , and all their Adherents by this direful Citation ; that they may repent and turn, and not be cast into the bottomless Pit, therein to burn, burn, burn, to all Eternity.

This Citation is added by reason of some, who being Usurers and Usurerers Champions, will not be answered ; nor convinced of the unlawfulness of Usury, by the strongest arguments from the holy Scriptures deduced, and by the greatest Wits and holiest men in the World ; such I mean as the Holy Fathers, and Godly Protestant Writers, were, and are, managed Syllogistically and otherwise, which hath inforced this Citation to come forth, citing them to answer to that which is laid to their Charge about Criminal and destestible Usury, before Jesus Christ, who will impartially decide this grand Question, whether Usury properly so called, and is now practised in the world ; with his own sacred mouth, according to his Gospel *lend freely* (as some render his words) *hoping for nothing from thence*, *Luke* 6. 35. To stop all Usurers mouths who then and thereupon will be judged to Æviternal Death and Flames, except they now repent. O direful, direful, direful, Desire !

Num. 17. I superadd ; and because some will condemn me for being singular, as if none did proceed so harshly against Criminal Usury : I will take Bishop † *Downam* for my second (as I am wont in all matters concerning Usury, to bring some of the holiest and learnedst men, that have flourished in the world, through the ages past, to stand by me, next unto God, and his holy Word) His going to work is this.

* Arch B. Usher *in his Body of Divin.* p. 300. † Downam *upon* Psal. 15. 5.

1. He

1. He frameth a Sylogism to prove the Usurers most certain Damnation without repentance, out of *Psal.* 15. 1, 5. *Lord who shall dwell in thy holy hill -- He that puts not his mony to Usury.*

And his Syllogism is this.

He that shall inherit the Kingdom of God, doth not put forth his mony to Usury.

But thou (say) to the Usurer, or him that lendeth for gain, dost put forth thy mony to Usury.

Thou therefore (unless thou repent) shalt not inherit the Kingdom of Heaven, but shalt be cast out of the heavenly *Jerusalem*, and * shalt have thy part in the Lake which burneth with Fire and Brimstone: Thus famous and learned Bishop *Downam*, Syllogiseth and writeth as bitterly as I; yea, much more against the wretched Usurer, which shews how my Doctrine concerning the Usurers Damnation is confirmed by this great man.

2. *He Citeth him to answer him at Christ's Tribunal, saying; Unto which Syllogism, let every Usurer Consider how he shall be able to* ANSWER BEFORE THE LORD. *Mark this, poor Condemned* U S. U R E R.

So that here two of us thus bring this Citation against the said miserable Usurer, and we have a Proverbial saying.

Ne Hercules quidem contra Duos.

Hercules himself cannot stand before and against two. And to make this a threefold Cord which cannot be broken, *I can add a third* viz. † Doctor Fenton *who saith, alas, poor Soul, whither wilt thou turn thy self for succour, when thy best Friends forsake thee? what wilt thou plead for thy self, when thou comest before the Eternal Judge upon thy Trial?*

But if God himself, besides us, be against him, and for us, as indeed he is, (as has been sufficiently proved) it must needs be worse for him to subsist, and to stand it out; *for if God be for us, who can be against us, Rom.* 8. 31. Where let this be thought upon also, What a dreadful day that great day of Judgment will be to the Usurer so cited; if that which some write of that terrible day should be true, *viz.* That it will last thousands of years, I say, if not the terminating a-

* *Revel.* 21. 8. † Doctor Fenton, *that famous* London *Minister.*

ny

ny thing about it, but contenting my self only with the naming the Authors of that Opinion, which are, * *Gemara*, All *Cabalists* , † *Carpentarius*, || *Rabbi Ketina:* And lest it should be thought strange that I mention this thing, I must and shall make this Apologie for my self, that the famous *Mead* also mentioneth the same in his Writings upon the Revelation. The poor cited Usurer may do well to pause a little upon this Citation.

---

* Gemera. Sank. Cap. Col. Israel. † Carpentarius.
|| Rabbi Ketina. *Though I do not deliver it as a Scriptural Verrity.*

The Usurers Last WILL and TESTAMENT,

Foregoing his burial which is to come, added, out of Thomas Beards *Doctors of Divinty Theatre of Gods Judgments*, p. 476.

Num. 18. MY Soul, quoth the Usurer, I bequeath to the Divel who is Owner of it, my Wife likewise to the Devil, who induced me to this ungodly trade of Life, and my Deacon to the Devil, for soothing me up, and not reproving me for my faults, and in this desperate perswasion died incontinently; which occasioned me therefore to reprove Usurers so sharply as I do, and to deal with Usury

Usury so roughly, and to Condemne it to the Pit of Hell; lest one Usurer or other that heard, or read me, should like this Usurer, bequeath me also, when he is dying, to the Devil, for soothing him up in his sin, as doubtless many Usurers do and will so bequeath, when they lye upon their death beds, those Ministers, which defend Usury, for soothing them up in that abominable sin, and not speaking, or preaching against it all the year long, as their Hearers tell me, who Condemn them for it here on earth, as God will hereafter in the place of his dreadful Judgment.

The NARATIVE,

Promised in the Title Page *of an Usurers burying by Satan. Out of* Lodowick Lloid *in his Pilgrimage of Princes,* p. 107. *Superadded.*

AN Usurer being dead, no man would bear his Corps to be buried by the Law of that City, but such as were of that faculty; all the just and good men of that City could not heave up the Coffin; at length came four of his own Science, I mean Usurers, which easily took up the

Coffin,

Coffin, and bare it; to whom one of the City ſaid; behold four Devils can carry the fift eaſily. (Note, they call theſe four Uſurers Devils, and the dead Uſurer a Devil too) and being brought to Church, the *Prieſt* knowing what he was, ſaid, that he ſhould not be buried in the Church, for that the Church is the houſe of God, and not a Grave for wicked men: His friends carried him unto the high way thinking to make his grave there; There the King's Officers withſtood, and ſaid, that the Kings high way was not meet to bury any man in: In ſtriving between themſelves, the Devil appeared, and ſaid, If they would give him leave, he would bear him into a meet place: They being well contented therewith, the Devil took him out of ſight, and buried him, where he uſeth to bury, in his Cheifeſt Chappel, in HELL.

This is inſerted to make way for the Uſurers future burying, which is to come, when my other Uſury books come forth, and to ſhew, what dreadful thoughts they had in old time of Uſury; that the poor and Condemned Uſurer may fear, and repent and not be buried in that woful place of torment, called Hell.

Which God in mercy grant.

My

Num. 19. MY Final Prayer now is to my God, who has carried me all along through the boysterous and controversial Sea of Usury, and graciously brought me to my desired Haven, that in mercy he would look upon poor Usurers Souls, and influence the Contents of this Book with his Celestial Benediction, as that they may look up to him therein, as calling them out of Darkness into his marvelous Light and so may repent with speed and live, I say with speed, because all mens lives, and so theirs too, do run not upon an Helixe, which still encreaseth, and enlargeth but a Circle, where arriving to their Meridian, they decline again, and at last fall under their by God destinated Horizon, which to they all press amain; so that their sitting and living here cannot be long, nor their sitting afar off, because their breath is but short of it self, also themselves make it dayly shorter by their execrable Usury, which will bring them, except they repent, quickly to their by God predestinated Doom, which is Death and Destruction Dolour and Damnation, to an endless Duration. O my God let Usurers and their Defendants imbibe this, and digest it thorowly, that they may not dye and perish suddenly, falling as Idolaters, into that Lake of Fire, which burneth with Fire and Brimstone everlastingly. *Rev.* 21. 8. For thou hast said of the Usurer that taketh encrease and giveth forth upon Usury, * *Shall he then live? He shall not live, he shall surely dye: His blood shall be upon him.* Ezek. 18. 12, 13.

O dreadful God, what a dreadful death, this death needs must be; because the poor damned Usurer will be always dying, and yet living in pains, in pangs, in torments, in flames of fire and insufferable burnings world without end. And therefore O most merciful God, have mercy upon him that truly and from the bottom of his heart he may repent, and not fall into that bottomless Pit, and suffer the vengeance of Eternal Fire. *Amen. Amen. So be it.*

---

* *(Or dying still) he shall dye, in Hebrew* מות ימות *meaning thereby Eternal Death.* Down. *in* Psal. 15.

Num.

TRANSCRIPTS Annexed against USURY: Stated,

1. *Out of the Institutions of the* * *Canon Law reviewed by* John Paul, Lancelot *the* Perusine. *The* 4. Book. *The* 7. Title *of* Usury.

Num. 20. USury is whatsoever beyond the borrowed Principal is taken, that is, saith the † Expositor of this Description, is taken by a compact for loane. And

The Sacred Canons do prosecute Usurers with a multiplicity of punishments. For, besides that they brand them with Infamy, they do not admit them to the || Communion, nor will they let any receive Oblations at their hands. And if they be of the Ministery, they shall hazard both their Office and their Ecclesiastical Benefices.

And yet farther, None may under the punishment in the * Gregorian Constitution comprized set unto Vsurers any houses, or if any be set, let them have them. And if any dye in that Crime, they shall be deprived of Ecclesiastical Burial. And this holds so firm, as that if Vsurers, when they are dying, shall in their last Will require * satisfaction to be made for Vsury taken, expressing a certain quantity, or indistinctly, yet till satisfaction be made they shall be unburied. But if any contrary to the said Sanction shall dare to bury

* *Which is so old as that that Ancient Emperour* Justinian *in his time did comprize it in a little Book saith* Franc. Mancinus ad Gambarum. *Who so highly prizeth it.* † Joh. Baptisto. || *That is to the receiving of the Sacrament of the Eucharist.* Inn. *And the Expositor addeth, that an Usurer must not be present in the Church when Sacred things and Services are there performed.* Cap. 1. Eod. in 6. * Quid sit satisfacere, vide L. 1 F. qui sat. cog.

 them

them, they shall be liable to the punishments by the Lateran Council promised. Their last Wills and Testaments also made * otherwise than according to the foresaid Constitution, shall be of no Validity; but *Ipso facto* shall be void: * nor will it avail any thing, if any do alledge that to redeem Captives, or to give Alms he lent upon Usury. Forasmuch as the Usurer is not to be dispensed the more for that, because a man may not lawfully make a lie to save anothers life, nor to rob. So bitter this Law is against the Usurer; What the Canonical Law here saith next, is of Restitution to be made, not only by the Usurers themselves, but also by their Heirs; Where this Law saith further thus: That if a man have borrowed mony upon Usury, and have sworn to the Usurer not to call for it again; yet the Judge may by an Ecclesiastical censure, compel the Usurer both to desist from exacting Usuries, and to remit the Oath, and also to restore what he has exacted, that none may gain by deceit and fraud, so exceeding strict is this Law: But yet it doth not take away a || free forgiving of Usury mony to be restored, saith the Expositor of this Law.

2. The second Transcript is out of the famous Doctor *Jer. Taylors Duct. Dubit.* added to the Canon Law, because some will be ready to say, observing the dreadfulness and bitterness of this Law, what are these Canons to us Protestants? therefore I subjoyn this great and renowned Protestant Doctor, his * words are: In things permitted for the hardness of mens hearts, or for publick necessity, the permission of the Prince is no absolution from the Authority of the Church, supposing Usury to be unlawful. Civil Laws permit Usury (meaning some, not all) and the Church forbids it, in Case the CANONS are to be preferred. For, tho it be permitted, yet by Law no man is compelled to be an Usurer. Let the Reader read the rest in the third Transcript out of holy Mr. † *Greenham*, who saith: Usury is the Devil's Mistery to turn Silver into Gold: It is a sin that has many Advocates and Patrons. They say, to the poor give freely, to the mean lend freely, of the rich take Usury. The Lord was never the Author of this Distinction.

---

* *Scilicet non facta satisfactione nec Idonea præstita Cautione.* John Bap. † *Which is proved by Scripture* Rom. 3. 8.
|| *Non inducit liberam remissionem. Idem* Iohn Bap.
* *Doctor* Jeremy Taylor. *in* Duct. Dubit. L. 3. C. 3. *mihi* p. 196. † Greenham p. 41. *In his Works.*

Dan.

Deut. 23. 19. The Jew of a Jew might not take Usury; but the link of a Christian is neerer than of a Country. Their brotherhood was by Country, ours is by Redemption. See the rest in his Works.

A Fourth, Out of the renowned and pious R. * *Capel*. saying, *Ainsworth* observs that Usury is fitly called biting, because it biteth and consumeth the borrower and his substance, and very few takers to Usury save their own by it, but the most of them are utterly undone and bitten, as it were, to Death by it. Doctor *Rainhald* (then whom the world hardly ever saw a better man and a better Scholar,) in his Book of *Divorce*. p. 8. Holds this Distinction between biting and not biting Usury, used by some late Divines, but a meer Flam. The best and best learned of our Prelatical and Antiprelatical Divines, saith he, (naming in his Margin *Jewel*, *Andrew*, Doctor *Py*. B. *Downam*, *Fenton*, *Bolton*) have taken good and great pains to prove Usury to be a thing utterly unlawful. Mr. *Dod* makes it a breach of the eighth Commandment; even † Theft. And *Uddal* in his Obed. of the Gospel is so severe and sharp against Usury, as that there he saith, that it is as clear in the Word, that Usury is a sin, as that Christ came into the World to save Sinners. Now here if any being contentious, and a Defendant of Usury; let him quarrel with these holy men, and the ancient Canons of the ancient Fathers. For their words I transcribe here, they are not mine, and therefore let them chide with them why they will be so bitter, so censorious, so harsh in their Writings against Usurers: Let him contend and dispute it with *Ainsworth*, the old Mr. *Dod*, with the learned *Capel*. with B. *Jewel*, B. *Andrew*, B. *Downam*, with blessed and holy *Bolton*, with the the unanswered Doctor *Py*, with that incomparable Doctor *Rainols*, with the renowned Doctor *Taylor*: With all the best learned Prelatical and Antiprelatical Divines in *England*; and with *Uddal* especialy, why he will offer to say that it is as clear that Usury is a sin, as that Christ came into the World to SAVE SINNERS.

And so I will leave him quarrelling with these men, let him come off as well as well as he can, and I will say no more but this: As *David* in old time. *Psal*. 139. 5. Thou hast beset me behind and before: So the poor Usurer whom *Da-*

* Richard *Capel*. *in his* Oppon. *to Usury*.

† *As also doth the Canon Law*.

vid condemns, may say to the Lord, now thou hast beset me, O Lord, now, behind, in the end of this writing against me, by all these men, who bring not only their own words, but thine also against me; and before too, thou hast beset me by that which in the beginning of this Writing is said out of both thy Testaments, even new as well as old, and out of all sorts of Writers ancient and recent. Good Lord, deliver me from this Usury, I humbly and heartily pray thee, *Amen, Amen.*

A fist out of the Famous * *Edward Cook*, by whom Usury is thus well stated against Usury ill stated, by *T. P.* Usury is directly against the Law of God, *Psal.* 15. 5. *Deut.* 23. 19. *Ezek.* 18. 12, 13. And ch. 22. And the reason why it was permitted to an Hebrew, or to an Infidel, was because it was a means, either to exterminate them, or to depauperate them. Thus he.

And again against all Usury he writes thus; and its adjudged by Authority of Parliament that A L L V S V R Y, being forbidden by the Law of God, is a sin and detestable; and he adds that also it is enacted by Parliament, that A L L V S V R Y (*N.* 3. twice) is unlawful, that is to say against the Laws of the Realm.

---

* Edward Cook *in his* 3. *part of his Institutions of the Laws of* England Edit cap. 70. Eliz. 13. *And* Jac. c. 17.

Godliness

GODLINESS Epitomiz'd

IN

TWO TABLES,

VIZ. FIRST, THE

RESOLUTION-TABLE:

EXHIBITED BY

CHRISTOPHER JELINGER, M.A.

WHICH

May be fixed on Mens Chamber-Doors for a Memorial.

CONTAINING

Twelve Gracious Resolutions for Walking in Newness of Life, every Morning to be taken up, as comprizing the Duty of Man.

I. I Will arise now, and by the grace of God, seek him whom my Soul loveth, in my Closet by private Prayer, and even wrestle with him as *Jacob* did, *Gen.* 32. 24. and not leave him till I have an answer of him; and after that I will joyn with my Family in the same duty.

II. I will read the holy Scriptures likewise, at least two Chapters

Chapters a day, one in the morning out of the Old Testament, another out of the New in the evening, to my Family and apart; and I will mark the chief contents thereof, and turn them into prayer, to help me in praying.

III. And I will delight my self this day and every day in my dearest Lord, as I am required, *Psal.* 37. 4. and as his Father delighted himself in him from all eternity, *Prov.* 8. 30. walking with him in my Chamber or elsewhere, Arm in Arm, as a Bride with her best Beloved; and talking with him and looking upon him by faith, *Isa.* 45. 22. *Heb.* 12. 2. and giving my loves unto him, *Cant.* 7. 12. even my love-desires, love embraces, love-kisses, *Psal.* 2. 12. *Psal.* 73. 25. and craving his loves of him, *Cant.* 7. 13. Thus by the Grace of God I will live the life of love with my dear Love, the Lord Jesus Christ.

IV. And because I do daily break Wedlock with him, by breaking his Commandments, I will daily return again unto him, he inviting me graciously thereunto, and saying, *Thou hast played the harlot with many lovers, yet return again unto me*, Jer. 3. 1. and I will even anew espouse my self unto him, in faith, in righteousness, and in truth, desiring him to return again unto me, and to espouse himself so too, according to his most kind promise, *Hos.* 2. 19.

V. And I will not so neglect as I have done, Meditating; but by the assistance of my God, Meditate this day and every day on the four last things, Death, Judgment, Heaven, Hell; and will have my Conversation in Heaven day and night, according to *Jos.* 1. 8. *Phil.* 3. 20. and when I awake in the morning, *I intend to be still with God both then and all the day long*, according to *Psal.* 139. 18. *When I awake I am still with thee.* which maketh me to break out into this acclamation, O sweet time so spent with God and Christ both day and night.

VI. And whereas my talk heretofore hath been but idle, vain, foolish, or impertinent, I will hereafter by the power of God, bridle my tongue, *Psal.* 39. 1. and speak as my Saviour of Heaven, and the things that appertain to the Kingdom of God, *Acts* 1. 3. and that at my Table especially, *Deut.* 6. 7.

VII. And by the same power I will keep my self from every evil way, like the same holy *David*, *Psal.* 119. 104. and like that Parabolical Merchant, sell all for the Pearl, for Christs sake, *Math.* 13. 45, 46. for it shall never be said that Christ and I parted for an odd Groat, I mean one sin or other, allowing my self in one odd ill favoured iniquity or other.

VIII. And I will make diligent enquiries, whether there be any in the place, or elsewhere about me, whom I may remember, relieve, and shew kindness too for *Jonathans*, I should say for Christs sake, like *David*, 2 *Sam.* 9. 1. Sith God hath gi-

ven

ven me an estate to do good with: so say (if thou hast this worlds goods) I am resolved to cast my bread upon the waters, and to provide my self Bags which wax not old, a treasure in the Heavens, which faileth not, where no Thief approacheth, neither moth corrupteth, *Luke* 12. 33.

IX. The Lords day I will observe, when it cometh by Gods help, so strictly and so holily, as if I were in Heaven with Christ that day; and there shall not come any worldly talk from me, nor will I do any evil or worldly work, nor have any earthly thoughts, but I will spend it wholly to and with the Lord, whose day it is, in holy exercises, as Reading, Singing, Praying, Hearing, Instructing my Family, and such like; being with blessed *John* wholly in the Spirit, *Rev.* 1. 10. and when I may conveniently, I will on the same day receive my blessed Saviour in the Holy Sacrament of his blessed Supper, labouring to be duly prepared for it, that I may not receive it unworthily to mine own eternal condemnation, 1 *Cor.* 11.29.

X. Fasting and Humiliation-days I will keep also, by the same divine power, to the Lord my God, at least once a month; and before the Sacrament of the Lords blessed Supper, and when there is great need, like pious Queen *Esther*, which so resolved likewise, saying, *I and my Maidens will fast also*, *Esther* 4. 16. and at other times also, yea always I will strive to be as sober, humble, and lowly, as God will enable me.

XI. I will moreover examin my self every Evening before I go to Bed (besides Praying, Reading, Singing, which at that time must be done also, with my Family and apart) what evils have I thought, done, and spoken, and what good I have done, that I may bless God for the one, and ask him forgiveness for the other, upon my humble confessions and deprecations made to his Heavenly most Sacred Majesty, *Lament.* 3 40. *Hos.* 14. 1. *Jer.* 3. 13.

XII. And I will not rest here neither, but by the help of God I will labour to be as chast, just, meek, patient under the Cross, as possibly I may be; and any other New Work that I have not yet done, and God shall command me to do in his Word, and by his Ministers; besides the forementioned, I will labour to do vigorously, constantly, and to his only praise and glory, and in faith, and out of my unfeigned love which I bear unto him: And when all is done, I will by the Grace of God not trust to any of my doings, they being all defiled and imperfect by reason of sin, *Isa.* 64. 6. but only and wholly to my dear and only Saviour, and to his blessed merits for life and salvation: *For there is no salvation in any other*, *Acts* 4. 12. *And in his name shall the Gentiles trust*, saith the Lord, *Matth.* 12. 21.

I add, But O let these good and gracious resolutions be endeavours also; and as a Merchant, when he is resolved to go to such a City, there to Trade, *Jam.* 4. 30. goeth and doth so; so do you, being so resolved to live so, to trade so, to walk so; go and do so, through Christ strengthning of you, *Phil.* 4. 13. and my most humble prayer to God for you is and shall be, that he will be your good speed, strengthen, settle, and stablish you, that you may hold out to the end, 1 *Pet.* 5. 10. Amen, So be it.

Deut. 6. 9. *And thou shalt write (these words) upon the Posts of thine House, and on thy Gates:*

THOMAS a KEMPIS de Imit. Christi, *l.* 1. *c.* 19.

Omni die renovare debemus propositum nostrum, atque dicere, Adjuva me, Domine Deus, in bono Proposito, & Sancto servitio tuo: & da mihi nunc hodie perfecte incipere, quia nihil est, quod hactenus feci. Et paulo post, *Justorum propositum in gratia Dei potius quam in propria sapientia pendet, in quo & semper confidunt, quicquid arripiunt.* In English thus:

Daily should we renew our Purposes and say, Help me my God, in this my good purpose, and in thy holy service, and grant that I may now this day begin perfectly; for that which I have done hitherto is worth nothing. *And a little after*, The purpose of just men depends upon Gods Grace, on whom they always relie for whatsoever they take in hand:

I superadd, But rest not here: but read over my whole Spiritual Merchant, in which this is included. Which may be had at the *Crane* in *Paul's Churchyard.*

SECONDLY, THE

EXAMINATION-TABLE,

OR

Examen Conſcientiæ,

OR,

SELF-EXAMINATION, Containing Twelve INQUIRIES.

I. WHat Evils have I thought, done, and ſpoken this day: and what good have I done and received?

II. More particularly: Have I not abuſed mine eyes by wanton looks, my tongue with vain, unprofitable, fooliſh, or unclean and filthy talking, and jeſting, and by cauſing my angry voice to be heard on high, or by lying, backbiting, ſlandering, ſwearing, calling of Names or ſpeaking evil of others? And have I not polluted my hands with uncleanneſs, or by taking Uſury, or by ſtealing, or ſome fraudulent dealing, or by ſmiting therewith wickedly? and have I not been exceeding angry, proud, luſtful, worldly, covetous, taking too much care and labour for and about the world? Is not my whole Nature vitiated, corrupted, diſordered, by ſin original, ſo that my heart is even deſperately wicked?

III. Have I not miſpent much precious time about and in idle and needleſs viſits, Playing, Carding, or Dicing, or too much ſleeping? and when I rode or did go abroad, by little or never minding God and his Word, and Heaven in all my journey, and going to and fro? and did I not exceed in eating, drinking, and company keeping?

IV. Have I not been ſhamefully brief, cold, dead, formal, cuſtomary,

customary, and exceedingly carried away with wandring thoughts in all my duties, and especially in prayer? do I not make a shew of godliness, denying the power thereof?

V. Have I prayed so often as I should, at least in the morning and evening solemnly, wrestling with God, and darting forth many ejaculatory prayers upon all occasions, besides joynt prayers with my Family, and was I thankful in prayer for the mercies of this day? nay took I any notice of them?

VI. Did I read Gods holy Word, at least evening and morning time?

VII. What time did I spend this day in meditating on my latter end, Judgment, Heaven, and Hell? any or none?

VIII. What mercy did I show this day to any, for *Jonathans*, I mean Christs sake? did I succour any by any corporal alms? or did I not cruelly shut up the bowels of compassion against some? did I visit any that needed it, according to my duty?

IX. And what have I been in company? did I reprove, instruct, admonish? had I any good communications with any of heaven and heavenly things? and what have I been in my house, place, and calling? and towards my Relations, Wife, Husband, Children, Servants, Neighbours, in order to the saving of their precious souls, as more worth than all the world?

X. And if the day did afford matter of Sorrow, did I fret or did I lie in dust before the Lord my God?

XI. Have I wrestled against Satan, and strcven against sin to overcome it, and his temptations, and that with success? have I left any sin, prevailed against any temptation, or have I not been shamefully rather foiled and defeated by this and that temptation?

XII. Was I careful to live by faith, and to be found in Christ, not having mine own righteous, but the righteousness of God in Christ this day? *Phil.* 3. 9.

I add, first, that this same directory may serve also for private Confession to be made upon this examination, as we shall be found guilty.

Secondly, *I add*, Not only the Philosophers have used the Examination of Conscience, as *Pythagoras*, *Seneca*, *Plutarch*: But poor *Barbarous Indians*, by the relation of *Apulejus*, took an account every evening of the good and evil they had done each day: and therefore for shame, Oh for shame, let not Christians, professing godliness, come short of these poor Heathens in this matter of Examination.

Thirdly, *I add*, One * *Deliro*, a noted Interpreter of the

* *Serm de Consc.*

Scrip-

Scripture, and after him, the Author of the *Holy Court*, relate both, the Vision of a Wise man, who on a day sought for the Court, or House of Conscience; and it seemed to him, he beheld a City built with goodly Architecture, beautiful with five Gates, which had as many narrow paths, ending in one large way: Upon this way stood a Register, who took the Names of all passengers to record them: Beyond that, he saw two Tribunes attended with a great concourse of Common People, who governed the inferior parts of the City: Above was beheld a Cittadel, wherein a great Princess commanded, who had a Scepter in her hand, and Crown on her head: By her side was a Lady very ancient and venerable, who in one hand held a torch, wherewith she lighted the Princess; and in the other a goad, wherewith she pricked her, if she governed not according to her discretion. The wise man amazed, asked in his heart, what all this meant? and he heard a voice within, which said unto him, Behold, Thy self, ere thou art aware, art arrived at the House (or Court) of Conscience, which thou soughtest for. The five gates which thou sawest, are the five senses. The way wherein they all meet, is common sense. All the people which thou sawest enter in by heaps, are the objects of the Creatures of the world, which first touch our senses, before they pass into the Soul. The Register is Imagination, that keepeth record of all things. The two Tribunes are the two Appetites; the one called the Appetite of Concupiscence; the other the appetite of Anger, extreamly striving to oppose all obstacles which oppose its good, real, or pretended. This Mass of people are the passions, which make ill work in the inferiour parts of the City. The Princess in the Cittadel with a Crown and Scepter, is Reason. The ancient Lady by her side is Conscience. She hath a torch to shew the good way, and the goad to prick those that wander: all which I apply thus: Answerable hereunto, I say to the Courteous Reader, who shall read this Table, and happily never was yet at this Court of Conscience here described, and at this Examination here *prescribed*; and so, just so art thou ere thou wast aware, arrived at the House or Court of Conscience; and therefore being thus entred into it, examine thy self, according to this Examination-Table, and according to the Order of the Court of Conscience here described, lying low *in thy very shame*, as *Jeremiah* 2. 26. Before the Lord; and yet, sitting withall like a Judge upon thy self, according to 1 *Cor.* 11. 31. For this sitting and

self-

ſelf-judging, and ſelf-examining, this Court permitteth, and no other beſides it. And that thou mayeſt do it effectualy and ſucceſsfully, is the moſt hearty prayer of thy moſt affectionate Friend, who hath penned theſe lines for thee, and who, when they dropped from his pen, beſought God in thy behalf that the ſame may be written by himſelf in thy very heart, *as with a pen of a Diamond*, Jer. 17. 1. And that as Juſtice ſits in the foreſaid Court of Conſcience, and even of thy Conſcience, inſcribing all thy ſins, ſo Mercy may ſit by her, blotting out all that Juſtice hath therein written, putting the point of its pen upon thy tender heart, it being become truly penitent by its ſelf-judging and ſelf-examining, and Gods bleſſing and mighty working going with it. So, even ſo be it.

Unto

Unto which twelve Resolutions *and twelve Examinations are now added twelve Holy Experimented Instructions, which this Author together with the foresaid two Tables Humbly Dedicates to the highly Honoured* HENERY CORNISH *one of the Sherifs of* London *and the Worshipful* JOHN UPTON *Esq; Whom both God bless and Preserve.*

THE 1. Instruction is, Be much with God in Praying, and praising. (1) in praying and as it were all prayer, as *David* was, who saith in *Psal.* 109. 4. *I am Prayer*, that is to say, be praying as Gods Elect, even day and night, *Luk.* 18. 7, 8. Crying to God by Night as well as by day; which I for my part cannot but practice still, according to *Lament.* 2. 19. Arise; crie out in the night; and that which is storied of Christ, in *Mark.* 1. 35. He rose a Great while before day, and prayed; For then none can hinder me, and then I shall have time enough, to performe all my Noctural Exercises, and to get an answer by craving a token for good, *Ps.* 86. 7. Which to me commonly is Triumphant shedding of leaves, which in such solemne praying I seldome misse, and to Gods Glory here do mention that others may do so to; and glorifie God thereupon, because that assureth them that their Prayers are

are heard, I add; that after such praying, we should still lay up something in store for the poor Saints according to 1 *Cor.* 16. 9. And 1 *Tim.* 6. And St. *Chrisostomes* pious Advisement.

2. In praising God; for how full are *Davids* Psalms of such praising, *viz.* *Psal.* 92. 95. 96. 98. 110. 150. And others, so also *Rev.* 5. and *Rev.* 19. So that I for my part, though I am but a poor worm, yet am emboldened thereby to get up to Heaven and to sing, as it were with those Heavenly Quiristers which there sing the Song of *Moses* and many others? and that by Night as well as by day, as also at *Constantinople* they were wont to do in the dayes of *Ennadius*; *Anno* 459. For which end I have learned sundry of *Davids* Psalms by heart, that in the dark I may sing them like *Paul* and *Silas*, *Act.* 16. to the praise of my Maker, as well as when it is light, which I intend to do as long as I live; and so till I enter ternity there to sing the Songs of *Zion* to all Eternity; and I have read of an Eminently holy man, which scarce had his like in the time wherein he flourished, that most of his work was Singing of Praises, and that, when he was near his end he cryed out, bring the Bible, and let us, sing the Psalms of *David*; and that, when he came to Halelujah, he doubled and trebled it, yea four or five times he would say it, and that when he did sing, the Angels would sing too by his Bed-side in the Chamber, which made him cry out I hear the Angels sing, and after a few hours are over, I shall stand in Mount *Sion*, and sing the Song of *Moses*, and of the Lamb, answerable whereunto, I also, who am but dust and ashes, yet hope, that I shall shortly, because I am grown Ancient, sing also with that multitude of singers which now sing in Heaven their Song, which is Hallelujah, praise the Lord our God, all ye his Servants both small and great, *Rev.* 19. 5. and my most hearty wish is that all my Readers may hereafter sing so here as that holy man did, that they also may hear the Angels sing, if God think it fit, as he, and befor him St. *Jerome* did, who calls God to witness, that he heard the Angels sing.

Secondly, Meditate Night and day, according to *Jos.* 1. 8. *Psal.* 1. 3. and especially, upon Eternity as *Paul* was wont to do 2 *Cor.* 4. 18. For Oh how that will keep you from sinning against God; I for my part do use my self to this Meditation, very much; if there were a law made, that whosoever shall perpetrate and commit the sin of Adultery or be drunk or swear an Oath, or steal, or lie, shall lie upon burning Coals for an hours space, and so be roasted like *Laurentius*, who

would

would dare to sin any such sin, now the God of Heaven hath made such a Law, that he who commits any such evil, shall lie in Hell fire it self, called unquencheable not for an hour only, but for ever and ever, *Rev.* 21. 8. *Esa.* 66. O dreadful! for this Eternity is such, as that it exceedeth all number, numbring and numbred, so called by the Learned; and that after the damned wretches have layen in that formidable and tremendous fire so many Millions of years as there are leaves upon all the Trees in the world, Haires upon all mens heads, Piles of grass in all fields, dust upon the whole surface of the earth, sands on the Sea shore, it may and will even then be said, now Eternity beginneth! now Eternity beginneth! and therefore who should not beware of the foresaid, and all such like transgressions! O mind the fire still.

3. Let your eyes be Doves eyes! *Cant.* 5. 12. They write that Doves love to look into Christaline Rivers, because therein them they espie their mortal Enemie the Kite, and evade him, semblably whereunto do you so look into the holy Scriptures and read you three Chapters a day, that thereby you may see and escape your mortal Enemy the Divel and his snares, which he laieth over all the world, 2 *Tim.* 2. but be sure to turn all your Chapters into Prayer, which will mightily help you in Praying, and the worlds and sins conquest in your fighting against both.

Fourthly, Be much in Love with God *Deut.* 6. 5. and with his Son *Jesus Christ* 1 *Pet.* 1. 7. 8. 1 *Cor.* 16. 22. I have read of one, that he was so in love with Christ: as that he would cry out, he hath Ravished me with his Beauty; Oh how glorious is the blessed Jesus! Oh what shall I do to speak the hundereth part of his praise! Oh he is sweet! he is altogether Lovely, O for words, O how Glorious, How Glorius is this pretious Jesus! Ah he is sweet, he is sweet, and now I am sick of Love, and shall die sick of Love, see *Cant.* 2. Thus he, and oh that all my Readers would be so taken too with this most fair, most sweet and pretious Jesus! be in fastings often, as *Paul* was 1 *Cor.* 9. 27. 2 *Cor.* 11. 27. But I will not press you with Holy *Calvines* example; who fasted from his dinner ten yeares together, spending his time in Holy Exercises, so as that even a Jesuite calls him a great Faster, it will be well for you, if you can Fast once a week, which I desire to do, if God help me, till death; let your talk be of Heaven and Heavenly things as Christs was, *Act.* 1. 13. After whom I will name *Ignatius Jordan*, who would Alwaies be speaking of Heaven too, and with him I will Joyne an other most eminent Servant of God, who would talk as

if

if he were in the third Heaven, thus did the Holy men talk, and so do you, and if you can meet no body to talk with, then talk with your beloved, Christ, I meane, as his Spouse in the *Canticles*; Walking with him Arm in Arm as it were, either in the feilds as *Isack*, *Gen*. 24. 33. or in your Chambers, yea in Heaven it self (mentally) where his Celestial Galleries and Walking places be, *Cant*. 7. 5. which sweet exercise I also desire to use daily for my delight, going as it were upon the Streets of Gold above, *Rev*. 21. 21. When I walk on the Streets of a City or Town to avoid the wandrings of my mind, and I wish also that all the Saints of God would do so, as also holy *Fulgentius* did.

7. Be much for Celestial visits, for Oh how pleasant they be! when the day Star from on high do visits us, *Luk*, 1. 79. Where give me leave to give you the words of a so visited gratious Soul; O Friends, stand by, and wonder, was there ever such kindness shewn and such manifestationss of rich grace made: Christs Armor and kisses and smiles turn Hell into Heaven: Oh he is come, he is come, and how sweet is the Blessed Jesus.!

8. Be as strict, as precise, as pure, as Seraphical spenders and Redeemers of your time as you can possibly be, *Eph*. 5. 15. 16. 1 Io. 3. 5. where let me add these two Councils, (1) Live as you will wish you had lived when you come to die, (2.) Leave such and such sins, as you shall wish you had left when you must leave the world.

9. Whatsoever you do for God, do it with all your might, and with all speed, as some Translators read the Hebrew, in *Eccles*. 9. 10. because there is no working in the Grave unto which we are all going.

10. Labour to be always ready to depart, by waiting for your change till it cometh, according to *Job*. 14. 44. and *Mat*. 24. 44. That is to say, from hour to hour, which both places do import, which makes me so to insist upon such an hourly preparing for death, because we know not what hour the Son of man will come, by death or Judgment, so as that I desire to put my self also upon the practice of it daily, as one that looks for his change hourly, and dares not promise himself one next day after the present, where give me leave to joyne with my self, 3. Noted men more and, 1. *Messidamus* who as *Guido Bituricensis* reports it, being invited to a Dinner for the next day, returned this Answer, I never promised my self a next day, looking for my change every hour. The second is *Ignatius Jyden* who, when he went from home, took his leave of his Wife still, as if he should

should never return to her again. The third is Mr. *Janeway* who when he went to his bed, took leave of his friends every evening, hoping to see them no more till the morning of his Resurection! and Oh that all my Readers would be such waiters and preparers too!

Omit nothing of all things here mentioned, and which God will have done besides, and the imitation of Christ by Name; which is grounded upon *Matt.* 28. 20. *Gal.* 3. 10. *Psal.* 15. 5. So that I for my part am exeedingly for the not omitting, and so much the more, since I read the dreadful saying of blessed *Ambrose*; *a slight neglect becomes an everlasting loss:* So as that I dare not omit the practice of that famous saying of that sweet Singer of *Israel*, which I use every night, as I awake out of my first sleep; whan I awake I am still with thee, or as the Hebrew also will bear it, I will be still with thee, *Psal.* 139. 18. And I must even marry my self anew to Christ, because I do dayly break Wedlock with him, and he bids me to return to him again, *Jer.* 3. 1. Which makes me then say, I will return to my first Husband, for then it was better with me than now it is, *Hos.* Nor can I leave undone any of my other Nocturnal exercises, but must also feed by Faith upon the bread of life, which is my Saviour Christ, both for my delight and strengthning, that I may be able to go thorow so much as I have to do: Which makes me cry out with that good People; Lord, evermore give me that bread, and a mouth to eat it, even the mouth of faith I humbly pray thee, *John* 6. 34. And because I do still meet with Enemies and Oppositions, I must needs fight also and wrestle with sin and Sathan, having before wrestled with God himself, see *Gen.* 32. 24. with *Eph.* 16. 11, 12. And I must even ascend into Heaven it self, and there sit down in those heavenly places in Christ Jesus, as the holy Ephesians did in their time, *Ephes.* 2. 6. And cry out again, Lord Jesus, make me also even now to sit down in those Heavenly places as thou madest the Ephesians sit-- and not being contented with this, I must cry again with *Moses*, shew me thy glory. *Exo.* 33. 18. for I must needs see it, and thy face too before I have done, that I may be able to say with *Jacob:* After all my wrestlings *I have seen God face to face; and the life of my soul is now preserved*, *Gen.* 32. 26. O sweet sight: O that all my Readers might see it and be able to say, we have seen his glory, as the glory of the only begotten Son of God *John* 1. And is not the sweet work to be done by night, and the Reward of it sweet?

12. And above all things, be much in believing, and even

 live

live by Faith, *Gal.* 2. 20. That you may rejoice thereupon with joy unſpeakable, and ful of glory, 1. *Pet.* 1. 8. Now this, Oh this is the principle thing, and without this all other things we need are as nothing, for without faith it is impoſſible to pleaſe God, *Heb.* 11. 6. Nor can we truly rejoice without it, but with it we may, and its done; for proof whereof, I will bring one, who in our time did ſo rejoice, even to the admiration of all that were about him, ſo as that a godly Miniſter that ſaw him and heard him, ſaid, I never ſaw, never read, never heard the like; for thus he ſpoke of his joy in believing, *I am as ful of joy as I can hold, O that I could but let you know what I do feel: This is a kin to Heaven, and if I were not to enjoy any more than this*, it were well worth all the torments that men and Divels can invent, to come through, yea even a Hell, to ſuch tranſcendent joys as theſe: I ſtand, as it were, with one foot in Heaven. I hear the melody of Heaven, I ſee the Angels watching for me *&c.*

But here a moſt needful Queſtion cometh to be anſwered. How ſhall I come by this Faith and rejoycing? I anſwer as the wiſe Virgins did the fooliſh, craving ſome of their Oyl, whereby we may underſtand Faith, which, like Oyl maketh chearful, 1. *Pet.* 1. 8. 2. *Go to thoſe that ſell*, *Mat.* 25. 9. And who be they? Secondly I anſwer. 1. The Holy Trinity, and firſt the Father ſelleth it freely, for he gives it, *Phil.* 1. 29. And therefore you muſt go to him for it, ſaying, Father ſell unto me this Oyl of Faith, giving it unto me, that I may rejoice with joy unſpeakable. 2. The Son ſelleth it; for he is the Author of it, *Heb.* 12. 2. So as that to him you muſt go and ſay alſo, ſweet Jeſus ſell unto me that Oyl of Faith, that I may rejoyce with Joy unſpeakable. And thirdly to the Spirit, who freely and givingly ſells it, 1. *Cor.* 12. 9. You muſt cry alſo, bleſſed Spirit, ſell unto me alſo that holy Oyl of Faith, that I may rejoyce glorioully! But hereupon another Queſtion ariſeth, How a man may know that he hath that precious Oyl of Faith and holy Joy which cometh it? Whereunto I anſwer, firſt if it purify his heart, *Act.* 15. 9. And ſecondly if he become a true Saint, and live a truly holy life, *Acts*, 26. 18. And thirdly if his faith work by love, *Gal.* 5. 6. And makes him love the Brethren dearly and unfeignedly. See 1 *John* 3. 14, 15. And fourthly if his joy be a glorious joy, 1 *Pet.* 1. 8. So as that he needs not be aſhamed to ſpeak of it, how glorioully it works in him and by him; and what glory is brought to God by it, and by the life which he now lives, living by the faith of the Son of God, and being crucified with Chriſt to the world, *Gal.* 2.

20. And

20. And yet I must answer one Question more: You said even now, that a man must imitate Christ too; and how and wherein may that be done? Whereunto I briefly answer, 1. in his godliness: For first, how that holy Lord Jesus went about doing good to souls by his powerful Preaching, *Mat.* 4. 23. Secondly, and how he fasted *Mat.* 4. Wherein, though we cannot follow him for so many days, yet may we according to strenth given us from above, for a day now and a day then, and even as often and as long as God shall direct us: and the like may be said by his praying whole nights upon a Mountain, *Luke* 6: 12. And secondly we should imitate him in his meekness, and not be so angry and provoking as many are. See *Mat.* 11. 29. Thirdly in his humbleness, for how he humbled himself by counting himself of no Reputation, and by coming in the form of a servant *&c.* *Phil.* 2. 7. and how he lay upon the very ground with his holy face; when he prayed *Mat*, 26. 3. Like *Joshuah* and the Elders of *Israel*, *Josh.* 7. 6. Which makes and moveth me, a poor Worm to do so too, by night in duty, as he did by night, counting it as nothing for me to lie so, when I consider how many of the most Eminent Saints did usually, and for many years together (some twenty, some thirty, some always till Death) did use themselves to such hardness; and so to lie upon no bed at all, having a stone for their Pillow, like *Jacob*, meditating upon, and scoping at their everlasting rest to come, and so forgetting, as it were, their natural ease and rest, which yet I do not press upon any, but only mention, as much thought upon by my poor and inconsiderable self, who am very much taken with the strict lives of such glorious Saints as have been Practitioners of such humble gestures and hard lyings; St. *Basil* I mean, who was as strict, as holy, and as zealous a man as any of all the ancient Fathers, so as that when one wisht he might but see that wonderful man, he was shewn him, in a bale of fire, and it was told him this is *Basil*; with whom I conjoyn *Udalricus*, *Lupus*, *Edmundus*, Master *Simpson*; *Clara* and *Brigitta*, weak and tender Women, which yet would lie so: But again I add, that I do not urge this as necessary for all; and so I shall end with praying that my good God (whom I desire to serve day and night in the best and humblest manner I can, by his enablement) that he will so bedew these lines with the dew of his celestial Benediction, to such as shall pervolve and read them, as that they may meet in them with that inennarable, glorious unexpressible Joy, which is mentioned, and sparkling forth therein, and thereupon may break out every one of them in-

 to

to the holy and triumphant Epiphonema's and Exclamations! is this reward and remuneration of believing and holy living, then do not I care how little else I do, for now Heaven is in my heart, and my heart in Heaven, welcome, welcome, unspeakable joy, long thirsted after, and longed for, thou hast ravished me by thy coming. For Oh the extatical leaps of my transported soul! And oh what an Ocean of unutterable delectations do now overflow me; and what a Globe of heavenly glory becircles me! O I do not care now, how soon I be unmanned by Death; that after my dissolution, I may be entranced into the joy of my Lord and Master, *Mat.* 25. 23. and may bath my self in that River of pleasures, and drink my fill out of that fountain and fulness of Joy which is at Gods right hand to an endless duration. *Psal.* 16. 17.

To God alone be all Glory to all Eternity. *Amen, Amen.*

This little Book was so contrived upon the request of some Noble Persons, and others, which desired me so to epitomize Godliness, that though it was printed with my book against Usury, yet it might be bound up by it self, to be carried as a little pocket Book, and read dayly, by such as cannot so carry about and read larger Volumes; written for and of the practice of that gainful trade of ever-blessed Piety.

The names of those Writers which this Author desired to Inspect for his own and other fuller satisfaction about Usury, besides the Holy Scriptures and has cited in this Book, are these following.

A

ABulensis, *alias Tostatus*
Rabbi Abraham
Augustinus
Agathense Consilium
Aristoteles
Aelianus
Antoninus
Andronetius
Acro
Apostolius
Agellius
Aquilejus
Ammianus Marcellinus
Ausonius
Aesclopiades
Auctor de imperio Mavis
Anianus
Thomas Aquinas
Aristarchus
Archidiaconus
Ambrosius
Alcasar
Allericus
Aristophanis Interpres Scholiastes Aristophanis
Alphonsus Mantuanus
Aristotelis Paraphrastes
Aristotelis Interpres
Arias Montanus
Aretius
Azoar
Arcadius Grammaticus
Agricola
John d' Abbia
Doctor *Abbot*
Mahomets Alcoran
Alex. ab Alex.
Tho. Annotat. of the Assembly
The Arraignment of *Usury*
Aubanus
Andreas Episcopus
Ainsworth
Axalla
Anna Maria Shureman

B

Basilius Magnus
Babington Episcopus
Bagshaw
Basilicorum Interpres
Baine
Bayley
Balsamon
Beroaldes
Beza
Doctor *Barnard*
Bartholomeus Cepolitanus
Doctor *Beard*

St. Bernardus
Bernardus Sylveſter
Bellarminus
Bartolus
Binny
Brooks
Betulcus
Bolſecius
Albertus Blanenberg
Petrus Pleſſeus alias Mornay
Bromyard
Bruce
Berifardus
Bodinus
Brimle
Brentius
Bruſius
Budeus
Bullinger.
Baxter
Bolton
Johannes Boemus
Brigilla
Burratius
Ponto Brumicenſis
Buxtorſius
Blaquerna
Boiſardus
Surius Baſtingius
Johannes Baptiſta
Briſonius

C

Cabaliſtæ
Cæſaris de bello Gallico Interpres Græcus
Cajus Imperator
Calepinus
Caſtalio
Caietanus
Caſtro
Clara
Camerarius
Carpentarius
Caniſius
Calvinus
Caſſ.n Jeſuita
Carion
Chriſtophorus Cartwright
Centuræ Magæ
William Chappel
Cicero
Cato
Doctor Chitræus
Conradus Paulus Brunſwicenſis
Cruciger
Conviction of Uſury
Clemanges
Copronicus
Cælius Secundus
Columella
Chryſoſtomus
St. Cyprianus
Clemens Alexandrinus
Conſtantinus Magnus Imperator
Clerk
Camphield
Craſius
Cujacius
Craſtus
Doctor Chemnitius
Chriſtiani Kumpt Codex

D

Dionyſius Halicarnaſſæus
Dioniſ. Halicarn.
Duodecim Tabulæ
Dionis excerptorum ex libro Conſt. πνοι ἀρετῆς ϗ κακίας Interpres
Downam Epiſcopus
Dalecampius
Dionyſius Areopagita
Dionyſius Carthuſianus
Demoſthenes
Demoſthenis Interpres
Demoſthenis Scholiaſtes
Dalmaſius
Danæus
Dod

De-

Democritus
Discipulus de Tempore
Dioclarius
Donarif
Durrham
Diogenes
Donatius
Diodati
Doctor *Didericius*
Deering
Dike

E

Elibertinun Consilium
Edward Cook is so bitter against Usury
Eusebius
Elias Rabbinus
Elephanus Egerton
Erpenij Interpres
Etymologici Magni Author
Eustatius
Eusebius
The Enlish *Usurer*
Escobar Jesuita
Erasmus Roterodamus
Edmundius

F

Fulgentius
Fabianus
Fabius Fagius
Farelius
Dr. *Fabricius*
Favorinus
Foxe
Festus Gratianus Comicus
Fabricius alter
Floid
Dr. *Fenton*
Filborn
Filliutius Jesuita
Fevardinus
Ferguson
Forbos
Foroneus

G

Galasius
Galatinus
Galenus
Gamfredus
Genianus
Glossarum Nomin. Author
Glossa quædam Antiqua Hæbr.
Glossarum Author
Glossarum Admirabilitas, et Admirator earum
Gei
Gratianus
Greenham
Gruterus
Guallerus
Gregorius Magnus
Gregorius Theologus
Franciscus de Gambara
Glanvil
Gregorius de Valentia
Geminianus
Gemara
Guido Bitriconsis

H

Hal Episcopus
Hamond
Haymo
Halburgensis Episcopus
Hadriunus junius
Harmenopolus
Harmenopoli Interpres
Harpocration
Harpocrationis Glossator
Hemingius
Hirn
St. *Hireonimus*
Hildeshemensis Synodus
Hostiensis

Herodoti Interpres
Hesychius
Horatij Criticus
Godofredus Hotton
Hugo
Humphrey
Thomas Hall
Huges

I

Jacobus Rex Angliæ
Juellus Episcopus
Josephus
Inscriptionum Interpres
Isidorus
Julius Cæsar Imperator
Justinianus Imperator
Justinus Imperator
Justinus Martyr
Jus Canonicum
Jus Civile
Jonas le Boy S^r. de la Revie
Justus Jonas
Janeway

K

King Episcopus
Keekermannus
Ketina Rabbinus
Doctor *Kimbus*
Johannes Knewstub
Keiserbergius
Rabbi Kimhi

L

Laurentius
Ladantius
Laertius
Langius
Lipsius
Legis Rhodiæ Interpres
Lampridius
Lavater
Legum Atticarum Enarratio
Leucrotarius
Lateranense Concilium
Lupus
Lake Episcopus
Comes de Leicester
Leo Juda
Leo Imperator
Leo Magnus
Lira
Laertij Interpres
Lorinus Jesuita
Petrus Lombardus
Ludolphus
Lucanus
Ludericus Galliæ Rex
Doctor *Lutherus*
Doctor *Luderus* I C.
Johannes Paulus Lancellotus
Lessius
Lactantius

M

Malvenda
Manichæus
Mansfeldensis Conscionatores
Marloratus
Muriana
Manchester
Petrus Martyr
Macer
Moses Gerundensis
Mave
Martoratus
Nonius Marcellus
Melanchton
Mercerus
Moad
Mayer
Mozia
Carolus Molineus
Mollerus
Monlanus
Mostellar

Doctor

Doctor

FINIS.

The TITLES, *of the several* BOOKS, *which this Author has in* English *and* Latin.

1. THE Rose of *Sharon.*

2. Christ and his Saints spending their time together Day and Night.

3. A Cluster of sweetest Grapes, or the Saints Assurance.

4. Fifteen Conferences with Jesus Christ, about the World's and Sin's overcoming by Faith, and about the Life and Joys of Heaven.

5. New and living way of Dying, in and by Faith.

6. Heaven won by Violence.

7. A New and heavenly *Cannaan* discovered, wherein a man may live with great Delight, as the Children of *Israel* did in the Earthly, flowing with Milk and Hony.

8. The Spiritual Merchant.

9. The precious Pearl Christ.

10. The Usurer cast.

11. A Latin Disputation, of and about the Lords Supper, and the Popish Mass, publickly Disputed by the same Author at *Geneva*, and turned into English.

12. And now Usury Stated overthrown.

13. And Godliness Epitomized.

14. And lately also a sacred Union in Enlish, proposing a way whereby the English Protestants agreeing in fundamentals, and dissenting only in Rituals and Ceremonies may Unite, bearing one with another in the said Ceremonials.

15. And the same in Latin, *mutatis mutandis*, changing what is to be changed, for the Protestants beyond the Seas, yea all good Christians besides in the world, which accord with us in the faith of Christ, perswading them all to Unite against that man of sin, which is against us all for the good and conservation of us all.

16. And the Protestant Religions Fundamenal Doctrine.

17. And

17. And four Tables containing Popish Religion at large, that all may see what an absurd Idolatrous and bloody Religion it is, and nigh to that the *Grecian* and *Armenian*, and *Muscovian*, and *Habesine*, or *Abysine*, that men may know how far they may Unite and have common with those Churches, that is to say, as far as they accord with the truth of Christs Gospel and no further, whereunto is added lastly the Confession of the Æthiopian Christians faith, published by *Claudius* King of *Æthiopia*, and a Description of the *Abysine* Empire, wherein the *African* Christians are, shewing also what their Religion is, in short, and what a goodly Country it is, so as that the Reader may read it all with great Delight.

www.ingramcontent.com/pod-product-compliance
Lightning Source LLC
Chambersburg PA
CBHW051526100726
47898CB00005B/1597

* 9 7 8 3 3 3 7 3 8 2 2 0 9 *